'This second novel from the [...] pin-sharp observations about [...] [destru]ctive nature of sexual attraction' *Observer*

'Shrewd, intelligent and very, very funny' *Heat*

'A treat . . . This is a laugh-out-loud rollercoaster of a book written with style' *Sunday Mirror*

'Biting humour, witty ripostes and the sharpest sarcasm since Eddie Izzard's last tour . . . It's big, it's clever and it's absolutely hilarious' *Daily Record*

'An original way of addressing the issue of what makes people unfaithful . . . Millington is good at getting inside his characters' heads and delivering smart, sharp dialogue' *Time Out*

'A brilliant look at instant love' *Marie Claire*

'The argument it posits is chilling enough to give the romantics among you nightmares!' *Metro*

'What defines compatibility? Is it the food we eat or the humor we indulge in? Millington explores these questions without succumbing to formula' *Entertainment Weekly*

'Sharp, hilarious . . . crisp, comic writing, which includes sardonic but believable dialogue and tightly focused, laugh-out-loud scenes. Millington augments this fun mix with a spot-on publishing satire' *Publishers Weekly*

'Scorchingly funny' *People magazine*

12641392

Mil Millington is the creator of the cult website www.thingsmygirlfriendandihavearguedabout.com and co-founder of www.theweekly.co.uk. He writes for various newspapers and magazines and was named by the *Guardian* as one of the top five debut novelists for 2002. Mil's first novel, *Things My Girlfriend And I Have Argued About*, is also available in Phoenix paperback. His latest novel, *Love and Other Near Death Experiences*, is published by Weidenfeld & Nicolson.

By Mil Millington

Love and Other Near Death Experiences
A Certain Chemistry
Things My Girlfriend And I Have Argued About

A CERTAIN CHEMISTRY

MIL MILLINGTON

PHOENIX

A PHOENIX PAPERBACK

First published in Great Britain in 2003
by Hodder & Stoughton
This paperback edition published in 2006
by Phoenix,
an imprint of Orion Books Ltd,
Orion House, 5 Upper St Martin's Lane,
London WC2H 9EA

An Hachette UK company

1 3 5 7 9 10 8 6 4 2

A CIP catalogue record for this book
is available from the British Library.

ISBN 978-0-7538-2072-8

Printed and bound in Great Britain by
Clays Ltd, St Ives plc

The Orion Publishing Group's policy is to use papers that
are natural, renewable and recyclable products and
made from wood grown in sustainable forests. The logging
and manufacturing processes are expected to conform to
the environmental regulations of the country of origin.

www.orionbooks.co.uk

To the most precious and adored things in my life:
Jonathan and Peter.
If I can leave you nothing else, at least let me
leave you the dedication in this book.

Oh and, incidentally, the way things are going
I probably *will* be leaving you nothing else, OK?
Bite the bullet, lads.

ACKNOWLEDGEMENTS

As usual, a big thank-you to the band. On bass, agenting, slanderous gossip and support and advice of absolutely, utterly, all varieties . . . Hannah Griffiths, ladies and gentlemen! On harp, commissioning editing, outrageous poshness and teary, romantic natures concealing an obsessive fascination with the raw details of sexual mechanics – please put your hands together for Helen Garnons-Williams! On some kind of horse fitted with microphones that, I don't know, probably convert the electrical impulses associated with muscle activity into musical tones or something, being illuminatingly funny and clever, standing back and letting me get on with this stuff with typical good manners and great forbearance, and the assassination of a string of Italian judges in the late 1990s – iiiiit's Mr Jonathan Nash!

Naturally, a spilling mouthful of thanks to Margret. Also profuse apologies for all the terrible things I've done up to this point, and for the additional terrible things I bet I'll have done since it. I'm so clearly lucky to be with you that it's actually embarrassing, and I will vacuum the house tomorrow. Or, you know, at least early next week.

Finally, my gratitude to the many, many scientists and researchers whose findings I've used here, often – so as to keep the prose moving – unattributed. Cheers. I'll probably come round and steal the food out of your fridge later too, then run a key down the side of your car as I walk away from your house, which I've idly set ablaze.

I

Hi there, I'm God. Yeah, yeah, I know, you thought I'd be taller. Cheesh, I created you people and sometimes even *I* don't get you, you know what I'm saying? Some joker's standing here – bit of a problem with his brakes and now he's the new kid in paradise – and he's all with the 'Yeah, right – *you're* God'; like there's a height restriction on creating the universe or something. So I'm a couple of inches shorter than he is, so what? I'm *God* – get over it.

Anyways, don't get me started down that road 'cause I'm here to explain some stuff. It's quite important stuff – kind of, you know, *sweeping*, if you get me. So, what I'm thinking here is that the best way to start doing this is to tell you about something that happened – you know, show it to you as an example of what I'm talking about. This is something that happened to Tom Cartwright. Tom's twenty-eight, he lives in Edinburgh, Scotland, and he's one of them – what do you call them? Them guys who do books for other people? – ghost writer, that's it, he's one of them there ghost writers. What I want you to keep in mind here is that . . . no, in fact, I'll come to that later. Right now, you just listen while I have Tom start to tell you his story.

Yeah, *of course* I can do that.

ONE

'Table for McGregor?'

'Let me see . . . Ah yes, just for two?'

Amy nodded and we were led through the restaurant to a table at the back, next to the toilets.

'I thought I'd better book,' she said as we sat down. 'It can be tricky to get a seat in the smoking area at lunchtime.' I glanced around as I shuffled my chair in and saw that, apart from a squashed little ghetto of smokers at the tables around us, the restaurant was entirely empty. The waitress gave us a couple of menus, an ashtray and a free, complimentary smile, and then turned to leave.

'Excuse me . . .' Amy called after her, arching back on her chair. 'Could we have a bottle of red and a bottle of white, please?' She turned back towards me, questioningly. 'Sorry – do you want anything?'

'No, I'm fine.'

'Just the two bottles, then,' she confirmed.

'Certainly,' replied the waitress, and headed away towards the bar.

Amy scrambled a cigarette out of its packet, chopped her lighter alight with her thumb and pinched her face up with the effort of a long, determined draw. With a slight pop, she pulled the cigarette from her mouth and let her hands fall down to the table, at which point she stopped completely. She sat there, eyes unfocused, without breathing or moving – as though she'd simply switched off – for a tiny eternity. Even though I was used to her doing this it still unnerved me and I was just about to reach over and investigatively poke her forehead with my finger when she finally relaxed and expelled the smoke with a noisy, swooping whoosh; like the valve on a pressure cooker releasing steam.

'So,' she said, 'how are things?'

Amy was my agent.

'Oh . . . you know,' I replied.

Once Amy is your agent, there's no going back. I don't mean that in a bad way. I'm not suggesting that Amy's contract specifies ten per cent of earnings and your immortal soul, or that trying to untangle yourself from Amy would mean her pursuing you, shrieking, through the night. I mean, well . . . I don't have a dishwasher, but everyone I know who does says that you can happily go for most of your life without a dishwasher but, once you buy one, that's it: life without one becomes unimaginable. Amy is like a dishwasher.

'I read the piece you did for *Working Mother!* – the "How to do your tax return" thing,' she said.

'Yeah. I just paraphrased the Inland Revenue's booklet, really.'

'No, you're selling yourself short again. The way you were struggling to run a small, ethnic rug shop while raising four children with eczema? I really felt for you. And your husband . . .'

'Brian.'

'Aye, Brian – what a dickhead. I'm telling you, when you were filling in the section on provisional figures, I was there with you.'

'Thanks.'

'And Hugh's really pleased with the way *Only the Horizon* is selling, by the way.'

This was the last book I'd ghosted. It was for a guy, Justin Lee-Harris, who'd sailed a small yacht between Ireland and New Zealand. I forget why. Lee-Harris was always doing this kind of thing. I'd only met him once because, by the time everything was agreed and I'd been brought in, he was just about to jump aboard another one-man yacht to do something admirable and vague in the South China Sea. It wasn't until after he'd gone that I discovered my Dictaphone battery had run out about halfway through our single meeting. Everything after Cape Town I just made up.

'I'm seeing Hugh later.'

'Really? Are you *sure* you don't want a drink?'

The waitress came back.

'Ready to order?' she asked, striking a pose with a pencil and pad.

'Ummmm . . . I'm sorry,' I said, theatrically pained by the admission, 'I don't really know much about Ghanaian cuisine . . . What's fufu?'

'It's cassava and plantain pounded with a wooden pestle and mortar until it glutinises into a ball,' the waitress replied, expectantly moving her pencil down to touch the pad.

'And cassava?'

'It's a root.'

'And plantain?'

'A bit like a banana.'

'Really? . . . Um . . . Can I have the roast chicken and chips, please?'

The waitress smiled, nodded brightly, scribbled something that looked rather like 'tosser' on her pad and turned to Amy.

'Oh, nothing for me, thanks,' she said, with a wave. 'No – could we have another bottle of red, actually?' She twisted back to me. 'So, what are you seeing Hugh for?'

'Oh, not *for* anything. I was coming out to see you anyway, I haven't seen him for a while . . .' I finished the sentence by waggling my hand about. 'I'll just pop in and say hello.'

'I thought you were there last week? I'm sure when I saw him he said you'd come into the office last week.'

'Yes, that's right. Now you mention it, I remember I *did* bump into him last week.'

'Where?'

'You know, in his office.'

'That's not really "bumping into" him, is it? "Hey! Hugh! Fancy seeing you here. At your desk." That's more "aiming at him", isn't it?'

'I suppose so . . . whatever.'

'Are you up to something?'

'Me? No, God no.' A specific pair of breasts came into my mind. Amy leaned forward slightly and peered at me: guilt whispered that she could see the specific breasts too; dangling there, just behind my eyes. 'No . . . What have you heard?'

'I haven't heard anything,' she said.

'There you go, then. You should listen to that.'

'OK, OK. But I've warned you before about getting too friendly with publishers, that's all. You know what happens every time you make friends with a publisher.'

'A pixie dies; yes, I remember. But Hugh *is* my friend, not just my publisher, Amy.'

'Friendship's cool, Tom. You can always cool a friendship. When you get too friendly with a publisher you just make my job of helping you harder. You keep a dignified distance. If anyone needs to make friends with them, *I'll* do it. I can do it better than you: I'm false.'

Amy lectured me about the risks I was taking by talking to, well, pretty much anyone. She continued doing this through a pack of cigarettes and all the wine – the number of adjectives increasing with each bottle.

'The usual pack of arrogant wankers, of course.'

'Yeah?'

'Abso*lute*ly.' She crushed the life out of a cigarette stub in the ashtray. 'London agents – bastards. They think I'm some kind of "plucky amateur" just because I don't live down there. You can actually see their body switch languages when I tell them; their shoulders unwind and they stuff their hands in their pockets. "Oh, so you *live* up here? How wonderful.

Wish I could, it'd be far better for my nerves." Twats. They need their shins beating with a spade.'

Every day I wake up and thank God that Amy's on my side.

'Well,' I sighed, glancing supportively at my watch, 'I'd better get off if I'm going to catch Hugh.'

'Aye, I'd better make a move too.'

She plunged her arm into her handbag up to the elbow and, after a brief chase, retrieved a hair tie. Both hands reached around the back of her head and pulled at her straight brown hair, binding it into the tie with a severity that tugged at the skin on her face so much her eyes narrowed. It was her battle ritual. Fearsome in any case, Amy McGregor with her hair tied back meant a Highland Charge was in the offing.

'What was it you're going to?' I asked.

'Oh, it's a magazine launch. Is my speech slurring?'

'A bit.'

'Good. Wouldn't want to look out of place.'

'See if you can hunt out anything for me. I've got nothing lined up and Sara's talking about new carpets.'

'Will do. Anything specific? Got any ideas for features?'

'Ha.'

'Yeah, sorry. I'll just wait for them to say anything about anything and then pipe up, "*Really?* Tom was just saying he'd got an idea for a piece about that." I've got a face to go with it . . . look.'

'Convinces me.'

'Hello, Tom.'

Hugh's face collapsed into a 'struggling on' smile as I approached. This didn't signify anything; it was simply his standard face. Hugh Mortimer always looked like a man who'd just returned to work after an embarrassing surgical procedure.

He was the Chief Commissioning Editor in the Scottish

offices of the publishers McAllister & Campbell. Depending on how Hugh happened to feel, an aspiring author could be set dancing with elation in his kitchen or left feeling utterly crushed and worthless, in the same kitchen. Many men (I know, I've met them) would be unable to control their erections at the thought of having that kind of power; it just gave Hugh ulcers. But then, pretty much everything gave Hugh ulcers.

'Hi, Hugh. Thought I'd just drop by and see how things were.'

'Oh, good. Good to see you . . . I've been having pains in my chest.'

'Really?' Hugh Mortimer was thirty-seven years old.

'Aye . . . *here* . . .' He rubbed his open hand over a liberal area, as though anxiously soaping himself. 'I was worried about my heart, you know, what with my being so sedentary. All I ever do is sit. Doesn't that worry you too? You sit.'

'No. But then I'm twenty-eight. Obviously, if I were thirty-seven it'd scare the crap out of me.'

'Mmm – anyway, I was worried about my heart, so I bought this rowing machine thing at the weekend. They're supposed to be very good for all-round health.'

'Yes.'

'Getting it in and out of the car damn near killed me.'

'Naturally.'

'I spent a stressful afternoon setting it up and I've been giving it a go each evening.'

'And now you've . . .'

'And now I've got these pains in my chest, that's right. The trouble is, doing the rowing really makes demands of your chest muscles. I don't know if it's the muscles in my chest aching or my heart.'

'Did you have any pains before you bought the rowing machine?'

'No. But that doesn't mean anything. It could still be my

heart. It has to give out some time, doesn't it? Its number might have been up and the fact that I happened to have bought a rowing machine now is just a coincidence. I missed my chance. I bought a rowing machine but my heart's already too far gone.'

'Did you keep the receipt?'

I'd known Hugh for six years, so I can say with some authority that today he was more upbeat than usual.

The accident of my knowing Hugh was simply part of the accident of my being a writer in the first place. I'd come to Edinburgh to study English at university. I wasn't, I must make it clear, fired up by any passion for literature. It was simply that, well, you have to study *something*, don't you? Once, in Miss Burston's class when I was ten, I'd been told that I was 'quite good at spelling', and I'd just sort of drifted along with that for the next eleven years. My academic career was indifferent to the point of beauty: I was so unremarkable, in every way, that the unvarying precision of my mediocrity achieved a kind of loveliness. The most middling student each year in Edinburgh really ought to be awarded the 'Tom Cartwright Cup'. Or, more fittingly, the '*Who?* Cup'.

Anyway, by the time I'd finished my degree I'd made some friends here and couldn't see any point in moving. I certainly didn't want to go back home (a tiny village located somewhere in Kent, somewhere in the seventeenth century) and the prospect of heading off to London to find glittering success filled me with a shrug. So, I hung around and got a job on a local advertising paper: wherever a cycle path was poorly defined, whenever a pensioner was doing something vaguely amusing for charity – I was there. I can't really see how I could have lacked any more flair, but I could spell and I worked fast; in journalism just one of those is often enough to build a career on. This all went along nicely for a time until an acquaintance of mine was asked if she'd ever thought about writing a book.

The friend, Janine, owned a shop that sold bollocks: reflexology charts, tarot cards, little statuettes of fairies ('faeries', probably) holding crystals, feng shui manuals, those pairs of shiny metal balls that always come in black, velvety cases – she stocked pretty much the complete range of pointlessness. Janine's speciality, however, was aromatherapy. Not only did she sell the oils, books and burners, but she was also available, for a modest fee, in a consulting capacity. Panic attack? Personal crisis? One phone call and Janine would race over so you could score some safflower oil. Tricky situation at work and you need to subliminally influence your colleagues in your favour? A few notes and Janine would see to it that you, quite literally, came up smelling of roses. Inevitably – I mean, *inevitably*, right? – some of Janine's users worked in publishing. One day, while Janine was giving her a hit of kanuka, one of these clients remarked that there was always a market for books about this kind of crap (I paraphrase) and had she, Janine, ever thought of writing one?

Janine was very taken with this idea, but didn't feel up to the task of putting all those words down on paper. As she knew I was a formidably mercenary wordsmith she asked if I'd ghost the thing for her – she'd give me the basic details and I'd work them up into a book. I said if we called it *Aromatherapy* I'd do it for a flat fee. If we called it *Sensual Aromatherapy* I'd do it for a proportion of sales. She went for the latter, which was a tremendous boon for me (ghost writers never get a proportion of sales – you get a one-off payment and that's it, no matter what). The book came out at a really good moment, just as aromatherapy was that month's top media fad (I want to say 'It was right on the nose', but I'm not sure I'd ever forgive myself), and it sold very well. We cranked out a follow-up, *Extra-Sensual Aromatherapy*, which didn't do anywhere nearly as well as the first book but still shifted enough copies to confirm that there is no justice in the world. More important was that during the process of doing the two books I met both Hugh (then lowly enough to have to deal with aromatherapy publishing) and Amy. With the odd lead from the former and the savage tenacity of the latter it was just about financially viable, within a year or so, for me to walk away from my job at the paper and ghost books more or less full time. I supplemented my income with magazine articles on how I'd coped with the menopause or what to do when your dentist is also your lover; even doing this, the money wasn't very good – and was very sporadic too – but it was enough to get me by. And I did have about twenty weeks off a year, which is an *excellent* holiday package by any standards.

Hugh sighed a long sigh. 'Confronting your own mortality, it really makes you take stock of your life, you know?'

'Does it?'

'Of course it does. I mean, when you're a bairn you have all those dreams. How you'll be a big star. How Parkinson will have you on all the time – and as the final guest too, not as the "*But first* . . .". You'll have really made your mark for something or other. Then, one day, it settles upon you. You're trying to get a bin bag out of the kitchen before the plastic stretches and comes apart at the top and you're thirty-seven years old and it settles upon you; the realisation that it's over. This is it. Not only are you never going to be as famous as Elvis Presley, but you're never even going to be as famous as the wee bald guy in Benny Hill . . . Christ.'

His head sagged down over his desk.

'Done any more work on your book?' I asked.

'Yes. It's crap. Utter crap.'

'Oh well, maybe you can sell it to another publisher . . . I can think of two names right now.'

I saw Fiona. She'd come into the office and paused to pour herself a drink at the water cooler.

'Awww, don't, Tom. It's easy for you – if you decided to write a novel . . .'

'Oh, don't start that again.'

'Well . . .'

'Can I just . . . ?' I hung a finger in the air, indicating Fiona. 'I just want to have a quick word with . . .'

Hugh let out another sigh as his only response. I took this as clearance to get up and quickly move over to where she was standing.

'Fiona!' I exclaimed with a grin. I meant it to come out convivial and engagingly larger-than-life. It just came out loud. She turned to look at me as you would at a person who'd come up to you in a quiet office and shouted your name at the side of your head.

She took another sip from her paper cup before answering, 'Tom.'

'I was just sitting over there . . .' I pointed. '. . . and I saw you.'

She glanced lazily over at Hugh's office. 'Did you? Must be all of four yards away . . . Be sure to leave your retinas to science.'

'Haha, nice one.'

Fiona Laurie. Early twenties. Around five foot five (without her heels). Star publicist of McAllister & Campbell. Her eyes were pale blue and her blonde hair was short – in that style which normally indicates that a middle-aged woman is having some kind of crisis, but she'd managed to conjure 'sophisticated' from it somehow. Like me, Fiona was English – originally from Hampshire, I think – and she had been with McAllister & Campbell for just a few years. Most of that time had been spent in their London offices, though. The word was that she'd been sent up here because she was still too new for it to be seemly for her to be elevated in a choir-accompanied ceremony of corporate apotheosis, yet she was clearly too big for her junior position down there. She'd come to Edinburgh in the same way that in former times a favoured son of the Empire might be given Canada to rule for a bit before returning to become Home Secretary.

I couldn't care less about any of that, though. The most impressive thing about Fiona, in my opinion, was her immaculate superiority. How *did* she get her whites that white? Why did she never crease? I'd never seen her look less than witheringly perfect: shiny or matt in all the right places. She moved slowly too. That's always arresting, isn't it? Everywhere she went, she looked like *she'd* decided to go there because it suited *her* purpose. She was cool. Aloof.

It had a potent effect – the flawless presentation and the easy condescension: an overpoweringly attractive combination. Oh, and she had great tits too. Really *great* tits. Tits Classic. Each one (tellingly) just the size of my cupped hand, firm as fresh fruit and possessing the kind of nipples whose very existence powered the invention of thin, white, cotton blouses. I was utterly – *utterly* – ashamed of the things I'd lately started thinking that I wanted to become involved in doing with those tits; it wasn't like me at all.

'I . . . er . . . just popped in . . . to see Hugh,' I smiled.

Fiona took another sip from her paper cup and raised her eyebrows at me in reply. It was an efficient and winning way of wordlessly conveying 'Yeah? How very, very interesting'. She was belittling me using nothing but the power of her eyebrows. I shivered and was unable to step in to block myself having an involuntary glance down below her neckline.

'Well . . .' I said, hammering it home by following up first with a long exhalation from between pursed lips and then, cleverly, a meaningless click of my tongue. 'Well . . . I . . . I'd better be getting back to Hugh. Things to discuss . . . You know . . .' I clapped my hands together and opened my eyes indicatively wide. '. . . stuff.' Suddenly, I reached forward, my hand having gone insane and made a break for it with the intention of patting her affectionately on the shoulder. I regained control just in time, however, and managed to turn things around by changing the movement into a thumbs-up sign. Situation salvaged, I judged that there wasn't much more

I could achieve today, so I backed away from her, returning to Hugh's office. ''Bye.'

'Goodbye,' replied Fiona, watching me evenly as I retreated. 'I'm glad we had this chance to talk.'

'Which arm is it that's supposed to hurt if you're having a heart attack?' asked Hugh as I flopped into the chair by him.

'The left, isn't it?'

'Hmm . . .' Hugh rubbed his right arm thoughtfully. 'What about the other arm? What does that mean? Have they discovered what that means?'

'I believe there is a school of thought that believes it's linked to reckless use of rowing machines, but supporting evidence is still sketchy.'

'Yes,' nodded Hugh, unconvinced.

'Well, as we've got a couple of minutes before the Reaper arrives for you, have you got anything for me? Any work on the horizon? Talk quickly and stick to the basic facts.'

'No . . . Well, aye. Maybe. I'd rather not say at the moment, Tom.'

'You'd rather not say? What does that mean?'

'There is *something* in the pipeline. But it's big – *very* big – and I don't want to raise your hopes.'

'Oh, come on, you tease. I'm damn near broke – throw me a crumb.'

'You know it's not my say, Tom. I can make a suggestion, put in a good word for you, but that's all. This is an A-list book and I don't want to get you all excited then have it come to nothing – have you mentally spending money you won't get.'

'It's a lot of money?'

'Oh, aye. A lot.'

'Tch – tell me. I promise to speak glowingly of you at the funeral.'

'No. I'll know in a day or so. I'll put them in touch with Amy.'

'OK.'

Hugh had become distracted again.

'You know, I think my legs are aching too now. What about legs? What does *that* mean?'

TWO

'Tom? Is that you?'

Sara was calling from the living room. We'd been together for five years and no one else lived in the house or had a key, yet every time I came in she always asked whether it was me.

'No,' I shouted back, 'it's your lover.'

'OK. But Tom will be back soon so we haven't much time. We'd better do it on the floor down here. Leave your socks on.'

I ambled into the living room. Sara was curled up on the sofa, watching TV.

'Some men take their socks off?' I asked, alarmed, as I pecked the top of her head and sat down beside her.

Sara kept her eyes on the television but nodded enthusiastically. 'Aye – I saw it in a film once . . . Good day?'

'Nyah.'

'Do you love me so much that my absence is like a weight on your chest?'

'Yeah.'

'So you should.'

She waited for an advert for margarine to finish then turned to look at me. Her eyes scanned quickly all over my face; I think she'd always looked at me like that after we'd been apart for a while, but I'd noticed it more lately. 'What have you been up to, then?'

'I had lunch with Amy, then went to see Hugh.'

'Any commissions?'

'No. Hugh told me that something's coming up, but he can't be sure I'll get it so he's not saying much.'

'We could do with some new carpets.'

'Yes, I told Amy.'

'You *didn't* ... Did you?'

'No.'

'Yes you did.'

'Yes, I did.'

'Tch.'

She gave me a poke in the stomach.

'Ugh ... She's going to hand out some flyers with my photo on them, "Will work for underlay" ... So – how was your day?'

'A freezer fuse blew in Fish. No one spotted it and we lost a pile of haddock.'

'I see. What's for dinner?'

'Haddock.'

Sara's concentration started to drift away from me because her favourite soap, *The Firth*, had restarted. It was set in a fictional coastal town and featured the harshly lit lives of the varied inhabitants. There was a marriage every year and a dramatic death every two – regular as clockwork. The gaps between these were filled with feuds, rivalries, affairs and some kind of storyline that could pick up extra publicity by being promoted in the media as the show 'dealing with issues' or 'helping understanding' or some such; a character having dyslexia, say, or the effect that a parent being convicted of cannibalism has on the wider family. The show had been running for about a million years.

'Haddock,' I nodded.

'Aye,' she replied, mistily, as if speaking under hypnosis. 'A haddock omelette in chicken gravy ... there's some spaghetti hoops too ...'

Sara had a very *promiscuous* attitude towards food: what might be called an unusually inclusive meal gestalt. She didn't like everything ('Olives – bleugh!', for example), but if she *did* like it, then that was that. If she enjoyed ice cream and she enjoyed fried eggs, and they were both in the house, then it was as likely as not to be ice cream and fried eggs for lunch. Being a writer (even if only a ghost-writing hack of one) and therefore fatiguingly condemned by my nature to look for causes, influences and even – in moments of particular weakness – *reasons* for things, I would have been inclined to put this down to her job. She worked as a supervisor in a food shop. PolarCity: one of those big, chuck-it-out/sell-it-cheap places that sells mostly frozen food. For Sara, I would have mused – had I been writing her rather than living with her – food is simply a continuum that goes from the baskets near the entrance to the checkouts by the exit: put into sections only for the convenience of storage – it all goes into the same carrier bags in the end. That's what I would have said. That would have been neat. The trouble with this wry analysis as applied to real-world Sara – Sara out of the laboratory conditions of a narrative – is that it would be utter bollocks. Sara had been like this with food before she'd ever gone to work in PolarCity. She'd been like it ever since I'd known her.

When I'd met Sara she worked in an off-licence. She worked behind the counter at my off-licence and I'd see her when I went in to buy a packet of fags or a few cans of lager. I thought she was attractive, right from the very first time I saw her there. OK, so the person she replaced was a sullen, bird-eyed Glaswegian who'd had one hand moving disturbingly in his pocket on every single occasion I encountered him, but she'd have caught my notice favourably even without the comparison. She wasn't beautiful as defined by the stag-night consciousness of magazines like *FHM* or *Maxim*, but had a kind of, well (don't laugh), a kind of *allure*. Charging down from her head like the Golden Horde was a boiling mass of ginger hair – yep, 'ginger'. I'm not going to resort to euphemisms here. I'm not going to drop my eyes and mumble something about Sara being 'a redhead' or 'flame-haired': she's ginger. Deal with it. In any case, the fact that she had ginger hair didn't jump out at me all that much. For a start, I was still only twenty-two and when you meet a woman at that age you don't think much about her being ginger; you're not remotely considering having *children* with her, after all. Also, I'd been living in Scotland for quite a while and there are so many ginger-haired people here that you become almost numb to it. Her skin was pale (some slight freckling, nothing disastrous) – almost bone white, in fact – and her frame heroin thin. Actually, I suppose she looked quite ill; but then I think, subconsciously, I find that kind of look appealing – it's probably the capital-'R' Romantic in me. The thing that struck me more than anything else, however, was her eyes. Pale blue, as clear and sparkling as the wineglass in a washing-up liquid advert and, even then, starting to line at the edges from smiling. Sara smiled all the time. She used to smile at me as I came into the shop, smile at me when I put the cans on the counter and smile at me when I said goodbye. *Knowing* smiles too, that was the thing. Her face smiled, but her eyes looked at me and knew, *told me* they knew. She'd smile as I gave her my money but her eyes would snag mine and say, 'I know you looked at my arse when I turned round to get that packet of Marlboro off the shelf just then. You stared at the contours of my thin, soft dress and wondered if that was a thong I was wearing, or if my knickers had just *really* ridden up there; and you thought that, either way, it was a pretty good state of affairs as far as you were concerned. I know you thought that and, guess what? That's fine. I'm OK with it. In fact, I even find it amusing and cute in some kind of schoolboyish way. What do you think about that, eh?' It's powerful stuff when a pair of eyes puts you on the spot that way.

At first I tried to put a cordon around her. It was trans-ference, surely? I associated her with lager and fags, *that*'s why my heart picked up speed and my mouth slipped into an involuntary smile whenever I thought of her. Falling for the woman in the off-licence? How sad was that? Textbook pathetic: like becoming smitten with your nurse or your mother. No, hold on ... not your mother. Whau for – you know what I mean. But it wouldn't go away. I found myself 'forgetting' things. I'd 'forget' to buy a box of matches, so I had to go back to the shop a second time. I'd suddenly decide at 10.30 at night that I needed to sprint over and get a single packet of crisps. Not because of her – no, simply owing to my sensing that my body wouldn't settle because it lacked salt. This madness continued for a while but things really became fatally unhinged when I found myself standing at the counter holding a bottle of dry white wine.

When she'd first started working in the shop I'd come in for a four-pack of lager produced by no one you've ever heard of – 'Weinermeister: brewed under licence in a big shed in Doncaster', that kind of thing. I'd scan the stock, ignoring everything but the price labels and the alcohol content of each item, do a quick 'cost divided by strength' calculation to work out the underlying Getting Pissed score of everything, and then go with whatever seemed most efficiently engineered. But then, one evening, as my fingers reached for the week's special offer, I happened to glance towards Sara and she, of course, smiled. My hand hovered uncertainly over the cans, then it reared up and began to rub my chin mendaciously: I was pretending to consider my choice based on more impressive criteria. 'Mmmm ... what *would* be an appropriate lager to accompany the *lapin à la moutarde* I'm having for dinner ... ?' And I picked up a four-pack of Carlsberg instead.

I'd crossed a line.

The next time I went in I bought McEwan's Export. Then Kronenbourg 1664, then just two cans of lager and a bottle (a *bottle*, mind – sophisticated) of Guinness, then ... well, basically at the end of the road I wound up standing at the counter holding a bottle of fucking dry white wine. I was trying to convince the woman who worked in the off-licence that I was urbane and multi-layered using some sort of alcohol semaphore.

Then the final phase hit me: I lost the ability to speak. Good job, you might think, when the only place left for me to go by this stage would have been to ask whether she perhaps had this wine in a 'carafe'. But, sadly, I don't mean that I went mute, just that I abandoned words in favour of making more or less random noises with my mouth.

I have a problem, you see. I'm a reasonably articulate person – no great raconteur or anything, but I'm passable enough at stringing phonemes together to convey simple ideas. I can talk to women without any problem; talk to them without either awkwardness or embarrassingly misjudged, bombastic shouting – I didn't go to a public school, after all. Even women I find attractive don't interfere with my communication skills (I am perfectly able to speak with my tongue hanging out). However, when and if I move from finding a woman attractive to having 'a thing' for her – even if I don't realise, consciously, that I *have* got 'a thing' for her at this point – then my ability to speak to her at anything approaching adult level simply leaves town.

I believe I was halfway through buying a cheekily crisp Chablis, twenty Marlboro and a bag of pork scratchings one evening when my evil, rat-bastard id decided – flick of a switch – that I'd now got 'a thing' for Sara and should therefore shed the English language. I could actually feel the words moult from me and fall uselessly to the ground; tumbling over my shoes, scattering across the counter like tiny ball bearings and bouncing randomly over the floor of the shop. I only had to say, 'No, that's fine' (because I *didn't* want anything else) and 'Thanks. 'Bye, then,' for Christ's sake. But every time I made a grab for the sentences, the effort of doing so blew the words out of my grasp – like when you try to catch a thistledown but the very movement of your hand through the air causes it to pull off an impressively rapid, evasive loop-the-loop and you open your hand to find nothing. I just stood staring at her for what seemed like most of the 1990s with a kind of vacant, hillbilly grin on my face (*'Don' you be payin' no nevermind to young Cousin Tom – ain't a scrap o' malice in the boy, but he done had a diff'cult birth'*) before I finally marshalled the array of forces needed to produce a noise like Goofy laughing, and then left the shop. I went home, drank the Chablis in ten minutes and woke up the next morning halfway up the stairs with my trousers round my knees. (I like to imagine – still – that I was trying to make it to bed.)

Things could have continued quite happily along these lines until either Sara got a job somewhere else or my liver exploded. I tried, a couple of times, to slip in (you know, pulling myself back just as I was leaving, as a sudden afterthought) a 'Do you live around here, at all?' or a 'So, what do you like to do when you're not working in this off-licence?' or even a 'What's your name, by the way?' On the first attempt someone else came into the shop just as I was about to begin speaking. Naturally, I fled. The second time I tried I ended up buying a box of fifty cocktail umbrellas. Having failed twice, wretchedly, I did what any sensible man would do: I retreated into a bunker and hoped for a miracle.

Later that week, there was a miracle.

OK, not quite a 'miracle', but a favourable coincidence, at least. I was still working for the newspaper at this time. A bunch of us had gone out to the pub after work to celebrate some occasion or other (I can't remember what it was now, but clearly to cajole a group of journalists into an evening's drinking it must have been something pretty special). We were sitting there, discussing the issues of the day, when Sara strolled into the bar enclosed within a semi-permeable casing of friends. A woman called Beverly had just had her decree absolute come through and they'd all dropped in for a few drinks before moving on to a club. Even better, one of Sara's friends turned out to be the cousin of our young production assistant. She quickly took the opportunity to come over and embarrass him and thus our two gangs intermingled. It was perfect. I was by Sara, in a social setting, but not under any pressure to form sentences for her. I could slowly ease myself in – the occasional 'Yeah . . .' or 'Haha . . .' from the sidelines being enough to keep me in the match. I even gleaned that her name *was* 'Sara'. (Make a note of that, I thought, that could come in useful later. There's no stopping me when I get going, there really isn't.)

When the women went on to the club a few of us went with them. This was a bit of a backwards step, really. By the end of the pub session I was doing rather well. I'd edged around to where Sara was standing so that, not at all infrequently, our forearms brushed. I'd uttered – OK, to the group at large, but my eyes paused on her – an entire phrase ('I'm just popping to the toilet'). I'd even offered her a crisp, and – get this – *she'd taken one*. The club, however, pulled the rug from under me and I was cast into a smelly, sweating, shuddering hell. Another hour or so in the pub and I could probably have pulled off a 'That's a lovely necklace' (at which point you're practically fumbling impatiently with each other's zips, of course). But that was irrelevant now because, even if I could summon up that kind of captivating patter, it was almost impossible to hear anything above the deafening roar of the music. Basically, anything that couldn't be shouted in fewer than five syllables was both too prone to sonic attrition and also too painful to be worth it. We can add to this the fact that I dance like a fool, and also that I seemed to be a catastrophic half a decade astray; I bumped against a group while I was getting a drink at the bar and one of them shouted, 'Watch it, Granddad!' Granddad. I was, I reiterate, twenty-two years old at this point.

It went on and on. For *hours*. I watched Sara dance and got so drunk that I came out sober on the other side. Every so often one of our party would leave off creating a humiliating spectacle amid the other dancers, come over to me at the bar, shout, 'Waaaah!' (I'd shout, 'Waaaah!' back), grab a quick drink and then rush back to abase himself some more. When it was well into the early hours, some kind of collective consciousness in our party eventually called a halt and we splattered out into the street – giggling, stumbling, hoarse, sucking greedily at the wonderful, cool oxygen. Taxis were summoned and, while some called it a night, quite a few of us went back – for 'a nightcap' – to what turned out to be the flat Sara shared with two friends.

And I slept with her.

Lord, she was pissed. More or less insensible and giving the acute impression that she might pass out at any moment. It causes a bit of an internal struggle when you're faced with a woman who's inviting you to bed while she's so clearly mentally incapacitated by alcohol; a real dilemma. How you resolve the situation in a way that allows you to feel comfortable is a purely personal decision, I believe; I'd certainly never judge anyone for taking a particular route. I mean, obviously, you want to have sex with her but, at the same time, you're a little uncomfortable with the idea that she might puke over you. I decided that the best thing for both of us was if I just had sex with her very quickly – then it'd all be seen to and if she *did* feel a bit nauseous later on, well, she wouldn't have me to worry about and that'd at least be one thing off her mind.

It started in the kitchen. Sara had gone in there to get a drink and I happened to be in there too, because I'd followed her. I made a fabulous joke ('Thirsty, then?' – which was quite funny, you see, because she was drinking a big glass of water) and, after just the tiniest amount of mumbling nonsense from both of us, we'd suddenly begun to kiss. (My memory of it is that Sara moved on to me rather than the other way round, and that's what will be recorded in history – as Sara herself can remember nothing

23

whatsoever about the entire evening.) After some really quite excellent snogging, she suggested we go to her room. Once there, without a word, she began to remove her dress – one of the thin, vaguely hippyish, cotton affairs she favoured. She grabbed it at the hem and pulled it right up over her head, turning it inside out in the process. She wasn't at her most balanced and dextrous, and it caught under her nose; the dress was off her body but still concealed not only most of her head but also both her arms which, raised up, were trapped inside. Trying to free herself, she swung and flapped the dress about – she looked vaguely like a huge, dancing cuttlefish. Finally, the edge of the neck hole pulling her face into the Phantom of the Opera, she managed to tug herself free and hurled the defeated garment across the room with a triumphant 'You *fucker*'. She wasn't wearing a bra – which at the very least saved us tens of minutes and quite possibly some kind of dislocation injury to her shoulders – so now she dropped backwards on to her bed and scrambled her knickers off in under half a dozen moves. So, there she was. Lying on the bed in front of me, completely naked.

Looking down at her, I knew that getting myself past the finish line in double-quick time really wasn't going to be a problem at all.

The next morning wasn't like one of those moments that those who've slept with *loads* more people than you have just can't stop themselves from telling you about (they're not bragging or anything, obviously; simply lamenting, oh-so-self-mockingly, how *awful* it is: 'it *always* is'). Moments when you wake up with someone and you can't remember their name or they're a singer who's at number four in the charts but you just hate their music really or they're triplets or something. There was no terrible awkwardness or backtracking. I could now articulate whole phrases, just like a real person. (Unless it solved itself less dramatically by my becoming distracted by a different woman, my speech problem always cleared up after I'd had sex with the person for whom I had 'a thing'. Funny, that.) Sara awoke perky and smiling.

'I don't generally go to bed with men I barely know – even if they are regulars in the shop,' she said, chattily more than anything else.

I could see it was a casual remark and she didn't seem to be suffering from any anxiety or anything, but I was keen to reassure her.

'Oh, God – *of course not*,' I replied. 'I don't think you're a slag or anything. You were just really pissed.'

'Cheers,' she said and – all potential misunderstandings now avoided – we thought about getting up and having some breakfast. I took a quick shower and, when I got out, Sara had already prepared porridge with tinned tomatoes and grapefruit. All in the same bowl. Obviously.

So, she's always been like that with food – which, you'll remember, was what I was telling you about.

'What are you going to do tomorrow?' asked Sara, sitting on the end of the bed rubbing some kind of cream into her feet.

'I'll probably go into M&C and badger Hugh some more – see if I can get any extra info out of him about this "big deal". Anyway, I think he likes me to drop in and keep him from his work. The more he works, the more books get published and the number of books being published already depresses him terribly. Maybe I'll have a word with Amy too. She went to some magazine bash today, so she might have scared up a little work . . . Why?'

'Och' (I still found it hard to believe that I lived with someone who said 'Och'), 'no reason . . . I just wondered whether you might remind Hugh about the video of the Dunkirk thing . . .'

She'd had Hugh (who had satellite TV, with its 800-plus channels of sport) record the cycling for her. And she was trying to be casual – a fatal mistake.

I toyed with her.

'The Dunkirk thing?' I asked, puzzled.

'Aye. Aye, you know . . .' She hurriedly finished off her feet, placed her watch on the bedside table and wriggled under the duvet: all without meeting my eyes. 'The Four Days of Dunkirk . . . the cycling.'

'Ohhh . . . the *cycling*,' I said. Handing my face over to a huge grin.

She finally turned to look at me and, my grin foremost, I leaned closer to her. She smacked me in the face with the pillow.

'Och, away with you, you fucker.'

It was Sara's Secret Shame: she liked to watch cyclists. What was at the heart of it, the aspect that really took hold of her, I don't know. Maybe it was those Lycra shorts, perhaps the rhythmic breathing, it could well have been the taut, rolling buttocks thrust up and exposed to the chasing camera on demanding hill climbs. It might even have been an association dating back to when she was young – some frantic moment behind the bike sheds or one Scottish girl's private discovery of how interestingly a well-placed saddle could translate the cobbled Edinburgh streets. I had simply no idea because, ludicrously, Sara denied that there *was* anything to it other than a sober interest in the complex and intriguing sport of bicycle racing.

'What?' I asked as the pillow fell away to reveal my face. I was surprise. I was innocence.

'You *know* what. I'd like to see the tape; the Four Days is an important event in the calendar, and a real indicator of form for . . .'

'Uh-huh.'

She hit me with the pillow again.

'Oh – just ask him, will you?'

'Yeah,' I said, pulling her over on to my chest, 'I'll ask him.'

She bit at me, gently. 'Do you love me in more ways than there are stars in the sky?'

'Yeah . . . sure,' I replied. And, well, *I really did.*

THREE

'Fio ... na!' I'd started to reach out and touch her arm somewhere in the middle there, and then thought better of it. 'I've just come.'

She raised a single eyebrow about a quarter of a millimetre. It was devastating.

'I mean, I've, er, you know, just come ... in ... here ... Just now. Walked in, through the door.' I mimed opening a door. 'Haha ... Yes. Anyway, I've come to see Hugh ... That's "*Hugh*", of course – not "*H-you*". Hahaha! ... Yes ... Well, suppose I'd better ... better ... you know ... "Thyme and parsley wait for no man." Hahaha!' What *the fuck* was I talking about? 'Yes ... well ... anyway. Better go and ... *heeere* I go. 'Bye, then. Good to see you, anyway.'

'Tom.'

I started to walk over to Hugh's desk. No, come on – let's be honest – I started to do a *little dance* away towards Hugh's office. I appeared to be suffering from an abrupt neurological impairment that had robbed me of the ability to process shame.

Hugh had a copy of the previous night's *Evening News* spread out over his desk and was revolving an empty coffee cup endlessly round and round in his hands as he pored over it. Thus wholly preoccupied, he hadn't noticed my approach and looked up only when I spoke.

'Oh, hi, Tom,' he replied, managing a weak, token curve in his lips. If some people's smiles are supposed to be able to light up a room, then Hugh's can dim one. 'What are you doing here?'

'Came to see you, obviously – who else would I have come to see?'

'I don't . . .'

'There you go, then. What are you reading?'

'What? Oh, I'm just going through the obituaries.'

'Who are you looking for?'

'Well . . . *me*, really. "Male, died aged thirty-seven." I'm comparing myself with the general state of play. You know: trying to get an idea of the form. If I see one "died aged thirty-five", then I think, well, that's pretty good. I'm not doing so badly – I'd have been dead for two years now, if I'd been that poor sod. That's something to be thankful for.'

'*Do* you?'

'No. No, I don't. I think, Christ – he died at thirty-five. I must be on an outrageous winning streak – it can't go on, how can that kind of luck hold out for much longer?'

'Good point. I'd get Satan on the phone: you need to cut some kind of deal – *now.*'

'It's like graveyards. You know when you're in a graveyard? Browsing in some country church or hanging around at a wedding, say?'

'Yes.'

'And you start looking at the inscriptions on the gravestones out of a vague curiosity or just to pass the time?'

'Yes.'

'And you calculate from the dates of birth and death how old each of these people was, so you can compare it to your own age?'

'No.'

'Well, it's just like that. If they're younger it's terrifying. If they're the same age, well, that's just rubbing your face right in it, isn't it? So, that's terrifying. If they're older, then that's . . .'

'Terrifying?'

'That's right. If they were forty-two, say, you think, that's just five years. Five more years: can I really achieve all the things I want to in just *five more years*? Considering I've been trying to achieve them for thirty-seven years now and I've got nowhere . . . I did some more work on my book last night, by the way . . .'

'Really?'

'Yes . . .' He let his head drop, as if this were explanation enough.

'Ahh . . . When *I* open the paper I always go straight to the personals.'

'What for?'

'They're fascinating. Addictive, even. I've been studying them recently and it's another world: all these people agonising over each word of the printed sound bite they have in which to define themselves utterly; who they are, why they're there, what they're hoping for. "Thirty-four-year-old single mum, five foot four, likes reading, keep-fit and Motown. Been hurt before, now seeking caring prince, 25–42." Tiny, two-sentence novels with the last few pages missing.'

Hugh grimaced, scrunched up his plastic cup and lobbed it into the waste bin.

'Sounds depressing to me . . .'

'Well, I can see how you'd think that – their not being dead and everything. In fact,' I nodded to myself, 'they're the true opposite of being dead.'

'Aye, I bet Sara often walks in when you're scouring them and says, "Tom! Going through the personals, eh? How delightfully life-affirming of you!"'

As it happens, I hadn't mentioned my newly discovered penchant for the personal pages to Sara; it just hadn't come up. I wasn't hiding it, you understand, I simply flipped to another page if she walked in so that she didn't misconstrue.

'Sara finds them intriguing too, actually, Hugh.'

'Really?'

'Yes, *really*. Anyway, never mind that: have you sorted out this commission thing?'

'I told you, as soon as I know anything definite I'll give Amy a ring.'

'When will you know?'

'I don't know.'

'When will you know when you'll know?'

'My God, you're annoying. Even for an author. Look, I'm seeing the people today; if it goes well, I'll put Amy on to it for you right away.'

'And if not today?'

'Then I'll escape out through the kitchens dressed as an old Mexican woman and you'll never find me.'

He clearly wasn't going to be bullied into giving up any information (don't you just *hate* people who are discreet?) so I reminded him about Sara's videotape and then went for an aimless wander around town. It was a warm, spring day and the streets were abubble with the usual mix of hawkers, tourists and homeless people. I collected fifteen flyers – tours, events, *Incredible!* and/or *Insane!* offers on new mobile phones; I didn't intend to follow up a single one of these things, of course, but I like to give the people handing them out a sense of achievement. I'm sure it must be spirit-crushing to stand in the middle of the pavement all day, a friendly smile fatiguing your face, trying to give out bits of paper to people who either refuse your offer contemptuously or take the thing only to scrunch it up and hurl it away four steps later. I always take the flyers. I like to think that it brings a little joy into the lives of the people distributing the things: they get home – weary, cold and reeking of traffic fumes – numbly cast their corporate-logoed jacket on to a chair, but then remember me and, with a smile, say to their partner, 'Today . . . I made a difference.'

With nearly twelve pounds burning a hole in my pocket, I meandered about, tried not to constantly think about Fiona's stern breasts, and did a little shopping. I bought some food, thinking I'd make the tea tonight. (I was inured to Sara's cooking by now, it's just that sometimes you like to sit down to a meal that's not quite so capricious. I got a frozen pizza and an M&S salad: in terms of steadiness, iconic, I thought.) By mid-afternoon I was back in my house with my laptop open upstairs in what I'm amusing enough to call my 'den' and had four hundred words of a magazine feature written. It was on 'shipboard romances' – I've never been in a dinghy, let alone a ship, of course, but I feel that being ludicrously exact about these things is best left to writers who already have new carpets in their houses.

I was pretty pleased with the raw material and was tapping away at the keyboard placidly when my mobile rang. I snatched it up from the table greedily. As I said earlier, my professional reputation is built on grim application – I'm The Deadline Kid – but this isn't because I'm keen or anything. I am – for a writer – very self-disciplined and diligent but I'm not some kind of freak. I'll always invite distraction in if it turns up, but it's doubly fatal if the intrusion happens to be my phone: I have a weakness for phones. Not just this particular mobile – though that would be understandable. It's not a top-of-the-range phone, but I did try to justify the expense of buying it with the desperate stand-by of saying to Sara, '. . . and then *you* can have my old phone!' which demonstrates quite how logically unsustainable the purchase was. (Especially as Sara already had her own phone and had no intention of changing it.) A slim, silver body, its contours erotic to eye and hand, my phone is as pleasingly light as if it were made out of meringue. A tiny LED blinks – what am I talking about? *Winks* – at me coquettishly whenever it's turned on. The instant a key is pressed, the display blooms into a liquid blue glow and all the buttons light up green from beneath. It's extravagantly triband, hints at a wonderfully louche sexual ambiguity by having both a phone *and* a SIM memory, and teases me with voice-activated dialling: I can call anyone in my phone book by simply pressing a single, quick key button on the side of the phone and then speaking his or her name. Obviously, I'd never do this in public – you might as well wear a hat with 'Twat' written on it – but, alone in the house, I'll often caress the soft rubber nipple on the edge and command, 'Amy' . . . a brief pause, then 'calling Amy . . .' appears on the display and I feel like Captain Picard on the bridge of the *Enterprise*. The fact that the phone vibrates too is simply sensual excess and, even before I evoked that feature, I'd already decided my mobile phone was alive, female, and called 'Natasha'. Anyway, as I say, my telephone weakness isn't isolated to this particular phone – and I wouldn't want you to think I was *obsessed* with it or anything – but is more general and long standing. I've always grabbed at ringing phones rapidly and instinctively. Perhaps because I have some vague feeling that it's the sound of Fate, or Opportunity, or Hope, knocking on the door. Who knows who will be on the other end and what fabulous news they'll have to impart – news that will change everything, for ever. If there's a better way of beginning a book than 'The phone rang . . .' then I can't even guess what it could be.

'Hello, Tom Cartwright.'

'Tooooooooom!' Amy, being an agent, always gave good phone. Even though *she'd* rung *you*, she always sounded surprised, yet delighted, to discover you were the person on the other end of the line.

'Hi, Amy, how are things?'

'Things are in a champagne Jacuzzi, shagging like baboons, Tom.'

'I see.'

'I've just had a call from a guy called Paul Dugan . . .'

'Who's he?'

'A wanker. London agent – so, a wanker, obviously – but we'll turn a blind eye to his stupid estuary English and his ridiculous, self-important lunches at the Ivy, because he happens to be *Georgina Nye's agent!*' She paused briefly for effect, and then elaborated. 'Georgina . . . Fucking . . . *Nyyyye!*'

A little tingle, I admit. Georgina Nye . . . this meant money. She played the part of Megan in *The Firth*, and Sara wasn't the only one who liked that particular show. It was currently the top-rated soap (and thus, by infrangible laws of the universe, the top-rated show of any kind) on television, and Georgina Nye was the star of it – she probably had more lingering close-ups just as the closing music kicked in than the rest of the cast put together (I knew because I'd sit by Sara on the sofa while it was on, pointedly reading the international politics section of the newspaper . . . but the damn programme sucked you in so unstoppably that half the time I'd even forget to tut theatrically when it finished). She was not merely a TV star, though: she was the UK's sweetheart. What's more, because of Megan's independence and her championing the rights of the women at the factory, she had become acknowledged – even in the broadsheets (though they protected themselves with the careful application of wryness) – as a working-class, postmodern, feminist icon. Women viewers loved her. The male viewers loved her too – both because she was undoubtedly a bit of a looker and also because she gave off the impression that, if it took her fancy, she could actually shag you to death. Full cross-gender appeal, then. If a book with Georgina Nye's name stuck on the front of it was coming out it would sell, everyone knew it would sell, and therefore the publishers would stump up an utterly obscene advance for it. And if Amy and I had anything to do with it, some of that advance would be heading right into our pockets.

'Georgina. Fucking. *Nyeee!*' she repeated.

'What's she thinking of doing? Glitzy novel set against the backdrop of a fictional television soap opera or something?'

'Autobiography.'

'Oh, nice – what is she? About twenty-eight? And she's been doing the same thing, three nights a week, for a decade of that.'

'So you'll need to make up half of the length entirely with adjectives? So what? With the money we're talking about here you'll be able to buy a fucking *huge* thesaurus.'

'What money *are* we talking about, exactly?'

'McAllister and Campbell paid one and a half million pounds for this book – I'll be after getting ten per cent of that out of her agent, even if it means fighting the bastard in the car park.'

'One and a half million? Jesus.'

'Abso*lute*ly. And there were other publishers offering not far off that as well. Apparently, they went with M&C because of the Scottish connection. The overwhelming bulk of their business might be in London now – the tossers – but M&C have that "Edinburgh born and bred" angle and actual offices still up here. The plan is to push the whole Scots thing, you see. Georgina Nye: Scots actress, in Scottish show, having her book published by a Scottish publisher. They want it to come out to coincide with the Festival too. I bet they even give it a tartan cover. Ha! Fuckers.'

'Mmmm . . . It's going to be tight if they want it on the shelves for the Festival, we're halfway through May now.'

'Nah – a publisher can puke out a book in six weeks if they have the will, a budget and somewhere to dispose of the bodies, you know that, Tom. But they need someone who – *definitely*: no scary doubts – will smack a completed manuscript down on their desk in about three weeks.'

I heard the fizz of a match and her speech became cigarette-in-mouth impaired.

'Dee tigh deadlinesh our aesh inna hole, Dom.'

Sucking breath. Whooshing exhalation.

'They can't afford unforeseen delays,' she continued, 'and you *are* Mr Foreseen.'

'So – when do we sign?'

'Ahh, now . . . we haven't quite got the bastards yet. Georgina Nye wants to meet you before she gives the go-ahead. Make sure she feels "comfortable" with your being the person who tells the story of her life, under her name. Some kind of fucking hippy, clearly. Anyway, she's staying in a hotel up here now, so: one p.m. tomorrow, by the Scott Monument – be there, and be charming.'

'In the park? Couldn't we have met over lunch or something?'

'*I* didn't pick it, you bamstick. That's where *she* wanted; who the hell knows what she's thinking – she's an actress. You just go and meet her. Figure out what she's looking for, then be that. OK?'

'OK.'

'Good. As soon as she's given the final nod, I'll set to work fucking over her agent.'

'Georgina Nye? Wow!'

'It's still not certain I'll get the contract, Sara. Don't go ordering new kitchen cabinets just yet.'

I was very excited about the prospect of a commission of this size so, naturally, I was deeply keen to keep Sara from getting excited about the prospect of a commission of this size.

'I didn't mean the money,' she said. 'The money's irrelevant . . . Well, except that if I know you've just got a cheque for a hundred and fifty thousand pounds I'm sure I'll suddenly find you hugely attractive, sexually.'

'Pah . . . you find me hugely attractive, sexually, already. We both know it, so it's foolish to pretend.'

'Not *a hundred and fifty thousand pounds* sexually attractive, though. Just sexually attractive at the level of . . . well, what have you got in your pocket right now?'

'A rocket.'

Sara raised her eyebrows and smiled mockingly.

'Aye – one of those that always explodes on the launch pad. No, really, Tom, I didn't mean the money. I meant, "Wow! *Georgina Nye*." Do you think I'll get to meet her?'

'I doubt it. She'll probably want to get the whole thing over with as quickly as possible. I reckon I'll have one afternoon noting down the name of her first hamster, she'll give me half a dozen photos of the "Here I am on the beach, aged six – little suspecting that . . ." kind, some instructions to subtly rubbish a couple of her co-stars and that'll be it.'

'Och – she won't have you rubbish anyone . . . She's really nice.'

'How do *you* know?'

'I read it in *Heat*.'

We both laughed and Sara dropped back on to the sofa, kicking off her shoes; one bounced under the table and the other landed in the magazine rack.

'Seriously, Tom, she supports campaigns to help working mothers and stuff like that, so she does. She's a . . .'

'Feminist icon – I know. The title of chapter fourteen, I'm thinking there.'

'You're cynical, that's your trouble.'

'Not by nature, only by experience.'

I sat down beside her.

'Wow . . . Georgina Nye . . .' She was staring up through the ceiling into some magical, unfocused distance. 'I'm really excited now.' Shuffling back a little, she put her head on my lap for stroking. 'Do you love me so much that my very name tastes sweet on your tongue?' she asked.

'Yeah, whatever.'

I wasn't sure of my timing. It's always the same with an important meeting, of course. There's something innately submissive about being there first. Yet, while being early can look a little desperate, being late might smack of arrogance or ineptness. You can pull it off if *you're* the important party (I

37

imagine, I've never been that party) by playing the endearingly scatty card: 'Sorry, I – *sorry* – phew! I just got caught up and – oh, don't ask! Phew! What *am* I like?' But, as the person who is (let's be honest) begging to be given a job, arriving late will never be a good move. Which leaves arriving *precisely* on time. Unutterably awful, that one, clearly. Might work if you're asking to be employed as a proofreader or an accountant, but otherwise you're going to look like a bit of a trainspotter – vaguely creepy, even. What I generally do – and I think this is the only thing you *can* do if you're an adult who's taken some time to consider all the issues and come up with a clear-headed course of action – is I arrive early, and then hide. I find somewhere close by and conceal myself: wait until I see the person arrive, pause for fifteen seconds, then march in – apologising *profusely* for being late. Works every time. Well, except for those times when the person you're meeting happens to walk up behind you while you're crouching watchfully behind a low wall across from the meeting place; if that happens you're pretty much into 'faking a seizure' territory, really.

So, bearing all this in mind, I took a taxi and got stuck in traffic.

I held out bravely for a long, creeping while, but at the bottom of Cockburn Street, I finally decided that there was no point sticking with the cab any longer: I paid the driver and raced across the bridge towards the Scott Monument as fast as I could. As I neared the other end, I abruptly changed my flailing run into a brisk stroll (I thought that'd appear more businesslike if Nye caught sight of me).

However, when I got to the monument . . . no Nye. I walked around the seated Scott, oh, let's say 'eleven' times, trying to pick her out of the people there. Not that difficult, really; I knew she wasn't male and I knew she wasn't Japanese so that narrowed it down to just two or three people each time I orbited. But, with each fruitless revolution, I became one level of certainty more convinced that she'd waited a little while and then, when I hadn't turned up, marched off in a colossal celebrity huff. I could get Amy to call her agent – 'Terribly sorry, Tom was at the scene of a road accident, couldn't leave the injured, or use his hands to phone without having to release the life-saving pressure he was applying to at least one person's artery.' They obviously wouldn't believe this, though – or even care. I'd lost the deal. *One hundred and fifty thousand fucking pounds.* I'd be kicking myself later – after Amy and Sara were both through kicking me.

I started peering around farther away from the monument. Maybe she'd left, but paused – to look in a shop window, say, or to read a mobile phone flyer – and I could still catch up with her and . . . well, and grovel.

I actually looked at her three times before I suspected it might be her. She was standing staring up at the statue of Livingstone, about twenty-five yards back along the way I'd come (I must have walked right past her). It was because you always expect famous people to look how they look while they're busy being most famously famous. Even if you're meeting them for lunch in Kentucky Fried Chicken, your brain expects David Bowie to have a coloured lightning flash across his face and be wearing a one-legged leotard, Harrison Ford to be running around avoiding some frightening peril and Dannii Minogue to be nude. I was looking for Georgina Nye dressed for *The Firth*: wearing factory overalls or a British Home Stores frock with her trademark coal-black hair washing animatedly over her shoulders. But here was a young woman in canvas jeans and a baggy Nike sweat top. She had sunglasses on – not Ray-Bans or wraparound shades, either; just the kind you'd reluctantly buy from a petrol station while cursing the drawer full of the damn things you had at home – and, crucially, her distinctive locks (a shampoo-endorsing gold mine, undoubtedly, if only *The Firth* didn't famously include a 'no adverts' clause in its contracts) were hidden inside a felt hat a little like the one Chico from the Marx Brothers used to wear. Anxiously, I walked over to where she was standing, all the time peering at her with an 'is it?/isn't it?' squint. I stood beside her and coughed.

'Um . . . excuse me . . . are . . .' I suddenly realised I didn't feel comfortable calling her either 'Georgina' or 'Ms Nye', and the full-blown 'Georgina Nye' made me sound like I was about to ask for her autograph so, even if it was her, she might simply lie to avoid drawing attention to herself. 'Um . . . I'm Tom Cartwright,' I said. (A world-class disconcertingly unbidden announcement to make to her if she was simply an unfortunate young woman standing there all alone gazing at a statue, but pretty much all I could think of that was appropriate to say if she actually was Georgina Nye.)

Thank God.

She beamed at me, displaying a quite impossible number of teeth, and replied, 'Oh – hi!'

I'd already prepared an affecting mini-drama where I'd double-take at the clock on the tower of the hotel across the road, glance – startled and appalled – at my own watch, press it to my ear, become spontaneously furious, tear it from my wrist and hurl it away down towards the railway tracks, cursing.

However, she seemed completely unconcerned about my lateness and before I'd even arranged my face into the prelude to horrified realisation she nodded up at the statue and said, 'Dr Livingstone, I presume.'

Quite the most hideously predictable thing it's possible for anyone standing at that point on earth to say. Statue Livingstone must hear that twenty thousand times a day, every day of the year. It's a wonder that the sheer, maddening repetition of the words doesn't cause Statue Livingstone to come to life, climb down from his plinth and savagely kick the speaker unconscious.

'Hahaha – nice one,' I said.

'What's that he's holding?'

'Erm . . . it's a book, isn't it? Probably a Bible, you know, with him being a missionary and all that.'

'Oh . . . yes.'

'Anyway, you have to hold something.'

'What?'

'If you want to be a statue in Edinburgh . . . You have to hold *something* – I reckon it's a by-law.'

'Really?'

'Yeah. All the people in the statues here have something in their hands. When they did the sittings I bet the instructions said, "Come to the studio at eleven. *Bring something to hold.*"'

She grinned at me again and, without a word, strode off purposefully down towards the Scott Monument. I was flat footed with confusion for a second, and then I trotted after her.

'*All* of them?' she asked, when I'd caught up.

'Um, I . . . yes. I'd say all of them.'

She paused and peered up at Sir Walter Scott, sitting under his monument, with his dog. 'A book,' she acknowledged.

'Yes. There you go. I . . .' But she'd taken off again. She was heading farther down the edge of the park, this time at a jog, to the next statue. Christ – actresses. I gave chase.

Adam Black. Hair a dignified white from copious amounts of pigeon crap: *easily* the favourite of all the crapping pigeons in Princes Park – don't ask me why.

'What's he got? I can't make it out.'

'A scroll, I think . . . some kind of document. He was an MP, wasn't he? So maybe it's a parliamentary paper.'

'He's absolutely *covered* in shit. Look at him.'

'Yeah, well – if you're a Scottish politician you're pretty much bound to get crapped on.' A winning joke in a fabulous number of ways, I congratulated myself. Before noticing she hadn't heard my off-the-cuff brilliance because she had already begun running along to the next statue down.

'Ah-ha! Got you. He's not holding anything.' She pointed triumphantly at John Wilson. 'You can't count that cloth, or whatever it is; that's just draped over his shoulder really.'

'No . . . look at his left hand . . . See? Another scroll.'

'Where? . . . Oh, right. Damn . . . Where's the next statue?'

'The next . . . ? Um . . . There – down across the junc . . .'

She was off.

Allan Ramsay. Staring across with huge gravitas at Barratt's shoe shop. And – I win again – holding a book.

'*Another* book.'

'Well, it's Allan Ramsay, he would be. But, anyway, Edinburgh is a town that takes books seriously,' I said, self-servingly.

'Next.'

'Next?'

'What's that up there?' She made off, at very nearly a sprint, up the Mound towards the Old Town before I could reply. I could have done without this. I'd had a big bowl of Sara's spaghetti and clotted-cream stew before I came out and it was lurching around in my stomach like I'd swallowed a moderately sized live dog. And they don't call it the Mound because it's flat, either, by the way. Nye, however, seemed utterly oblivious to its being leg-defeatingly steep and sped up the thing like a scampering rodent. I had to will myself to catch up with her; overruling my muscles with every stride and picturing £150,000 floating slightly above her head.

'Erm . . . can I just . . . you *are* Georgina Nye, aren't you?' I asked as I drew up, gasping, alongside her.

She grinned at me again. 'Do you generally follow women round Edinburgh at random, then?'

'Much less since the injunction,' I tried to say, but I think it was lost in the wheeze.

'Mmm . . .' She pulled to a halt. 'A rifle. I *suppose* I can let you have that one.'

'It's the Black Watch . . . It'd look stupid if he were holding a cake.'

'Right. Let's carry on round. I bet there are some more up there.'

'No!' I instructed. Well, OK, 'pleaded', then. 'No!' I pleaded. 'We can cut through there . . . if we *have* to c . . .'

She went bounding away up Lady Stairs Close.

I'd pointed out the short cut hoping to plant another psychological suggestion in her mind by taking her past the Writers' Museum, but she was five yards ahead of me and I didn't have the chance, nor anywhere near the breath for that matter, to point it out.

She was glancing up and down the street when I reached her. I had half a second to gather myself before she cried, 'There!' and sped away towards David bleeding Hume. (A tablet of some description – damnably, as his being empty handed would have been a desirable defeat for me because it would have brought this nightmare to an end. Sodding philosophers.) 'There!' again, and – faster, if anything – she shot off across the road. I was beyond the farthest shores of knackered. I wasn't running in any accepted sense of the word any more. You know how children gallop odd-legged – like Igor crossing Frankenstein's laboratory carrying a torso – when they are pretending they're riding a horse? That's how I was moving.

She was standing squinting up at the statue carefully.

'I think I've got . . . Oh, bugger it!' she said. 'A pair of damn gloves! Where's the next one?'

'That's it.'

'What?'

'That's it. Really, that's it – there are *no more statues in Edinburgh*. I swear to God . . .' I slumped to the ground below the 7th Duke of Queensbury, sweating like a pig. 'That's it.'

My heartbeat was hurting my eardrums and there was this buzzing noise that seemed not to be localised in my head, or even simply my body, but engulfing Scotland generally. I sat gasping on the cobbles, my forehead inconsolably sobbing tears of perspiration that wriggled down my nose and dripped on to the stones. Georgina Nye leaned back against the plinth and tugged a packet of cigarettes out of her pocket. Great: she smoked. She smoked, and yet she'd reduced me to this. Either she had the lung capacity of a whale or I had no more than five working red blood cells in my entire body.

'Want one?' she asked, offering the cigarette packet down to me.

'No thanks, I gave up years ago.'

'Sensible. I wish I could.'

'Yes . . . I'd take today as a warning shot across your bows, if I were you.'

She laughed. 'Oh, I try to do five miles a day – that and some aerobics keep me slim. Well: that and some aerobics and the cigarettes keep me slim.'

'A three-point plan. Maybe that's the book we should do?'

She smiled at me. She was friendly enough, but I couldn't read exactly what she was thinking. Still a bit wobbly, but at least no longer feeling like someone was sandpapering the inside of my chest, I pulled myself to my feet.

'I'd like to see the city,' she said, blowing out cigarette smoke with more vigour than my smoke-free lungs could dream of. 'I've only been here once before, and I was four years old at the time: all I can remember is people's knees. I was thinking we could go up the Scott Monument – you can do that, can't you? That's why I suggested meeting there, so we could look over the whole city.'

I might have been up for that, but only before I'd made a casual remark about statues that had resulted in a near-death experience (I was sure I was floating at one point, because I *definitely* couldn't feel my legs). The very last thing

I wanted to do now was go all the way back to where we'd started, and then climb about three hundred steps. This book might be worth about fourteen years' worth of money to me, but it was no use if I were dead before I'd signed the contract.

'Going to the top of the Camera Obscura is higher, if you want a view of Edinburgh,' I replied.

'Really? Where is it?'

'Just up the road there – it's really close.' Better for her *and* not requiring anywhere near as much exertion from me. There was a bit of luck, eh?

'Cool. Let's go, then.' She bounced off again. Where did she get this kind of springy energy? It wasn't normal. She was like a woman in a tampon advert – she even had the white jeans on, for God's sake.

We made our way up the road, paid the entrance fee and climbed up inside the Camera Obscura building. I was pretty smug, I don't mind saying, that I got all the way up to the rooftop viewing area without passing out. Nye leaned against the rail and lit another cigarette.

There were only a few people up there: looking at leaflets and talking excitedly in Italian. We stood silently side by side for a few moments and gazed out across the stony browns and greys of Edinburgh towards the distant cranes pinned along the waterfront. I wanted to get down to business, of course, but I thought that if I stared wordlessly over the rooftops for a bit I'd come across as contemplative.

'So, you want to write my autobiography, then?' Georgina said suddenly.

'Yes. I think I could do a good job of it. I've had a lot of experience of ghost writing, for all kinds of people, so you can be sure that I'd produce something you wouldn't be ashamed of.' Ugh! What a moron. I should have said, '. . . that you'll be proud of,' that would have sounded far more emphatic:

45

'Sara, I've just lost us one hundred and fifty grand. Yeah . . . litotes again.' Hell and arse.

Nye, however, seemed focused on other things.

'Hugh Mortimer recommends you highly.'

'Well, that's very . . .'

'He says you're a genuinely talented writer.'

'I've never missed a delivery date yet.'

'No, not just efficient. He said you were a natural, that you could be an author in your own right.'

'It's awkward for me to say I'm great, of course,' I replied with a smile. 'But I like to think that I'd produce a book for you that read well. That had a little flair in the prose.'

'That's not what I'm getting at. I'm wondering why you don't write for yourself.'

She didn't have much of a Scottish accent. It was there, if you listened, but distant or vestigial. The accent of her character in *The Firth* was far broader – like Sara's. I realised that she must put it on for the show.

'Oh, don't worry.' I smiled again. 'I won't leave you in the lurch because I've suddenly dropped everything to go off and write the classic, epoch-defining novel.'

'Are you deliberately being evasive?'

She managed to say this without it sounding accusative or irritable – simply innocently curious.

'Um, no . . . I just meant – I ghost-write. I ghost-write books, or do magazine features where my name, some other name or no name gets a byline – as needs be. It's what I do.'

'No desire to make your mark? No yearning for fame?'

'Fame's bollocks.'

She simultaneously smiled and looked like I'd just said the Pope was really a woman called Trixie who used to work down the docks. I backtracked a little.

'Well . . . not *utter* bollocks. You know, I don't want to *ban* it or anything. It's just . . .'

'Worthless?' I think she was teasing me.

'Illusory. You know why I think most people want to be famous?'

'Um . . . money? Power?'

'No, not . . .'

'Adoration? Respect? Getting to refer to Denzel Washington as "Washy"?'

'No – that's not the main thing. Ask most people if they want to be on TV and they won't even *think* of asking if they'll get paid – let alone respected, sexed or drugged. It's the fame itself they want, for its own sake. And they want it because, on some level, they think it'll make them immortal.'

'So?'

'Well, that's not true, is it? We're in the twenty-first century now, and people remember some twentieth century figures. What about in the twenty-*fifth* century? Who'll they remember? Hitler, maybe? And in the four hundred and seventy-second century? In historical time Elvis is only a heartbeat away from anonymous. A billion years of celebs will pile on top of each other, burying the ones below, then the earth will be consumed by the sun – after that, just voiceless time until the universe ends it all utterly. It will be as if I'd never appeared on *Me and My Pet* at all.'

'Well, you certainly like to think ahead. I'll say that for you.'

'I'd just prefer to pass on the whole fame business, thanks. Write the words; collect my cheque; buy a carpet. Fame's just wrapping paper: a few seconds and then the wrapping paper's in the bin.'

'Right.'

'Well . . . not if it's really good wrapping paper, and you can get the Sellotape off without causing too much damage – then you'll store it under the bed thinking you can reuse it. But it's still quite a good metaphor.'

'I see.'

'Especially as you never *will* actually reuse it. It'll just lie there for years, forgotten about, until you have a big clear-out one day and throw everything away in a cathartic orgy.'

'Hmm.'

'And, yes – OK – I bet *the very next day* you suddenly need wrapping paper, and now you have to go out and buy some. But that's hardly the issue. I didn't say you could just keep extending the metaphor for ever, or anything.'

'No.'

I thought I'd now made my point pretty skilfully, so I fell silent.

She stared at me for a few moments with that unreadable expression again and then turned away, looking out over the city once more.

'I've always wanted to be famous,' she said. Then, after a pause, 'Are you married?'

'Er, yes. I mean, as good as. Sara. We've been together for about five years.'

'Is she a writer too?'

'No. She works in a frozen food store.'

'God – a proper job . . . I've wanted to be someone famous for as long as I can remember. Not famous for anything in particular. I didn't stand in front of the mirror pretending to be an actress or a singer or a model. I just used to have fantasies where I was being interviewed.' She slipped into a, very well executed, performance of playing someone being thunderously nonchalant. 'You know, "Hahaha – well, that's a question I'm *often* asked, Lionel . . ." *Nothing* is more conclusively validating than being interviewed. People actually wanting to know what you think – what you think about *yourself*, even.'

Or just the fruitful collision of people's morbid curiosity and the strategy of some publicity department, I thought. But I didn't say that. Instead I said, 'Yes.' (But retained my integrity by giving it an ambiguous inflection.)

'Sometimes I think I only see my therapist because it's like being interviewed – all that talking about yourself.'

She saw a therapist. Jesus.

'Right,' I said. Same inflection.

'Anyway, there was nothing I wanted more – no, there was nothing I wanted, *full stop* – except to be famous. Being interviewed. Photos in the Sunday supplements of me chatting at exclusive parties. People stopping me in the street and saying, "Wow! You're *Georgina Nye*, aren't you?" Meeting other famous people and being somebody other famous people wanted to meet. Yet now, if there was a button I could press and it'd all go away – I'd be a normal person; a normal, non-famous person just by pressing a button – then, do you know what?'

'You wouldn't press it.'

'No bloody way.'

Again her toothacular grin.

'I suppose you think that makes me shallow or something? Needy?'

'Not at all,' I said, shaking my head with emphasis. 'I don't think fame's desirable, it's not something *I'd* want . . . but I feel the same way about anchovies on a pizza – and I don't make moral judgements about people who order the Neapolitana.'

She scratched her nose.

'I like you . . . Do you like me?'

'Well, I don't really know you . . .'

What a *stupid* answer to give at this proximity to £150,000. I should have just said, 'Yes,' why didn't I just say, 'Yes'? This is why I needed Amy – Amy would have said 'Yes' *right away*, without even having to think; it'd have sounded sincere too. I quickly recovered, though.

'Um, I mean, yes.'

She turned around, leaned back on to the rail and pushed her hands into her pockets.

'I'm going to tell Paul that I want you to write my book.'

'Excellent.' Axminster, Wilton – here we come!

'I like you; you're clever – which means you'll make *me* sound clever; and you're normal – which means you'll make *me* sound normal. I don't want to come over all showbizzy, and I think you're the ideal person to see to that.'

'I will – if that's what you want. Thanks, that's brilliant, Ms-um-Ny-Georgina.'

'George. Call me George.'

'OK. George. You can call me Tom. Obviously.'

'Tom.'

'George.'

'Brilliant.'

I reached out, grabbed her hand and shook it. Which was an idiotic thing to do, of course, but I was realistic enough to realise that there was no way I could possibly stop myself from doing it. If all went according to plan, this meant well over a dozen times more money than I'd ever got for a commission before. She was lucky I just *shook* her hand, rather than falling to my knees, pressing it to my forehead and beginning to weep.

'Right,' she said, 'what do you want from me?'

'I'll need to go through everything with you – get all the basic biographical facts, any anecdotes you have lying about, that type of thing – and for this kind of book they'll want some photos too. Not publicity shots, but more personal stuff: family snaps or behind-the-scenes pictures.'

'Right, I think I can arrange the photos at some point. When do you want to start hearing my life?'

'Whenever suits you best.'

'Tomorrow?'

'Sure, if it's OK with you.'

'Well – as you know – I simply *hate* being interviewed, so I'd prefer to get it over with.' She grinned. Hugely winningly.

'Look . . . here's my phone number,' I said. 'Just give me a call – tonight maybe? – and we'll sort it out.'

'OK.'
'Right.'
'Yes.'
'Brilliant.'

II

Hiya, God here again. Forget I was watching, did you? Yeah – that happens a *lot*. Ha ha! Relax, relax, it's OK – I'm just kidding with you. I got to tell you, one of the real drags about being God is being, you know, misunderstood. You know what I'm saying? It's like I crack a joke and everyone's, 'What did he *mean* by that? Should we laugh? Or is he going to smite us or something?' I'm telling you, it'd really get me down if I let it. And expectations too. Man, you wouldn't *believe* the expectations people have of you when you're God. They can come to you with a real attitude because you don't do things just the way *they* expected. Sometimes I have to get a bit heavy, you know – remind them of the lines. 'I hear you're upset, and that's OK. But lose the attitude or you'll find yourself in a situation – you hear what I'm saying?' Like, say, when they die. Some of them stand there shooting their mouth off. Real *obstreperous*. They're like, 'Hey, Tony – we followed this religion or that religion and this God or these Gods, and it turns out you're nothing anyone's ever *heard* of! Why didn't you tell someone, eh? Do you realise the time we've wasted panicking about certain days and what to wear and how to do things and what we could say? And don't even *start* us on the nightmare we've had keeping to the *diet*.' You know, like that's *my* fault. I have to try to calm them down, yeah? Say I can see where they're coming from, but *I* didn't make all that up and, frankly, some of it . . . Well, for ages I didn't think anyone actually *believed* that stuff, I thought they were just pretending to believe it for a joke. You know, being kind of ironic. Anyhow, eventually I generally get them to calm down. It's a bit of a kicker wasting all that time (though, I tell you, mostly I think they're angry just because they're embarrassed) but that's over. Put it behind you. Fresh start. They usually come around in the end. It's a pretty good place here, all things considered – we even have mini-golf now.

Whatever – let's stick to the matter in hand, yeah? The tale I'm laying on you here, with Tom and all those guys, I'm showing you it so you understand a few things, OK? I'm trying to show you why things happen the way they do. It's about how stuff works, basically – that is, it's about how *you* work, that's the thing I'm trying to explain: the reasons you all behave a certain way and how you stick to the path, even though you can't *see* the path. Some of you may not like what I have to tell you, but it's for the best that you understand the situation. So, for now, I just want you to watch the people, yeah? I know how you guys tend to get, well, 'distracted', right? You look at what work people do and where they are and all that kind of thing. The scenery. You get all caught up with the details and can't see beyond them. Well, don't, OK? What's happening here is what always happens. And there are reasons for that, but I'll come to those later. Just don't get distracted by any of the background noise, OK? Watch the people. Don't think about who they *are*, watch what they *do*. It's the people: the people is always the important thing.

FOUR

I rang Amy about four seconds after I'd said goodbye to George. She was pleased with the way the situation was progressing and commended me on my personal diplomacy.

'Yessssss! Way to go, you fucker!'

Amy said she'd get in touch with George's agent and start working through the details right away.

Sara was also pleased.

'What was she like?'

'Damn quick on her feet.'

'See – I told you she was canny.'

'No,' I said, shaking my head, 'actually I meant that literally. It nearly killed me trying to keep up with her running all over town – she's like a bloody whippet.'

'What else? Tell me everything.'

'There's not a lot to tell; I haven't really got a handle on her yet. She likes the whole celebrity game, certainly, and I think she might be a bit of a thesp on the sly, but that's about it.'

'What was she wearing?'

'Sara, can I just mention that it would make my working relationship with her tricky if you're going to start stalking her, OK?'

'Och – I'm just *interested*. You don't usually have proper stars. You have boring adventurers or people who've suffered huge personal tragedies . . . but this is real *interesting* stuff – she's on the telly.'

'Oh, right. She was wearing meaningful canvas jeans and a thought-provoking sweat top.'

'Wow. That's just the kind of thing anyone would wear. *I* might wear something like that, even . . . Wow.'

'Would you like me to get you a glass of water?'

'Tch – you *git*.' She punched me playfully in the ear, then rested her head on my shoulder and said, almost sleepily, 'I suppose, what with her being so famous, that she can get loads of complimentary things . . . You know, a wee enquiry about something and they just give her the stuff . . .' She drew swirling patterns on my chest with her fingertip.

'I am *not* asking if she can get you free bicycle race tickets.'

She lifted her head off my shoulder abruptly and sat up again.

'It could be a way of getting her to talk,' she said. 'You never know, she might be interested in the sport in the same way as I am.'

'Interested in it *in the same way as you are*, eh?' I replied, grinning.

'I have no idea what you're implying there . . . but you're a wanker, OK?'

I kissed her nose. She rubbed it off with her hand, extravagantly, but returned her head to my shoulder.

'Do you love me so powerfully it dizzies you like a glorious drug rushing through your bloodstream?'

'Yeah, I suppose so.'

'Good . . . well, keep the tickets in mind – just in case the subject ever comes up in general conversation with her.'

George rang at about half nine. (When I heard her voice, I spontaneously stood up. Tch.)

'Tom?'

'Oh, right – *George*,' I said, trying to affect a 'lots of other business deals on my mind' nonchalance. 'Hi there, I was just . . .' I waved a hand in the general direction of the curtains. '. . . you know . . . So, how are you?'

'I'm fine, thanks, fine. Look, does it matter where we do this interview?'

'Well, not really. Best not to do it at an all-nighter really – my Dictaphone has a poor bass response – but as long as it's not too noisy and we can talk freely, it doesn't matter. Over lunch in a hotel room, say, or in a quiet restaurant, perhaps . . .' I was, obviously, gunning for being fed on someone's expense account.

'Right. That's great – I thought we'd do it on Carlton Hill.'

'Great.' Yeah – great. Not only did it look like I wouldn't be scrounging a meal but she was getting me to climb God knows how many steps as well. Couldn't the woman function at sea level? If this carried on I'd be calling Amy and getting her to add the purchase of a bloody mule to the commission.

'Great,' I repeated.

'OK, I'll see you there at, say, two o'clock? The weather's supposed to be good tomorrow and I hear the view's lovely from there.'

'Yes. Great. The view. Yes – I look forward to it.'

Jesus.

I did a bit of research on the Internet in the morning. As you'd expect – what with George being a feminist icon and all – there was a good selection of sites offering photos of her naked. After checking out just thirty or so, however, it became clear that all the pictures were fakes. There was one picture that took a great deal of studying, but in the end I concluded that the shadows were wrong and that it was also pretty unlikely anyone would have that kind of wistful expression on their face while performing the act shown. The only genuine thing on offer appeared to be a shot up her skirt as she was getting out of a car at some premiere or other – her crotch helpfully magnified as a detail to the side of the main photo. She was, in any case, wearing knickers (pretty mundane ones at that), so it would only be of interest to people who got off on seeing that her legs joined at the top. Oh, I learnt that she was thirty years old too. The Internet really is a tremendous resource.

I took the bus into town early and made my way up to Carlton Hill. My being late for our first meeting was a factor in making sure I was there ahead of time, but not the main one. It's a steep walk up there and, when George arrived, I wanted to be already at the top of the path, lounging nonchalantly against the railings like Marlon Brando leaning on the jukebox in *The Wild One*. Rather than appear on my hands and knees, gasping for air, like, um, well, like Marlon Brando trying to walk up Carlton Hill, later in his career, I suppose. I strolled up, spent a little time enjoying a search for my breath, and then picked myself out a good spot. I tried several positions: back to the path, gazing up at the Observatory; one hand clutching the black iron railings, the other pensively at my chin; looking over the graveyard and the river and the castle; lounging back, hands deep in my pockets, eyes closed as my face tilted up to accept the warmth of the sun. After a good deal of experimentation, I decided on the final pose but – fatally – shuffled about a lot trying to find a place where I was angled just right and the spikes on the railings weren't spearing me in the back too severely. Too much careless shuffling. When George arrived I was doing a little slap-drag-look-slap-drag dance in an effort to get a great, sticky, ochre dog turd off my shoe. Right up in the arch it was: it's a bugger to get them off when they hit there.

You know what I think the worst thing about smells is? An unclear provenance, that's what. Smelling of garlic is unpleasant, of course, but I'd far rather have someone think of me 'He smells of garlic. He's been eating garlic, and now he smells of it' than 'My word, what *does* he smell of?' At least if people know then they'll make allowances, accept that, well, these things happen. Far better that, in my opinion, than being someone who is giving off a mysterious odour. I mention this because I hope it explains why, when George strolled up to me, smiling, and said, 'Hi there,' my reply was, 'I've got dog shit on my shoe.'

A gambit I followed immediately by lifting my foot up to show it to her.

She looked down at the turd squashed out beyond the sides of my sole and nodded.

I moved off a little to scrub my foot against some longer brushes of grass while George waited patiently for me to return. She had on the same sunglasses and hair-concealing hat that she'd worn yesterday but now she was wearing them above a pair of – pre-aged, no doubt – jeans and what looked like a man's white cotton shirt (it was too big and the cuffs reached almost to her fingertips). She also had trainers on again. I hoped this wasn't a bad sign.

When I made myself acceptably shit free I trotted over to her.

'OK – all done. Shall we . . . ?' I offered the hill to her.

'Would it be all right to sit up there?' she asked, pointing to the National Monument (a recreation of the Parthenon: inspired by classical Athens, but imbued with a distinctively British quality by having run out of funds and been left half finished).

'Yeah, I suppose so.'

Young people tended to gather on the steps of the National Monument and 'hang out' in the early evening. God knows why they couldn't do this outside McDonald's or at the bus station like youths everywhere else in Britain but, in any case, none of them was here at this time of day. A few tourists wandered around taking pictures of each other standing in front of things but, other than that, it was pretty quiet. We strolled over and scrambled up on to the monument, plonking ourselves down between two of the pillars.

'Gorgeous view,' she said.

'Um, yeah, I suppose so.' And, I suppose, it was. Edinburgh's an extraordinarily spiky city. There's little of the thudding, sterile blocks you see when you look out over many modern places. It looks more like the stalagmite-strewn floor of a cave: random and pointy and crystalline. 'I'm a bit blind to it, maybe, having lived here for ages,' I admitted.

'Whereabouts do you live?' She swept her eyes back and forth, waiting for me to tell her where in the vista she should look.

'Ha! Nowhere you can see from here. I live way out over there – in a grey-walled semi that used to belong to Sara's parents. Absolutely *anything* you can see from here we couldn't remotely afford . . . Anyway, is it OK if I . . . ?' I pulled the Dictaphone from my pocket and waved it questioningly. She shrugged amiably and I started recording.

'Right . . . Hold on – one, two, one, two . . . OK. So, I take it you don't come from Edinburgh, then?'

'No. I come from a village in East Ayrshire called Mauchline.'

'I see – interesting place? Anything we can use?'

'Robert Burns lived there for a while.'

'Ahh . . . so rare to find a place in Scotland that boasts a Burns connection. Anything else?'

'Nothing springs to mind.'

'Never mind. I'll investigate – see if I can flannel something up.'

'I left when I was seven years old, you see, so I can't really remember all that much about it.'

'Oh, right. Where did you move to?'

'Coventry.'

'Jesus.'

'It was for the work.'

'I imagine it'd have to be.'

'My father got a job in the car plant there.'

'I see . . . and how long did you stay in Coventry?'

'Until I was eighteen.'

'Uh-huh.'

'Then I moved to Stoke Newington.'

'Right . . . right. Where do you live now?'

'Chiswick.'

I rubbed my nose a bit.

'Mmm . . . don't take this the wrong way . . . but you're not *tremendously* Scottish, are you?'

'I was born here. And I still come up nearly every week for filming – the studios are in Glasgow.'

'I'm sure it'll be OK. "Give me the child until seven . . ." as the Jesuits say, eh? It's just that, if we're going big with the whole Scots angle, I'll have to play up Mauchline, and play down Coventry and Stoke Newington.'

'I see.'

She looked sort of apologetic, as though she was sorry for causing me the bother. It was obviously false, of course – polite, professional regret; precisely the face a shop assistant gives you along with 'Oh, I'm *so* sorry – that item isn't in the sale. It was simply displayed right in the middle of lots of other massively more rubbishy items that are . . . by some regrettable quirk of fate.' It was quite endearing, though. She could easily have just shrugged: she was paying me to do the work, after all.

'Not that playing down Coventry and Stoke Newington is ever going to be that tricky,' I said.

'And Chiswick?'

'Mmm . . . Let's see if we can avoid mentioning Chiswick altogether, shall we?'

I questioned her methodically to find out the basics: parents, siblings, friends, education, names, dates, and all that kind of thing. After that I let her ramble, with just the odd nudge in some direction here and there. She did, indeed, like talking about herself so it wasn't the draining ordeal I sometimes had. I could get a rally driver, say, who would talk excitedly for *hours* about axles, but when you tried to find out some details of his schooldays (so the reader would find him human and engaging, and thus *care* about what axles he had used in later life) you'd get 'My schooldays? Pretty normal. Same as everyone else's,' and then silence. (And then more axles.) George, in contrast, was almost embarrassingly forthcoming. I got her first sexual encounter (that'll be 'First Love' in the book, I can tell you now) related to me in evocative detail when I'd only asked her what she did after school in Coventry . . . I mean – she even did the voices.

The tape came to an end and I paused to turn it over. Always an awkward moment, oddly. People feel they should say *something* while you do this – just as you feel the need to make a comment to the barman while he's pouring your Guinness or the mechanic who's taking a first look into your engine – yet, given that this is the point where the tape's not recording, they want to be sure that what they say is something of no significance or interest whatsoever.

George said, 'Lovely day.' Then, however, she did something that quite shocked me. It shouldn't have, of course, but it did, so I was further quite shocked that I was quite shocked by it. She pulled off her hat and then, placing it down next to her like a bowl, took off her sunglasses and tossed them into it. Instantly . . . she was Georgina Nye. Her distinctive dark, bubbling hair poured out across her shoulders like a pan of jet-black milk boiling over and there – *there*, right in front of me – were the eyes that the camera held in close-up so many times as they looked out of frame at a villainous factory owner, a tragic car crash or an unexpected pregnancy. The famous usually don't look quite right in real life. They're often shorter than you expected, or oddly brown, or tired or old or – most often – jarringly ordinary. But George – perhaps because I'd got used to her half hidden under her hat and glasses and now here she was unexpectedly complete – didn't have disappointment lying a single glance behind her celebrity at all. In fact, I suddenly 'got it': I understood why she stood out from the countless other pretty, but unemployed, actresses in the country. I couldn't say precisely what 'it' was – some subtle combination of things, a magically winning constellation of tiny flaws, perhaps – but 'it' was got now, definitely. I summed up all these thoughts in one, involuntary, exclamation.

'Fuck.'

'What?' asked George. She saw my expression and quickly scanned her top – presumably looking for stains or escaped breasts – and then, finding nothing, went cross-eyed trying to examine her own face.

'Sorry. You just turned into Georgina Nye – I wasn't expecting it.'

She grinned at me. 'Oh, *darling*, that's so sweet . . .' She rested her thumb and finger on the palm of her hand, miming a pen and paper. '. . . who would you like me to make this out to?'

'Yeah, yeah . . . OK.' I smiled back. 'I didn't say I *liked* you or anything, I was just surprised to *see* you.'

'Sure, back-pedal all you want. You have this whole anti-fame thing going on but then you encounter my . . . um, my *presence*, and your entire philosophy lies in ruins.' She plucked a packet of cigarettes from her shirt pocket and lit one. 'Is it running yet?'

'Uh?'

She nodded towards the Dictaphone.

'Oh, right, hold on . . . OK. We're going.'

More biography poured out. Ironically – as I'd just seen how remarkable she was to look upon – what she was saying was deeply *un*remarkable: to be honest, I was going to have to work pretty hard at making her life remotely book shaped.

I tried to keep from just staring at her and drifting off. It was an added difficulty when I really needed to hunt out anything useful I'd be able to put down on paper. One problem was that there wasn't a stand-out incident to work around. If you're doing an autobiography because the person has taken gold in the World Nude Hula Hoop Championships (which I've just invented, of course, but which I suddenly realise is actually something that's a very good idea indeed) then there's your story: I dreamed, I practised, I competed, I won – hurrah! The same thing, just a different shape, if it's the tale of a lottery winner or someone succeeding after a debilitating accident or having been born with ridiculous ears. George wasn't really like that: she was just persistently famous. What everyone wants if the person is persistently famous is 'revelations'. Something shocking about their co-stars or a nice little Percodan addiction that they've struggled to hide, overcome and which, 'in some ways, readers, has made them a stronger person'. George, on the other hand, was telling me how she'd had real trouble with the people who'd fitted the shelves in her flat. I was beginning to feel that I'd have to pay someone to trick her into smuggling a plaster Buddha stuffed with heroin out of Malaysia so I had any sort of third act. It was almost as though she was doing it deliberately to wind me up: her parents hadn't abandoned her, none of her boyfriends had abused her, all her friends were really nice and she'd never had anything worse than chickenpox – what kind of a life was that? Maybe I ought to push her off the National Monument right now? It was a good six feet to the ground and at least a nasty fall would give me *something* to work with.

I realised I was just staring at her and had drifted off again.

The interview went on for almost two hours before she had to leave for another appointment. I'd got lots of facts, and I enjoyed her company immensely – she was remarkably charismatic, and talked with an intimate, easy confidence; it wasn't at all that she was dull, personally, absolutely the opposite – but she hadn't given me a single thing I could get any mileage out of. The damn book was going to read like Pinter.

'Well, I'd better get going,' said George, tapping the face of her watch. 'You'll want to do another one of these, I suppose?'

'Yes . . .' Yes, give me a chance to uncover the bombshell of that time you went up to someone in the street and touched their shoulder but it turned out not to be the person you thought it was, just someone who looked quite like them from behind. That can be our big finish. '. . . yes. I'll go off and work on some things and that'll probably throw up a few questions. If we could meet up again to go over them, that'd be great.'

'OK. I'll give you a ring, then. Look forward to seeing you again – it's been fun.'

'I've enjoyed it too.'

She put her hat and glasses back on, leaned over, gave me a media-issue kiss on the cheek and then, with an easy athleticism, jumped down on to the grass. I watched her walk away towards the town – she turned back just before she went out of view and waved; I held up a hand in reply. She was an interesting woman. Pity she didn't do any interesting things.

'Oh, Hugh, *don't*.'

I was in Hugh's office at McAllister & Campbell for an initial state-of-play meeting. I'd arrived a few minutes early so, predictably enough, Hugh was using the time until the others arrived to tell me about his prostate.

'No, no, listen . . .' he continued. '. . . I'm just telling you so that you'll know when you start having prostate examinations yourself.'

'But I don't *want* to know about them until I actually start having them, Hugh. It'll spoil the surprise.'

'Though, you might want to begin having your prostate checked out even at your age, you know – you can never be sure,' he went on, not listening to me. 'So, you know how the doctor checks your prostate, right? He, or she, pokes a finger up your rear.'

'Nice one. They use the same method to cure a stutter, I believe.'

'OK, you might say "Fair enough" . . .'

'My very words.'

'. . . but do you know what I find the biggest problem is?'

'No.'

'Guess.'

'Hugh, my head is already full of the most frightening images – things that could haunt a person for years. I *beg* you not to make me think about it any further.'

'Chatting. I go into the doctor's office, pull my trousers down and bend over the examination table . . .'

'I've heard this one – it turns out to be a chip shop, doesn't it?'

'. . . and he – or she – slips on a rubber glove, applies a bit of lubricating jelly and then inserts his – or her – finger. *That*'s when it starts getting awkward.'

'Surely not, Hugh? That's *the best bit*.'

'The doctor is feeling around in there, I'm bent over the table . . . and I feel I should say something.'

'Reminds me of Georgina Nye and my Dictaphone.'

'*What?*'

'Never mind, it doesn't matter.'

'So, I feel I should say *something* – you know, to break the silence. But, well . . . what do you say? If you're hunched forward with someone's finger up your bottom and you say to them, "Did you see the football last night?" it just sounds kind of odd coming out of your mouth. I desperately want to say something to fill this terrible silence, but I simply cannot find the right level of informality for the situation.'

'Don't they have an etiquette column in the *Daily Telegraph*? You should write in.'

'And the worst of it is, it starts to play on my mind even while I'm waiting outside for my appointment. I get all tense.'

'Which is something of a hindrance to what's coming next. I see the problem.'

'I get all tense, and I panic over what I should say. I run all the different subjects through my head. Nothing feels appropriate. If you went in with a bug you'd probably make small talk by asking if it was going around at the moment, but you don't feel right asking someone with their finger stuck in your behind if they've been doing it a lot recently. And there's not only what to say, there's when to say it. Leave it too long and the silence has become an issue already, but start right away and, well, you feel like one of those dolls where you push a button and they start talking . . .'

'Now *that*'s the Barbie I want.'

'. . . How long after insertion is *just right* to ask if they get much chance for a holiday in their job?'

'I don't know, Hugh. And I'll tell you something else: I'd be profoundly worried about myself if I did.'

Hugh gave me a pained expression – though I couldn't say whether this was due to the conversation we were having now or simply his mentally reliving his last prostate check. He opened his lips to say something further but just then Amy burst into the office and his mouth snapped shut immediately.

'Hiya, Tom! Hugh! Hi! You miserable fucker!'

'Hello, Amy.' He began tidying some papers that were already tidy.

'Right,' said Amy. 'If we're all here then we might as well . . .'

'Oh, Fiona's not here yet,' Hugh pointed out.

Amy knew perfectly well that Fiona wasn't there. 'Fiona? . . . Och, *Fiona*.' She took a cigarette from her handbag and placed it between her lips. 'Should we start without her?'

'Sorry, Amy, you know you can't smoke in here.'

'I'm not smoking, Hugh. So, should we start, or is it important we wait for her . . . for some reason? I mean, she's clearly late. Because I was late, and she's not here yet.'

Hugh looked at me pleadingly. I turned away and let my

head drop to the angle that indicates you're fascinated by seeing what titles are on someone's bookshelf.

'Um, she *is* head of publicity, Amy. I think . . .'

Fiona swept through the door at just that moment and some of the tension left Hugh's shoulders – though he still had enough to keep him going for a week or so. She wasn't exactly flustered, but she was a little agitated and had obviously hurried over from whatever she'd just been doing.

'Sorry,' she said, without especially looking it. She rolled her eyes and shook her head – 'Phew! My frantic world, eh?' – before repeating the apology. 'Sorry – I appear to be all behind.'

'Oh, *no*,' replied Amy, reassuringly. 'Just a bit heavy around the hips, that's all.'

Fiona looked at Amy. Amy looked back at Fiona with an innocent smile on her face. Fiona continued to look at Amy. Finally, Fiona dug up a good-natured grin from somewhere deep, deep inside and said, 'Hahaha' (just like that; she didn't actually laugh so much as *say*, 'Hahaha'). 'I get it.' She walked to her chair, going around behind Amy (tugging the sides of her skirt down as she did so), and added, 'Yes, very funny.'

I joined them around Hugh's desk, taking the free seat between Amy and Fiona.

'Right . . .' began Hugh.

'I'm *terribly* sorry, but you aren't allowed to smoke in here,' Fiona smiled at Amy.

'I'm not smoking, Fiona,' Amy smiled back.

'So then,' continued Hugh, 'Georgina Nye's book. I believe it's all sorted out between you and her now, Tom?'

'Abso*lutely*,' replied Amy. 'Just dotting a final few "i"s and crossing a couple of "t"s.'

'So, you haven't actually signed yet?' Fiona asked.

'As good as.'

'But not actually?'

'As good as actually.'

'I . . .' said Fiona, writing something on her pad. '. . . see.'

Amy took the cigarette from her mouth and tapped it on the top of the table. 'Georgina Nye,' she said, talking to Hugh, 'has told her agent to commission Tom. They've met twice already, Tom has a good angle for the book . . .' I didn't, of course, but at this point Amy looked at me with a secret eyebrow arrangement she had, so I nodded to everyone reassuringly. '. . . and time is a real issue here. Anyone who thinks Tom isn't going to be the person to do this book is, well . . .' She looked over at Fiona and waggled her hand a little, as though the word temporarily escaped her and she was asking Fiona for help locating it. Just as Fiona began to open her mouth, Amy continued. '. . . an arsehole. Georgina's agent, Paul Dugan, and I are simply nailing down the details.'

'Good,' said Hugh. 'Fine.'

Fiona ostentatiously brought the tip of her pen down to rest on her notepad. 'You say you have an angle, Tom?'

'Yes,' I replied.

'Abso*lute*ly,' added Amy, but Fiona kept her gaze on me. I thought she looked a little tired, though, actually. Her eyes hadn't got quite their usual penetration; it was as if her pale blue irises were, well, *pale* instead of icy. Maybe she'd been working too hard and it was catching up with her.

'Yes,' I repeated, with a smile.

She peered at me, and something between surprise and confusion ghosted across her expression for just a moment before irritation settled in and made itself comfortable. 'Well, would you mind telling me what the angle *is*, at all? Because – who knows? – I might want to mention it in some small way during the publicity campaign.'

'The whole Scottish thing is already a given,' I said, playing for time. 'That's all going to be there. George as a Scottish actress, *The Firth*, a big launch to coincide with the Festival – I don't have to tell you all this, Fiona.'

'But you seem to be doing so anyway, Tom. And don't think I'm not grateful for that.'

'But – *but* . . .' I held out my hand, index finger and thumb slightly apart, as though showing the exact, yet deceptively small, size of 'but' . . . or something . . . God, I don't know *what* I was doing. '. . . what's the problem with the Scottish angle?' I sat back in my chair, smiled and folded my arms, clearly waiting for her to give the obvious answer. Which I'd then repeat because I certainly had no bleeding idea what it was.

Amy popped her cigarette back into her mouth and stared at Fiona expectantly.

'Um, well . . .' Fiona glanced across at Hugh.

Hugh turned away and let his head drop to the angle that indicated he was fascinated by seeing what titles were on his own bookshelf.

'. . . well,' Fiona continued falteringly, 'it's Scottish. The Scottish angle is a good angle, but it won't be a hook everywhere.'

'Precisely,' I replied.

'Abso*lute*ly,' confirmed Amy.

I really felt I'd done enough now, so I leaned forward and, moving on, said to Hugh, 'Will you be doing bound proofs?'

'Oh, I don't . . .' began Hugh, but Fiona rapped her pen on the desk.

'I'm sorry, but I think I missed the bit where you explained what angle you've got lined up, just now. Could you go over that again?'

Amy saw me hesitate in replying and, rightly, guessing that this hesitation would last for between four and six weeks, took over. 'The thing you appear to be missing, Fiona, is that Georgina Nye is a woman . . .' She took an exaggerated breath before she would have gone on to say '. . . with lovely hair' or '. . . who can juggle oranges' or I don't know what because suddenly I had a tiny spark of inspiration and jumped in.

'A *woman*. Georgina Nye is a *woman*,' I said.

Fiona affected astonishment. 'And you coaxed this information out of her after just the *two* meetings, Tom? Wow. With that in our pocket the bidding war for newspaper serialisation rights will be savage.'

'I meant . . . Fiona . . .' I said, using her name like a criticism. '. . . that *The Firth*, like all soaps, is especially strong with women viewers. Not only that, but Megan is seen as a crusading female character and George herself is known as someone that even the *Daily Mail* regards as the acceptable face of feminism. Go with that angle and we can keep the hard-core fans on board but broaden the book's appeal far wider.'

Fiona stared at me intently. Hugh raised his eyebrows and nodded thoughtfully. Amy reached across and ruffled my hair. Fiona didn't speak for a moment or two.

Eventually, she found her reply. 'Are you ill in the head?' she said flatly. 'This is a star autobiography. What do you think will happen if we promise a star autobiography and then turn up carrying a book? Just decide what the revelation we're going to use in all the press releases will be, and build the rest of the damn thing around that.'

'There *are* no revelations,' I explained. 'The woman is completely sensation free.'

'What about her father?'

'Lovely man. Gentle, always did his best – they're still close now.'

'Former lovers?'

'From what she's told me, there have only been a few, and they've always parted amicably.'

'Christ almighty! Are you telling me that no one's beaten her up *at all*?'

'Seems not.'

Fiona looked at Hugh in bewilderment. 'Did we know this when we signed the contract?'

'Um . . .' Hugh began, but Fiona wasn't going to wait for him.

'Self-harm? Miscarriage? A brief period hooked on anti-depressants?'

'Nope.'

'Jesus – what's the woman been doing for the last thirty years? We've got nothing here – *nothing*.'

'Not unless you let me go with the thoughtful, feminist line.'

Fiona was still examining me for signs of weakness but now I could see she was also slightly desperate to believe that I was right. 'And you think you can pull that angle off?' she asked.

'Definitely. I won't just crank out a by-the-numbers celeb autobiography here; this'll be something really special.'

Fiona didn't reply.

'*George* is really special,' I went on. 'It's too good an opportunity to waste: a celeb book with genuine merit.'

'Has she had some kind of eating disorder, maybe?'

'No.'

'Right . . .' she said, slowly: forcibly psyching herself up. 'Merit . . . I can do a campaign with that. Yes.' She actually started to become a little enthusiastic. 'Yes – "not just another celebrity cash-in". I like it. "Brave." "Intelligent." "*Unique.*" "A celebrity autobiography that dares to be different – like nothing you've ever read before!" In fact, I've still got some stuff from the last time we ran that campaign: a couple of years ago – it was for that cricketer with the lisp, but the framework is transferable.'

'Do you think Georgina Nye will be happy with going in this direction?' Hugh asked.

'Why shouldn't she be?' I said. 'If we do it well, that is. In fact, she actually said to me that she liked the idea that I'd make her look clever. And I'll keep in lots of showbiz anecdotes and fashion tips too, of course.'

'Of course.'

'Of course.'

'Abso*lutely*.'

Everyone seemed in agreement.

Amy threw open her arms. 'Nye will love it. I mean, who'd complain about being portrayed as smart and socially aware on the one hand and having a one-and-a-half-million quid advance thrown at her on the other?'

'Where did you get that figure from?' Hugh said to Amy uncomfortably. 'We haven't disclosed the actual sum.'

'Bill told me.'

'Bill?'

'Bill – the guy who delivers the sandwiches here.'

'Oh, right,' Hugh nodded, '*Bill*.'

I'd forgotten it was Sara's birthday in two weeks.

'Have you remembered it's my birthday in two weeks?' she said.

'Of course,' I replied.

Sara loved birthdays. She loved any kind of celebration, in fact – and they loved her too: they played to her sunny disposition. Sara and celebrations fitted together as perfectly as, well, as perfectly as any food items she prepared for them almost certainly wouldn't. On her twenty-seventh birthday we had literally danced all night, the two of us . . . at home . . . alone. Well, *Sara* had danced all night, at least. As far as I know, that is: I'd passed out on the sofa at some point, but the last thing I could remember was her dancing; and when I woke up the next morning, she was still there in front of me, still dancing.

Sara, irresistibly, is just the right side of being a nutter.

'It's a bit special, you know.'

'Special?'

'I'll be twenty-nine.'

'Yeah, I know that. But why is that special? *Thirty*'s special.'

'Tch.' She shook her head, amazed that I was such a dullard.

'Twenty-nine is the last birthday you have in your twenties. That's really special.' She fiddled with the buttons on the old-fashioned, almost Victorian, nightdress she was wearing – I was still sitting in front of my computer, thrashing out an introductory chapter for George's book.

'And thirty?'

'Aye, that's special too,' she said.

'Though not as special as thirty-one – you don't get to be another prime number for six years after that. *That*'s the kind of thing that'll really make you take stock of your life.'

'Noooo . . . my sides!'

'So, what do you want for your *special* twenty-ninth birthday anyway?'

'Something I'll remember.'

'What? Like a damn good beating, you mean?'

'A clever tongue is a wonderful gift, so it is . . . but it always holds the danger of making me come over there and thump you, you wee English bastard.'

'Yeah, yeah . . .'

'Och – *brave*, are we?'

'Come on, tell me what you want.'

'Surprise me. Surprise me with something fabulous.'

'Yeah, right. Just tell me what you want. I don't do surprises.'

'You used to surprise me when we were first going out with each other.'

'Only accidentally. I simply did the same things I've always done, but you didn't know me so well, so they looked surprising.'

'Yeah . . . *terrifying*, some of them. Come on – do something extravagant. Something romantic. Do you remember that film the other night where he . . .'

'Oh, no. Oh no you don't. How many times do I have to say this? "Films aren't real." That big, romantic gesture stuff only ever happens in films. Normal people don't do things like that

– picking you up from the pub in a candlelit helicopter stuffed with Turkish delight or some such bollocks. You think Hugh Grant's like that in real life? Is he arse. I bet his girlfriend thinks herself lucky if she gets a kiss on the cheek and a ten-pound gift voucher for Boots.'

'Well, you see, that's where you're wrong. Because it's not just in films. You know Sadie, from work?'

'The one with the thing?'

'Yes, that's the one. Her boyfriend called me up and arranged it so she'd have two weeks' leave booked – but she didn't know about it. Then he turns up at work one Monday morning – she thinks she has a day at the checkout ahead of her – but he just turns up at five past nine, goes up to her and asks her to marry him. She says yes, and he says, "Right, this position's closed, then." He's got a taxi waiting outside with a suitcase of her clothes that her friends have secretly been round and packed for her and they're off to the airport right away for a holiday he's booked in the Balearics. There wasn't a dry eye in the shop.'

'Now *that* . . .' I said, with some degree of righteousness. '. . . is pure bloody arrogance.'

'You *what*?'

'Well, for a start, think of all the things that could have gone wrong there – from Sadie saying, "Actually, it's your brother I'm really after" downwards. It takes an awful lot of ego to think up something like that and imagine it'll be a perfect romantic moment and not a disaster. *And* I'll tell you something else – and this is the thing it's really worth keeping in mind. The bloke who did it? He did it for *himself*. So that *he'd* look really great. Why did he have her friends do the packing for her?'

'Because he wanted to be sure the perfect things were packed, of course; just what she'd have packed herself. If you packed for me before a holiday I'd have one dress – which you'd choose at random – and you'd fill the rest of the suitcase with stockings and suspenders.'

'Pff. The reason he asked them was so that he involved as many people, for as long as possible, in knowing how simply *marvellous* he was. He didn't call her outside, did he? Didn't ask her there, where – if there was any problem – she wouldn't be so embarrassed? No, he did it in front of all the people in the shop, because he wanted the biggest audience for *his* performance. I bet every time she starts to tell the story he's right there by her side, isn't he? Grinning like a twat.'

'You know what?'

'What?'

Her reply was to hoist up her nightdress and moon at me.

Bit of an own goal, though, of course. Men can moon and it's funny or abusive or whatever. If a woman bends over and shows her bare bottom to you, well, the worst that can happen is you'll be too choked up with gratitude to get the words 'Thank you' out properly. And, what's more, Sara's gesture was especially doomed to failure because she was unfortunate enough to possess a particularly fantastic bottom.

She waggled it in my face a little, to emphasise the insult she was making.

Yup.

'Well,' she said, letting her nightdress fall back down, '*I* think what he did was great, and so did all the girls at work. I know you're English and everything – but it'd be nice if you did something like that, just once. Just to show you love me.'

'I do love you.'

'Tch – I *know* you love me.'

'So, what are you . . .'

'I said to *show* you loved me.'

'But, if you know anyway, then . . .'

'To *show* it.'

'But you've said you kn . . .'

'Christ, Tom.' She smiled and kissed me on the top of the head. 'It's not science, OK – it's art. You're a lovely man, a wonderful boyfriend, a talented writer . . . and a complete fucking idiot. Anyway, I'm off to bed now.'

'I'll come too . . .' I said, starting to shut down the computer.

'I thought you said you'd got work to do.'

'Yeah . . . well.'

'Well?'

'Well, that was before you got your bottom out.'

'Ahhh . . .'

'You had this incredible bottom hidden under your nightdress – who knew?'

She walked away into the bedroom, calling back, 'And suppose I'm not in the mood?'

'Oh . . . right. Well, I have got work to do, so I can . . .'

She appeared back in the bedroom doorway.

'Tch. I said *suppose.*'

FIVE

'You could do with a haircut,' said Sara. She'd bent down to give me a peck on the neck on her way out to work.

'Could I?'

'Well, unless you're going to grow it long – are you going to grow it long?'

'I'm too old to grow it long.'

'What does that mean? You think your twenty-eight-year-old scalp wouldn't take the strain?'

'I mean that only under-twenties can have long hair.'

'You can have long hair if you want.'

'People would laugh.'

'Fuck 'em.'

'Yeah, you're right, of course . . . I sound like Hugh. I can do what I want: it's my hair. I wasn't put on earth just to behave how *they* want me to . . . Fuck 'em.'

'You look better with short hair, though.'

'I'll go to the barber's today.'

After Sara had left I went up to my room and scratched at the book a little more. I was trying to get the feel right. Unusually for a ghosting, I was inventing the voice I wanted – creating George, rather than aping her. I wanted Romantic, but not dreamy. I thought that her voice should sound idealistic, yet practical. And strong. And Scottish. And I was digging myself into a hole. I pecked at the keyboard, just to see what happened.

> When I was a little girl in Mauchline, I used to stand on the corner of Loudoun Street and look up at the post office. I thought it was an enchanted place: a

mystic portal to the rest of the world. The Masonic Lodge was above it (and who knew what strange wizardry went on in there?) but the magic of the post office was its own, and far exceeded anything that men might achieve through the power of rolled-up trouser legs. Parcels were passed into its insides and there, hidden behind the imperious, red-brick Victorian walls, amazingly – impossibly – they were given the means to travel to anywhere in the world. The power to be in Laggan or London, New York or New Delhi. Standing before the post office, in the drizzle, with my wrinkled woolly tights, my scuff-toed shoes (despite my mother's repeated urgings, I was addicted to dragging my feet) and the big raincoat my sister had been rather too keen to hand down to me, I couldn't imagine anything more magical than being able to go to all those different places. Now, of course, I know that the truly magical thing isn't the places you go to, it's the little bit of your home you always take along.

Dreadful. Trite, saccharine, the joke about the trouser legs was impossibly weak and, in any case, coming after the 'who knew what wizardry' bit awkwardly smudged the child-George/adult-George voice. The hand-me-down coat was a nice image (I quickly double-checked my notes to confirm that George *had* got an older sister – she had. Phew.), but a bit obvious, really. And my information about Mauchline was from a 1950s tourist guide to Scotland I'd dug out of the attic. George certainly hadn't mentioned the post office at all, so before I went building her psyche around it I really ought to have a look at something more recent. It'd be a bit embarrassing if the book came out and someone said, 'Er, the post office was demolished in 1961 . . . Georgina Nye must have been looking up wistfully at the front of *Safeway*.' So: pretty much uniformly risible, then.

I'd show it to George and her agent and, if they liked it, carry on in the same vein.

My phone rang; the caller display read 'Anonymous'. (Note to self: not only begin a book with a phone call, but with one where the caller display reads 'Anonymous'.) I snatched it off the table and 'yellowed' into it.

'Hi, Tom – it's George here.' She was phoning from her hotel.

'Hello, George. How's it going?'

'Fine, fine. I just wondered if you needed another interview now? I'm off to Glasgow for filming tomorrow and I'll be heading back to London when that's done. This afternoon might be the last face-to-face opportunity we have for a while . . .'

'Oh, right.'

'I'm free this afternoon. You could come over to the hotel, any time after three.'

'Yes, that'd be useful. There *are* a few things I'd like to go over.'

'OK, I'll see you here, then.'

'Righto.'

''Bye.'

''Bye.'

That was quite exciting. Well, not *exciting*, obviously. Useful. It would be quite *useful* to get to see George again: to get the chance to check up on some facts at this point. I was clearly 'excited' simply to have such a 'useful' opportunity.

I needed a haircut.

I'd better get a haircut before I met George. It'd be very unprofessional to turn up at her hotel room poorly haired.

I called around but, even on an unremarkable Wednesday, it was tricky to get an appointment. The best I could do was a place that said they could 'fit me in' if I turned up at two o'clock. That was tight if I had to be at George's hotel by three, but it'd have to do.

'That's cutting it fine,' I said. 'But then, I suppose doing fine cutting is your business.'

'. . . So, do you want the two o'clock or not?'

'Yes . . . Yes, please.'

A man walking into a women's hairdresser's is treated with wariness and suspicion. In the eyes of the women in the shop I was almost certainly some kind of pervert and needed to be dealt with strictly so I didn't try to get away with anything. 'Yes, I'm a hairdresser,' the body language of the woman tying a plastic apron brusquely around my neck was saying to me, 'but I'm *not* easy.'

She pushed a toe on the pedal of my chair and I descended with a hiss. 'What do you want?' she asked me in the mirror, her eyes adding, 'As if I didn't know – you weirdo.'

'Um . . . can you just, you know, tidy it up a bit?'

She stared at me. I lifted up my arms and indicated my requirements by the vaguest of actions – as though both my ears were hot and I was fanning them with my hands. She nodded and set about her work. Pointedly, she didn't say anything to me, not even asking whether I was going on holiday this year. All around us the other women hairdressers and their women clients bubbled with talk. One of about fifty (with small locks of hair teased out of the holes in a rubber highlighting cap, so her head looked like a semi-flaccid, balding porcupine) was relating the trouble she'd had with the council about that hedge. Her hairdresser spent as much time paused, arms akimbo, shaking her head at the astonishing twists and turns of the story as she did doing any actual bleaching. Another was worn out with everything that needed to be done for the wedding; she didn't know how she was going to organise it all – and Jimmy was useless, of course. And I was just becoming quite enraptured by the whispered tale of someone else's sister from Spean Bridge when I heard the sirens.

Through the plate-glass windows at the front of the shop

we could see that people had stopped in the street and that police cars were pulling up on to the pavement. While we were still wondering what had happened, an officer opened the door and leaned in.

'We've received a bomb threat. I need everyone to evacuate this area now. If you've seen any suspicious packages or people, please let us know.' He leaned back out of the doorway and darted off to the next shop. There was a pause inside the hairdresser's: a silent suspension of everything. Then a loudspeaker outside began repeating pretty much the same message as the officer had given and we all flicked into action. The overriding desire of everyone present was to begin, as quickly as possible, to complain. Sighing, tutting and moaning that somebody had to plant a bomb . . . *here* . . . *now*. It was just typical. Making us get up and traipse down the street halfway through a haircut? Well . . . it had just better not turn out to be a hoax, that's all.

Now, while it was patently ridiculous for a woman having her roots done to complain that she was being interrupted by something as trivial as a bomb, *I* was due – in less than twenty-five minutes – to see Georgina Nye. I couldn't turn up at Georgina Nye's hotel room with my hair halfway through a cut – I'd look like a mental patient.

'Couldn't we just finish off?' I pleaded to the hairdresser, who was tugging her coat on.

'What?'

'Couldn't you just finish doing my haircut, before we go?'

'There's a bomb scare.'

'Yes, yes, I know. But you, well . . . look at my *hair*.'

'Tanya – come *on*,' an older woman I guessed was the owner called from the doorway.

'I'm coming – this gentleman was just trying to persuade me to stay and finish his cut.'

The owner squinted at me.

'What is it? A dry cut?'

'Aye,' Tanya nodded. 'I was trying to leave some of the length on top.'

'Mmmm, don't overdo it, though. His hair hasn't got the thickness.'

'OK.'

'Now, come on, for God's sake – we could all be dead any second.'

I hurried out into the street, pausing half in, half out of the doorway and shouting after them.

'Couldn't you take some scissors?' I pleaded. They were hurrying off up the street and didn't' reply. I sprinted after them. (Hoping that all was not lost and wanting to keep the atmosphere, I was still wearing the plastic apron. It flapped around at my sides as I ran along: imagine Batman with bed hair and his cape on backwards.) 'We could get to a safe distance and you could finish off . . .'

'Sorry,' said the owner without looking back at me. 'Can't have Tanya cutting hair out in the street – our insurance won't cover it.'

'What insurance? It's a *haircut*. Nothing can happen to . . . well, bombs aside, obviously – nothing can happen to you getting a haircut.'

'And suppose Tanya took your ear off?'

'Is that *likely*?'

'Who knows? She could just be tidying up when the bomb explodes . . . gets hit by the blast wave and . . .' Still without turning round, she touched her hand to one of her ears, and then flung it away to illustrate a pinna being severed by scissors.

'I'll sign a waiver.'

'Pfft,' spat the owner, 'I've heard *that* one before.'

'Well . . . er . . . argh . . . OK! Yes – OK, here's what we'll do . . . I'll run to the nearest shop and get a pair of scissors and a couple of mirrors, right? I'll set up the mirrors and *I'll* cut my hair – following your instructions. You can talk me down. Yes? Eh? *Yes?*'

The owner and Tanya just looked at each other and shook their heads. Like I was some kind of fool or something. They weren't going to budge.

Shit and bee stings – what was I going to do now? I glanced at my watch. Crap. My mind howled as I tried to think of another hairdresser that was close. Where? Where? *Where?* Ha! *There.* It was a good distance, on foot, but I might be able to make it *just* in time for them to salvage my head and get to George's hotel on time if I really, really ran as fast as I could.

I clawed my way through the small crowd of people who were standing there waiting to see whether they'd be able to return to work, or at least get the chance to see it explode. The second I was beyond them I put all my hopes into my legs and sent them haring off across Edinburgh. Bloody *Edinburgh* – why couldn't they have built the place somewhere flatter? In fact, it's not just that it's not flat, but that everywhere you go in Edinburgh – there, and back – appears to be uphill; I think the city must have been designed by Escher. I pounded along the pavement, jigging and weaving in between pedestrians who seemed to be going to supererogatory lengths to GET IN MY DAMN WAY.

After about five minutes and what I judged to be between four to six breaths away from the point when I was actually going to cough up my lungs, I collapsed against the door of what I knew was, as far as I was concerned, the Last Chance Salon. I staggered in and half flopped over on to the counter. The startled receptionist stared at me with an expression that said, 'OK, OK – take what's in the till, just don't hurt me.'

'Need . . . haircut . . . now . . . desperate . . .'

The receptionist bit her lip.

'I'm afraid we're fully booked . . . I could fit you in, um . . . Friday afternoon?'

I looked at her with eyes that would break your heart and animatedly jabbed a finger at my head.

'. . . *desperate.*'

The door to a small office was open behind her. Turning slightly, so as to face a little more in that direction but not allowing her eyes to leave me for a moment, she called out towards it.

'Mrs Connelly? Mrs Connelly? There's a gentleman here who says he needs a haircut.'

'. . . *Des* . . .'

'Desperately. He says he needs a haircut . . .'

'*Des* . . .'

'*Desperately.*'

A faceless voice called back from the office.

'We can't fit him in today. Tell him to make an appointment.'

I held out my hands to the receptionist, imploringly.

'He seems to want one *right now*, Mrs Connelly.'

'Right now?' the voice replied, with an edge of irritation.

'Aye, Mrs Connelly. *Right now.* I mean . . . he's even come in wearing his own apron.'

Ah, yes – I'd forgotten about that. Oh well.

There was a pause, the sound of a chair scraping across the floor, and then a woman wearing more make-up than an entire Parisian chorus line appeared in the doorway. She saw me, took a step back into the office, steadied herself for a second and then walked out and up to the counter.

'I'm sorry, but we're completely booked up until Friday afternoon.'

I'd regained some of my breath now, so I was able to be a bit more articulate.

'Bollocks to bastard Friday afternoon,' I explained. 'I need this repaired *now.*'

Mrs Connelly stiffened further.

'Well, there's simply nothing we can do about that. Look – all our seats are full. You don't expect me to get someone up halfway through their session, do you?'

I used every facial muscle I possessed to indicate that I'd make it financially worth their while if the three of us just grabbed that old woman over there having the rinse and threw her out into the street.

'I'm sorry,' added Mrs Connelly, with a stern, definite finality.

My lips squirmed. Eventually, struggling out from between them, emerged, 'You . . . *you* . . .' but anger and frustration had brought down a barrier my vocabulary simply couldn't penetrate. I huffed furiously and slapped my open palm down on to the counter top as hard as I could. A display can of styling foam wobbled, slightly. After a single accusing glance into the eyes of each of them, I marched off back towards the door. I wrenched the handle towards me then paused, in the open doorway, looking back over the entire shop.

'I am *never* . . .' I announced, holding a hand, Lenin-like, high in the air. '. . . coming here again!' This bombshell didn't seem, noticeably, to break the spirit of anyone who was looking, but I held the pose for a couple of seconds anyway, just to drive home the point. With that, I grabbed at my plastic apron, flung it up theatrically over one shoulder, and swept out into the street.

Arse.

Arse, piss drips and chips.

I snatched up a sleeve and looked at my watch. My stomach fell into my bottom. I began to trudge, broken, in the general direction of George's hotel, cursing towards my shuffling feet. But then, I looked up once more. And I stopped.

I ran, as fast as I could, across the road into a shop.

'I need a hat.'

'And what kind of hat did you have in mind, sir?' replied the assistant, a middle-aged man with a quite impossibly refined Edinburgh accent.

'Any kind. Any kind of hat.'

'Erm, well, is it for general use, or a formal occasion or . . .'

'Look – I'm meeting a woman in . . . oh, *Jesus*. Look – I'm meeting a woman in a hotel in about *two* minutes and I need a hat.'

'I see . . . Sir.'

'Hfff . . . Do you see my hair? I was having a haircut and someone made a bomb threat and I ran like a bugger across town but they haven't got a free bloody slot until Friday afternoon and I'm meeting someone in *two* minutes and I need a hat – do you *see* my hair?'

'Yes, of course,' nodded the man. He peered around the shop. 'A fedora, perhaps? Classic, stylish – just a touch . . .' He plucked at the air with his thumb and forefinger. '. . . bohemian.'

'Will it cover my ears?'

He looked at one ear then the other, his eye-line dipping noticeably as he took in the point at which my hair ended by each.

'Mmmm . . . Maybe one of these?' he said, uncurling his fingers elegantly to direct my attention towards a large bin close to the counter. 'I believe they originated as "snow" "*boarding*" headwear, but they've become quite fashionable with young people generally now.'

I stood, peering down into the bin.

'Warm, of course,' he continued, 'lightweight, highly washable . . . they exclude one's ears from public view entirely.'

'How much?'

'Twenty-nine pounds ninety-nine pence . . . Or "p", as I believe we are now required to say.'

'Thirty quid for a woolly hat?'

'Not wool, sir: they are one hundred per cent polyester.'

'I . . . oh, yes – whatever . . . I'll take one.'

'Excellent. The "electric orange" or the "shrieking mauve"?'

'Are they the same price?'

'Precisely the same, sir, yes. It's merely a matter of personal preference.'

'What do you suggest?'

'Well, the orange has an energy – a *vitality* – to it. Perhaps that would be the one most fitting for a meeting with a young lady.'

'It's . . . look, she's an actress: I'm an author – that's all.'

'Ahh – the mauve, then,' he nodded sagely.

I began to scramble around in the bin.

'One size fits all, sir.'

I pulled out one of the fashionable among young people shrieking mauve snowboarding hats and jammed it on to my head, down over my ears.

'How do I look?' I asked.

'Equally at home on the piste at Davos or strolling along the Royal Mile, sir.'

I feared even the briefest of checks in a mirror: I just paid him the money and left to make a dash for George's hotel. (Pausing only once along the way: to ram into a bin – with exceptional fury – the hairdresser's apron.)

'Huh.'

'What?' I asked.

'Oh . . . nothing,' replied George, opening the door wider to invite me inside her room. 'Please – come in.'

'Sorry I'm a bit late. There was a bomb scare – it's affected the traffic.'

'Yes – the Animal Liberation Front, they mentioned it on the radio.'

'Is that who it is?' I said. 'The ALF? Sods. I'm going to spend all day tomorrow drop-kicking squirrels into the river.'

It was a posh suite in a posh hotel: you got the feeling you'd stepped into a Victorian drawing room. No, actually, that's not quite right. How it really felt was as though you'd stepped on

88

to a film set of a Victorian drawing room. Even though I'm sure the writing desk was a genuine antique, it appeared fake – too pristine, too carefully placed. It was a room that was flushed out after each guest left to be fresh and untainted for the next one. Consequently, it had a sterile, unlived-in and unloved atmosphere.

'Do you want to take off your coat? And hat?'

'I, er, no . . . thanks. I think I've got a bit of a chill coming.'

'Oh, really?'

'Yeah . . . *brrr*.' I hugged myself, rubbing my arms and generally making every effort to reinforce the message. It was about 25 degrees Celsius in the room – George was barefoot and wearing just a T-shirt and jeans cut off into shorts.

She took a step towards me and placed her hand on my forehead. It felt cool on my skin – which is probably why the hairs on the back of my neck prickled as it touched.

'Wow, you're cooking. I think you might have a fever.'

'Well, I certainly have an erection now . . .'

Yep. That's what I said. Excellent. I'd like to say that it just came from nowhere: fell out spontaneously after being planted in my head the instant before by aliens or witches. The frightful truth was, however, that it was the result of a long process of inner debate. Maybe not long as measured by the disinterested ticking of a watch but, inside my mind, it felt like a million years had passed while I considered it. George had reached up, in slow motion, and placed her hand on my forehead. It was probably so swift as to be almost a gentle slap, but I felt it as many distinct phases. I felt her fingertips touch, and pause for a moment, before her hand folded out, so her palm lay flat across my head. After it had rested there a while, I felt it retreat slightly and move across to a slightly different position as she explored the temperature in another area, for comparison. Finally, it lifted gently away – her fingertips had been the first to arrive and they were the last to leave: they brushed across my skin, moving just slightly down towards the side of my face, before losing contact completely. It was around now that I experienced some stiffening in the groinal region. I looked across at George, and was very conscious that just a few dozen inches below our eyes my penis was making a bid for freedom. I dared not glance down to assess the size of the problem – for fear of George's eyes instinctively following mine – but it certainly felt about the length, and rigidity, of a descant recorder: if I turned around quickly it'd surely give itself away by sweeping a host of small ornaments from the table. I could try simply ignoring it and carry on as if nothing were amiss – as long as carrying on didn't involve walking, or sitting, or standing straight. Or I could try to make things less awkward and visible down there. Perhaps shout, 'Look at that!' and, while George's gaze was away from me, have a frantic wrestle to rearrange myself into a more comfortable position. I discarded that idea *right* away: it's not the kind of operation I'd want her to glance back and discover me halfway through performing. *Or* I could simply exorcise the whole problem by bringing it out into the open. That's sometimes the best way, isn't it? If you turn up to an important meeting with a stain on your tie you can't ignore it, and trying to hide it will often just make the situation worse. The best option is to say, 'Tch! Look, I've just got a stain on my tie.' Acknowledge it, show it's not an issue for you, and everyone can forget about it and move on. So, you can see that I'd thought this one through, carefully, before I opened my mouth and said to Georgina Nye in her hotel room:

'Well, I certainly have an erection now . . .'

Her eyes widened and her face mixed an expression of surprise with one that said, 'Oh. Congratulations. I'm pleased for you.'

'. . . hahaha,' I added, hoping to, well . . . Oh, Jesus, I don't know – whatever alternative there was to her screaming at the top of her voice and hitting me in the face with the telephone receiver, *that*'s the one I was hoping the 'hahaha' would edge us towards.

Suddenly her grin appeared.

'Sorry,' I shrugged.

She grinned even more blindingly.

Still our gazes remained fixed, however. I was trying, by keeping my eyes looking right into hers, to *prevent* her glancing below, even for the briefest moment. If I even blinked it might break the connection – it was like trying to stare down a bear. Finally, her face softened and she began to turn around to head over to the sofa. But – arrgh! – there it was! Just as she was twisting away, she flicked her eyes down for the tiniest of looks. My shoulders slumped in exhausted defeat. Even worse, immediately after she'd peeked at the situation in my trousers, she gave a little, snorty laugh. Now *that*'s irony: crippling panic at the idea that she'd view my feral, uncontrollable erection and, the second she *does*, she produces the snorty laugh that was the single thing on earth guaranteed to break its spirit. The instant my ears registered her reaction, my penis fainted; I felt it begin to shrink so rapidly that it's a wonder it didn't make a hissing sound.

She sat down on the sofa, curling one leg under her bottom.

'So, then . . .' she said.

'Yes . . .' I scanned the room hastily. There was no way I was going to sit down on the sofa beside her – not with the messages my genitals had just been sending out – so I grabbed a wooden chair from over by the writing desk and placed it down opposite where she was sitting. She twisted her lips as I did this, trying not to smile. A coffee table separated us: on to which I placed my Dictaphone. '. . . OK. Are you ready?'

'Sure – do you want anything, before we start?'

'What?'

'Do you want anything? Shall I call room service for tea or coffee or something . . . ? Before we start?'

'Oh, no. I'm fine, thanks.'

'Some paracetamol?'

'Sorry?'

'For your chill – it keeps your temperature down.'

'No, no, I'll be OK – thanks all the same.' I ran my hand up across my forehead to wipe away a little perspiration – the action reminding me that I was wearing a 'shrieking mauve' snowboarding hat (ace) over an 'under construction' haircut (double ace).

I sought refuge in professionalism and immediately began asking some questions that had arisen since I'd made a start on the book. She answered them cheerily, and gave me lots of extra material too; we'd got all the biographical facts pretty much covered now, so she came up with some good anecdotes and a bit of behind-the-glamour-of-showbiz stuff I'd be able to weave in – hopefully using a voice sufficiently conspiratorial for them to appear far more excitingly confessional than was really the case.

We talked for hours. She got through about half a packet of cigarettes and at times not only did I forget that I had a stupid hat on, I also forgot I was interviewing her for the book: we were just chatting. She'd ask me about myself or writing or publishing in general and fifteen minutes could go by before I realised I'd been telling her *my* life story instead of the other way round. Not really a very efficient use of the Dictaphone tapes – I already knew my life story, and I *definitely* knew there wasn't a book in it. It was the tapes, in fact, that brought us to a halt. When I came to the end of the final one I had with me, that was that. A slight irritation crept through me – a bit like the feeling you get at school at the end of an exam – 'Everyone put their pens down now, please' – when you finally, remarkably, know where the essay you're writing is going and suddenly have a head full of things to say.

I picked the Dictaphone up off the table and patted it.

'Well, that's it, I suppose,' I said.

'It's a bit depressing, really, isn't it?'

'What?'

'All my life being able to fit on a few tapes.'

'Good Lord, no. First of all, it's not *all* your life. It's simply all your life that's . . .'

'Fit to print?'

'Exactly. Next, you're only thirty, after all. And finally, I have to say, if the situation were reversed I'd be able to give you all *my* life just by leaving a message on your answerphone.'

'Ha – I don't believe that.'

'Oh, it's true. Pretty much the most interesting thing I've ever done is meet you.' Which I'd meant to sound gently self-effacing but, after I'd loosed it into the room, I realised seemed sickeningly fawning and then, after you'd thought about it for a bit longer, actually mildly insulting.

'Thanks,' she replied, with a smile. (She obviously hadn't reached the 'insulting' realisation yet. Doubtless she'd wake up abruptly in the middle of the night a few days from now and mutter, 'Wanker.')

I gathered up the used tapes from the table top as George twisted her cigarette to death in the ashtray. We rose, made elaborate displays of stretching, and drifted towards the door. She opened it for me and I went out into the hallway, turning back for the final goodbye once I was there.

'Like I said, I've already got a few bits you can read through, just to give you an idea of the tone I'm using. I'll send them to your agent – any problems, just get back to me and I'll rewrite.'

'OK,' she replied. She was standing in the doorway, leaning with her cheek against the edge of the open door.

'And the sooner I can have those photos the better,' I added.

'I'm back in London after filming, so I might be able to get them to you by the weekend.'

'That's great.'

She smiled. There was surely some clear signal that we'd both recognise as marking The End (allowing her to close the door, and me to walk off down the hall, without any lingering awkwardness) but we appeared to be having trouble locating it.

"Bye then,' I said.

'Yes, 'bye,' she echoed, but she didn't move from her position at all.

'Perhaps I'll see you again. To talk over rewrites and amendments.'

She didn't reply, but instead lifted herself off the edge of the door and stepped closer to me. She reached up and laid her hand across my forehead.

'You feel a little cooler now . . . that's good.'

I said something in reply, but I don't know what it was. It certainly wasn't a word.

"Bye. You get yourself to bed,' she said as she closed the door, looking at me through the narrowing gap right up until it shut.

I stood there motionless for a few seconds, then turned and headed for the lift. I did consider the stairs, but thought the lift would be easier. What with the erection and everything.

III

Right, now I know what you guys is like, so I think I need to step in here
– just quickly – and get something straight. 'Cause I can just see you all
sitting there going, 'Yeah, I know what's happening here,' and starting to
invent this big theory that I'll never be able to get you off of. You just can't
stop yourselves – that's part of the problem, in fact. I don't know about
what George said back there a ways about wanting to have a shrink, but
I *do* know that every one of you secretly thinks you could *be* a shrink: you
just love to analyze each other. If I don't step in here, you'll be giving it all
the 'this means that' and 'he does such because she does whatever' and
'it's all to do with unfulfilled needs' and 'faulty images of self' and 'the table
represents his mother' and who knows *what* you'll end up believing. Well,
before you start doing that, I'm going to say one word to you, OK? Here it
is . . . 'monoamines'. Got that? Monoamines.

I'll explain this more later – now's not the time. But I want you to stay
focussed, you hear me? I want you to keep on the path and, if you ever
find yourself wandering off into some tangled forest of theorizing, you just
say to yourself, 'Monoamines,' and get yourself back on course. Think you
can do that for me? Yeah, well . . . at least try – OK?

SIX

'Is that you, Tom?' Sara called from the kitchen as I came in through the front door.

'No. Axe murderer. Nothing personal – I was just in the area.'

She came out into the hallway – carrying what looked suspiciously like a bowl of lime jelly and tuna – and paused, looking over at me. I heaved my coat off and hung it up.

'You're back late.'

I sighed.

'Yeah, sorry – I got tied up in town,' I said, taking off my hat and tossing it aside. 'First there was this ALF bomb thing . . .'

'Och – sweet Jesus!' cried Sara, looking at me and beaming with amusement. 'The Animal Liberation Front have bombed your hair!' She moved over and poked the top of my head.

'I was halfway through having it cut when the police evacuated us,' I mumbled.

'You poor wee dear . . . and the authorities *swore* to us this kind of thing was all in the past, after it happened to Phil Oakey all those years ago.'

'I'll go somewhere and get it fixed tomorrow.'

Sara, still brushing at my hair, wrinkled up her nose. 'You smell of smoke . . . have you been with Amy?'

'Yeah.'

Odd. I wonder why I said that?

'The Georgina Nye book?'

'Yes. Just contract stuff – little details, but you know how these things drag out. I was with her all afternoon going through the fine print.'

Sara nodded absently, gave my hair a final ruffle and headed off into the living room. 'There's food in the fridge, if you want some,' she said as she moved away.

'No thanks,' I replied. 'I'm not very hungry.'

Amy, not exhaling her smoke until she'd got it lined up precisely how she wanted it, placed her lighter on top of the packet of cigarettes she'd put on the table.

'He's a formidable wanker, even by the high wanking standards of London agents,' she said, shaking her head. 'It's like haggling with an East End fruit seller. Never mind a literary agent – never mind even a general *showbiz* agent – Paul Dugan not only *is*, but seems to be positively *proud* of being, a "right old cockney geezer".' She attempted to send her accent down to the market stalls of London for this last phrase. It crashed somewhere on the outskirts of Carlisle.

I'd called her the previous night and asked if we could meet up in a pub at lunchtime, saying I wanted to talk about the book deal. I was interested in the deal, of course, but more than that I kind of wanted to erase the – pointless, utterly pointless – lie I'd told to Sara by *actually* having a meeting with Amy. OK, not quite when I said I had – I was having it a day later – but, still, that changed it from an outright lie into more of a trivial discrepancy about the chronological details of the statement really, didn't it? Wednesday? Thursday? No big deal.

'He didn't like our call for ten per cent of their advance, then?'

'He did that thing where he pretended it was so outrageous that he actually found the idea funny. Laughed out loud.'

'Tosser.'

'Abso*lutely*. He said he was thinking more along the lines of seven per cent.'

'What did you say?'

'I laughed out loud.'

'Good for you.'

'So, I asked him how many books he thinks they'll sell. Being a chancer, he naturally goes over the top: instead of being realistic he says, tear in his eye, he doesn't reckon on more than about seventy-five thousand.'

'Bollocks.'

'Boll-abso*lute*ly-ocks. But that's where I have him. I say, OK, we'll take seven per cent . . . but if we produce something with such a broad appeal that it far exceeds his expectations – say, oh . . . combined format sales of 200,000 – then we get *thirteen* per cent. "Surely, Paul," I say, "*surely* the extra publicity having such a massive hit would generate is worth the money on its own?"'

'And?'

'Shits himself, obviously.'

'So what happens then?'

'He goes off on a long tale about all sorts of arse – really, stuff even I wouldn't try to get away with. Finally, we settle on nine per cent but – "Oh, the agony – me poor ol' sainted mother'll be selling matches on the street this winter, she will" – eleven if we shift over two hundred k.'

I nervously drew a circle of moisture on the table top with the bottom of my glass of lager. 'And will we?'

'Georgina Nye? Aye . . . *Easy*. Her publicity machine will be smoking, so will M&C's. You knock out a good read – interesting, funny; something anyone will enjoy – and if they haven't shifted *at least* two hundred k by this time next year then we'll come back here and I'll blow you, on top of this very table, in front of the whole pub.'

'You're still the only agent in Edinburgh to include that clause in their agreement, you know.'

'Fucking right I am.'

She stubbed out her cigarette and leaned back in her chair.

'Oh, there's another thing that came up while I was talking to Paul,' she said, leaning forward and lighting up again. 'M&C are having their in-house sales bash down in London at the end of July. Naturally, they've asked Nye to go, but she's away in America. She suggested you as a stand-in, so Paul asked if you'd be up for it.'

'Did he also suggest any theoretically possible ways in which that might not be the worst idea ever? I can just see the faces of the people expecting to meet Georgina Nye when they find I'm there instead. And I'd have to slog down to London and back too – quite apart from my having to spend an evening being nice to people.'

'Oh, they aren't likely to care about not meeting a celeb – they'll all be from sales or marketing and burnt out *years* ago. And Paul did point out that if someone needs to talk to the people who are going to have the job of selling the book to the shops, then you'd be the right person – you'll have the best idea of what's going to be in it. Plus you'd get a hotel room and travel expenses.'

'Would *you* do it?'

'Would I bollocks.'

'And I see no reason to question your judgement.'

'OK. I'll get back to Paul later and say we're very flattered that they thought of you, and you'll do everything you can to ensure the success of the book, but they can both fuck off and die.'

'Cheers.'

'Hey – it's my job.' She took a drink from her glass of wine – impressively managing to swallow gulps of it down with her mouth while at the same time exhaling smoke out through her nose. I tapped along to the song playing on the jukebox; chinging my nail against the side of my glass for the few moments it took for her to finish.

'So,' she said, once more leaning back in her chair, 'I've

held out for as long as I could . . . what's with the stupid fucking hat?'

'Oh. Haircut situation – I'm getting it fixed later.'

Sara had to work on Saturday. She had to work a lot of Saturdays – it being the busiest day at the shop – but she always hated doing it.

I heard her downstairs – performing her Symphony of Irritation for low, grumbling noises and slamming cupboards – until she finally left the house. Meanwhile, my famously disciplined regime extended to not working on Saturdays – whether I wanted to or not – and lying in bed until about 10.30 – whether I wanted to or not. There's little as pleasing as waking up on a Saturday morning and realising it *is* a Saturday morning, and you can therefore continue to lie there. I wasn't about to give that up just because I was my own boss, didn't have to work office hours and could, in theory, lie in bed *every* morning. You have to work at pleasure, you see, invest effort in it. It's like damn well going on every ride in the amusement park, say, now you've sat in a car for three hours to get there and paid twenty quid for it: it doesn't matter that you're cold, tired, every queue is forty-five minutes long and you have a pulsing headache that you rather suspect won't be improved by being strapped into a cage and flung around upside down at 30 mph. No, you're here now and you're going to have all the fun you can, however unpleasant it might be. So, I sprawled in bed, resignedly gazing at the clock-radio digits climbing up to 10:30. When they finally made it, I got up without having to suffer any self-recrimination about having succumbed to weakness and cut short my weekly lie-in.

I ambled downstairs into the kitchen, picking up the morning's post from the floor on my way past the front door. Three letters went straight into the bin, unopened, as they all had on them the telltale signs of junk mail – two implied I'd won something and the third declared, 'Open immediately:

time-critical documents enclosed'. The fourth was a Jiffy bag; I flicked on the kettle and then set about tearing at the lavish amounts of Sellotape that had been used to fasten it shut. Inside was a brief note ('*Hope these will be of use. Let me know if you need any more. Love, George xxx*') and about a dozen photographs. Two or three weren't really personal – pictures of George at parties chatting to major international celebs – but they would be useful for the book in any case; the rest were family photos. She'd been an ugly baby.

I couldn't say how long this had lasted. However, she'd certainly started on the way to the arrestingly attractive Georgina Nye we knew today by the time she was eight or nine. The photos of her at this age (one at a picnic with her parents and siblings, another posing with a sporadically-toothed grin by a birthday cake) included her masses of black hair, and the seeds of her later features were discernible in her round child's face. George had written brief notes on the back of the photos for me. She'd loved that dress and refused to take it off, even for bed; her mother had to remove it each night after she'd gone to sleep. The dog was called 'Snowy' (it was black, so clearly someone in the Nye family had a powerful sense of humour) and had been run over by a Hillman Avenger shortly after the family had moved to Coventry – it being that particular model had seemed to have an occult significance to the young, newly transplanted Georgina and she said she'd felt a final, loosening relief when she'd learnt that production of the car had ceased in 1981. Her brother had taken the Christmas one with the Polaroid camera he'd had for his present; later, she and her sister had found a big pile of the tear-off, black backing strips in the bin. They revealed, in eerie negative, what a sporting sort his girlfriend clearly was. (Until he'd eventually managed to find and destroy the evidence, they'd pretty much ruined his life using them for close to eighteen months. Whenever she and her sister got together, they still laughed about it.) The inevitable holiday beach photo was not George aged four, patting a sandcastle with her plastic spade. It was George aged about nineteen, running out of the sea in a black one-piece bathing suit. Her legs and arms glistened, her face was jewelled with droplets of sea and her wet hair ran down over her upper body like sticky, shining tar. Perhaps she'd fallen over, or leapt recklessly into the water. Whatever had happened, she was running towards me grinning the type of grin you only brought out after some kind of impulsive, splashing, visually exciting, Pepsi-advert moment, and only if the person holding the camera was your lover, with whom you would be having the most riotous sex back in the hotel that evening. I felt a pang of . . . well, I supposed it must be hunger. So, I put some bread in the toaster and made myself a cup of tea before shuffling into the dining room and tossing the envelope full of photos on to the table.

As it was getting awfully close to Sara's birthday – and I still hadn't got a clue what to get her – while I was waiting for the toaster to finish I brought my laptop into the dining room and connected to the Net.

Nibbling toast from one hand, I used the other to guide the mouse around; leaping from one hyperlink to the next in search of something I could get for Sara as a present. Two hours later I was still in my nightclothes, I hadn't got any closer to finding a present for Sara, but I'd seen poorly drawn versions of all the characters in *The Simpsons* in every kind of sexually compromising situation you could imagine. It'd be pleasing to say that, ultimately, I tired of this trudge from one image to the next and disconnected with a weary huff, berating myself for wasting so much time. In fact, I had to stop because I was desperate for a piss.

That's the problem with John Stuart Mill's vision of Utopia, you see. He had this dreamy belief that his Utilitarian ideal would work because, given time and education, people would prefer the 'higher pleasures'. However, when foreign powers attempt to suck secrets from the finest minds in science and politics, I note that they tend to use the lure of sex far more than the promise of a really good anthology. The thing about humans is that they are, ultimately, only human.

Nevertheless, after I'd been to the toilet, I did at least decide on getting dressed and going out, rather that returning straight away to more cartoon fellatio . . . you know, for J.S. Mill's sake.

'I need something for Sara's birthday,' I grumbled into my mobile.

I was wandering randomly around town, growing ever more fed up. No, not fed up, *annoyed*. I was getting more and more annoyed with Sara for having a birthday. It was so selfish. I'd been with Sara when she was buying presents for friends and, first off, she enjoyed searching for them. The act of needing a present, but not having found one yet – how can you *enjoy* that? It makes no sense. It's like wanting to sit down in the cinema but not being able to find a seat and yet thinking this is splendid as looking for one is half the fun. Madness. Still, she does indeed *enjoy* the lack of satisfaction that comes from trying to find something but not achieving it. And when, eventually, she *does* locate the present she's going to buy, there's a kind of euphoria there. She pays over the money flushed with pleasure at the purchase. When *I* eventually find the present I'm resigned to buying for a friend I pay the shop assistant with nothing but a kind of angry, nihilistic despair: 'Well, that's *it* now. *That*'s what they're getting. I've had enough . . . and I've bought this now . . . and *that*'s the end of it . . . and if they don't like it they can just fuck off.' Moreover, I'm additionally irritated by having spent twice what I intended to, and I *always* spend twice what I intended to – out of guilt about buying them something that's crap. Unpick that one.

So – 'I need something for Sara's birthday,' I grumbled, broken, into my mobile.

'Mmmm . . . have you thought of getting her one of those

spa things?' said Amy. As I've hinted before, in return for taking ten per cent of everything I earn, Amy gets to be my mom.

'No. What spa things?'

'Where you buy someone a day at a beauty place, out in the country somewhere.'

'Isn't that just like implying you think they're ugly? And anyway, what's the point of it? You can get all the stuff from Superdrug for a few quid – if she wanted to lie in a bath, she could lie in the bath at home.'

'I think the whole point is to get away from your home.'

'Why? What's wrong with our home?'

'Och . . . Tom – and I promise you I'm not saying this just because you're an Englishman – but you really are an utterly clueless fucker.'

A bit harsh, I thought. I am a writer, after all. I think about things deeply, and from various perspectives, day after day: it's my job. It's unavoidable that I'm going to be pretty damn insightful and sensitive – I'm a *writer*.

'Look, Amy, just tell me what to do. Sara's birthday's only a week away.'

'Surprise her. Plan some really big surprise – horse and carriage, new dress and shoes inside it, she can change as you ride along to the box you've secretly booked at the ballet . . . Tom . . . ? *Tom?*'

'If you're going to take the piss, Amy, then . . .'

'I'm not taking the piss. What's wrong with that?'

'The ballet? I *hate* ballet – don't say it. Don't say it: because I've never heard *Sara* rave about ballet either – I don't think she's ever been in her life, in fact.'

'Ah-ha!'

'What?'

'It's one night, you twat. And it's something she's never done before.'

'And supposing – as seems pretty inevitable to me – she

doesn't like it? I want to get her something I *know* she'll like. I don't want to risk disappointing her.'

'Even if she hates it, she'll always be able to say, "I don't like ballet," and she'll go straight from those words to the wonderful memory of how she learnt that – with you whisking her away to an evening there on her birthday.'

'Are you . . . ? "Whisking her away"? What *the hell*? Are some people from Mills & Boon threatening you, Amy? They've got you tied up right now, haven't they? Cough once for yes.'

'You called me, you know.'

'Yes, but not for Gothic fantasies. I didn't expect you – Christ, you of *all* people – to turn into Mrs Radcliffe. Can we please keep our feet on the ground? There are about a billion things that could go wrong with a grandiose scheme like that and, anyway, Sara's a modern woman – she doesn't want "whisking away". I mean, OK, she might *say* she does, sometimes – but that's in the abstract. Nice as a fantasy, but she wouldn't want it really: she likes us to make decisions together, she'd hate to simply have to go along with what I'd decided was best for her.'

'You . . . Oh, Jesus – just buy her a dress, then, OK? Buy her a fucking dress.'

'Right . . . What size would you say she is?'

We needn't concern ourselves with Amy's reply here. Evidently the contract negotiations had put her under more stress than I'd realised.

A short time later it started to rain: that dirty, tepid rain you're sometimes cursed enough to have soak you in a city in May. The air became sticky and streets smelled like wet denim. I continued to trudge around all the shops but nothing seemed right for Sara. My wet clothes held in the heat and before long I didn't know what was rainwater and what was sweat. In misery and defeat I caught the bus back home.

As soon as I arrived I struggled out of my soaking clothes,

got into the shower, had a quick wash, and then exited in the standard fashion: one leg out – other leg inside slips – Jesus! – Fuck! – phew, caught myself in time – whoa, adrenalin rush – I've never *felt* so alive! . . . crap, where are all the towels? I picked up my mobile (*yes*, I take my mobile into the bathroom with me – so?), went and rummaged a fresh towel out of the chest of drawers in the bedroom and gave myself a brief scrub dry. Then, seeing my crumpled, filthy, wet clothes lying on the floor of the bedroom and the washing basket nearly full, I decided to go downstairs and dump everything in the washing machine. I hoped Sara would note this thoughtful, Domestic Prince-style act and remember it next week, when I'd utterly failed to have found a birthday present for her. Passing back through the kitchen, I flicked the kettle on and padded into the dining room to collect my mug from the table where I'd left it that morning. I put my mobile down by my laptop. Ahhh . . . naked I might be, but here was a laptop, a mobile phone and the promise of tea: this was how Man was *meant* to live. You could keep all the frivolous ephemera of modern society, I thought, *this* was all I needed. I noticed the envelope lying on the table too, and idly pulled the photographs out for another look. George's life in a bag; it vaguely reminded me of when you see people in movies finishing a prison sentence and being handed back an envelope containing who they were twenty years ago. A baby. A girl. An adolescent. A nineteen-year-old emerging wet from the sea. I held on to this particular photo, and sat down. George really was very . . . and she'd not gone downhill, either. In fact . . .

I laid the picture down on the table in front of me and started up my laptop. It took me a few minutes of searching but, yes, there it was. Just for comparison, see how her legs, in this photograph of her in a clinging bathing costume, are no less well formed than they are in this other photograph on the Net where we can look up them to her knickers as she gets out of a car. Interesting. I flicked my eyes back and forth between the two images, pondering how photography captured instants like this – sealed moments in amber. I was thinking about the way future generations would have access to these unposed, unguarded insights into our lives in a way we never could for the people who'd lived before the advent of the camera. It was a fascinating line of thought and I was a little annoyed that I was being hampered in pursuing it by the irritating distraction of my erection twitching against my stomach. I reached down and moved it around a little, trying to manoeuvre it into a less intrusive position. It remained determinedly vertical and skittish but, not to be outdone, this only made me redouble my efforts to wrestle it into submission.

Relatively quickly, this became an end in itself.

Time took on an indistinct quality. Despite this dreamlike dimension, however, in some respects I was remarkably lucid and focused. Here was this stubborn erection that simply refused to go away – either after my initial mental requests or, now, owing to my later attempts at a police action using increasingly rapid and vigorous hand intervention. There was clearly only *one way* I was going to rid myself of this unwanted intrusion. Once I'd realised this, I resolved upon a plan of action and strove towards its conclusion with great vim and determination. I was, I had *no* doubt whatsoever, very close to my destination when my mobile phone rang. As always, I snatched it up off the table and answered it. Habit. Completely reflexive, no brain function involved at all: the extreme limit, in fact, of the left hand not knowing what the right hand is doing.

'Hhhhhello,' I said. (OK, 'gasped'.)

'Hi, Tom,' replied George.

Oh, Jesus. An avalanche of the most horrific thoughts imaginable fell from my head and plunged icily into my stomach.

'Oh . . . Geor . . . um . . . 'lo, George. How are things? Going?'

'Fine, fine. Look, the reason I'm calling is this publisher's thing they're having while I'm in America. I know you said you didn't fancy it, but I really would appreciate it if you went for me.'

'Mmm ... I don't really ...' I noticed, absently, that despite the trauma of the situation my hand still appeared to be moving down there. It had stopped very briefly when it had first heard George's voice, but had managed to retain its grip. And now it had begun moving again. I was, of course, utterly *appalled* by this. I could only imagine it was doing it out of some kind of rebellious thrill at the thought of trying to get away with it: the frisson inherent in (oh dear) trying to pull it off.

'I really would owe you one,' whispered George, simultaneously on the phone, in a bathing suit and flashing the most *fantastically* prim white knickers at me as she got out of a car.

This was just awful. I *loathed* myself. If *only* there was something I could do to change this situation. Surely there was something I could do to stop this? Sadly, nothing occurred to me.

'Yeah ... well ...' I replied, leaning back in my seat slightly.

'Go on, Tom. Go *ooooooooon* ... for me?'

Terrible. A truly terrible state of affairs.

It's amazing how fast the human mind can go. I don't mean go *somewhere*, reach a conclusion, but just race along; sprinting through thousands of thoughts, picturing hundreds of possibilities, conjuring up a countless number of spinning images. If there's a record for the speed of thought, I broke it. I broke it sitting there at the table in the dining room, naked, a bathing-suit photo spread out by my laptop – which was displaying Dave's Upskirt Pics Page – Georgina Nye on the phone, a thumping erection in my hand and, from the front door, the voice of Sara calling, 'Tom? Are you in?'

'Fuck!'

'What?' replied George, a little surprised.

'Oh, Jesus! Fucking fucking *fucking* . . .'

What do you do first, eh? Stuff the photo back in the envelope? Turn off the laptop? Try to wrench your erection agonisingly down out of sight between your legs? Hang up on George? Look for something to wear? If your girlfriend is only moments away from the door and you won't have time to do everything, which combination of things *unarguably* hangs you? Leaves you without any hope whatsoever of being able to give a plausible alternative to 'Hello. I'm in the dining room naked having a wank over Georgina Nye'? You might say the erection – think about it, though. No erection, but bathing photo, upskirt.jpg and dining-room nakedness are going to ring bells with Sara, she's no fool. If I had only the erection to contend with at least I could try to bluff it: 'Ah! Sara!' (Sweeping, theatrical hand movements.) 'I've been waiting for you!'

'Are you OK?' asked George.

I slammed the lid of the laptop shut. 'Yes! Fuck. *Fuck!*'

'Tom?' Sara called, queryingly. She'd obviously heard me scrambling about. Or possibly heard my heartbeat, which was surely a single decibel of loudness away from shattering all the windows in the house. 'Tom?'

'Yes,' I called back. I tried to inject it with a kind of off-hand, casual, no-need-to-come-into-the-dining-room-there's-nothing-interesting-happening-here tone.

'Yes what?' asked George.

I looked around the room frantically for something to wear. Not a bleeding thing. Well, that wasn't strictly true: there was my mobile phone case. I suppose I could slip that over my erection. Sara would come in, there I'd be with a Simpsons mobile phone case on my penis, I'd shout, 'Ta-da!' and then, all being well, instantaneously have a seizure and die. It was easily the best plan I had.

'Nothing,' I whispered to George. 'Look, I have to go, I . . .'

I could hear the rattle of coat hangers by the front door. 'Tom,' Sara shouted, 'I've got Lindsey and Beth with me – I said we'd look after them for an hour while Susan does some stock-taking.'

Susan was a workmate of Sara's at the freezer store. She had two daughters: Lindsey (6) and Beth (4).

So, that was it, then. I was going to jail.

'Tom? So . . . will you go to the publisher's evening?' George asked.

'What? Yes, whatever, yes . . .' There were the French windows. '. . . anything. *Yes.*'

'That's great!'

'Yeah, it is. I've got to go. Love you, 'bye.'

'Ha – love you too.'

'Sorry, I'm not . . . it's . . .'

'It's OK,' she said, a laugh in her voice, ''bye.' She hung up.

So, I could get out of the French windows into the garden. I walked over to them. Yes. *Yes!* Because then I'd be naked in the garden, with no way of getting back into the house other than to stroll back into the dining room, naked, through the French windows.

The door opened. I dived to the floor, pulling the photographs off the table as I did so.

Fortunately, because the table was between us, I was not immediately visible to anyone standing in the doorway. I poked my head up into view.

'Hello, Lindsey,' I said. 'Hello, Beth – I've just knocked some papers off the table . . . and I'm picking them up.'

'Do you . . .'

'*No!* . . . I don't need any help, thanks. Why don't you two go into the other room? You can watch a video.'

'What videos have you got?' asked Lindsey.

'Oh, I don't know. Loads of them.'

'Any children's videos? Only Mom doesn't like Beth seeing scary things – it gives her nightmares.'

Well, she'd definitely be better off with *any* of the videos in there than she would be glancing under this bloody table, then.

'I'm not sure what's there, Lindsey. You take Beth and have a look.'

'OK.'

'You're sweating,' said Beth.

'Yes. Go with your sister now.'

They left. But where was Sara? I strained my ears and picked up a tinkling of cutlery coming from the kitchen. I was in the dining room; to my left lay Sara; to my right Lindsey and Beth. Could I get through the hall and up the stairs without being spotted by either? If they stayed in their rooms, and had the doors closed, certainly. But, though I didn't know about Lindsey and Beth, I was sure Sara's door would be open. Sara had never closed a door in her life (being a devoted door-shutter myself, it drove me mad). Still, who knew how long I had even this half-chance? I had to make a break for it – there wasn't a moment to lose. So that I had at least *something* to cover my shame if the worst happened and Lindsey and Beth spotted me, I unplugged the laptop and pressed it over my groin.

I'm no saint, I'll freely admit, but I'm not an evil man. I'm not a mass murderer or a tyrant; I've never made off with the pension fund of a group of war widows or sent a tiny child to an orphanage so I could steal its inheritance. Given this, I think that I really didn't deserve, at this moment, what with all my other troubles, to burn my genitals against the extremely hot plastic on the bottom of an improperly ventilated laptop case. Is there anyone who would not concede me this point?

You unexpectedly burn your genitals, you say, 'Fuck!' – I don't care who you are. How I managed to bark it so quietly,

I still don't know. My *word*, it stung. I grabbed at my scorched erection and gripped it tightly – my face scrunched up, my eyes closed and my lips twisted back to expose my gritted teeth as I hissed, 'Grrrrrrrraaaaaaahhhhhh': had anyone walked in at this instant and taken in the tableau I fear they might have jumped to entirely the wrong conclusion. Thankfully, no one did and – despite the clock ticking – I took a few seconds to examine myself for heat damage. (However busy a man might be, he will always find the time to check his erection if he's burnt it on a laptop case – it's common knowledge.) I couldn't see any marks. From the pain, I'd expected to see the laptop's serial number, in reverse, and the ventilation grille branded on to it: my speeding mind had already played awkward host to the somewhat tricky problem of how I might explain to a doctor, and to Sara, why it was that I'd seemingly bar-coded my own penis. Luckily, though, burning your genitalia always feels worse than it is and there were no visible signs of harm. As with any injury, however, the blood was rushing to the site. As it happens, that particular site had not been short of blood rushing to it before this, so now it was like it had been allocated its own heart. It bobbed. In time with my racing pulse, it bobbed up and down; repeatedly flicking its chin up in recognition of someone I couldn't see – 'Hey – how you going?' I flattened it, struggling, under the laptop (carefully turning the case round first so I used the cool upper side this time).

Laptop clasped over my groin, I crept to the door and, like someone opening a package to see whether there was a bomb inside, warily eased it back so I could peer outside. I couldn't see the living room from this position – it was right next to me, its door in the same wall – and I'd just have to hope that either the door was closed or the girls were too busy looking through videos to notice a naked man running through the hallway. I could see into the kitchen, though, because it was at the end of the hall, perpendicular to my room. The door, of course, was open and Sara was in there preparing some food. I closed my door until it was open about the width of a single human hair and watched her through the crack. She was by the sink cutting up cheese and placing the slices in to a bowl that looked as though it contained some kind of fruit yogurt. I was sufficiently far behind her to be out of her line of sight, but certainly not enough so that she wouldn't notice the movement out of the corner of her eye if I attempted to leave the room. I needed to wait until she was in a better position before making a run for it.

Then she turned round to face right at me. My soul left my body. Really – it was as though something deep in the heart of me was abruptly sucked clean out: I went cold, I stopped breathing, all my limbs sagged – it was like someone had flicked my power off.

She popped a yogurty cheese slice into her mouth and placed the bowl down by the cooker. Obviously, though I could see her plainly, she couldn't see me – not even my wide, terrified eye – beyond the tiny sliver of a gap I was looking through. I ordered my lungs to start working again and, with not a little pride, noted that I hadn't pissed all over the carpet. Sara started to hum a tune to herself ('Champagne Supernova', I think, but I couldn't swear to it) and moved over to search for something in one of the overhead cupboards. Her back was to me. This was my chance, and who knew whether I'd get another? Over the top, lads.

Clutching the laptop hard to myself, like a security blanket, I whipped open the door as quickly and as quietly as I could. With my jaws locked tightly together from tension, I sprinted out into the hallway, past the living room (the door was open but the girls weren't anywhere in view), round the newel post and off up the stairs.

No one squealed behind me: I'd made it.

I ran into the bedroom and threw on the first pieces of clothing I found in the drawers. When I stood there finally – undiscovered and fully clothed – I felt like the KING OF

THE FUCKING WORLD. I made a little fist and shook it: 'Yessssss!'

I wandered casually back downstairs. Sara was no longer in the kitchen. She was sitting at the table in the dining room with her bowl of cheese and yogurt, absently flicking through the photos of George from the envelope I'd left lying there.

'Hi,' I said, pecking her on the top of her head.

'Where were you? I thought you were in here.'

'Tch – I've been for a pee. Is that OK?'

'Aye, of course – I just didn't see you go past.'

'I said hello.' I sighed. 'You were humming in there in your own little world, though.'

'Oh, right . . . these for the book, are they?'

'Yep. Publishers always like them. A picture is worth a thousand words, and nearly as many extra sales, I reckon.'

She leafed past the childhood stuff and paused on the swimsuit picture.

'Nice figure,' she said, admiringly.

I leaned over her shoulder and squinted at it to convey the impression that I hadn't really given the photo more than a casual glance before now.

'Hmm . . .' I shrugged, unenthusiastically. '. . . she's not really my type.'

IV

I'm sorry you had to witness that, I really am. You're classy people, some
of you, and you shouldn't have to be confronted with that kind of thing. If
it's any consolation, just think how Tom's going to feel when you all meet
up in the afterlife and he learns that the lot of you sat there watching him
trying to get a quick one off the wrist, yeah?

Of course, I've got to take some responsibility myself, and I'm big enough
to put up my hands and accept part of the blame – that's why I'm here
telling you all this now. When I started this whole thing – you know, the
universe and all that stuff – I thought it'd be a nice little distraction. I'd set
it up, leave it running . . . sit back and watch it like a lava lamp: kind of
fascinated, kind of just letting my mind drift. You know what I mean? But,
anyways, to keep it working you need to have the whole sex thing, and so
I put that in the mix. Never thought it'd be such a big deal, I swear to you,
I really didn't. It's like, OK, I heard this thing about Rachman and Hodgson
the other day. These guys are scientists . . . I'm a real science freak, by the
way. Do you watch the Discovery channel? It's great – I *love* that stuff. You
see, I didn't have a clue about how anything works – why would I have, yeah?
I want a whale, I go, 'Boom – whale,' and that's it – bada-bing, bada-boom.
I'm not going to get all caught up in the details, am I? I mean, the devil's
in the details, right? Ha ha – 'the devil's in the details' – get it? No, no,
I'm kidding with you again: relax, there's no devil – why would I make a
devil? What am I? Stupid? But that's a good one, right? 'The devil's in the
details.' Ha ha. Anyways, what I'm saying is, these scientists come along
and they study stuff and investigate and explain how everything works. And
I'm, like, 'Wow! A whale. So *that's* how I did that . . . cool.' So, same thing,
these guys Rachman and Hodgson – Stan and Ray – Stan and Ray do these
experiments to see if they can persuade people to have, you know, 'a thing'

for boots. They're basically seeing if they can grow a fetish in the lab, right? Because, they're thinking, some people have these things anyways, so let's see if we can understand how that could happen by trying to make one of our own. And they chose to make one for boots. Don't ask me why. Maybe they think using underwear would cloud the issue, you know, and trying to get folks to have the hots for a gas turbine engine is just making things hard for themselves – so they settles on boots. Whatever – ask them if you want: it's not important to what I'm telling you here. Anyways, they do it. Stan and Ray do these, you know, kind of, conditioning things with volunteers and eventually they get guys to go, 'Phwoar!' when you show them a picture of a boot.

So, back there, Tom was doing a bit of conditioning of his own. Self-condition: reinforcing his attraction to George by looking at pictures of her while . . . you know . . . 'applying stimulation'. He didn't know that, of course, he didn't intend to do it; but that's what he was doing all the same. Maybe some of you might want to bear that in mind, yeah? Be aware of what you're doing sometimes – just so you avoid getting yourselves more in to spin-dryers or certain kinds of fruit or socks full of Jell-o than you ever intended. It's OK, I'm not going to name names: you know who you are.

But that's not the most important thing here. The most important thing is what happened *after* Stan and Ray worked their shoe trick. You see, they got a result, and they're happy – they go out for a meal to celebrate, maybe, I don't know – and then, because they're straight-up guys, they set about *de*conditioning the volunteers. Ridding them of this unfortunate boot attraction that's been created for the purposes of scientific investigation. And here's the thing, right . . . a lot of the volunteers don't *want* to be 'cured'. They're into it now. I mean, you can imagine how it is for them. It's like they've discovered a whole new sex or something. They can probably spend the entire afternoon standing looking through the window of a shoe shop: it's probably like watching an orgy for them, right? It's just a programmed reaction . . . but *that's all 'normal' attraction is*. I simply put it in there to make sure you kept things going – but, to guarantee that, it needed to be powerful. So powerful it has Tom playing five-knuckle shuffle in his dining room when the house is empty. So powerful, right, so *powerful* that it seems more than functional, it seems precious and mystical to those who feel it.

The boot squad don't want to have their desire for a nicely turned insole taken away from them, but would *you* want *your* desire removed? If some doctor said to you, 'We're going to do a desire-ectomy on you, so that all those feelings you have looking at a film star or a singer or a model or the person across the road no longer get in the way and you can live your life undistracted by such urges,' would *you* go in for the operation? Like I said, this is partly my fault. I make things important for you lot, and then I'm all surprised when you feel they're important in ways I didn't intend. I needed them to be strong; I never intended them to be special.

I'm sorry about that. Really, I am.

SEVEN

'What did Tom get you?' asked Hugh's wife, Mary.

We were having a small party for Sara's birthday. Sara's friends and a couple of her less dangerous relatives were wandering around with precarious paper plates of sausage rolls and crisps in one hand and glasses of sparkling wine in the other – asking each other what they did for a living, responding, 'Oh, *really*?' and then falling silent. Sara had friends from all sorts of places: I had Hugh. I knew a few other people – old colleagues from the newspaper and so on – but no one I saw regularly or felt any need to invite round because it was my girlfriend's birthday. That was fine by me, incidentally. I'm not hugely gregarious and it was quite enough for me to have Hugh, and Amy. Except, Amy wasn't really my friend: she was my agent – a thing simultaneously less and more than a friend. Amy I hadn't invited to the party; she would, I knew, have felt uncomfortable about it. Like it was crossing a line. She'd have felt that there was a kind of non-specific, visceral ickyness to her being there – in the same way as there might be if a man were having a birthday party and his wife invited her gynaecologist.

Hugh I'd expected to be a damper on any reckless attempts at celebration, but I hadn't thought Mary would come in and almost immediately turn down the ambient joy.

Sara and I had had a row that morning. We didn't have many rows – Sara's too upbeat and good natured and I'm too lazy – so, when we *did* have them, we tended not to know how to have them properly. We were under-rehearsed and no one was sure of their lines or their cues and there was confusion about who should start bits and, crucially, we had no idea where the end was.

It had begun almost first thing in the morning. I'd been working on the book until very late the previous night and because of this I didn't wake up early so I could rouse Sara with a kiss and a breakfast tray, as is a birthday requirement in our house. Sara was determined to get her due, however, so instead of getting up she sat there, in bed, for God knows how long, waiting for me to wake. I think she grew irritable during this period. In fact, I have a suspicion that the reason I woke even when I did was owing to her finally losing patience: I know for certain that I awoke with a start, my ear was unaccountably painful and Sara was rubbing her elbow.

Anyway, once I was awake, I got up and did my duty. I returned with the tray and her birthday card. The card turned out to have an ill-fitting verse inside it, which annoyed Sara further, but, really, what kind of freak reads the verses in cards before he buys them? Sara carefully stood the card on the bedside table.

'Present?' she said – noting that I hadn't brought one in with the tray and card, and glancing around the room a little for effect.

'Ah,' I replied, remembering I'd prepared something. 'I've got you a present, but it's nothing I could wrap.'

Sara sat up straighter in the bed and cheered a little. She wriggled expectantly. 'What is it?'

I popped out into my den and returned with an envelope. 'It's a thing that's going to happen later,' I continued, 'but I did do this envelope. Just so you had something to open now.'

She took – snatched, in fact – the envelope from my hand and flexed it with her fingers in examination. 'Tickets?' she offered.

'No,' I smiled back, 'not quite tickets.'

'Ohhhh . . .' she squeaked, girlishly excited. She tore open the envelope wildly and unfolded the piece of paper inside as fast as she could.

'It's a year's subscription to *ProCycling*,' I said, in confirmation (even though she had stared fixedly at it for what I judged was long enough to read it five times over). 'I did it over the Web, but I thought I'd print out the e-mail confirmation of the order, just so you had something to open this morning.'

She reread the print-out in motionless silence, oh . . . perhaps another twelve times.

Finally, she placed it back in the envelope, put the envelope on the bedside table by the card and said, 'Thanks.'

Over the course of the following twenty minutes or so – from nowhere – an argument developed.

And it never really ended. We'd prepared everything for the party by running on a kind of chill professionalism – 'I'll grate the cheese with you, but it doesn't mean I *like* you, OK?' As we moved about the house getting things ready we never missed an opportunity to pass each other soundlessly in the hallway without making eye contact.

This is the context, then, in which Mary had asked Sara, 'What did Tom get you?'

'A magazine subscription,' she replied, with a smile that gave everyone goose bumps.

'Oh,' said Mary. 'That's nice.'

'Yes. Isn't it?'

'It's a cycling magazine,' I cut in, defensively. 'You know how Sara loves cycling. And this is an American magazine – I had to do the subscription on the Web.'

'Oh,' said Mary. 'That's nice.'

Hugh, sensing an atmosphere, changed the subject. Though, of course, Hugh only had one subject he was capable of changing to, so it didn't give a huge lift to the mood.

'Twenty-nine, eh?' he said to Sara. 'You've still got a little chance left at life at twenty-nine. You probably don't realise it – probably think you've already let all the good years slip away – but, really, you've still got at least one more shot, trust me.'

'I'm fine about being twenty-nine.'

'That's the spirit.'

'Georgina Nye is *thirty*,' I said, hoping this would encouragingly illustrate a point but, simultaneously with uttering the words, completely forgetting what that point could possibly be.

There was a short silence, after which Hugh said, 'Exactly – there you go.' Everyone looked into their wineglasses for a moment, and then Hugh started raising our spirits once more. 'Of course,' he mused, 'a lot of people think it's all over and done with bar the credits when you hit thirty . . . but that's not true at all. No, complete nonsense. Your life's not really finished until you reach thirty-five.'

'Thirty-five, eh? You're thirty-seven, Hugh,' I said, 'and you're still talking.'

'Oh, you shuffle on, of course you do – but it's just waiting, really. Once you hit thirty-five your body starts to fall apart; simply *careers* downhill faster than you ever thought possible. All of a sudden you notice your scalp shining through your hair when you look in the mirror, and you begin collecting fat – which you can't seem to lose whatever you do – and comprehensively, body-wide, you sag. You can stand there in the shower for ages, just grabbing great bits of yourself, pulling them up, and then watching them drop, heavy, lifeless and wobbling the second you release them from your grasp.' Hugh was staring down, but his eyes weren't focusing on anything. 'You start to squint at things, you start to drift towards elasticated waistbands, you start to think about your joints, you start to worry about what you eat, you start to fall asleep during the evening news, you start to say things like, "Ohhhh . . . I've been sitting in one position too long." At thirty-five it all unravels so rapidly you can't even take it all in. That's why . . .' He raised his sad eyes to me. '. . . Have you ever filled in a survey or a questionnaire? They have age categories: "Under a year", "1–7", "7–14", "14–21",

"21–34" . . . "35–70". That's the last category, "35–70".
Sometimes they don't even bother softening the blow at all
by writing the "70", it's just "35 and over" – "35 to death".
"35" – whoosh!' He swung his arm out and looked off into
the distance, like he was throwing a frisbee, '. . . to infinity.
Welcome on board the number 35 – next stop the grave.'

Hugh took a sip from his glass and sloshed the wine around
in his mouth while he gazed down at the floor again and slowly
shook his head.

'Well,' said Mary, 'I think I'm going to grab something from
that buffet – it all looks delicious.'

'Mmmm . . . yes,' I said, leading her away towards the table.
'Dive in – everything needs to be eaten.'

'What's in the sandwiches?'

'We have salmon, cheese and jam,' I said, then leaned closer
to her and whispered, '*I* made them so don't worry: that is
three *separate* types of sandwich.'

Sara's uncle Tam and his wife, Lizzy, were the last people to
leave, at around eleven o'clock. Lizzy apologised, again, for
Tam and thanked us for the bag of leftover cakes. Tam stood
behind her, wriggling with surprising fluidity for a man his
age, and singing 'Do You Think I'm Sexy?' We told Lizzy
it was fine and thanked her for coming – and for the Ikea
token – and said we really must make an effort to see each
other more often this year. She steered Tam down the drive
towards their car, hissing, 'You do this *every* time.'

'Quick,' he hissed back, grinning. 'Get us home – I've a yen
for some lovin'.'

We waved them off, closed the door and silently set about
tidying the house. I gathered up the rubbish from the table
and Sara stood next to me, putting all the leftovers on to as
few plates as possible. There was more silence than could
comfortably fit into the room. Then, without glancing away
from the trifle, Sara finally spoke.

'I'm sorry.'

I stopped my tidying and looked at her. She spooned the remainder of the trifle into a smaller bowl: each scoop coming up with a sound like a wellington boot being pulled out of deep mud. When she'd finished, she too stopped and looked back at me.

'Oh, I'm sorry,' she repeated, smiling sadly. 'It is good that you ordered the magazine for me, I know I'll enjoy it. It's just . . . you know, I was *expecting* something really . . . *unexpected*. I must have seemed very ungrateful, but I'd dropped you all those hints and I'd worked myself up to the point where I was certain you'd got something *unbelievable* planned. I convinced myself so much that I even started to sense you were being secretive and . . .'

'Secretive? How?'

'Well, that's the point, I can't even say precisely how. I just had the feeling you were up to something, that there was something going on that you weren't telling me about, and that confirmed to me you'd got a big surprise in the offing. I must have been imagining it simply because I wanted it so much. I got angry because I was disappointed . . . but I disappointed myself, really.'

'No . . . It's my fault.' I felt awful. And why hadn't I apologised first? What a twat I am. 'I'm just shit, Sara. You know what I'm like, I can't bring myself to do the big set pieces, I simply *can't*. I can't do the carriage and the ballet . . .'

'The *what*?'

'Oh, just for example, you know – the fairy-tale stuff. And, yes, I do think they're stupid, and I do think the men who do them are self-serving egomaniacs, but I should have tried anyway: I knew how much you wanted something like that. I'll make it up to you, somehow. I just messed up this time because, well . . . you know . . . I'm shit.'

She moved the couple of steps needed to cross the huge distance that had been dividing us all day and put her arms around me, laying her head on my shoulder. I pulled her to me even tighter and combed my fingers through her hair. She smelled of home.

'Oh, well,' she said, 'maybe one day.'

'Ewww . . . don't. Can't we just agree I'm completely shit and draw the line there?'

She laughed. 'OK, OK – you're shit. At the end of the day, I'm very happy with what I've got . . . and it's you, Tom . . . and you're shit.'

'Utter shit.'

'You shitter.'

I kissed her head.

'Do you love me beyond the edges of reason and beyond the walls of time?'

'Yeah,' I replied, 'sure.'

By the time the McAllister & Campbell thing that I'd promised George I'd attend in her place came round I'd delivered the manuscript of the book to Hugh. In truth, I could have delivered it a little earlier. I'd gone back and rewritten parts of it what was, for me, an extraordinary number of times. Normally, I raced through the process of slapping the words down and then reread the completed manuscript once to check for unbearable uglinesses (sometimes I didn't even do this: that's what editors are for) and clumsy typos or embarrassing factual idiocies (sometimes I didn't even do this: that's what copy-editors are for). I'd then plonk it on Hugh's desk, whoop with joy and never think about the damn thing again. For some reason, it was different with this book. It was now officially titled *Georgina Nye: Growing*, by the way. As she was still only thirty, it seemed fittingly apologetic as a title for an autobiography, and it also gave the sense that the book covered the period of her growing up. Moreover, it hinted that she modestly felt she was still growing, um, 'spiritually' or something, and, finally, our all-purpose subtitle was actually a reference to a Burns song, 'Green Grow the Rashes' – which jammed in not just the Scottish angle but also George's perky, chat-show-friendly feminism: a quote from the song began the book.

Auld Nature swears, the lovely Dears
Her noblest work she classes, O;
Her prentice han' she tried on man,
And then she made the lasses, O!

I'd simply been unable to leave the text of the book alone. I recast bits. I threw out whole sections: disgusted with myself because of their crassness. I did research – *proper* research. I fretted over single words. Often I'd even get up out of bed and start writing, unable to sleep because a flawed passage was reading itself over and over in my mind. In the end, I practically had to *force* myself to deliver the manuscript: it was never going to be good enough to satisfy me, but the deadline had arrived.

When he got to read it, Hugh was 'a bit concerned'. A ghost writer is usually required to sound like the person whose book he's writing. Not completely, of course – you don't want the footballer you're being on the page to be the mumbling, drunken twat that's on your Dictaphone. But enough so that the people reading it can comfortably match the image of Wayne Centre-Forward with the voice of the simple, unpretentious geezer in the prose.

And that was why Hugh was concerned.

He felt that *Growing* read rather more like Susan Sontag than Georgina Nye. It was a mismatch. I countered by saying that I quite fancied Susan Sontag – going so far, in fact, as to ask if he knew of anywhere I could find nude photos of Susan Sontag on the Web. He remained concerned. (Actually, he looked somewhat more concerned.) Eventually, he called in support from Fiona, who – with typically unattractive snottiness – informed me that viewers of *The Firth* and big fans of *Against Interpretation* were two 'largely distinct demographics'. So, in the end, I took out nearly all of the section about how one could use the collapse of Weimar as a metaphor for personal conscience being ever open to the atavistic demons of the id, lost the chapter on Teiresias, and we added lots of photos of George at showbiz parties.

George's agent had approved everything – 'Terrif choice of photos! Cracking!!!' – and so the manuscript went off to the copy-editor (copy-editors, like, say, computer programmers or proctologists, are the kind of people you're hugely thankful exist, but whom you can't help worrying about at some very deep level), and I got a hotel room booked for me so I could attend the McAllister & Campbell in-house party in London.

I wasn't looking forward to the party at all, and the day before it I got some news that made me even less keen to go. I was in the bedroom packing my overnight bag and Sara came in from the shower.

'Don't forget to bring back the hotel shampoo,' she said.

Sara had pale skin. In fact, with her see-through-you eyes, pale skin and red hair, you could easily think that one of those tragic, fey heroines from a Waterhouse painting had attempted to evade her fate by sneaking off the canvas and hiding out as the supervisor of an Edinburgh frozen food store – perhaps a Danaïd placed there by some Olympian witness protection programme after grassing up her murderous sisters. However, after a hot shower Sara went bright pink (or, if she took a bath, pink everywhere below the waterline – just a white head and knees): fresh from the shower, she looked like the kind of exotic dancer you'd find in a bar in *Star Wars*.

'Sure . . . shampoo, soap, maybe if we're lucky I'll get some chocolate and a sheet of notepaper too.'

'Newspaper?'

'Nah. The place to collect newspapers is on the train – wait long enough and you can get one of everything.'

Sara laughed and scrubbed her hair with the towel. 'Good thinking. You can get a few tabloids that way – you'll be able to see what else Georgina Nye has been up to in America while you're here doing her book promotion work.'

'Yeah,' I laughed back, then paused my packing and asked, 'What do you mean, "what *else*"? What has she got up to already?'

'Och,' Sara shrugged. 'She's shagging Darren Boyle, isn't she?'

Darren Boyle was a comedian turned game show host turned actor. (He could, as far as I was concerned, keep turning.)

'What?'

'It was in the paper the other day.'

'Which paper?'

'I can't remember – one of the girls at work was reading it. The *Star* . . . or the *Sun*, one of those kinds of papers. The *Daily Mail*.'

'What did it say?'

'Just that they were both in America at the moment and had been seen together. Having dinner, in clubs . . . you know. I think we had the usual quote from "a friend" saying they couldn't get enough of each other or something.'

'And what the *hell* does that mean?'

'I don't know. Jesus, Tom, calm down.' She laughed again. 'What does it matter? She's not your girlfriend or anything. Who cares if she's having a bit of a wriggle with Dazza?'

'It's just . . . I mean, obviously, I don't care who she sleeps with – the tart – it's the book I'm thinking about.'

'Isn't it good publicity for the book?'

'No.'

'No?'

'Well, yes, it is good publicity in that sense . . .'

'In the "publicity" sense.'

'. . . in the sense that she's in the news. But Darren "Oh, I'm so fucking hilarious" Boyle isn't even mentioned in it. People will be disappointed not to find him *anywhere* if they buy the book because they've been swept up by the excitement of George's whirlwind romance and marriage to the gurning little ponce.'

'I don't think anyone's mentioned marriage – they've just had dinner.'

'Well . . . that's how it starts, believe me.'

Sara peered at me.

'Are you all right?' she asked.

'Yes, I'm fine.' I noticed I'd very nearly shouted this. 'Yes,' I repeated more sanely, 'I'm fine. It's just all the work and having to go to this stupid party . . .'

'You didn't *have* to go.'

'I did. I told you – Amy committed me to it as part of the contract.'

'You could have told her to go back to them, because she didn't check with you first.'

'No, I couldn't, because . . . well, it doesn't matter now: I'm just a bit wound up, that's all.'

'Perhaps you should call and cancel. Say you're sick.'

'Mmmm . . .'

Sara pulled on her nightdress.

'No,' I replied, 'I'll go. I've said I would.'

'Well . . . please yourself,' she said, and headed off to take the wet towel back to the bathroom.

I began jamming the rest of the things into my overnight bag, *really* hard. 'I'll do the bloody party, you just hump your way round America, George,' I muttered venomously to myself. 'I hope you feel massively fucking guilty about it, that's all.'

In-house publishing parties work like this: drink. It's an opportunity for all sections of the organisation – management, editorial, marketing, sales, authors, etc. – to come together for one evening and get savagely pissed on an equal footing. This one was being held at some venue in London that I knew must be very fashionable at the moment because in any other city in Great Britain no one would have stepped into the place. Ageing metal handrails came out of dusty, grey concrete and ran alongside narrow steps gorged with people shuffling between levels in the desperate hope that above, or below, or above again was where the fun was actually happening. (It was probably designed to be 'minimal' by people whose vocabulary tragically ended before the word 'grim'.) London, because it's where the media lives, truly is the only place where you can get away with this: in Leeds people would simply say, 'Eh? They've just put some garden chairs out in an old fooking abattoir.' And it didn't help that I really wasn't in the mood for it anyway: after doing the minimum permissible amount of shouting how very big *Growing* was going to be at the sides of people's heads, I spent most of my time simply trying to keep out of the way.

I was sitting alone in the corner of the bar, drinking a lager and watching a group of young women from M&C's London offices – every single one of whom was called 'Emma' – dance while holding bottles of Smirnoff Ice, when my mobile got a call. I whipped it from my side and slammed it against my ear. I didn't even bother to glance at the caller display, as I knew it must be either Amy or Sara.

'Hello. Tom Cartwright can't come to the phone right now, as he is currently in fucking hell. Please leave your message after the gnashing of teeth . . .'

'Erm . . . ? Tom?' It was George.

I rammed my finger into my other ear so that I could hear her better. 'George! . . . Sorry . . . I was . . . expecting . . .'

'Oh, sorry – I won't keep you, if you're waiting for another call.'

'No . . . I – *no* . . . You're, not . . . no . . . Hahaha,' I explained.

'I've still not quite got my head round the time difference – I think it's five hours, or maybe six . . . or is it eight? Anyway,

I just wanted to call you to say thanks again for filling in for me and ask how it was going.'

'Fine . . . You . . . Fine,' I said.

'Great, I'm glad. I'm having a wonderful time here.'

'Apparently,' I replied. I intended this to come out flatly, but it seems that instead it took along enough bitterness to last twelve thousand miles, because after I'd said it there was a pause at the other end of the line. I went cold.

I was expecting George to hang up on me, or break the silence with either 'How is it any of *your* business who I sleep with?' or, equally justifiably, 'Twat'. Yet, when she did speak again, her voice was apologetic. 'Oh, sorry, Tom. I know you didn't want to go to that thing, and here I am ringing you up and telling you what a great time I'm having while you're doing it for me.'

'I . . . um . . .' I clarified.

'Look, I'll make it up to you somehow when I get back, OK? Promise.'

'I . . .' A man's voice called her name, impatiently, in the background.

'Yes, yes – OK,' she called back to him. 'Look, I've got to go, Tom. Thanks again, though – see you soon, yeah? 'Bye.'

She hung up.

'Yes, see you soon. Sorry about snapping there – just a bit stressed out, nothing to do with you. We'll have a meal when you get back, yes? It'll be fun. 'Bye,' I said, to the dead-line tone.

I drank some more lager and, later, swore at a poet. It was the early hours of the morning when I eventually shuffled back to my hotel room.

I was a little drunk.

There were three or four porn channels on the TV, but you had to pay for them and – as McAllister & Campbell were picking up the bill – I didn't dare. You could see the names of the films that were showing on them by glancing at the on-screen menu, though. I sat on the edge of the bed in my underpants, scanned the titles and tried to imagine how they might look if I could access them. Every one of them was, as I pictured it, quite astonishingly and unremittingly filthy. That's quite terrible, really. I mean, this was supposed to be a respectable hotel – young children, unbeknownst to their parents, might accidentally bring up the channel menu and imagine exactly the same relentless depravity that I was. Something ought to be done.

I thought about George saying she'd 'make it up to me . . . somehow'. Perhaps it was a prank and she wasn't really in America (being repeatedly penetrated by Darren Fuckwit Boyle) but just down the road, waiting. Perhaps, two seconds from now, there'd be a knock on the door and in she'd come, laughing and teasing. And wearing that bathing costume from the photo. (But not wearing it for long.)

I picked up my phone, pressed the voice-activated dialling button on the side and spoke the name with my eyes closed.

'What? Erm, ah, I mean . . . hello?'

'Hi, it's me,' I said.

'Christ, Tom – what time is it?'

'Um . . .'

'It's twenty past four. *Jesus*. Are you all right?'

'Yeah, I'm fine.'

'Well, you shouldn't be. If you're going to phone me up at twenty past four in the morning you should bloody well be being cut out of a car by the emergency services or something.'

'Sorry, Sara . . . I just missed you, that's all. I wanted to tell you I missed you.'

'Are you pissed?'

'No.'

'So, you're not pissed and you're not dying, but you're calling me to tell me you miss me at four-twenty a.m.? What are you—' She stopped abruptly. 'Have you copped off with someone?'

'No, of course not.'

'Well, the three reasons I've just listed are the only ones for an "I miss you" call at this time of night: that's just a simple fact, Tom.'

'Don't get ratty. I missed you – that's all it is. I missed you and I wanted to tell you so.'

'I've got to get up for work in three hours. Didn't you miss me at ten o'clock last night?'

'Sorry.'

'Oh,' she sighed, sleepily. 'I'm glad you miss me, Tom, and it's lovely of you to call and tell me so . . . Now fuck off, eh?'

'Yes – sorry. 'Bye.'

''Bye.'

She hung up.

I looked at the phone in my hand for a while – pondering on it as though it were some kind of surrogate Sara – then put it down on the dressing table. The names of the porn films were still cycling around on the TV screen. I sat on the bed in my underpants, read through the titles, thought about George coming into the room wearing, briefly, her bathing costume, and wondered how I might pass the next few minutes.

EIGHT

To celebrate the acceptance of the manuscript, Amy took me out for lunch. It was this kind of thing, the little bits of extra attention she gave her clients, that made you feel such a loyalty to her.

You can gaze out over a small section of Princes Park if you sit by the window on the upper floor of the McDonald's in Edinburgh. It was a sunny day and, beyond the ferocious congestion at the intersection (it's a matter of some pride, locally, that Princes Street has the highest mortality rate of any road in Britain), people were sitting on the benches eating ice cream or wandering around in pairs, looking at maps. I popped a chicken nugget into my mouth.

'It's a huge fucking comfort for me to know,' said Amy, digging around in her tiny tub of ketchup with the end of one of her fries, 'that at nearly any time of the day, and almost wherever you are, there's always a McDonald's within easy reach should you ever be swept by the desire to hear Whitney Houston singing "I Wanna Dance With Somebody".'

She reached over to her drink, pushed in the little plastic bump on the lid that's used to indicate whether something is 'Diet' or not, and then stroked this newly concave area: she matched thumb to indentation for size and shape, and seemed pleased with her work.

'The Nye woman's back from America now, you know,' she added.

'Yes, so I understand. She hasn't called me, though.' Not, of course, that I'd been waiting for her to or anything. I quickly continued, 'Had quite a time over there, so I hear.'

'What do you mean?'

'The papers said she was seeing that irritating twat Darren Boyle.'

'You know Darren Boyle?'

'No.'

'Oh, well,' Amy said, sweeping specks of salt from the table with her hand. 'I'm not sure about that – could be bollocks, you know what the papers are like. But, as long as it gets her *in* the papers, eh? That's what matters.'

'So you don't think it's true?'

'I've no idea – can't say one way or the other.'

'Right.'

'It's probably true, though.'

'Why do you think that?'

Amy leaned across to me and lowered her voice. 'Well, our Georgina's supposed to be a bit of a Fuck Monster, isn't she?'

'Says . . .' I started to snap back, but wrenched the wheel away in the direction of surprised curiosity for a last-minute, second-word recovery. '. . . who?'

'Um . . . No one . . .' She shrugged. 'You know . . . *Every-one.*'

'I see.'

'It's simply what you hear.'

'From whom?'

'*People* . . . I can't remember anyone in particular saying anything: it's just the word on the street, man. She's supposed to be a flirt.'

'Is that right.' I couldn't make it sound like a question; I just tried to keep it flat enough not to become a snarl.

'Yeah, kind of a prick-teaser . . . Except, when she's finished teasing, she'll likely as not take it home and sit on it.'

'Uh-huh.'

'Did she strike you as coquettish at all?'

'Why ask *me*? Did she strike *you* as coquettish?'

'I've never met her, have I? Not face to face – we've only spoken on the phone.'

'And if you *had* met her – face to face – then you'd know?'

'Of course.'

'How?'

'Christ, Tom: under this calm, professional agent's exterior there's still a fully working woman, don't forget. I'm not so short of oestrogen that, given the chance of seeing a woman for a few minutes, I can't immediately divine to my own satisfaction whether she's a right slag or not.'

I tore at another chicken nugget.

After a pause, Amy continued, casually, 'I spoke to Paul the other day.'

'Why did you call him? There aren't any contract problems, are there?'

'I didn't call him. I don't want to speak to him any more than I absolutely have to. I didn't call him at all – he called me.'

'OK, so why did he call you?'

'They've got a TV interview lined up. *Barker*.'

Benny Barker: chat show host and wit – a bit in that wanker Darren Boyle's mould, actually, but much sharper, and funnier, and not such a wanker. His show, *Barker*, was on weekly. Good ratings: he was cool enough for the twenty-somethings, wry enough for the thirty-somethings and twinklingly charming enough to attract women all the way from forty-something up to lying-in-state. He effortlessly got any of the upper B-list celebrities, but also A-listers who wanted to appear hip or 'just normal people' – sometimes even visiting American actors.

'Nice spot,' I admitted.

'Barker's relocating up here for the Festival: doing the shows live in Edinburgh, getting the Fringe comics on, local colour – all that stuff. As the book hits the shops right after the first show airs, they've lined up a mutually beneficial interview.'

'Good,' I said, without much feeling.

'Paul said Nye wanted you to go to it with her. I mean, not appear, obviously, but go to the studio. Moral support, I suppose.'

'Really?' I shuffled excitedly in my seat.

'I told him to fuck off, of course.'

'Did you?'

'Aye. I said you'd already hauled yourself down to London and back to attend that publishing do for her. That was going the extra mile. They could fuck off if they thought you were going to lose another evening hanging around like an idiot just so you could hold Georgina Nye's hand if she got nervous.'

'I wouldn't mind, actually.'

'What?'

'No, I mean – pfff – it'd be a bit of a bind and everything. I wouldn't really *enjoy* it . . . but it could be quite interesting. I've never seen behind the scenes of a TV programme.'

'And why would you want to? You know what they say about people who work in TV.'

'Yes, but, even so . . . I just think it'd be quite, um, "informative".'

'Really? Well, I didn't think you'd see it like that.'

She fished around in her bag for the few fries that had escaped into it when she'd taken out the box holding the others. There were seven of them. She ate them in two twos and a three. Then she wiped her hands and mouth on the paper towel, scrunched it up, placed it on the tray, reached for her drink and began sucking it up through the straw.

While she did all this I watched her and clicked the nails of my thumb and index finger together.

In the end, I burst. 'So you'll call back and say I'll do it?'

'Eh? What? Oh, the interview thing? You want me to phone and say you *would* like to do it after all . . . ? Really? You're that keen?'

'Well – I wouldn't say *keen* . . .'

'Makes me look a bit of a twat, after I've suggested they were pushing their luck even asking, doesn't it?'

'Well, maybe "keen" *does* convey it: I'm very *keen* on seeing the process of television production, close up.'

'I don't mind looking like a twat, of course – if it's for your benefit. I'm that kind of agent.'

'I know you are.'

'Abso*lute*ly.'

'You'll do it, then?'

She sighed.

'OK, yeah, I'll do it – of course I'll do it.' She got up and began to carry her tray over to the bin. 'But you remember that I do things like this for you, OK?'

'*Definitely.*'

'You wee English fucker.'

And so it was arranged. Amy sorted things out with George's agent and I was placed on a guest list. The show was going to be broadcast from one of the many venues that Edinburgh uses for Festival shows. Well, during the Festival, only the top-level performers get a proper 'venue' in the sense of it being a theatre or a club. Others make do with 'rooms' or tents or any space at all in which you can place a few people and be physically able to stand in front of them. During the Festival the tired homeless people have additional competition for shop doorways from desperate dance companies.

I think 'experimental dance' ought to stop now, by the way. I'm not going to make a big thing about this; I just think it ought to stop.

Benny Barker, of course, had got a prime place right on (appropriately) George Street. His show was on the Friday – national TV – and George's book went on sale on the Saturday. It was great publicity, especially as both Barker and George would be keen to ride the Scottish wave. George had been given a list of the questions she was going to be asked – this suited everyone: George wouldn't get to face any awkward enquiries or things she was uncomfortable talking about, while Barker knew that she'd have the time to prepare some snappy answers which was good for the show in general and therefore, naturally, for him personally. Amy had e-mailed me the list of questions, because she said George's agent wanted to make sure the ones about the book got suitably clever replies. I'd e-mailed back some quietly brilliant off-the-cuff responses for George to make.

I was, um . . . 'niggled', that'll do – I don't want to over-state the case – I was niggled that all this was going on via Amy and Paul. George could simply have talked to me herself, couldn't she? That would have been easier. Still, I didn't let this niggling impact on the quality of the sparkling retorts I prepared for her: I'm a professional. She can do everything via our agents, if that's what she wants. And she can go off to America and let Darren Grinning-Twat Boyle fuck her brains out too: it's nothing to me, it won't affect *my* work.

Where Sara was concerned, on the other hand, I did rather get it wrong with my nonchalance level about the evening. I'd played it cool with her. My going along to the show was no big deal, I'd shrugged . . . that, in fact, was why I'd forgotten to mention it to her until the day before it happened. Why should I have mentioned it earlier? It was a trivial thing. I upgraded it from 'mundane' to full 'wearisome' when Sara continued with her line that it *was* quite exciting: Benny Barker, watching a live TV show being made, from behind the scenes, all that.

'Why didn't you ask if I could go too?' Sara had said.

'Well, like I've told you, it'll be *sooo* dull. I was just keeping you out of being caught up in the tedium of it. You know – protecting you, really.'

'I'm sure I wouldn't find it dull, and you know I'm desperate to meet Georgina Nye,' Sara had replied, before pulling a really dirty trick by adding, 'And, anyway, you could have asked me what I wanted, couldn't you? Not just decided for me.'

Low blow or what?

'Well, yes . . .' I'd replied, changing tack, and pausing for a moment or two while I looked for another tack to change to. '. . . but there's also the security issue.'

'What?'

'Security. And popularity. *Everyone* wants to get to see the show . . .'

'Fools – clearly we're the only ones who know how dull it is, eh?'

'It's a . . . look – there's everyone and his mom trying to get in, and only a limited space, and the security people really don't want to let *anyone at all* in . . . do you think *I'd* be there if I wasn't needed for the show? They're allowing me in, grudgingly, because they have to so I can support Georgina. So what chance do you think I'd have with "Oh – and can my girlfriend come too, please?", eh?'

'You could have *tried* . . .'

'I . . .' I held on to the 'I' for a long time, and then just released it as a defeated sigh. 'Yes, you're right. Sorry. I wasn't thinking.'

Sara had looked at my penitent face for a while, and then rolled her eyes. 'Aww . . . never mind. Just promise me you'll have a really shite time.'

Then she'd smiled. Christ, but she was beautiful.

'Done.'

'No – listen to me: a *really* shite time.'

'I'll probably attempt to take my own life as a cry for help – I promise.'

After this I'd continued – spontaneously – to remark upon how boring it was going to be. Unfortunately, all my efforts to convince Sara that I was off to spend an evening equivalent on the excitement scale to watching the bite in an apple go brown while listening to Portishead worked against me when the time came around and I turned into the bride's mother. I tried to label my obvious, jittery excitement 'huffy irritation' in the hope that it would get by on false papers, but I don't think I got anywhere near pulling it off. I paced around and fussed over my shirt and checked my watch every couple of minutes – and this was *hours* before the time I was due to leave. Eventually, I simply bolted. A good hour and a half ahead of the time I'd been told to arrive, I got myself into the city centre and flung myself into the pub nearest to the hall.

The place was a boiling soup of people, but I got myself a lager from the bar – impressively, after being overlooked only four times in favour of people who'd arrived after me and whom I hoped fucking died; their slumping corpses pinning down the barman in such a way as to hamper his respiration until he, too, fucking died. Then I sat down on a chair that had been left on its own by a small table.

There's a strict limit to the amount of time you can be in a pub alone before every single person looks at you and thinks, 'He's been stood up, he has.' In the UK, the time limit currently stands at sixteen minutes. You can try to affect that you *haven't*, in fact, been stood up. That you are (1) a desperate, desperate man out on his own hoping to pull – please God – tonight and thus bring an end to the years of agonising loneliness and nightly, mechanical yet frantic, masturbation sessions followed by self-loathing and late-night TV until briefly given some reprieve by a sweaty, fitful sleep, or (2) an incorrigible alcoholic. Option (2) is the popular choice. Either one is better than being stood up, though. Having no partner is, at least, nothing personal: it's really just a general state of affairs, rather than a slight aimed at you in particular. Being stood up, on the other hand, is the most unambiguous, targeted comment it's possible to make. It's not blurred or diluted by the presence of everyone else in the world (because you're basically being rejected from a short list of one). It says that, although someone has made a commitment to see you – perhaps after suffering a head injury or as a practical joke – when it came to the crunch they couldn't go through with it:

they simply could not bear the idea of being with you. With *you* – solely and specifically.

After sixteen minutes, I noticed the people in the pub flicking glances at me and welling up with pity. Had I set out a hat and a cardboard sign, 'Stood Up', I reckon I could have made quite a decent amount of money. Instead, I chose to smile wryly – indicating that I knew they were thinking I'd been stood up, but that nothing could be farther from the truth and, in fact, the irony of their thinking it amused me greatly. This tactic worked for a little over a minute and a half, after which I left to sit in another pub. Fortunately – and this may surprise you – Edinburgh isn't a place where it's difficult to find a drink, so I easily went through three more lagers in three more locations until it was time for me to turn up at the Benny Barker show.

The doorman called some kind of assistant to take me into the green room they'd set up inside the theatre. Here, back-stage, I could have a glass of wine, eat nibbles and watch the show on a TV monitor. Some might say that these are precisely the same things you could have done had you stayed at home, but that would make you some random punter on the 'outside': here you were bathed in the specialness of being on the 'inside'. Other than me, the only people there were the members of this week's boy band (who were in the charts with a song that I'd never admit to liking and looked a lot uglier in real life), a few of their entourage and an anxious-looking Benny Barker show helper wearing a headset into which she periodically shouted, '*What?*' They all ignored me, and I was happy to be ignored. Nerves and four quite rapid lagers had left me feeling a bit sick, as it happened.

It was telling that no one else was in the green room. Benny Barker usually had several guests, but George was big enough for it to be her alone tonight (the band would simply be miming to their single halfway through the programme, as is traditional on chat shows). It was a Georgina Nye Special.

One, it seemed to me, that was rather short on the Georgina Nye. There wasn't long to go before the show started – where was she?

I ate some peanuts, which did wonders for my nausea, and strolled around the room slowly, pretending to be fascinated by things: the flower arrangement; the wine bottles; random bits of wiring. I was looking at the place where two sheets of wallpaper met and running my finger along the join with an apparent mixture of scientific scrutiny and childlike awe when the door opened and George finally arrived. She was, as always, frothing with controlled energy and easy, unshowy confidence. Dressed in a pair of jeans and a T-shirt, she looked utterly spectacular. She glanced around, saw me, grinned, rolled her eyes and then came directly over – seeming not to notice that there was anyone else but the two of us in the room. This, I must admit, made me feel pretty spectacular too. It's completely astonishing what four lagers and the attention of a soap star can do for your self-esteem.

'Just our luck, isn't it?' she said, laughing.

'Yeah.' I laughed back. Then I cleared my throat and asked, 'What is?'

You know that phrase, 'It's the beer talking'? It felt like I was bringing that to life in an unusually literal way. It wasn't that the quartet of lagers had loosened my verbal restraints. No, that wasn't how it felt at all. When I saw George come through the door, if you'd asked me what I was going to say to her when she got over to me I'd have been at a loss to give you any response whatsoever. I simply couldn't find any words within me: my head had been scrubbed of them. At any other time, I'd probably have had no choice except to just stand there and bark at her. However, though my brain and mouth weren't up to stitching vocal sounds together in any meaningful way, it seemed that the four bottles of Stella I had on board were relaxed and chatty. *They* were doing the talking for me. Odd as it sounds, that was the sensation: *I* was, unaccountably, tongue tied, but these things were coming out of my mouth – they didn't pass through my brain at any point and I had no inkling what the lager was going to say until the words had stepped out from between my lips and into the room.

'Oh, haven't they told you?' said George. 'Benny Barker's sick.'

'Since when?'

'Since yesterday morning, apparently. They're saying it's a stomach virus.'

'They're *saying*? What is it really?'

'Um, a stomach virus – it's the doctors who are saying it.'

'Oh, right . . . So, what's happening, then? They clearly haven't cancelled the show.'

'They've got one of the comics who was up here for the Festival to do it. He's a pal of Benny's . . . damn. Can't remember his name now . . . He's been tipped for the Perrier, and – Paddy! That's it, Paddy Adams.' She repeated the name to herself five times, insistently hammering it home.

'Paddy Adams.' I nodded.

'You've heard of him?'

'Yeah. He's pretty funny. Very surreal. Clever. Students like him. Though, obviously, that's not his fault.'

'Right.'

'He's a good choice. He's likeable, but he's still reasonably unknown, so there'll be no sense of competition – it'll be your show.'

'They tell me he's been briefed and has worked really hard to prepare himself. It's his first major TV show and he's nervous . . .'

'Christ, so am I. And all I have to do is stand here and eat peanuts.'

'It'll be OK, though. I hope.'

'Did you get the replies I did for the book questions?'

'Yes, they're great.' She reached out and squeezed my arm. 'Thanks.'

At this point the lager ran out. I pleaded with it to deliver just one more sentence, but it'd talked itself dry. I stood there and grinned at her. A big, dopey, idiot grin that just went on and on: I could see the boy band glancing over at the two of us, and I could tell they assumed that George was meeting me for charity. Thankfully, the woman with the headset – who I'd believed was climactically nervous before, but who I now realised had many higher levels of quivering, frantic distress yet to tap – juddered over and, shouting, near tears, into her microphone ('What? I'm . . . *What?*'), led George out of the room.

I had a glass of wine. It was awful. Simply dreadful – I'm not big on wine to start with, and peanuts don't really improve the taste of it, but I'm sure anyone would have found this particular stuff just as unspeakably appalling as I did. I had another glass.

Before long, the show started. I sat down on a tubular steel and black leather chair that was probably worth more than all the furniture in my house combined and watched the monitors. Adams came on and did a minute or so of stand-up using the fact that he was hosting the show instead of Benny Barker as a basis for the routine. He seemed a little over-anxious to please and he was obviously an unknown to most of the audience, but he was funny and had a kind of bemused-looking charm and it didn't take long for everything to feel comfortable. Good for him. And, more importantly, good for George. After this, he sat down on the big curved Benny Barker sofa and introduced George. To a jazzed-up version of the theme to *The Firth*, she trotted in from the wings – looking for all the world as though she were just turning up to a party at a friend's house, rather than stepping out in front of a big studio audience and millions of television viewers to chat to a man she'd never met and whose name she had difficulty remembering. However silly and pointless this celebrity nonsense was, there was no denying that it was still difficult to do it with the apparent ease and naturalness that George could. That in itself required real skill: she had a talent for being able to seem normal in the most abnormal circumstances.

And just *look* at her arse in those jeans too. Wow.

There was a little preliminary chat – Isn't Edinburgh great? Aren't Scottish people great? Isn't this old Scottish theatre, in Edinburgh, great? – then Adams pulled out his intrigued eyebrows and asked his first proper question. At which point every single muscle in my bowels fell limp. It was astonishing in the most horrific way – a nightmarish turn of events that no one could have predicted.

'So,' said Adams, 'in your autobiography, *Growing* – out tomorrow – you're quite dismissive of Klaus Theweleit's so-called "feminist" interpretations . . .'

Shite. *He'd read the book.* The chances of being interviewed about your book on television by someone who's actually *read the thing* are incalculably small – no one could have predicted that Adams would be so hysterically fastidious in his preparation as to have done this. Moreover, even if the interviewer *had* read your book (accidents happen), it would take a sick mind indeed to imagine the possibility that he would be so deranged and graceless as to ask questions about it based on this, rather than sticking to the prepared list. George was stunned into what I can only call 'an episode of dual audio-visual ventriloquism': her mouth moved and the word 'Yes' came out, but simultaneously her eyes shouted, 'Fuck!'

It was quite clear to me . . . Adams might have read her book, but *she* hadn't.

Well, *of course* she hadn't – why should she? Reading books takes ages, and she had an agent to check that I hadn't sneakily slipped in that she enjoyed kicking homeless children or something. If the person you're ghosting for reads the book you've written for them it's very nearly insulting –

like they don't trust you not to have made a pig's ear of it. George had been dropped into this through no fault of her own, but *Adams*, well . . . I was trembling with rage. Surely he couldn't believe the country's top soap star had written her own autobiography? No one could be that stupid. So, this could only be malicious: he was trying to make himself look clever at George's expense.

However, being a pro and a trouper, George had reset her face in an instant. Quite possibly, I may even have been the only one who'd noticed her brief flicker of astounded fright. She smiled and shook her head gently. 'Ah – Klaus, Klaus, Klaus . . .' The impression was that the old rascal being mentioned amused her, but I could tell that really, inside her head, she was racing around like a maniac to try to find any clue to who on earth the man was. An actor she'd worked with, perhaps? A minor clothes designer given to sociological contemplation?

'What was it you said?' continued Adams. 'That you found his "magpie blend of literary, historical and psychoanalytical interpretation too selective to be persuasive and, in any case, too analytically subterranean to be of use to the woman in the street"?'

George leaned forward, picked up a glass of water from the table, took a long drink from it and then placed it back down again. She turned back to face Adams.

'Yes.'

Adams nodded thoughtfully.

'Something else that struck me,' he began, 'was your reference to Sandra Gilbert as . . .' But here he cut off abruptly and grabbed at the side of his head, wincing. It didn't take a genius to guess that this was because the show's director was screaming into his earpiece. (Screaming so loud, in fact, that it actually picked up on his mike as a scratchy, high-pitched squeal – like the sound of a terrified mouse being cast into hell. You couldn't distinguish the actual words, but it was

precisely long enough to have accommodated – for example
– the set of phonemes: '*Just ask the prepared questions, you
cunt!*') Adams, still clutching his ear and his eyes watering
slightly, squinted at George and said, '. . . but what I'd *really*
like to know is whether you think of the cast of *The Firth* as
your family now?'

'Oh . . .' replied George – surprised and needing to consider
the question for a moment. 'You know . . .' and she set off into
the answer she'd prepared.

Adams had been defeated and the rest of the show went
off without additional scariness. His questions were delivered
very carefully, with a sort of timorous apprehensiveness, and
he sat mute and perfectly still while George gave her replies. It
was almost as though someone, somewhere, had hissed to him
that they'd called in an electrician to make behind-the-scene
modifications and, if he went off ad-libbing just once more,
then the flick of a switch would send 240 volts, via his earpiece,
directly into his head. I was still nervous, though – the whole
time willing Adams to keep to the script using only the power
of my clenched buttocks. It was therefore a fantastic relief for
me when the show finished. The house band started to play
the title music and, exhaling for the first time in about forty
minutes, I hurried over to pour myself yet another glass of
wine. I hurled it down and was just about to do the same with
a second when George – rubbing make-up off her face with
a handful of wet wipes – burst into the room and grabbed
me by the arm. She was laughing in the kind of breathless,
manic, release-of-tension way you see people doing as they're
scrambling out of the cars at the end of a particularly terrifying
theme-park ride.

'Quick!' she said. 'Let's get *out* of here!' She dragged me
hastily through the building and out of a back door, where
a cab was waiting. 'You know the hotel, yeah?' she called to
the driver as we fell inside. He nodded and we pulled away
almost the instant we'd hit the seats.

'My *God*,' George shrieked, burying herself in my chest. 'Can you *believe* that?' She lifted her head up to face me again. Her hands were clapped to her cheeks and she was grinning and flushed and her eyes were wide lights shining fright and thrill and amazement at me.

I was still unaccountably unable to speak, so I just grinned back, rolled my eyes skywards, and made that noise small boys use when they need to imitate the sound of a depth charge going off: 'Pchhhhhhhhhhhffff!'

'I nearly wet myself when he started making up the questions at the beginning. My God. My *God*. Live TV, Tom, eh? There I am, supposed to be talking about my autobiography, and I can't think because my whole life is flashing before my eyes – how ironic is *that*? My *God*!'

She laughed again, looked into my eyes and drew a breath, waiting for me to respond with my feelings and thoughts on the matter.

'Pchhhhhhhhhhhffff!'

Taking this on board, she nodded in agreement and then peered down at her hands. 'Look,' she said. 'Look at my hands. Can you believe it? I'm shaking – I'm actually *shaking*.' She lifted them up and placed them against my face so I could feel them tremble. But I couldn't feel them tremble, because I was trembling a hundred times worse than they were – the skin on my cheeks where they touched was fizzing.

And then she stopped laughing.

Just like that. Abruptly, almost within a breath: it was as though her excitement-fuelled emotional train had suddenly jumped the tracks – and she was now heading in a different direction *entirely*. Her expression changed and her movements stilled. All sound left the area around us. Well, I'm sure it didn't – the cab driver's radio probably hissed and popped with fares waiting for collection, the engine surely thrummed and I have no doubt that my breathing must have sounded like a set of bellows being operated by a hyper-active child. But none of this made it to my ears. As far as my ears were concerned, there had been something akin to explosive decompression; except instead of it being air that had been lost, it was noise. George, her hands still on my face, paused for a moment. She looked right into my eyes – and I mean precisely that. She didn't 'make eye contact' or 'look *at* my eyes': she looked right *into* them. It felt as though she saw down far, far beyond the transparent lid of the irises and the pupils – could peer deep behind them and see where I was standing, exposed. She searched me for a while – sitting motionless in this serious silence. Then she leaned forward and pressed her mouth to mine. The instant her lips touched a shock wave of goose bumps swept out across my skin from an epicentre somewhere at the back of my neck. My head was a fog of buzzing through which no coherent thoughts were visible and, muscles instantly losing all power, I fell back deeper into the corner of the cab under George's delicious weight.

Now – and I must make this clear – I'm very much a critic of society's expectations of gender roles. I'm no supporter of a view of the world in which men are decisive and powerful and proactive while women wait and hope and respond. Not only is that picture demonstrably forged but, more importantly, neither do I secretly harbour any ugly little longing for it to be genuine. It's not that I reluctantly accept that things aren't like they were when wives had fourteen children, husbands died down the mines and there was none of this nonsense about polysaccharides, but rather that I cheer it along. You sense a 'but' is arriving any second now, don't you? Yes, well, though I don't – I swear – go in for any of this ludicrous stereotyping, I couldn't help but have the vague feeling that I was being a little . . . well – you know? I mean, look at it: I'd sat there, meek, while George had *cupped my face in her hands*, and then advanced upon me with her lips – to which it's disingenuous to say I did anything else but 'surrendered' . . . Then I dropped over – 'swooned' wouldn't be far off – on to my back against the door of the cab . . . Under her. Not a great deal to be proud of there, I think you'll agree. Christ – why didn't I just flop my head over, fan my face with my hand and breathe, 'Oh, Miss Nye – my heart is beating like the wings of a tiny, frightened bird'?

In the next moment, in fact, I as good as did that. George was manoeuvring my face in her grasp so that it sort of danced against her own. Her lips slid and pressed and drew mine between them: the intensity of this grew and grew, and then stopped. Her lips withdrew, the movement ceased, and I felt her tongue move forward. Slowly, carefully, *immaculately*, its tip traced around the edge of my mouth. It circled my lips, then moved like a dare against the sharpness of my teeth, and finally paused – just for an instant, but with calculated teasing – before sliding inside. It was at this point that I squeaked. A little, high-pitched, nasal 'Mmmm . . .' of yielding ecstasy. If I'd had a shred of self-esteem left, simple shame could justifiably have been expected to have incinerated me right then: leaving nothing but a fine ash. However, as I lay there giving a pretty passable impression of Meg fucking Ryan, two factors saved me from such a fate. The first was that my objective analytical capacity was, at this juncture, 'a little fuzzy' – I was, frankly, rendered pretty much insensible by euphoria. The second thing was that, though in many ways I was not entirely broadcasting my masculinity (and I was *also*, it must be acknowledged, happily 'putting out' in the back of a cab. Ah, well, like Lisa Stansfield says, 'I may not be a lady – but I'm all woman'), I was certain that George could be in little doubt of where I really stood. She was pressed against me, and there was simply *no way* she could have failed to notice that my trousers were now home to something easily rigid enough to have been used to lever up a manhole cover.

I'll skip the bit that contains the details of the rest of the cab journey through Edinburgh's sometimes tricky road layout, the paying of the fare, getting the key from hotel reception and going up to George's room: I'll be buggered if I can remember it very well and, anyway, I'm sure you want to get up into the hotel room now only a little less keenly than George and I did then.

It was surprising how we didn't talk, though. Well, I couldn't talk, as you know, but George was almost completely wordless too. Things were assumed: George, when we arrived at the hotel, didn't ask me whether I'd like to come up to her room, for example, she just walked ahead and assumed I'd follow her . . . OK, *yes* – not the greatest intuitive leap ever on her part, but you get the idea. There was a kind of pact of silence. When we got into George's room and closed the door, making ourselves secret, it was even more apparent. I think it was because any words at this precarious point would have shattered the moment and the momentum: which felt like it was – which I *wanted* it to feel like it was – a momentum so heavy as to be inevitable. The likelihood was that (out of tension) one of us would say something over-conversationally ludicrous – 'Oh, they have this carpet at my bank,' or something equally tragic – or, even worse, give voice to the thing that must surely have been on both our minds . . . 'God – what are we *doing?*' More than anything else in the world at this instant I didn't want George to ask me, 'Oh, Tom – is this wise? Should we be doing this?' I knew there was no way I could possibly have brought myself to give any reply that would have brought it to a halt: 'Yes . . . you're right. I'll go now: let's put a stop to this before it's too late' – there was *utterly* no way I could have wrestled such a sensible thing out of my mouth. But, at the same time, I didn't want to be made incontrovertibly complicit by *explicitly* brushing aside even the most cosmetic and shallow expression of doubt. I wanted this to be madness or, rather, to appear to be madness. And I think George also wanted to keep the icy clarity of words out of it. We were both far more comfortable with the conceit that we were temporarily insane, and our silence allowed us to maintain it.

George, kissing all over my face, backed towards the sofa and lay down on it, pulling me over on top of her. I cracked my shin on the corner of the table as I went past it: it really, really hurt, and I couldn't have cared less. I lay on her, spread my fingers through her endless, overflowing, sin-black hair and plucked at her ear with my lips. She arched her head over and began doing some seriously thrilling mouth work along my neck – sinking her teeth in beyond the point of affection but just short of the point of pain: precisely hard enough to bite through some neural tie and allow a nest of shivers to fall tumbling down my back. Then she reached downwards with both hands and pulled at the button on the front of my trousers. Her fingers slipped and fumbled and failed . . . I decided to step in and help her out – after politely waiting (for the look of the thing) for about three-eighths of a second.

I jumped up and began having a bad-tempered scuffle with my own clothes. Every button and zip seemed to be in favour of abstinence – I was, apparently, wearing celibate clothing. (Get *off* me, you fucker! Loosen! Undo! Tomorrow – I'm telling you now – it's Velcro for the bastard *lot* of you!) Men, if they have their wits about them, should always take their socks off *first* – it's an aesthetic thing. Socks, then top, then bottom. It goes without saying that *I* started with my trousers – pulling them down, then realising that they wouldn't come off over my shoes (which were now stuck three inches up inside my trouser legs), then trying to tug the whole shoe-trouser-pants tangle off together. Finally (after moments when I scaled the heights of fury and moments when I plumbed the depths of despair) succeeding, I stood there: near-exhausted, but triumphant, with my trousers a crumpled ball in my hand, my shirt dangling too high for modesty yet too low for flamboyance, and one sock on. George, thankfully, didn't really notice as she had her own trousers to battle. She'd kicked her shoes away into two opposite corners of the room and whipped off her T-shirt with the easy, assured skill of a duchess, but her jeans were giving her a bit of trouble. They were pretty tight around the . . . well, around the everything, and she was having to lie on her back on the sofa and pull and wriggle herself out of them using quite a degree of effort. She was like a butterfly frantically trying to struggle out of its chrysalis. I stood, completely naked by now, and watched her finally pull the last ankle free: she hurled the jeans right across the room, like the limp corpse of a defeated monster, looked up at me, and smiled. She was naked, I was naked – we really ought to get closer together before we caught a chill.

I swung myself on to the sofa with great enthusiasm. So much enthusiasm that it toppled over backwards and, clasped together, George and I rolled off across the floor. We were racing ahead before we'd even come to a stop, however. Everywhere skin slid against skin, there were lips and tongues and fingertips, hair being stroked and grasped, breath rushing hot on to us, hands running desperate over us, everywhere, as far as our bodies could feel, farther than our minds could think, we were the entire universe, together, electric to the touch, everywhere. More than anything else, it was *real*. It had such immediacy, and every sensation was so intense, that it was real in a way that made the normal experience of reality seem blurred and pale and muted and laughable. If I had to write this moment for characters in a book, I know what I'd do. If I were doing my job and inventing it as fiction, rather than describing it as fact, I'd conjure up a storm of thoughts: the conflicts, questions and self-doubts. Because that's what you do when you're a writer, that's the artifice – always highlighting the inner world. Even in the most primal situations – *especially* in the most primal situations – you have your characters examine and interrogate themselves. And the more complex, multi-layered and subtle you make the thoughts of a person at the moment when he's engaged in some raw, feral activity, the better a writer people say you are. It's a lie that readers and writers happily conspire in together. So, if I were writing this moment, I'd say that 'Tom noticed how George was a million tiny differences. Everything she did – the way she moved and the way she touched him – the way she smelled, the way she tasted: everything defined her not simply as George, but as not-Sara. It was impossible for him to experience anything without experiencing it in comparison. Each new surprise of George was simultaneously a joy of otherness and a guilty reminder, a thrill and a sting.'

In fact, as – naked on the floor of a hotel room – I was being spectacularly unfaithful to Sara, this is what was going through my mind: 'Yaaaahhhhhhhhhh!' That's it. There was nothing in my head but a dull roar: we rolled about together without ever exchanging a single coherent sentence and while fucking like wild dogs.

It was fan*tastic*.

'I thought you didn't smoke?' George said, as I reached over and plucked one of the cigarettes from her packet. We were huddled together on the sofa, under a duvet that George had hurriedly gone and pulled off the bed. (It wasn't really cold in the room, but it's just nicer to huddle together *under* something. And anyway, there's something slightly awkward about staying completely nude after sex. Like you've finished doing everything now but, rather inelegantly, appear to have some nakedness left over. It's the kind of feeling you get looking at the food remaining on a table after a party's ended.)

'Yeah . . . well,' I shrugged, pulling the lighter in George's hand across from her cigarette to mine.

I gave up taking sugar in my tea many years ago. Question people who've done this and they'll all say the same thing. At first the tea tastes *awful*, it's an effort of will just to force it down, but, imperceptibly, over the months, you become used to it and it starts to seem perfectly fine. Then, one day, you accidentally take a gulp of someone else's tea – someone who still takes sugar – and, 'Yeugch!' It's nothing but warm, wet sickliness: you can't imagine how you ever liked such an unpleasant drink.

Giving up smoking is the polar opposite of giving up sugar in your tea. For a start, you can avoid the initial dreadfulness of sugar-free tea very simply: don't drink tea. To give up smoking is to experience every second, every part of every second, as a misery of smokinglessness – there's no avoiding it. More important is that fact of sugary tea becoming repellent to you after a few months. Once a smoker, months can pass, years can pass, but you never lose the knowledge that it'd be great to have a cigarette right about now. You long for all bets to be off, if only for a moment – for something to give you a perfectly legitimate justification to smoke just one more cigarette. There are times when you fantasise about being involved in an especially traumatic car crash, just so you'd be well within your rights to have a cigarette for your nerves.

I was busy rationalising this cigarette I was smoking (this post-sex cigarette: most celestial of all the cigarettes) as a, perfectly legitimate, palliative given the frightening hugeness of the situation. It was really the joyous return of a prodigal son, the secretly welcomed triumph of pleasure over common sense.

I glanced at my watch: 12.34 a.m.

George caught me checking.

'Sara?' she asked, quietly. She needed only that one word. In fact, I'd have preferred her to have phrased any number of questions in any number of probing and uncomfortable ways, had they only been free of Sara's actual name. But she'd used it alone, so I couldn't avoid it. I suppose it was, really, all the questions that could be asked combined.

'Yeah,' I replied, hurrying my cigarette back to my mouth.

'Will she wonder where you are?'

'Maybe. I'm not sure. Maybe. I could be at an after-show party, though, I suppose. It's not *that* late, really.' I hadn't given Sara the impression I'd be away for a long time. I imagined her asking me, when I got back, why I hadn't phoned to say I'd be staying a while. Not angrily, just a bit miffed because it was such an easy thing to do and I hadn't done it and it was a little, you know, 'thoughtless'. Naturally, the idea of calling her now gleefully mocked me with a knowing smirk. It wasn't *that* late, but it was still after midnight and it knew I'd be reminded that the last time I'd woken Sara with a call the first thing she'd asked was whether I'd slept with someone. My nerve wasn't up to playing the double bluff right now. And, anyway . . . Christ – you know what I mean. Putting on a slightly fed-up voice ('It's a horror, Sara – insufferable media types – I simply couldn't get out of it, though . . .') and explaining how I was stuck at some tiresome party ('Look – I've got to go. I have to talk to some awful producer – 'bye . . .') while I was actually sitting here naked next to George? How nauseatingly grubby would *that* be? There's a code of decency even in lying.

'I love Sara, you know,' I said.

It was a pathetic thing to say. A pathetic, ridiculous cliché – exactly the same sad, stupid thing that everyone says at this point. Saying it made me ashamed of both my hapless idiocy and my risible banality. How could I utter such a hoary old standard, when the situation itself with George and me was so unique and special?

'I know,' replied George. Supportively showing that she could keep up with me if I really wanted to stick to the script.

I tapped the ash off my cigarette with quite astonishingly excessive thoroughness. 'What about you and Darren Boyle?'

'Me and *Darren*?' She laughed a little and put on a talking-to-the-press voice. 'Darren and I are just good friends.'

'No, really – is it serious?'

'No, *really* – we're just friends. Friends and conspirators.'

'What does *that* mean?'

'Oh . . . just that we deliberately let the press jump to the wrong conclusion. It was a bit of pre-book publicity, and it didn't hurt me as a general thing. If you even use the *word* "feminism", there's a section of the media who immediately look for signs that you're a joyless, bitter lesbian.'

'Surely they must know you're not?' I said. (On a hunch, pulling myself up before adding, 'Amy told me that everyone says you're a Fuck Monster.')

'What they know and what they wish were true are two separate things – and it's the second one that tugs at their hearts the most. They're infinitely happier with the idea that everyone is hiding something. Which makes it really annoying when they're right – like with Darren – of course.'

'What's he hiding?'

'Oh, come *on*, Tom . . . Darren was over there trying to make some kind of dent in America – perhaps even get himself involved in a TV show. The American media won't touch you if you're a gay man. There'd be riots in Iowa. And if you have an English accent, then they already assume you're gay until proven otherwise.'

'So you were basically there to compensate for Darren Boyle's pronunciation?'

'Yes . . . well . . . Darren has other things I needed to weigh against too, obviously.'

'Like actually being gay?'

'He's not *gay*, no – not strictly speaking.'

'Not "strictly speaking"?'

'He's just . . . you know. He's just been experimenting with homosexuality.'

'Experimenting? He thinks . . . *what*? It may provide the world with a new source of propulsion?'

'Have you got a problem with this?' She laughed at me. 'I really didn't have you down as homophobic.'

'Well, normally I'd say that it's no issue for me at all whether someone is gay or straight, but, on this occasion,

I have to admit I'm absolutely *delighted* to find out he's gay.'

'Because you thought I was having a fling with him.'

'Do people say "having a fling" any more?'

'You read we were having a fling, and you were jealous?'

'Not *jealous*, no.'

'Ha.' She gave me her huge Nye grin. 'You were jealous – and here I was, not even sure that you fancied me.'

'Yes, tough call. I can see how anyone might have assumed that I had some terrible, incessant-erection condition – the hospital wards are full of people like that.'

'It's a flattering suggestion, of course, but I don't spend my entire time examining men's crotches for signs of arousal. Oh, I remember you *telling* me about it on that one occasion, obviously. But men get erections all the time. They can get an erection if you bend over in front of them, but you can't really take that as meaning much – not when you know that they can quite easily get an erection if they accidentally brush up against a low wall too. I thought your blurting out that you had one was your technique.'

'Yeah – the ladies love that line.'

'No, no, not that – your *professional* technique.'

'You thought that my telling you, apropos of nothing whatso-fucking-ever, that I had a stiffy was my professional technique? I am, unequivocally, agog.'

'It seemed to be the only explanation that made any sense at all. You were trying to get me to talk, frankly, for the book . . . and isn't it a standard tactic to make potentially embarrassing confessions about yourself in order to encourage the person you're interviewing to open up?'

'Gosh, you're right. Without even knowing it, I'm a bleeding *genius*.'

George wriggled under the duvet and turned to face me more head on. She adopted a mock-interrogating tone. 'So, when *did* you start to fancy me, then, Tom Cartwright?'

'Well – sorry – I wasn't a big fan of yours or anything. Which I suppose is a good thing, right? Less creepy.'

'Yeah, *definitely*,' said George, playing offended. 'There's simply *nothing* worse than being screwed by someone who thinks you're good at your job.'

'Oh, don't get me wrong – I didn't think you were crap.'

'If *this* is your technique, Tom, then I'd advise actually going with the "I have a stiffy" routine.'

'OK. I'll start again. At first, before I'd met you, I couldn't picture you in any way except as a massive bag full of money.'

'I'm *so* glad you started again.'

'Then, the first time we met, I was completely preoccupied with trying to avoid blowing the deal. That and not dying of explosive, gruelling exhaustion . . . I'm not really sure when I . . . You see – how stupid is it for someone like me to get a thing for Georgina Nye? I was trying my very best to avoid admitting to myself that my interest in you went beyond the standard desire to shag any number of actresses, singers or weathergirls. Right up until tonight, in the cab, I was trying to look the other way rather than admit I was . . . But, I suppose, now I can be objective, it *started* that second time I met you. When we were up on Carlton Hill and you took your hat off – and you turned into Georgina Nye, right before my eyes.'

George didn't say anything for a moment.

'It was important that I was "Georgina Nye"?' She didn't look at me as she said this, instead reaching over to the table to get another cigarette.

'Oh – *no*,' I laughed.

'You brought it up twice just then.'

I smiled and leaned forward, running my hand across her cheek and brushing her hair aside.

'Hello?' I said. 'Have you forgotten who you're talking to here? There cannot be a single person in the English-speaking world who rates celebrity as any less important than I do. I just meant that you went from a tiny, fast-moving thing – more lucrative commission than woman and hidden under that hat and dark glasses – to . . . *you*. I abruptly *got* the whole Georgina Nye Experience. I suddenly saw why you were a big deal: but it was the *why* that impressed me, not being the big deal.'

'That's . . .' She didn't seem to be able to find the word for what it was, but she pulled up my hand and kissed it. '. . . I'm probably a bit wary. With everyone. My therapist says I need to give myself permission to receive more often.'

It sort of shows you're sensitive if you have a therapist, doesn't it? Thoughtful and complex. Selfish, mindless thugs don't see therapists, do they? Well . . . not unless it's a requirement of their sentence, obviously.

'So – when did *you* start to fancy *me*?' I grinned, and George grinned back. It was like being sixteen again. Like being sixteen and sneaking off at a party with a girl: sitting in semi-darkness, smoking naughty cigarettes and talking about sex. Low voices and prickly-heat excitement. Though, admittedly, George and I had just been all over the room in an unrestrained, feral journey through every obscene, filthy and glorious sexual act we could think of, which – when you're a sixteen-year-old boy – is more where you'll hope the conversation will lead than its prelude. And yet, somehow, the feeling of intimacy, and of flirtatiously playing with fire, was the same.

'Um . . .' George took a long draw on her cigarette and looked up at the ceiling, considering my question. 'I found you a bit *intriguing* on that very first day, but I didn't really find you attractive – not physically.'

'Cheers . . . Did I mention that you're a massive bag full of money?'

George laughed. 'Not *then* . . .' she said, coquettishly, and she lifted up my hand again – this time sucking on my finger, sliding it in and out of her mouth.

'So when?'

'I'm not sure. I just sort of found myself attracted to you, after the event. It happened slowly. I *knew* I fancied you when I decided to ask you to come to the Benny Barker show, but I can't think of any big moment when it started.'

'Why did you know when you asked me to come to the show?'

'Oh, because it was *obvious*. There was no need for you to come, none at all. What were you going to do? Shout prompts from back-stage if I got an awkward question? *And* I couldn't even bear to call you myself and ask you to come: I made Paul call your agent. *God* – it was like being at school and having your mate ask someone out for you.'

'Ha. I just thought you were being aloof.'

'Aloof? Did you? I thought I was being so obvious that I must look absolutely *desperate*. I was too scared even to see you before the show. I hid back-stage and just popped into the green room at the last minute – so I'd got an excuse to leave again quickly. I imagined you standing there with a glass of wine and a knowing smile . . . "Hi, George – you've clearly brought me here to shag me, haven't you?" I was more nervous about you than a live TV interview.'

'You didn't show it.'

'An actress, me, pal.'

'So, then what?'

'What do you mean? So, then, we came back here and did all those *disgraceful* things.'

'We came back here after you jumped on me in the cab.'

'Thanks, Tom. Nice. Letting me keep my dignity. Cheers for that.'

'I simply meant: what changed between the show and the taxi?'

'Oh, I was buzzing with adrenalin after the interview, and that cancelled out my nerves a bit, I suppose. And then, in the cab, I just looked at you and knew. I knew that you wanted me too.'

'How?'

'I just *knew*.'

'Yes, but *how*? I can't remember doing or saying anything, so it's obviously a message I was unaware of sending. I'd simply like to know what it is so, you know, I don't accidentally send it out to the man who reads our gas meter or someone.'

'I *just knew*. I can't say what it was. Maybe it was lots of tiny things, or magic, or telepathy or something . . . I just knew.'

We talked on and on. Talked for many times longer than we'd spent having sex, and, in its own way, it was better than the sex.

Jesus. What *am* I on about? No it wasn't – the sex part was fucking *stupendous*. I appear to have started talking bollocks: sorry – that's the writer in me coming out, that is.

But the talking *was* wonderful. So wonderful I didn't want it to end. It was also – and this *is* true – it was also the part that made me feel the most guilty. Sex is . . . well, *sex*, isn't it? A powerful, primal, natural force. I'm not saying I couldn't help being unfaithful to Sara, that it was beyond my control, but it did . . . I mean, it's like you might say someone is a bit clumsy for falling over through not picking their feet up properly, yes? But you don't blame them for *hitting the ground*: that's gravity. You see what I'm saying? Good. So, the sex part you can kind of excuse, can't you? But the talking – and my *enjoying* the talking so much – well, that was an unforgivable betrayal of Sara. Doubly so, because how often had she lamented that I never wanted to just sit with her and have a long, long, long talk? That three or four sentences after we'd finished exchanging strictly factual information she'd see my eyes start to drift in the direction of the TV guide? It wasn't that I *never* talked with Sara, you understand, and certainly not that I didn't enjoy it. It's just that, well, Sara and I had been together for years. I didn't need to ask what she thought about most things – I already knew, or could guess. And I didn't feel I needed to keep telling her that I loved her either: we were beyond that, *deeper* than that. She could rest assured that I loved her. She could be so confident of it that she didn't need to have me constantly restate it, night after night. That was true love, in my opinion. And Sara and I were together too – completely together: if I didn't talk to her much one day, well, I could talk to her the next; there was no urgency about it, was there? Still, I couldn't help thinking about how Sara would regard all this talking I was doing, and how I was enjoying it. Talking to George like this now was bad enough, but my finding it so intoxicating felt like an outright declaration of contempt for Sara: a slap in her face. It was, quite simply, appalling.

George and I talked until after 4 a.m.

Though, to be fair to myself, it wasn't quite as bad as that – because we did have sex again too, so that took up part of the time.

Finally, I said, 'I'd better be going.' We'd just smoked the last cigarette: George had crumpled the empty packet and tossed it on to the table. Obviously, I'm not suggesting that I was cynically staying until I'd smoked all her fags – it's just that the end of the cigarettes is always a watershed, a sign that the evening is over. George went to put a dressing gown on and – thankful that she wasn't there to watch (I was, ludicrously, self-conscious) – I got dressed. Then, very slowly, we walked to the door. Arms around each other, like moony adolescents. I opened it and stepped out into the hallway.

'So . . .' I said.

'So . . .' agreed George.

I was getting a little choked. I'm not sure there's a word for the precise emotion, or mixture of emotions, I was experiencing. If you force me to pick one, though, I'd probably have to go with 'frightened'.

'So . . .' I said. 'What happens now?'

'What do you *want* to happen now?'

I looked away down the corridor. At nothing.

'I love my girlfriend . . .' I began. There are times when someone *really* ought to hit you across the head with a shovel. '. . . but . . . the thought of not seeing you again is just unbearable.'

George didn't say anything. I assumed she was simply appalled speechless by my trite dialogue.

'I . . .' I started again, but I didn't have anywhere for the sentence to go and I just – and I'm not kidding here – 'hung my head'.

I felt George's hand under my chin. She raised my face and it lifted up to find her mouth waiting there for mine. She kissed me so perfectly that when she'd finished there wasn't any of me left. I'd dissolved and left only my shell.

'I've got a book signing tomorrow,' she said. 'Two p.m. I'll be at Waterstone's in Princes Street.'

'OK.'

V

Well. I've got to be honest with you here . . . I feel a bit of a jerk right now. Kind of like when you play a practical joke on someone – thinking everyone will get a blast out of it – only it goes wrong and people get upset. I mean, sure, I feel responsible – I'm God, right? It comes with the territory. But I got to assure you that, for what it's worth, I had only the best intentions. You got to believe what I'm telling you when I say that I never intended things to get messy like this.

Oh, I don't mean for Tom or Sara or George, obviously – I knew about that; *that's* the very reason I'm showing them to you now, so you can see what I'm talking about. No, I mean not for *anyone.* Because, like I say, Tom and Sara and George could be *anyone.* I have to check that you understand me, here. It doesn't matter, for example, that George is a famous actress, yeah? I know you people are built to understand complex stuff and be able to see patterns and meaning – and that's good. But, the trouble is, it makes you *want* to see patterns and meaning, and *hate* to think you're not complicated. If that terrible Fiona chick had been willing, then Tom might easily be in a hotel with her now. And later, he'd think that maybe it was some indefinable connection they had – both being English in Scotland or both working in publishing or whatever – that was the critical thing. But that ain't it. Remember: filter out the scenery. Remember: Sara or George or Tom or A. N. Other or *you* – it's all the same thing, OK?

Look, when I set this universe up I was kind of making it up as I went. There was no 'Creation 101' I could have attended beforehand, you know what I'm saying? Sure, so I could have done a few things better, I'm the first to admit that. Don't no one ever say I ain't prepared to stick up my hand and say 'mea culpa' when I screw up, 'cause that just ain't right. And I'm at least trying to make up for things best I can – I mean, that's why I'm here now, yeah? We got to deal with the situation we're in: we can't go back and rewrite the book, but I can at least read you the rules we have, so you know where you stand. Should have done it a long time ago, I admit – strike two against me – but you know how you put these things off.

OK, enough with the beating myself up: let's get on with business.

You remember what I was saying about the whales? How I just kind of thought up all this stuff and went at it? Sometimes I got a bit carried away – got into a groove and kept pumping out these ideas. I'm like, 'Yeah, that's good! Woah – and I know what else would be cool . . .' and I don't know when to stop. They call it plenitude: I just kind of thought of it as 'being on a roll'. Well, I don't want you getting the idea that I simply threw you guys together, OK? I was really on the case, thinking about all these angles and stuff; all these possibilities. Like I say, though – like with the whales – I don't really know how I do stuff; I just, you know, want badgers and – there you go – badgers. Which suits me, by the way. If I have this great idea for a plant, I don't want to have to figure out cell division and invent osmosis and stuff first – who has the time, right? But, as I told you earlier, I'm totally into all these scientists of yours getting out their microscopes or whatever and working out how I did everything. That gives me a real kick. And – I'm guessing here, but I figure I'm right – I think it helps you to understand what's going on if you look at it like that. So, that's how I'm going to explain all this to you, OK? So you kind of hear it in your own language, you know what I mean? And also, so you can check up on it and see I'm telling you the truth here. I'm showing good faith by making sure you can do that.

Now, first off, I thought you'd mostly all be dead by forty. Let's get that straight right from the start. That was the time frame I was working in, and I don't think anyone can accuse me of not doing enough to make this reasonable. Natural disasters, disease, wild animals, cold, starvation

– the list goes on. So, I don't think that any charge of negligence is going to stick, yeah? And, until fairly recently, it worked: how was I to know you'd start coming up with all this stuff to keep yourselves alive? Flood warnings and antibiotics and office work. You think it's reasonable to blame me for not guessing that some wise guy would go and invent a *dialysis machine*, eh? So, for a start, any problems with your love life when you're over forty . . . 'not my fault', OK? Out of warranty. Stuff you do beyond thirty-nine you do at your own risk, you know what I'm saying?

So, anyways, I'd got this sex stuff – which, I think you'll agree, is kind of neat – and my only problem was how to . . . um, how to *implement* it. You have fourteen years to get a chance to stop being stupid (OK, OK – third strike, there: let's push on anyways), a bit of finding your feet, then all the sex while you try to defy the odds against dying for a decade or so. Now, it was kind of important you had sex. I was worried you might not do it enough to keep yourselves in offspring, so I put a lot of work into getting you to go for it. (Well, *yes*: I went over the top, obviously. Everyone can be smart in retrospect, can't they?) First I made you want it – badly. How? 'Gonadal steroids', apparently. As I say, I'm just using your words here – if *I'd* have been naming stuff you can bet I'd never have come up with 'gonadal steroids'. I mean, 'ugh', right? Anyways, you have these gonadal steroids – oestrogen and testosterone – to get you all fired up and looking for sex. Off you go.

Now I need to refine it a bit or . . . well, I'll let you picture what happens if I don't – but the queues would move even slower at the post office, if you know what I'm saying? So, I get you to be attracted to someone, rather than absolutely *everyone* (I'm going to come back to this later, so remember it, OK?). I'm pretty clever here, even if I say so myself. I throw in a bit of that brain chemistry that you people call 'psychology' – basic stuff, but I do it real smooth like, so you don't notice. For example, I make you most attracted to faces that are similar to your own. That's to say that, if you're a man, you like your own mug, only in a more feminine style, and the same if you're a woman – you go for the structure you see in your mirror, but with the manliness turned up. (You didn't even know that, did you? You think I'm making this up. I'm not – ask the people at the University of St Andrews, in Scotland, if I'm just making this up: they'll smack you right in the face.) Better, I thought, that you're drawn to faces like your own than if you're drawn to faces like your dogs'. Tell me I'm wrong. Mostly it's very simple rules that I come up with. You don't know about them, but they're pretty formulaic. Symmetry: you prefer physically symmetrical people. Smell: women prefer the smell of men whose immune systems are different from theirs. Oh, and they go for male pheromones pretty reliably too. (I got a bit carried away with women and smelling, to be honest. Ended up with women being a *thousand* times more sensitive to some smells than men. No need for that, really. Just on a roll, again.) And all the time I'm seeing to it that you get really excited about this by doling out the monoamines.

You remember the monoamines, right? Remember I mentioned them a while back – just so you wouldn't start giving some kind of spiritual agenda to the woody that Tom got while he was interviewing George? Yeah, sure you do. Well, let me clue you in on the monoamines.

Monoamines are a collection of chemicals – neurotransmitters – and they, well . . . they *are* sexual attraction, basically. What happens when you feel attraction? Nah – don't give me any of that 'Oooh, I go all tingly' or 'It's like tiny little bunnies are hopping around in my stomach and my mind starts twinkling' stuff. Not only are metaphors part of the trouble here, but I asked you what happens, not how you 'interpret' it. Attraction isn't controlled, it couldn't give a damn about your morals or your world view and it *definitely* isn't the work of Cupid, tiny pink fairies or magic of any kind. It's monoamines. You've got your serotonin, your norepinephrine (that's adrenalin to you and me) and your dopamine washing about in your head. Your brain's lighting up around the medial insula, the anterior cingulate cortex, the caudate nucleus and the putamen – while it's 'goodnight' to the posterior cingulated gyrus, the amygdala and, right-laterally, the prefrontal, parietal and middle temporal cortices. What the hell does all that mean? It means you're as mad as a crab, basically. I'm not kidding here – you're *clinically* barking:

you really shouldn't be allowed to drive. Monoamines are the ruthless, amoral storm troopers of sexual attraction: these things really do take no prisoners – dopamine alone buys your entire better judgement in exchange for a warm glow and, together, they make the kind of cocktail that can, say, lead to you ending up in a hotel room on top of a soap star.

But, as you'll have guessed, all of this is no good if, when you manage to *get* sex, you find it's about as appealing as chewing a truck driver's sock. So, stage three: neuropeptides. What we have here, basically, are your standard oxytocin and vasopressin. You have sex, oxytocin hits the pleasure centres of your brain, and you think, 'Woah. *That's* something I'll be doing again.' But – and this is where I got *real* smart – oxytocin also encourages you to be faithful. I really put in the effort with this one. Did the road work. I tested the idea of faithfulness with prairie voles first – to see if it was possible. Didn't know I was using oxytocin, of course, but that's what it was, and I tried faithfulness with Midwestern prairie vole males and skipped it with the Northwestern ones. I have to tell you, with prairie voles, it was fine either way. But, for you, I went for the faithful approach – figured you'd enjoy the grounding. So, I hit you with oxytocin when you had sex *and* I made its release what the white coats call a 'classically conditioned reflex'. What that means is you get oxytocin when you have sex, but if you have sex with one person enough it gets so as a bit slips out when you just *see* them. If Tom thinks he feels guilty now, just wait until he sees Sara again and gets a shot of oxytocin to hammer it home.

So, there you go, pretty well planned, I think you'll agree. You don't have to bother about sorting yourselves out to reproduce, 'cause I've set up everything for you – no thought required on your part.

Then you go and begin moving the goalposts.

I didn't know you were going to change from small groups to cities of eight million, did I? I thought you'd be very lucky to reach the four-decade mark before you died from the flu or were eaten by a wolf – so why bother about the long-term durability of faithfulness? The effects of the monoamines only hold out for – best-case scenario – thirty months. After that your body becomes 'tolerant' to the neurotransmitters and, well, passion fades. That's the end of the running through parks in rainstorms, laughing – there's only reflexive oxytocin holding you together now. And how well do you think *that's* going to hold up when another round of dopamine and serotonin arrives? And I didn't even think it was important to fix that glitch where women – whatever country and culture they've grown up in – have a cycle of about four years from getting together to thinking about finding someone else. Serial monogamy seemed to be fine: chances are that within four or five years either she or her partner would have succumbed to appendicitis or been carried off by an avalanche or something ... and even if that didn't happen, well, there'd hardly be *four million* other people hanging around within an hour's drive for her to move on to, would there? And why not give men an extra helping of testosterone to keep their eyes open? Better to have loved and lost, right?

And this is where it starts to get *very* embarrassing for me. 'Cause I didn't think infidelity would be a big issue – I *certainly* couldn't have guessed that more people would be, would even get the *chance* to be, unfaithful than faithful: you really shot me down in flames there, didn't you? – 'cause I didn't allow for it, it's all done really, really badly. I never thought to throw in a bit of sleight of hand to make it look random or varied ... I didn't even give it the thought I put into snowflakes, is what I'm saying. It just runs on the basics, it falls back on to the low-level, unrefined chemistry and psychology (and psychology is nothing but chemistry in a groove, of course). That's why every affair is like every other affair. It doesn't matter whether it's an infidelity between two people who make the same bolts at the same factory, or an English writer living in Edinburgh colliding with an actress from the country's highest-rated soap ... it's always the same. The trivial details vary and the settings are different but the people go through the same thing time and time again. I know you must have spotted this, which is partly the reason why I felt I should own up here. Admit what you all knew anyway, just to clear the air.

I messed up. But I got lots of other stuff right – take bananas, for example. Bananas I got spot on. OK, OK, I sense the hostility, and that's fine: best to acknowledge it. If we don't both acknowledge it, we won't be able to move on.

And you know, I think we *can* move on, a little. I'm not going to discuss that now, though. Right now I think you need some time to yourself, a little bit of space.

We'll talk later, OK?

NINE

I slept on the sofa.

I'd like to think that this was a bit of auto-flagellation: that I was punishing myself on Sara's behalf. I certainly tried this line on my conscience – had a bash at seeking forgiveness in masochism – but I saw through me with damnable ease. It really had very little to do with an attempt at punishing atonement, it was simply cowardice. I couldn't face the possibility of Sara waking as I slid, holding my breath, into bed. Of her rolling over, looking at me and sleepily asking, 'Where have you been?' It was a stomach-churning prospect. So, I slept on the sofa, in my underpants, with a coat pulled over me.

I didn't sleep very well. However, even *I* didn't have the cheek to try to make the residual decency in me believe that I was twisting and rolling, unable to get comfortable, because the cold realisation of what I'd done was forbidding me to sleep. The – vulgarly obvious – fact was that I couldn't get settled because I was on a sofa that had little room for manoeuvre and I was there carrying another erection. I'd lain down in the darkness and, naturally enough, my mind had fallen to replaying what had just happened. The replay had barely begun when my erection turned up to watch.

I'd had *hugely* extensive sex with George twice that night, and yet I was still easily able to get another erection almost instantly and retain it pretty much until dawn. I'm not proud of this, obviously. That'd be unbelievably crass, wouldn't it? Trying to get out some kind of idiot message about my sexual stamina in the midst of a situation like this. Still, there it was. Kept it until daybreak. I'm just stating the facts, that's all.

Anyway, what with erections and so forth, not only didn't I sleep very much or very well, but I was also up again by 6.30. I wasn't tired either. I was quite hyper, in fact, and also bobbing atop that one-step-removed, gently swimmy high you get when you've had virtually no sleep. I did think about avoiding Sara. I considered leaving a note on the table about having to go out somewhere. Somewhere that sounded logical and innocuous to be going before 7 a.m. on a Saturday morning when you'd barely come back at all the previous night. You will, I trust, already have spotted the difficulty with that plan. So, instead, I ate a bowl of Cinnamon Grahams – which I detest (both taste-wise – I hate cinnamon – and in a broader, sociolinguistic sense: as we don't have the word graham in its 'wholewheat flour' meaning, then they're surely vicious, bludgeoning, American corporate cultural imperialism, in cereal form, right?), but I couldn't be bothered making toast. I also drank several cups of coffee. Wandering into the living room, I turned on the TV. It was the Saturday morning kids' slot. I sat there, cupping my drink in anxious hands, while hyper-ventilating presenters shouted at me for forty-five minutes solid: it was probably what I deserved.

When, eventually, I heard Sara stir upstairs the sound ran through me like a jarring electric shock.

I pushed at my ears with my brain, trying to force them to venture out and pick up more noises. I was shaking. Not visibly, but on the inside. The slow, soft thuds as she descended the stairs seemed to me not like the half-asleep footfalls of a smallish Scottish woman but rather the consciously and gleefully audible approach of some occult beast in a horror movie. I stared, unseeing, at the television screen as the living-room door slowly opened and she entered.

'Awwwhen did you get back last night?' she asked, segueing into the sentence from a yawn.

'Hmmm . . .' I shrugged, so casually that I was practically boneless. '. . . I'm not sure . . . Quite late, I think.'

'When was it – roughly?'

'No idea. Like I said, I didn't really notice the time.'

I still hadn't looked at her. I was staring intently at the television and speaking in a distracted, staring-intently-at-the-television voice. (I couldn't have told you what was on the television if you'd offered me a million pounds.)

'Aye, but *roughly*.' She didn't sound angry or chiding, just sleepily curious. She was simply interested in a conversational kind of way. The best answer to give would be 'Oh, after four – I know it was after four', or something like that: answer her perfectly reasonable question with a non-evasive reply. That was the way to go.

I said, 'Jesus – *I didn't notice*, OK? Why? Is there a curfew or something? Does it *matter – at all* – what time it was? It was "late", OK?'

I spoke this brilliance to the TV. Beside me, I heard Sara not answer. Immediately after this, she didn't answer again. Her silence began to pull at my face, twisting it in her direction. I was terrified of what might be in the box: this was forcing me, against my will, to look in the box.

I wasn't sure which I expected or dreaded the most: an expression that told she knew, in some way, what was going on, or a hurt look. She completely threw me by having neither of these arrangements of features. What she was doing was smiling. Smirking, in fact.

'Bit tired, then, love?' she said. 'Been out late, and not really up to it any more?'

As you can imagine, I leapt at this with both arms and hugged it to my grateful chest.

'Yeah . . . sorry.' I rubbed my hands over my face, as though trying to wash away a bit of fatigue. 'I've clearly turned into a sickening lightweight.'

She grinned. She stood by the door, grinning. With her hair straight out of bed and still in open revolt and pillow marks across one of her cheeks; wearing a big, baggy T-shirt with a design faded almost to invisibility and holes in both armpits that was bravely hanging in there like some kind of stunt nightie. She was beautiful. Beautiful and beatific: she was the Madonna, Ophelia, Sybil Vane and Alyson Hannigan all rolled into one, and I collapsed inside just looking at her. How could I have betrayed this . . . this . . . *angel*? You know, I don't think I'd ever loved her more than I did at that moment. A fantastic night fucking a gorgeous woman against every solid surface in her hotel room really *does* make you appreciate how lucky you are to have your regular partner. I smiled at Sara. You know a 'wan smile'? Like they say in books? It was one of those.

'Och . . . Give me your cup, my little soldier,' said Sara. 'I'll make you some fresh coffee.'

She went into the kitchen and I sat there, alone with my agony. I thought about how sensitive I was – I bet some men could be unfaithful and not even think twice about it. Not me, though. My guilt ran knives through me, it clawed at my heart and its sheer, glutinous weight closed my eyes and bowed my head. Christ – why did I have to be so deep?

Somehow – for Sara's sake, really – I disguised the tortured, personal hell that was Tom and forced on a tranquil façade when she returned with coffee for us both. She sat down beside me on the sofa, curling her legs up inside her nightshirt and blowing into her mug.

'So, what happened, then?'

'Happened?'

'At the show. I watched it on TV here, of course – but what happened behind the scenes? Any gossip? Was Benny

Barker really "ill"? How many of that boy band were there with their boy-band-friends?'

'Oh . . . There's . . . Nothing happened really. Or, if it did, I didn't see it. I just watched the recording from this poky little room and ate peanuts.'

'And then went to a party.'

'A party? Why do you say that?'

'Hold on, let me think . . . Georgina Nye's book is coming out tomorrow, the Benny Barker show is in town, you don't come home all night and, when you do . . .' She wrinkled her nose. '. . . you *stink* of smoke.'

'There was a party. Yeah. It was awful, actually. Just, really . . . well, it was really smoky, for a start. I felt obliged to stay, though.'

'Where was it?'

'The party?'

'Aye – obviously.'

'Right. I thought that's what you meant. It was at the theatre, everyone stayed on there after the show.'

'Did any extra celebs turn up?'

'No, not really.'

'Not *really*?'

'No, not really. They *really* didn't. Turn up.'

'What about that Paddy character? The one who was standing in for Benny Barker. I thought he was quite funny. Is he funny off-camera?'

'No.'

She sipped her coffee.

'You could have phoned, you know. I was a bit worried.'

'Yes, sorry. I simply lost track of the time because I was so . . . bored.' Christ. Move on, Tom, move on *quickly*. 'But I left my phone on – you should have given me a bell. Why didn't you call, if you were worried? I left my phone on so you could do that.'

'Oh, *right* . . . So it'd look like the clingy girlfriend was calling to check up on you? A newly twenty-nine-year-old woman sitting at home brooding: timing how long you're staying out of a night by her biological clock?'

'I wouldn't have thought that at all.'

'No, but the people with you might have.'

'Not tremendously likely, is it? And even if they did, none of them knows you, so what the hell would it matter?'

'OK, so I was over-thinking a bit. I was lying – alone – in our bed, I was twenty-nine years old, my boyfriend was out at a glamorous showbiz bash and I came over all defensive.'

'You missed me?'

'Let's say that I recall thinking, "Well, I'm not ringing the fucker. That'll be just what he wants me to do." It was that kind of mood, you know?'

'Ah.'

She lifted a minor chaos of hair away from her face and took another sip of coffee. 'Why did you sleep on the sofa, by the way?'

'Oh, it was late. I didn't want to wake you.'

'I wouldn't have minded.'

'And, you know – eugh . . .' I waggled my shirt, fanning it. '. . . I stink of smoke.'

'Awww . . .' She leaned forward and kissed my cheek. 'But next time . . . phone – you wee English twat.'

'Next time? What "next time"?'

'Well, whatever . . . But you're still a wee English twat, OK?'

'OK.'

I kissed her nose.

'Do you love me more than the moon loves the sea?'

'Twice as much.'

She moved over to rest against me and I nuzzled the top of her head.

Inside, of course, I was churning with self-loathing. I mean – I don't even have to tell you that, right?

* * *

177

'Where are you going?'

'Oh . . . only into town.' I was pulling on my jacket as I spoke.

'What for?'

'Just a few things.'

It was, of course, perfectly legitimate to be going to see George at her book signing. To have a look at how things were going and say 'Hi' to her (without letting any of the punters know who I was, naturally). I knew Sara wouldn't have thought it remotely odd or suspicious. What I knew also was that she would have wanted to come along – because she was desperate to meet George. I really didn't want this. The exact reasons I didn't want it sank through two levels of vileness. Allow me to share.

The first one was simply that I'd be worried about taking her to meet George at all. George had sensed I was attracted to her, maybe Sara would sense it too. Even if she didn't, it would still be an awkward situation for George and me: playing innocent just makes you feel all the more guilty. The second reason was easily more odious. Quite simply: with Sara there, there'd be no chance of anything happening after the signing. If I was alone, maybe George and I could go back to her hotel afterwards. You know, if it felt right – I wasn't counting on it or anything. But if Sara came along that was a complete non-starter: 'Right, off you go back home now, Sara – I'll be staying on for a while so that George can sit on my face.' It was simply repugnant to be thinking this way. I didn't even have the psychological salve of it being unconscious, of not being able to see my motivations clearly – it was all perfectly plain. Jesus, I thought, I'm utterly worthless.

I thought again about George sitting on my face and hurried frantically out of the door, calling goodbye to Sara.

I'd never been to a book signing before. Most of the authors

I really admired didn't do book signings, on account of their being dignifiedly dead for at least a century. I like to think that the authors I admired wouldn't have wanted to get involved in them anyway – what is more evocative of the concept of 'celebrity' than the notion of 'the signature'? No, all my favourite authors would have fled at the very idea. Well . . . except Dickens: Dickens would certainly have done signings in Borders bookshops, and readings, and the odd *Hello!* photo spread – but I bet it would have been to raise awareness about something or other. Anyway, there'd never been a reason for any publicity people to hurl *me* bodily into a branch of Blackwell's because none of the readers of the books I'd written wanted *my* signature scrawled across the inside (a state of affairs – let me be clear about this – that suited us both).

Even though I'd never been to any signings, I had a picture of them in my mind. An author, sitting behind a table, with a stack of books neatly piled to one side. That's it. Not a prospective purchaser for ten thousand miles. It was more, even, than a lack of people who wanted his books – let alone his signed books – no, what I pictured was an actual exclusion zone of embarrassment around him. Bookshop staff, heads furiously down, busying themselves so as not to accidentally catch his eye and have to join him in yet another 'Tch – it's a lark, eh?' click of the teeth and a smiling roll of the eyes. Customers bunched up together, as distant from where he was sitting as they could make themselves and too fearful even to walk past him to the section they wanted because of the screaming statement of non-his-book-buying, non-his-book-wanting-signing this so clearly made.

You won't be surprised to discover that George's signing was nothing like this at all. The shop was simply churning with people. There were far more than could fit inside. The pavement was completely blocked by those waiting to be let in: they were craning their necks and regularly pushing themselves up on to tiptoes to see over heads and deeper into the shop – desperate for a glimpse to sustain them until the big moment. A couple of police officers were there. One was talking into his radio and I wondered whether there was going to be some trouble with the crowd causing an obstruction – the police officially intervening because of such a problem was just the kind of unfortunate event about which the McAllister & Campbell publicity department would be overjoyed.

It was simply idiotic that all these people had turned up just to see George. What was actually *annoying*, though, was that they were preventing me from getting in to see George. I tried the line 'Let me in – I work for the publisher' on the people at the door, but they weren't convinced enough to let me pass. (Though I admit that, when they asked the question 'And what are you here for?', I really ought to have come up with a better reply than 'It's a secret'.) In the end, I couldn't think of any other option but to phone George's mobile. Fortunately, she had it on and she sent someone out to get me.

She *was* sitting behind a table with a pile of books stacked to one side, but nothing else matched my vision – as I knew it wouldn't where she was concerned: she was a celebrity, not an author. Instead of repelling customers, they all wriggled to get next to her. Not simply out of competition to get their book signed first, but out of a raw desire to be closer to her, physically. While maintaining their places in the queue, they still shuffled and leaned and pressed to be as near to her as they possibly could be at any given moment. Those who'd reached the front and were standing there – *with* her – exchanging words, smiled. All of them. Male and female, young and old: as soon as she looked at them directly – personally – they smiled. And it wasn't even a smile of pleasure, I don't think. It seemed reflexive – I reckon if you'd asked them *not* to smile when she looked at them, they really couldn't have managed it. It was an offering to her: an offering that they, unconsciously, felt compelled to make. It was creepy. Something else that was creepy was standing beside her . . . Fiona.

It's not at all unknown for the area sales rep to go to a signing with an author, I knew, but I didn't imagine that the head of publicity would go along (and on a Saturday too) very often. Fiona had obviously awarded herself the job. I could just see her saying, 'We need to show George that we're giving one hundred per cent . . . so I think *I* should accompany her.' Meaning, really, that she wanted to stand there beside her: 'Look. Georgina Nye – and *I'm with her* . . . I must be pretty great too, then, right?'

I didn't want to get in the way, so I walked over to stand with Fiona, behind the table. (As I passed George, she flicked her eyes up at me and smiled. Just for a fraction of a second, but it was enough to make something in me start to hum.) Fiona looked at me evenly as I approached and said, 'Hello, Tom. What are you doing here?', her intonation wavering uncertainly between contempt and suspicion.

'I just thought . . .' I began but, as I started to reply, she took several steps back away from me. This somewhat threw me. It was rather like those scenes in Mafia movies where they've arranged to have someone killed: they meet, nothing overtly threatening, but then the one who's organised the hit steps back, because he knows someone is about to appear and rake the person he's talking to with machine-gun fire. Would Fiona have me killed simply because I'd turned up unexpectedly at a book signing? It was certainly the kind of thing that would be good to have on her CV if she went for a publicity job elsewhere. I glanced over my shoulder, quickly scanning the crowd for Joe Pesci. Fiona stared at me and wordlessly folded her arms – adopting the traditional 'Well – I'm waiting' stance. It finally became clear that she just wanted us to stand farther away from George so that the book-buying public couldn't hear what we were saying. (The implication of this, naturally, being: 'Because, Tom, I judge it highly likely that you'll say something inappropriate.') I sighed to myself and walked forward to where she was now standing.

'I just thought . . .' (If Fiona had any sense of humour *at all*, she'd have taken another several steps backwards at this point: she didn't.) '. . . I'd drop in and see how it was going,' I said.

Fiona nodded. Then, still nodding, said, 'Why?'

'Why not?'

'Good point. I mean, it's not busy at all, is it? Why doesn't absolutely everyone who fancies dropping by wander in?'

'We're not talking about everyone. It's just me. I'm not going to make any difference.'

'Hff.' She gave a tiny, bitter laugh. 'That's what people say about cars and the ozone layer.'

'You drive that big, blue cabriolet thing, Fiona – I came here on the bus.'

'Jesus – I was just speaking metaphorically. I don't give a shit about the fucking ozone layer, do I? I was simply using that as a comparison.'

'Oh, right,' I said, placidly. She really was very easy to wind up: I can't imagine why I used to think her so unassailably cool and imperious. Maybe she was losing it, or perhaps it was that I'd matured as a person. Whatever. Either way I didn't have any desire to argue with her; all I wanted to do was hang around until George had finished. I changed the subject.

'The reviews have been good,' I said. 'You must be pretty happy with the way it's all going.' I used a kind of congratulatory tone: hoping she'd pick up that I was being positive in a general way – a way that very much included her – rather than merely implying I'd done a good job with the writing. Fortunately, I don't think the idea that good reviews were anything to do with me even crossed her mind; my role had ended with delivery; everything beyond that was down to her.

'Yes,' she replied, noticeably loosening. 'It's been a book that's resisted pigeon-holing . . .' This, I must make it clear so you don't misunderstand her meaning, was said with a concerned frown. A book that resists pigeon-holing is Marketing's worst fear. In fact, if an editor gave someone in marketing *two* pigeon-holing-resistant books in a single year he'd probably find himself up in front of an industrial tribunal on a harassment charge. The bulk of Marketing's job is concerned with actively pigeon-holing a book as comprehensively and narrowly as possible: they must convince everyone – the booksellers and the public – that it's *precisely* the same as whatever other book has recently been a huge success. Fiona continued, '. . . but I've actually made it work for us. What we've got, effectively, is *two* books: and everyone is pretending to buy one of them – the feminist treatise – so they can read the other – the showbiz autobiography. We'll be number one for *weeks*. I bet they'll use what we've done here as a model for celebrity autobiographies for the next two hundred years.' I waited for her to follow that final sentence with a smile or something but, nope . . . she really meant it, apparently.

'Good work,' I said, not caring about anything but when George would be finished. She continued to sign books and exchange a few words with the public for what struck me as a creeping age. The event had been designed to run over by half an hour so that George could visibly insist on continuing when it was announced the signing had finished. This she did, but finally – amid much moaning from the punters – it had to be brought to an end because George 'had another engagement'.

Fiona escorted George to a room beyond the public area of the shop, and I went along with them. George then had a little chat with the staff. I glanced at my watch and tried to calculate how long these courtesies needed to continue before, without anyone being offended, they could all just piss off so I could fuck George like a howling, maniac coyote.

'Well,' Fiona cut in, at last, 'I'm afraid you have to leave now, George – the cab's waiting to take you.'

'Oh, OK – thanks,' George replied, and then she turned to me. 'So, Tom . . .'

'George,' I replied, with a broad grin.

She held out her hand. I looked down at it – I thought that she was perhaps showing me something . . . that it was swollen from signing books, maybe, or, I don't know, that she'd had a tattoo done. Then I realised she was holding it out so that I could shake it.

She might as well have simply punched it into my face.

Never mind that, just a few hours ago, we'd been on intimate enough terms for me to keep needing to lift my head up slightly in order to be able to take a breath – even excluding that – this was an unmistakable personal rejection. At the edge of my vision, I saw Fiona widen her eyes with surprise, and then allow herself a smile.

Men and women kiss each other's cheeks in publishing – it's how we know we work in a creative field. You don't have to be great friends or anything: it's just like saluting in the army or the strictly defined forms of address used in parliamentary debate. It's what separates us, as a community, from people who slaughter pigs for a living or work in building societies. If you don't like someone very much, you might just kiss the air, or only one cheek, or even simply walk away. You don't *shake their hand*, though. Christ. Why didn't she just pull a disgusted face while poking me with a stick?

In a mute daze, I didn't reach out and grab her hand so much as simply watch my own unrelated-to-me arm do it on autopilot.

'Thanks for all the work you've done,' she said. 'I really appreciate the effort you've put in and the time you've taken to get things right.' I wasn't listening. At first, I wasn't listening because I was too shocked by the completely unexpected insult of having my hand shaken, but this faded. I noticed that George wasn't just holding my hand. While my hand remained in hers, her thumb was gently stroking my wrist. And when, realising this, I raised my eyes I found that hers were there to look into them unwaveringly. She was trying to be very formal and distant for the people there, while making it quite clear to me how she felt. This was a fantastic relief. And *tremendously* exciting – everyone watching us, but unaware of our feelings. This was *great*.

Oh, and it was also not working.

That's to say, I think it was working with regard to the few bookshop staff who were there, but Fiona had begun to peer at us with a curious expression on her face. I don't know whether she'd picked up something in our body language too, or whether she actually caught sight of George wooing my wrist, but I glanced across at her and saw that her former expression of *schadenfreude* had given way to suspicious peering. I hastily pulled my hand away from George's and said, 'Well – keep in touch!' – as you would to a couple from Goldalming you'd met on holiday.

Fiona stepped forward and, placing a guiding hand on George's arm, said, 'We'd better get to that cab, George,' while giving me a penetrating stare. They left together, briskly, but, just beyond the doorway, where no one else could see, George glanced back at me and mouthed, 'I'll call you.' I grinned delightedly and raised my hand. Fiona looked back at this point, so I turned it into a little wave to her that was the single most unconvincing thing since the dawn of the universe. She looked at me, at George, at me again, narrowed her eyes and then continued to the cab.

Maybe she thought something suspicious was going on, but she couldn't know precisely what it was – much less have any proof of it. And anyway, even if she did, what could she do about it?

I started to make my way home but had to stop and return to town again. Luckily, I remembered in time that I'd told Sara I needed to buy a few things, so it'd look odd if I came back without anything at all. Back in town, I ran into the two nearest shops and hurriedly bought a packet of anti-diarrhoea tablets and a Swiss Army penknife, and then returned to the bus stop energised by my narrow escape.

Actually, I also bought a packet of cigarettes and a lighter.

I smoked half a cigarette while waiting for the bus to arrive – smoked it nervously. I held it down by my side in between drags, in the schoolboy style. My eyes darted around; I was fearful of being spotted by someone who knew Sara. It was an edgy and uncomfortable experience, smoking that cigarette . . . yet, curiously, one that I preferred to the idea of not smoking it.

When I got back home, Sara heard me opening the front door and shouted from the kitchen, 'Tom? Is that you?'

'Yeah.'

She remained out of sight. 'Georgina Nye in a cab yesterday, then, eh?' she called. 'Already at it like rabbits in the back seat – so God knows what went on in her hotel room . . .'

My response to hearing this wasn't emotional, or even broadly psychological: it was overridingly physical. I don't want to go into specifics.

I stood in the hallway, completely still apart from a slight wobbling at the knees, staring at the doorway into the kitchen. I felt as though the kitchen itself had spoken through its open-doorway mouth. Sara was no mere mortal now: she had been transformed into a vengeful spirit, a disembodied force that communicated with mankind via the oracle of my kitchen. Something was wrong, though. No, hold on, that's ambiguous: what I mean is that something wasn't right. There was an uncomfortable juxtaposition – elements of this didn't fit together properly. I don't know whether my silence made Sara poke her head out and look at me, or whether she was attracted by the deafening, wet thud that was the sound of my stomach turning over with fear: whatever it was, her face appeared in the doorway and I saw what it was that was making the situation feel as though it had been incorrectly assembled. She was grinning. That had been what felt curious about her words – they'd been delivered with a playful, laughing tone. Now, the thought that Sara had discovered my infidelity, and found it amusing, did wander through my mind . . . but it found nowhere to stay. Every respectable synapse slammed shut its door and drew its curtains at the approach of this insane, pestilent concept. Sara standing there, tutting and ruffling my hair, as she said, 'Been fucking Georgina, then? Och, you wee lovable rogue, you' wasn't a picture that stayed in focus for very long. So, I was at a bit of a loss here.

Sara continued to grin at me.

Trying impossibly hard to imbue my voice with no kind of inflection whatsoever, I looked at her and said, 'What?'

'Your *girlfriend*,' laughed Sara. I'd clearly been sucked into some surreal, David Lynch dream sequence. Something – possibly my head – was sure to burst into flames in slow motion any moment now.

I pressed on.

'What?'

'Your girlfriend's been at it in the back of a taxi with some bloke – and on the way to her hotel together, apparently. I wonder what Darren Boyle will say when he finds out.'

'Yes,' I replied. Then, 'Um, how did *you* find out?'

'It's in the paper.' She nodded across at something out of my field of view.

Walking a bit like the Tin Man still waiting for the oil to fully work, I moved forward into the kitchen. The local paper was there and on the front page – though not the main headline (which was just about the economy collapsing or something) – was 'Nye-t on the town!' Which, I like to think, I'd have found offensively appalling on a professional level even if I'd been a disinterested reader. Whether the cab driver had gone directly to the paper or whether the story had travelled a little through his fellow drivers first, it was clear that he was the ultimate source. (I bet George had already seen this before the book signing – no wonder she was so anxious to remain formal.) The story contained everything we've come – depressingly – to accept as news. It was just the headline and a couple of sentences on the front page before a *continued on page 7*. And even there it continued for only another fifty or so words because it was, of course, a fundamentally trivial event. Nevertheless, they managed to cram every piece of journalistic tiresomeness into the small space available. We had a good selection of those words that are kept from becoming outright archaisms thanks solely to their incessant use by the press: 'canoodling', for example, and 'beau'. In addition to being her 'beau', I had extra aesthetic misfortune heaped upon me by also being a 'mystery man'.

I read through the piece. Several times, in fact – each time expecting to discover a tiny, throwaway fact that revealed my identity. The kind of thing everyone overlooks until Poirot says, 'But, *of course* . . .' just before the denouement.

'Do you know who he was?' asked Sara.

'It wasn't me,' I replied, instantly. Like a twat, instantly.

Sara huffed with laughter and glanced up from where she was slicing tomatoes, grapes and onions, and dropping the pieces into a bowl of strawberry-flavoured Angel Delight. 'You don't say? Georgina Nye whisking you off to her hotel room? Yeah – *you wish*.' She popped half a grape into her mouth. 'I just thought you might have seen who she left with.'

'No. I didn't notice. I stayed there at the party – as you know – and George left. I was so far away from her when she left I didn't even see her leave, let alone see who was with her. It wasn't until hours afterwards when someone said, "Where's George?" and someone else replied, "She's gone," that I knew she wasn't there any more, in fact . . . I imagine she left with someone very famous, though.'

'Why?'

'Well . . . because George is famous. Celebrities always have sex with other celebrities, don't they?'

'Special celebrity sex, I bet,' laughed Sara. 'This really well-choreographed, non-squelchy sex that's lots better and sexier and loads more photogenic than the sex we have.'

That sent a shudder through me. 'Better than the sex we have.' The sex had been pyrotechnically fabulous with George, but it wasn't better than the sex Sara and I had. Or was it? And it didn't matter anyway – this wasn't simply about sex. But – even looked at purely in sex terms – then the sex I had with Sara was great. Really lovely. It was a different kind of sex, perhaps, but still quality sex, no doubt about it. I'd be terribly hurt if I thought that Sara thought that I was having better sex with George than I had with her. Hmm . . . what I really needed here was to *Stop Thinking.*

'Why don't you pick out the carpet you want?' I said. 'We can afford to buy it now.'

Sara waggled her head and then looked at me. 'Whoa – from sex to carpets . . . What worries me is that I *can* see your train of thought there.'

'I was just thinking that I'm getting the book money, and you wanted the carpet, and I love you and, well . . .'

'No, no, I wasn't criticising. Christ – you express your love for me in carpet form just *any time you fancy.*' She leaned towards me and gave me a quick kiss on the lips. 'Phew – you smell of smoke.'

'Oh, yeah, it's this jacket. It needs airing after last night – it *reeks.*' I fingered it and grimaced.

God, I could do with a cigarette.

I spent the whole of the rest of the day repeatedly checking that my phone was working. George had said she'd call and I was so hyper with expectation, longing and frustration waiting for her to ring that you'd have thought I was trying to get my own syndrome. I couldn't sit down, or watch television, or read, or concentrate on anything. I drifted off halfway through whatever Sara was saying and every single thing in the world – presumably owing to the simple fact of it not being George calling me – was unbearably irritating. Only yesterday I'd started smoking again: right now I really could have done with hitting the town and scoring some Ritalin. Except that was probably being optimistic. Attention Deficit Disorder *and* obsessive compulsion? I was bringing together two disparate dementias. Yeah, check me out – very experimental, very cross-over.

Sara couldn't fail to notice that I was agitated and prickly. I told her it was just because I was over-tired and kept apologising. When we went to bed, it was obvious I wouldn't be able to get to sleep, so I had sex with Sara in the hope that it might help. That sounds dreadful, doesn't it? Cold-bloodedly having sex with your girlfriend, just so you can siphon off some of the tension that's there because you're thinking about another woman. Well, it wasn't as black-and-white as that. I got some pleasure from the sex with Sara as well. Hmm . . . that sounds even more dreadful, doesn't it? OK, listen, I'll tell you something: even though I might have started it just to help me sleep, and even though I was getting enjoyment from Sara while deceiving her, I tried the best I could to give her simply excellent sex. Really. I thought I owed it to her. I was having this extra sex, so I owed it to her to make sure the sex she had was perfect. No thought of myself. My only purpose was to serve her. If need be, I was going to be there for her until my jaw locked. Making sure she had great sex was my duty: a penance I gladly performed. Ahhh . . . now *that* sounds just about the most dreadful perspective of all.

I should have stuck to talking about giving myself a wank – that way I'd have retained your respect.

What you have to remember is that *I* was the victim here. I don't think you could say I was having an 'affair' – it was just the one incident. That's not an 'affair', is it? That's what you call a 'slip'. OK, I'll admit, I was, um, less than resolute that it would end with that single night, but that's all there'd been so far. You can't go all hysterical and over the top and start giving labels to things simply on the basis of what they *might become*, can you? That's unfair. But anyway, even if we call it an 'affair', purely for rhetorical purposes, it wasn't an affair like other people have. For one thing, I'd simply been caught up in events – and unlikely events at that. If George's agent hadn't decided it would be good to do a book, if they'd gone with another publisher where Hugh wasn't in place to suggest me, if I'd missed our meeting that first day (as I very nearly did), etc., etc. – forwards and backwards. An almost incalculable number of ifs *all* needed to have been linked in a chain to allow this to happen: for a nobody from Kent to end up with a woman from East Ayrshire who was now probably the biggest celebrity in the UK. This wasn't bloke; married; has affair with his secretary. This was almost as if Fate had forced me into the situation against my will, because it was *destined* to happen. And I felt completely different to how I'm sure other people feel when they have affairs. *I* was suffering horribly. Suffering while everyone else was fine, too. George certainly had nothing to feel miffed about. She'd made the first move, and if I'd seemed to encourage her at all it was unintentional. I hadn't lied either before or after the fact. She knew I was with Sara – I'd talked about her a lot: in fact, if anything, George had been keen to hear about Sara and me, and our relationship – and I hadn't said I was going to leave Sara, or that I was unhappy or any of that stuff. What's more, *she* didn't have to worry about being discovered as I did. She didn't have a relationship to lose, nor did she have to keep herself alert and be constantly wary of slip-ups. No, George had been dealt a good hand. As for Sara, well, yes – I was being unfaithful to her. But *she* didn't know that. *I* was the one who had to endure life under the weight of that knowledge: *I* was the one who felt guilty. If anything, things were better for Sara because I was trying hard to make sure they were. So, you tell me: who was getting the worst deal out of all this? And yet I was keeping it all to myself – living with the turmoil inside, unable even to share my burden. My philanthropy was going completely unrecognised. Good God – people had been sainted for less. I was practically a modern-day Sydney Carlton. Here I am suffering silently to maintain the happiness of others, and all you can do is despise me for ensuring that my girlfriend has wave after face-crushing wave of orgasms: you ought to be bloody ashamed of yourself.

Anyway, as I was saying, George didn't call. Nor did she call on Sunday morning. Sunday afternoon snailed by – and you know how Sunday afternoon drags even under normal circumstances – and my phone stayed silent. Except for the half-dozen times I called myself from our land line, just to make sure there wasn't a technical fault. Sara accidentally made the whole experience all the more harrowing by watching the omnibus edition of *The Firth* on the TV. It was having George rubbed into my face in entirely the wrong sense. I sat beside Sara on the sofa while the landfill of Sunday afternoon TV gently gave way to Sunday evening TV's stumbling confusion: dead and letting it bury me. One of the evening's succession of atrabilious detectives adapted for television from a series of novels was moaning about something or other to his subordinates when, at last, my mobile trilled for attention. I whipped it up to my ear with fumbling speed. (This might have looked suspicious had someone else done it, but Sara was used to me doing that all the time anyway, of course.)

'Hello? Tom?' It was George. She sounded naked.

'Oh – hi,' I replied, casually. I rose and walked towards the door. 'How are you?'

'I'm fine,' she said. She was marking time: I could tell she didn't want to say anything that wasn't completely bland until I gave her some sort of clue that it was OK to talk.

'Good.'

'You?'

'Oh, you know . . .' I was out in the hallway now, but still didn't feel completely safe. '. . . fine. Just watching a bit of telly.' I mounted the stairs and went into the bathroom. 'Some detective show is on.'

'Right – if you're watching it . . .'

'No, no, no. I'm not watching.' I sat down on the toilet. 'It's just on . . .' My voice became whispery. '. . . I've missed you.'

'Have you?'

'*Christ*, yes.' I realised my sitting there might look odd if Sara came up. 'Hold on, let me take my trousers down . . .'

'That's OK – you've missed me, I believe you.'

'Ha. No – I'm hiding in the bathroom. I just want to make it look convincing.' Trousers now vouchingly round my ankles, I sat down on the lavatory.

'It's a romantic picture you're painting.'

'Sorry. I . . . oh, bugger.' (If anyone's devised a workable solution to the problem of sitting on the toilet with an erection, I wonder whether they'd be good enough to send me a schematic.)

'What is it?'

'Nothing. I just noticed we're out of conditioner.'

'Have you seen the papers?'

'Yeah. Tossers.'

'Scared me to death. Can you imagine what the press

would do to me – what with the book just out and my banging a feminist drum? They'd make it a whole "betraying a sister" issue. Not to mention that they'd have a good time talking about you and how much of the book was really my work.'

'And there's Sara too.'

'Hmm? Oh, yes – exactly. It'd be awful for both of us.'

'So . . .' I picked at the toilet roll. '. . . are you saying you want to stop?'

'Is that what you want?'

'Is it what *you* want?'

'If it's what *you* want.'

'I didn't say I wanted to stop, I just asked if you did.'

'So, what do you want?'

'I want what you want.'

'Well,' said George, 'I don't want to stop, but if you want to . . .'

'Jesus, no! *I* don't want to stop.'

'Really?'

'I couldn't bear it.' I was sweating. I didn't tell George this. It might convey how intense my feelings were, but it was a less than ravishing concept: let her just keep the image of me sitting, unsweaty, on the toilet. 'I want to see you again as soon as possible. Sooner than possible – I want to see you impossibly soon.'

She giggled. *Giggled*. How can you hear even the fading echoes of your reason over a noise like that?

'I've got to go to Glasgow tomorrow,' said George.

'I'll sneak over.'

'No, I'll be tied up all day.'

'Even better,' I purred. (Christ – I can *purr*: where'd that come from?)

'Oh, *don't* . . . No, really, I have to do a couple of things at the studio. They'd arranged it so I had time off from filming to promote the book, but I need to go back and do a few loops.

Then I've got another signing, two radio slots and a pile of interviews. I don't have a second free. But on Tuesday we're getting together at the publisher's for a meeting. Kind of a launch post-mortem.'

'They didn't tell me that.'

'Your agent will be there – Paul mentioned she would be.'

'Ah, right. Probably thought there was no need for me, then.'

'If you turned up, though, that'd be perfectly fine. We could go off somewhere and have lunch afterwards; there'd be nothing remarkable about that. Lunch could run on – happens all the time.'

Sara opened the door.

'Right. OK. Yes,' I barked into the phone. 'Five per cent. Yes. Tuesday. Yes. Goodbye, then.'

George understood. ''Bye,' she cooed, and I hung up.

'Oh,' said Sara, 'you're here.'

'Yes.'

'Who was on the phone?'

'Georgina Nye.' I sighed wearily, and wrinkled my face.

'Why did you come in here to speak to her?'

'Because of the TV – I couldn't hear properly with the TV on.'

'No, why did you come in *here*? I wasn't suggesting you'd *snook off* . . .' She said the words in an elaborate hiss and waggled her fingers in the air, to emphasise the fact she was only joking. (I wondered if she *was* only joking.) '. . . I'm simply curious as to why you decided to talk on the lavvy.'

'*Ohhhh* . . .' I said. '. . . *Riiiiight*. I just wanted to use the toilet.'

'That desperately? Eww . . . weren't you afraid she'd hear?'

'Well . . .' Occasionally, you just get lucky. '. . . I've got a bit of a stomach thing. I've had it all day.' Of all the random things I could have bought – just to have bought *something* –

what did I get? Sometimes, blind chance helps you out. 'I got some tablets in town – they're in my jacket. You couldn't go and get me a couple, could you?'

'Why didn't you say?' She turned and began to make her way off down the stairs to the coat rack.

'I'm too dignified.'

'Ha.' She reached the bottom of the stairs and pulled down my jacket. 'Which pocket?'

Oh, my mistake – this wasn't one of those times when blind chance was helping me out.

Fuck.

'No! Actually – forget about it.' The chances of Sara finding the anti-diarrhoea tablets were *exactly* the same as those of her finding my cigarettes. 'I'll come down myself.'

'I'm here now.'

I yanked at my trousers, flushed the toilet (for effect) and bunny-hopped frantically towards the door. 'Yes, but . . .'

You might think that I was overreacting, especially as I had a rather more devastating secret under my hat. You might think that flying into a panic at the thought of Sara discovering my cigarettes was a bit needlessly hysterical. In which case, I'll use my mysterious psychic powers to somehow . . . inexplicably . . . know that you are not someone who is in a long-term relationship with a non-smoker: a relationship that you entered as a smoker, but from which position you moved in step with your blossoming love. In those circumstances, being uncovered as apostate chills your blood even as a purely theoretical prospect. The (admittedly similar) situation of being found in possession of a bacon sandwich by your vegetarian partner – even *that* – is better. In that case you will be judged to be simply evil: nothing more stinging than a treacherous, lying murderer. The non-smoking partner, however, will be 'disappointed with you'. Not only can they never trust you again, but you've also broken their heart, and also 'really let yourself down'. What's more, you have no case. It's easy enough to plead that the pig was already dead anyway and, you know, tastes *great*. You have none of this ratiocinative moral armour to protect you with smoking, however. You'll have to face 'Do you *want* to kill yourself?' and 'Are you stupid?' and 'What's so good about it? Tell me. *Go on*', and all you'll be able to do is mumble, 'Sorry,' and hope you get sent to your room as quickly as possible so it'll all end. Oh – and it won't *ever* end.

So, hurling myself out of the bathroom with my trousers halfway down was actually a perfectly measured response.

'Yes, but . . .' I scrambled down to her at the top speed of a man descending a flight of stairs without his trousers on properly. '. . . I've finished on the lavatory now and . . .' I finished the sentence by turning her around and kissing her greedily.

She smiled. 'Hmmm – nice. Even if . . .' She slapped my face, playfully. '. . . it's not the most romantic thing ever to put me in second place after the lavvy.'

'No.' I put my hand on her face. 'I'd never let you be second to anything, Sara. Never.'

You can imagine the silent, lonely anguish I had to endure telling her this, when its deeper meaning was apparent only to me. I managed it, though: sometimes you find an inner strength that you never suspected you had.

Monday was a hell that wouldn't end.

It had no purpose, no reason for being: it simply insisted on hanging around like a tedious, unwanted guest, keeping me from Tuesday and George. I tried to do a bit of work – sorting out my files – but I couldn't stay focused. With Sara at work, I could at least go out into the garden and have a smoke, but only carefully as I was worried one of the neighbours might see and grass me up. There was also the bother of digging little holes to bury the dog ends, and then I had to brush my teeth, take a shower and change my clothes. If I'd simply told myself I'd smoke all day it wouldn't have been so bad, but every one was a just-this-one, so I had to keep changing back into my smoky clothes before having another cigarette and then showering again afterwards. By teatime I could have assisted at an operation.

The evening was slightly less awful. Not because I was closer to Tuesday (the tantalising effect of this counteracted any possible satisfaction) but because Sara was there. I had something to concentrate on: i.e. trying my hardest to be as nice to her as possible. As there was every likelihood (at least, I hoped there was) of my being unfaithful to her again the next day, I was keen that she should want for nothing this evening. Television? What did she want to watch? Cup of tea? I'd get it. This wasn't for my own benefit, by the way. I didn't have any inchoate notion of being able to build up a karmic stockpile that I could draw on to balance out tomorrow's infidelity. It was, as I've said, purely because I felt I owed it to her. If you love your girlfriend, but you're planning to have sex with another woman the next day, then you feel a responsibility to massage her feet for absolutely however long she wants you to. It's all about respect, really.

Tuesday finally saw fit to arrive and I warmed up with a bit of pacing around in the living room before somehow convincing myself that it wasn't too early to begin heading for McAllister & Campbell.

Nobody sat by me on the bus. That's unremarkable – but I couldn't help feeling that *today* people weren't sitting by me because they could see into my head. It was messy in there. There's a whole world of difference between being unfaithful unexpectedly – in the disorientating swirl of the moment – and catching the bus across town to be unfaithful. This was calculated. You can't dismiss as temporary insanity an infidelity for which you've made sure you have the correct change.

The writer in me pleads for lies again here, incidentally. He wants to play up that standard story point in the second act where the protagonist – *after much internal struggle* – finally commits to a course of action. He wants me to say how I nearly turned back: how I even rang the bell and moved to stand by the door halfway through the journey . . . before my desire stared me down and, finally – broken and accepting – I returned to my seat through the curious looks of the other passengers. That never happened. I felt guilty, yes, and I was harried by the realisation that I was doing this calmly and thus culpably. But I never once made a move to abandon the path I was taking or embarked upon an unsuccessful attempt to pull back from the brink. Terrible really, that – on top of everything else – I could also have used some work on my character arc.

Moreover, the thing that was playing on my mind even more than the formalisation of my infidelity was how things would go with George. I didn't have to consider how things would go the last time: they went before I knew they were going at all. Now, however, I was worried. What would I talk about? Should I make 'advances', or wait for her? Would she still feel the same, seeing me again in . . . well, in daylight? The first thing I did when I got off the bus was to have a cigarette and another little pace.

I'd intended to stroll in to the McAllister & Campbell offices when everyone was already having the meeting – 'Oh! You're all here! What a surprise!' – but I couldn't endure the waiting and so I turned up early. Hugh was in his office, alone, staring out of the window.

'Hi, Hugh.'

'Ah, Tom, hello. How are you?'

'Fine, fine. You?'

'Oh . . .' He looked down into his lap and shook his head, slowly. '. . . you know.'

'Right.'

'I did some more work on my book last night.'

'How's it g—?' He interrupted my question with a simply heartbreaking facial expression. 'Oh. Well . . .' I have no idea what words of consolation I was hoping to find, but I was saved from the trauma of looking for them because Amy, George and a man I guessed was her agent, Paul, strolled brightly into the office.

'Tom,' said Amy, with an oddly large amount of surprise. 'What are you doing here?'

'Oh, I just popped by. Why?'

'No reason. It's just that we're having a meeting. I didn't expect you.'

'Should I . . . ?' I made a vague, proto, thousandth of a step in the direction of the door.

'No.' Amy waved me down with her hands. 'It's fine. I didn't mention it because it's only a general, post-launch chat. I didn't think you'd be interested. Stay, though – we can sit at the back together and make farty noises with our armpits.'

'Hello, Amy,' said Fiona, entering the office.

'Fi!' Amy peered at her. 'Have you done something with your hair?'

'No, it's . . .'

'I thought not – but you said you wanted to.'

'I didn't.'

'*Didn't* you?' Amy bit her lip and then questioned herself thoughtfully. 'God . . . who *was* talking to me about your hair, then?'

Fiona marched to a seat. 'Shall we get on?'

'I like your hair, love,' chirped up Paul with what I suppose in London they'd call a cheeky grin. 'Lovely – a proper posh bird's cut.' Annoyance sprinted briefly across Amy's face, Fiona thanked him unenthusiastically and we all made to sit down at Hugh's table (I sat between Amy and George). As I was halfway to being seated Fiona said, 'Tom? Turned up unexpectedly again, then?'

I don't think she anticipated my answering at all so, to show I could hold my own if we were going to exchange snide comments, I replied, 'Yes.'

One all, I reckon.

The meeting started and almost immediately became very dull indeed. It was uniformly good news about the book; all sorts of things were going as they should, new opportunities were presenting themselves and, if you're the kind of person who gets a buzz out of the flawless execution of a business plan – Fiona, let's say – I'm sure you'd have had a great time. To 'keep up the momentum', they'd decided to have some sort of belated launch party in a couple of weeks, around the time the Festival ended. It'd be billed as a celebration of the success of the book – a 'thank you' to George from McAllister & Campbell – but it was basically a way to get some people from the media around and manufacture another reason to have the book mentioned everywhere. A very grim prospect for an evening, if you ask me. I said it was a great idea and I'd look forward to it. Really, I had my mind on more human matters, however. Jesus – I wasn't hypnotised by sales figures or percentages of net or promotional parties. At the end of the day, it was just money and marketing and what did that matter when, right next to me, George had on a short denim skirt?

Hugh said how proud he was of everyone. Lots of times. This was my first contact with George's agent, Paul, and he struck me as not only the wide boy Amy had described, but also quite dangerous. He was stocky and wide necked and prone to weaving his head as he spoke – like a former boxer who now 'sorted people out' for some firm that specialised in delivering meat and extorting money from betting shops: I suspect he had that combination of physicality and easy arrogance that some middle-class women find 'awfully thrilling'. I imagined him to be agent to the Krays. Also, he was keen to haggle over things. There wasn't really anything to haggle over: I think he simply enjoyed the haggling experience. Amy kept spinning glances at him, but didn't send any acidic comments in his direction (I was so proud of her professional restraint). Fiona repeatedly and variously told us what she thought the thing we must remember was. Like almost every publishing meeting, fifteen minutes of stuff was said, it took an hour and a half, and someone provided biscuits. When we hit something like the seventy-minute mark, however, I couldn't have cared less if everyone had begun speaking in tongues: because, at that point, George started to feel my crotch under the table.

There was something quite inexpressibly exciting about this. George feeling my crotch under the table . . . Partly, I think, it was the secrecy of it – everyone else there having no idea what we were up to. The other great aspect of it was that she was feeling my crotch. I think that bit would have worked anywhere, really. It felt thrillingly daring. It wasn't: no one around the table looking at us could possibly have seen that anything was going on (though they might have suspected that I'd popped a few tablets of ecstasy before arriving). It just *seemed* daring.

After a while, George stopped – carefully placing both her hands on top of the table. While everyone else was concerned with some marketing detail, George gave me a look which included subtle performances from both raised eyebrows and dropped eyes. I glanced quickly around the table, and then slid my hand down on to her bare leg. It was cool – or my hand was hot: whatever the precise balance it felt absolutely right that they should join together in search of equilibrium. I pretended to stare down at some papers that Fiona had given everybody. They contained a few good review quotes from various sources, some tables of figures, a sales projection and were of no interest to me at all at this point in my life. I couldn't even see what was on them, in the sense of the marks that were the letters and the numbers being interpreted and given meaning by my brain. My brain was concentrating entirely on the sensation of my fingers running over George's leg. I had no spare capacity left to faff around with requests from my visual cortex, because my mind was filled utterly with the experience of George's skin. Like a snake moving over a branch, I curved my hand across the top of her leg a few inches above her knee. It slipped easily down over on to the other side so that my palm lay against the inside of one leg while the inside of her other brushed lightly against the back of my fingers. Then, subtly – appearing to everyone else at the table as though she were merely adjusting her position slightly as part of a movement that was really more concerned with shuffling the papers in front of her – she opened her legs wider. Maybe I've got an especially highly attuned ability to pick up clues from body language, I don't know, but somehow I knew this was an invitation. Gently, slowly, in a series of advances and retreats, I moved my hand up along the inside of her thigh. Her legs were firm: I could tell she ran all those miles every day and blessed every treadmilling inch of them. They were smooth too, but not lifelessly so – not like plastic or enamel: there was still friction as my skin ran over hers, and I could feel a tiny, light, down of hair prickling against my touch. I could even lift away from her skin, glide a fraction of a millimetre above it, yet still remain connected as I skimmed across the ends of those soft hairs with my fingertips. And as I moved farther up between her legs, it grew hotter. I'm sure there was an identifiable difference in temperature even half an inch one way or the other: the heat didn't rise in a gentle slope but leapt along in an ever-steepening curve as each cautious edging of my fingers moved them into an area wildly hotter than the previous one. I could even feel the heat radiating now. From just a short distance farther up, from the point where her legs joined, came a heat whose source I wasn't touching, and yet it was a glow that even now fell warm against the back of my hand – it was like the sun on my skin in summer.

George jerked her legs away, crossing them at the same time – she did this so violently and abruptly that her chair made a scraping noise across the floor. As her legs crossed and shifted my hand very nearly got snared between them and I came close to being dragged off after it like a man whose arm has got caught in machinery. I looked at George, but she was determinedly staring away from me, apparently completely fascinated by something her agent was saying about cross-marketing. I had no idea what I'd done, what line I'd overstepped (a bikini line of some sort, I imagined). It wasn't until I pulled my eyes away from George that I saw the cause of her sudden explosion of chastity. Fiona was bent over towards the table. It was no consolation whatsoever that I could see down her top, because she wasn't bent down, heading *down*: she was bent down, heading *up*. I'd no idea why – my attention was elsewhere – but Fiona was obviously sitting upright again after reaching under the table for something. What it was that had made her descend – to retrieve a dropped pen, or a piece of paper, to attend to an itch, to dip a loosening finger into a shoe, or maybe just to sneak a crafty look at Paul's groin – I didn't know, but, whatever it was, her head had been sub-table. It was, of course, possible she hadn't seen anything. Her eyes may simply not have glanced in the direction of George's legs, or George could have spotted her ducking in time and made evasive manoeuvres before she was sufficiently submerged to be able to see anything. Both of those things were possible, but neither of them was true. A fraction of a second with Fiona's face dismissed those possibilities instantly. As she moved back into an upright position, her eyes remained zeroed on me in the same kind of way you see a lion maintaining its lock on a gazelle while moving through tall grass. If that wasn't enough – and it was more than enough, I can assure you – she was smiling at me. A wholly humourless smile. If it contained any emotion at all – other than a soulless, icy maleficence – then it was simply a whiff of something like, but not quite, triumph.

I tried to meet her look with a counter-countenance of blankness. Not guilty, nor embarrassed, nor angry, nor anything at all except resistant. My eyes fell first, though. You can't bluff when your opponent has seen your cards. I avoided eye contact with her and feigned interest in what Paul was saying. The final ten minutes of the meeting seemed to last about twenty-eight years and take place in a room that was a dozen degrees hotter than before. Hugh had barely got a third of the way through a speculative sentence tentatively suggesting that we might think about drawing to a close before I was up out of my seat and heading towards the door at a brisk trot. Fiona – poisonously casual – called out to me, 'Tom . . . ?' as I shot out of the room, but I pretended not to hear her and raced off towards the water cooler like a man with a thirst borne of the desert.

I poured myself a cup of water and used it as a thing to look over at the rest of them leaving the office. Hugh stood in the doorway, like a host bidding farewell to his guests. Fiona, Paul and George paused just outside the office, chatting cheerfully about something, but Amy broke away from them and made her way over to me.

'So,' she said, 'that went pretty well.'

'Hm,' I replied.

Amy looked back at the group. 'I must say I'm glad you've got over your Fiona thing.'

I arranged a couple of bemused eyebrows and a surprised mouth for her. 'Eh? What Fiona thing?'

She was digging around in her handbag. 'None of my business, I know . . .' She pulled out her cigarettes and put one in her mouth. '. . . but I don't miss much. I couldn't help noticing, really.'

'Noticing what?'

'Oh – the gormless expressions, how you lost brain cells as she approached, the way you stared at her tits . . .'

'I stare at everyone's tits: I stare at *your* tits – all the time.'

'Yeah, yeah.' She had her lighter in her hand and was absently flicking it on and then letting it go out. 'But only because they're tits and they're within view. You look at my tits like some people would watch a football match between two teams they don't support: you'd bought a season ticket and a club shirt for Fiona's tits.'

'You reckon, do you?' I said, dismissively.

'Whatever . . . Like I say, it's none of my business: but I'm glad that you've recovered – you couldn't even bear to look at her by the end of that meeting. I don't miss much, you see.'

'Apparently not.'

'You're far better off with Sara, you know. How long have you two been together now?'

'About five or six years.'

'There you go. You've got yourself a nice-looking woman – a nice-looking *Scots* woman, too: which is a prize no Englishman really deserves – and you're happy together. You're far better off than most people.' Fiona, Paul and George left Hugh to seal himself in his office and mope about his book and his mortality, and began walking over to where Amy and I were standing. 'If you're going to risk what you've got, then at least do it for someone who's worth it. At the very least, you ought to consider someone whose arse isn't visible from space – oh, hi, Fiona!'

Fiona ignored Amy, but now she did so with a superior, invulnerable air. She didn't say anything to anyone: she just stared at me, smiling.

'You ready, love?' Paul said to Amy.

'Sure,' she replied.

I looked at her, pleased to have a reason not to look at Fiona.

'Paul and I are having lunch, Tom. I've booked at that Bosnian place – we'll never get extra seats there at this time of day: sorry – I didn't think you'd be here. We could go somewhere else, though – that's OK, isn't it, Paul?'

'Erm, yeah, sure – I'm easy.'

'No,' I insisted, 'it's fine.'

'Why don't you and George go somewhere together?' said Amy.

Fiona coughed. I didn't look at her. More surprisingly, neither did I beat her to the ground with a fire extinguisher.

'Leave us to talk business,' continued Amy, 'and you two have a nice "Job Well Done" meal. You both deserve it.'

'Yeah – good thinking,' said Paul.

'And I'm sure Paul will pick up the tab as a thank-you,' added Amy.

Paul seemed to experience a sudden, sharp constriction around his heart, but he managed to reply, 'Yeah' weakly and shoot George a glance that read, 'Please God, George, *please God* guide Tom in the direction of sitting on a park bench with a saveloy and a can of Fanta.'

'Sure,' George nodded. 'How does that sound to you, Tom?' I think she'd decided that the way she was going to play it with Fiona was to carry on as if nothing had happened. Show no sign of concern whatsoever.

'Well . . . yes. Why not?' I said.

'I'll leave you all to eat, then,' Fiona said. 'I've got things I need to get on with here.'

'Don't you . . . ?' began Paul, but Amy stomped over him immediately.

'You're a real trooper, Fi. You almost make me feel guilty. Right – let's the rest of us go and stuff our faces.'

Fiona stood and watched me all the way out as we left.

* * *

It was really so that we could have some privacy, but I'm sure it was also a great relief to Paul that George and I rejected all of the restaurants in town in favour of some Marks & Spencer's sandwiches on the scrubby grass of Arthur's Seat. George suggested it, saying she'd heard the view of Edinburgh was wonderful from up there (she really did seem to have a thing about views). I wasn't bothered one way or the other about the view but I suspected that, if you want to get a sense of perspective about things, then it always helps to be sitting on the side of a volcano. So, we took a taxi out to the bottom, hiked up to the top and, with no one passing within a hundred yards of us – and George in her Nyeness-concealing hat and glasses anyway – we were hidden on the most exposed place in Edinburgh. Nearly bleeding *killed* me walking up the damn thing, of course, but, once there, my wheezing had subsided enough to allow me to talk after only about ten or fifteen minutes.

'No,' I said, 'you did exactly the right thing.'

'You're sure?'

'Definitely. *You* can stare Fiona down. She wouldn't *dare* do anything to offend you – you're Georgina fucking Nye, for God's sake.'

'What level of celebrity do you have to be to merit the "fucking", then?' She laughed.

'Hu-fucking-*mongous*,' I replied. 'Nothing can touch your tmesis-grade celebrity.'

'Your *what* grade celebrity?'

'Tmesis – when you split a compound word with another word.'

'Tmesis?'

'Tmesis.'

'Did you use that just so you'd sound clever?'

'Did it work?'

'Yeah.'

'Phew. Because I'm not sure it is tmesis, technically, when

you say "Georgina fucking Nye". I was a bit scared you'd pull me up about it.'

'With good cause . . .' She teased a slice of cucumber out of her sandwich, popped it into her mouth and became serious again. 'She could tell people, though. Even if she's scared of me – and my fearsome tmesis – she could start rumours that'd wind up with some reporter.'

'No. Not Fiona. She defines herself too much by her job: it's how she measures herself against others and the universe. It would be unprofessional of her to let the info out, so even the *faintest possibility* that any leak would lead back to her – and people would therefore think she was flawed as a head of publicity – even that would be more than she could bear.'

'So she's got to pretend she didn't see anything, then?'

'Oh, no – I bet she'll use it to torment me: as a stick to poke me with. She'll always make sure *I* know that *she* knows something I wish she didn't, but she won't mention a thing to anyone else.'

'Right . . . Thank God. We need to be careful.'

'You said that before, and the next thing I know you're feeling me up under the table at a sales meeting.'

She did her grin. 'I know, I know. I couldn't stop myself. You know how it is sometimes . . . the very fact that something is so *obviously* dangerous and a bad idea just makes it all the more irresistible.'

I started to consider this notion, but quickly switched to taking a bite of my sandwich. I wonder who first decided to cut sandwiches diagonally. I bet that at the time, when they first displayed their triangular slices to a stunned world, they were thought of as subversive, shocking and anti-Establishment. There were probably furious editorials in all the papers and, when the initial scandalous platters were carried in, men led their fainting wives from the room amid chaos and uproar. Now, of course, it's a mark of the most twee kind of refinement: they've gone completely mainstream. Just like trousers arriving in respectable society – as an outrageous fashion that referenced the leg-wear of the French revolutionary peasants – to appalled howls, and now being the norm. I bet diagonally cut sandwiches have an outlaw past.

Right: I think all that's distracted me sufficiently from what George said.

'Are you free for the rest of the day, then?' I asked.

'Day . . .' she replied. '. . . and night.'

'The whole night?'

'Yes. Can you get away?'

'Away where?'

'I don't know where, I just meant . . .'

'Oh, right. Away *from* . . .' I didn't say 'Sara'. But even the tacit acknowledgement of her existence blew a kind of sadness over us. Not that I wished that she didn't exist, that she *wasn't* – absolutely not: I loved her. It was simply . . . oh, the *pain*.

How cruel were the sightless stumblings of Fate – how unpitying the heart of Chance to torment us thus! We were sensitive people. I ached with guilt and sorrow not as other men, but deeper and more profoundly. My conscience was in anguish. My soul wept. George and I, alone – our feelings a fire whose flames at once warmed and scorched us: the most wonderful of emotions intertwined inextricably with the worst. My throat swollen with a dizzying melancholy, I leaned across and kissed George's lips. She responded without hesitation and, mouths accepting, we wrapped our arms about each other and lay back on the harsh ground. High above, the sky looked down on our joyous, tragic embrace and sought in pity to hide us for a moment from the spiteful gods.

'It's a pisser,' I said to Sara, pressing my phone harder to one ear and sticking a finger into the other to hear over the noise of the traffic. 'I can't complain, I suppose – Amy has never overlooked any details before. But she missed this one and now I've simply *got* to get my initials on the amended contracts while we've got Georgina's agent off balance.'

'Aye, of course,' she replied. 'You get it sorted out. You've *promised* me that carpet, remember.'

'I'll be back tomorrow afternoon.'

'OK.'

'I'm sorry.'

'It's no big deal, you're only away for a night.'

'Yeah, but I hate that I couldn't warn you. We only realised at the meeting today.'

'Och, relax, Tom. You're off to London for a night – I'll cope. Hell, I'll probably hunt out that old electric toothbrush I had, rent a couple of John Cusack videos and have a scorcher of an evening.'

'Sure – you do that.'

'I was kidding.'

'I know . . . but I'm just saying it'd be fine if you wanted to do that. What with me having to be away for the night like this . . .'

'Tom?'

'Yes?'

'Get a grip . . . Did you have a few lagers with lunch, at all? You know how they make you all . . . odd.' She laughed.

Christ, what a complete bastard I was.

'OK, OK. I'll see you tomorrow,' I said.

'OK.'

'Love you.'

'Well, *obviously*.'

I hung up. I made something of a long-winded performance of doing this very simple thing because I was aware that when I'd said 'Love you', I had – conscious that George was walking next to me and could hear – blushed extensively. It wasn't because I was ashamed of her hearing me say that to my girlfriend as part of setting up the means of being unfaithful to her. (It would have been perfectly understandable if this *had* been the reason – being observed performing that kind of calculated treachery is shameful even if the person watching is in league with you.) Oddly, the reason I'd flushed awkwardly was that it felt mean to tell Sara I loved her within earshot of George. I was concerned and embarrassed about the hurt it might cause *George* to hear me say it to *Sara*. This was complicated. Some people might think that complications like this proved they were an interesting person with an interesting life and relish it. But not me. No, I only wished things could be simple, that I didn't have to carry around the curse of being interesting and exciting. Look at all these people walking past me – *they* were the fortunate ones. If only they knew the anguish of being interesting, they'd thank their lucky stars they were dull people with mundane lives. But they didn't know, of course. They had no idea who walked among them.

Despite what I'd told Sara, we weren't in London, of course. We were in Bathgate. Bathgate is about twenty miles outside Edinburgh and, quite probably, George and I were the only people in the entire history of the British Isles who, when arranging a night of illicit passion, had *ever* settled upon speeding away to Bathgate. But it takes thirty minutes on the train and they run regularly, OK? It's all very well following your heart, but you still have to be practical about some things.

After a little searching around, we found a place to stay (I booked a double room for the night while George kept out of sight). Once I had the key, George and I waited for an opportunity and then sneaked up to the room (in a series of little dashes, eyes scanning each area – like saboteurs infiltrating a building). We made it up the two floors, stormed in – laughing from the tension – slammed the door shut behind us and had the most frantic, hungry and thrashing sex. After this we made ourselves two cups of tea. (Tea-making facilities were provided in all the rooms at no additional cost.)

George sat in bed next to me, blowing thoughtfully into her cup. I stared dreamily across at the television. It was off, but had one of those set-top portable aerials that never quite get any station clearly and which, therefore, no mortal man can help fiddling with in addictive, perpetual hope. During the course of events, my underpants had somehow got draped over this aerial. It was the most curious thing but, from where I was sitting, the arrangement of folds made a near-perfect likeness of the head of Richard Nixon, in profile.

'What shall we do tonight?' asked George.

I looked at her precisely as I imagine Cary Grant would have, had he been asked that question in this situation.

'There's no need to leer,' she said, laughing. 'I think we can assume *that*'s a certainty. I mean what *else* shall we do?'

'What would you like to do?' I asked, silently hoping that her reply was going to include a rubber nurse's uniform in some way.

'Hmm ... I'd like to go out to a pub. Go out to a pub for a drink and then get a kebab on the way back.'

'Right ...' I pondered this unexpectedly exotic request. 'Isn't that a bit risky, though? Being seen out in such a public place together? Rather than just staying here and smearing each other with fruit.'

'Smearing each other with fruit?'

'Or whatever.'

'I see. But anyway, I think we can get away with it. We won't be doing anything in public that's ... you know. So, it won't be risky like that. And I'll keep my hair under my hat – that always seems to be enough to prevent most people recognising me. What's more, if anyone asks, I can say that I just *look* like Georgina Nye: that, "I *know* – people are *always* mistaking me for her." I do that sometimes anyway.'

'Yeah ...' I nodded. It would be quite exciting. A bit like being spies in occupied France – adopting assumed identities, having a cover story. 'I could say you were a prostitute who played on your similarity as a selling point – you know, men hired you so they could pretend they were having sex with Georgina Nye.'

'Yes. Or we could just leave it at saying that I looked like her.'

'Oh, yeah – OK.'

'We'll be normal people tonight, then? Out for a few bevvies and a kebab, eh, lover?'

'Och, aye – Ah wouldna say no, hen.'

'That is *the* worst attempt at a Scottish accent I've ever heard.'

'Yeah, yeah, what the fuck do you know? You live in Chiswick.'

She laughed, then leaned across and bit my ear.

'Ow!'

I put my cup of tea down and began to extract my revenge on her in nibbling ways.

You know, maybe this would all work out fine after all. It felt so wonderful, so natural, here with George. As for Sara, well – she didn't know anything about us, and it wasn't like she and George would be constantly bumping into each other. I could carry on just as before with Sara – which was important to me as I loved her and certainly didn't want to do anything that might jeopardise our relationship – and see George, say, three nights in the week. Everyone would be happy. And people did that kind of thing all the time, didn't they? You're forever reading about some bloke who's died and it's only then that they discover he'd had two wives, in two different parts of the country, for thirty years. I'd got it far easier – as I didn't have to hide Sara from George – and there was less travelling involved too. Christ – it was hard to see a way in which this *couldn't* work. Why did I insist on giving myself such a hard time about it? If I simply accepted the situation, it was fine.

*   *   *

'Can I have . . .' I'd now got to the stage of waving my money in the air as the barman walked past (to somebody else): it wasn't helping a great deal. Barmen do it deliberately. If they can see you're out with a woman, they deliberately pass you over in favour of everyone else, so you look like an ineffectual twat. It's a warped, power thing. I bet there's a correlation between involvement in animal torture and getting a job as a barman. And women are simply unable to respect you if you can't get served at the bar. Oh, sure, some of them will pretend it's not important, or even make a joke about it, but deep down they can never feel the same way about you again. If I didn't get two lagers in within the next minute and a half, George would be looking elsewhere for sexual fulfilment – I'd be a fool to kid myself otherwise.

'Excuse me! Do you think I could get some drinks, *please*?' Shouting at the barman is a hazardous tactic. It's likely to make him respond by not serving you even more flamboyantly, just to re-establish his position in the hierarchy. And you'll get no support from the other punters – quite the opposite: they'll all glare at you and tut, hoping that the barman will see this and favour them. They don't care about justice – it's all politics. If shouting at the barman is high-risk, then shouting at the barman with an English accent in a Scottish pub is positively reckless. Perhaps it was the sheer obviousness of this that helped my cause. The barman peered at me for a moment, concluded that all the evidence pointed to my being some kind of lunatic and – reasoning that his careful torments were wasted on a madman – served me.

I swaggered back to the table carrying the two bottles of lager like a prehistoric hunter returning to his woman bearing an elk on his shoulders.

'Thanks,' said George.

I merely smiled in response.

She lit a cigarette and showed me the packet. I took one, and she offered me the flame of her lighter (allowing me to do that 'steadying her hand' thing: and we all know how hot that makes both of the parties involved). This was great. In a pub, with Georgina Nye, having a fag. Life didn't get much better than that.

'What are you going to do now, then?' I asked.

'Worried I'll start feeling you up under the table again?'

'No, I meant – that would be great, by the way – but I meant, what are you – really fantastic, actually – I meant what are you going to do work-wise? Now the book's done.'

'Oh, right. Well, there's *The Firth*, of course – I think I've got a health scare coming up, which'll be cool – but, long-term, I really want to break into America.'

'Why?'

'Erm. Because it's big.'

'Not as big as China.'

'Who wants to be famous in China?'

'Interesting.' I nodded in a scientific manner.

'What?'

'That it's not just numbers. That it's no good a third of the world knowing who you are, if it's the "wrong" third.'

'Well . . . America's the dream, isn't it? As a teenager I always dreamed about Hollywood – I'm sure everyone does.'

'I dreamed about Madonna.'

'Ha . . . and what do you dream about now?'

'Madonna.'

'My, how you've grown.'

'Oh, we do different things nowadays. Oddly, as we've aged together she's actually become even *more* supple.' I rocked forward at this point, missing the ashtray with my suavely flicked cigarette ash because somebody had barged into the back of me. I turned round, glowering. Behind me was a man with a head as solid, as battered and as misshapen as a champion conker. His bright blue eyes were poorly focused in that way that tells you a person is an idiot, but they were definitely looking right at me. I didn't know why – perhaps he didn't like my accent, or my 'attitude', or the fact I was with a beautiful woman: morons really don't need sturdy reasons to take exception to you. In any case, I flung aside my glower, speedily whipped my view away from him and, by way of a pretext, glanced up at the clock over the bar – pretending to check its time against my wristwatch using these expressions: 'agitated', 'thoughtful', 'annoyed' and, finally, 'resigned'.

'Well, it sounds like you and Madonna are very happy together,' George said as I turned back to face her, 'but I've got an uphill struggle in America. We were over there trying to make some headway – get me a *tiny* part in *something* – but it's brutal.'

'Yeah, I . . .'

'*What* did you just call me?' said the tight, angry little mouth of Conker Head Man. He'd banged his drink down hard on to our table as he rapidly pushed his face to within a quarter of an inch of mine.

I leaned back in my chair to be far enough way so that I could see him without it making me go cross-eyed. 'Pardon?' I said.

'Oh – "*Pardon*",' he replied, putting on a caricature effeminate voice and pursing his lips. '*Pardon*,' he repeated, this time to his two friends, who were standing a little behind him. They all laughed – revealing that, between them, they had enough teeth for a wily dentist to salvage a single mouth. Conker Head Man turned back to me (his companions seemed content merely to stay back, watch and concentrate on lowering the collective IQ of Scotland). 'I *said* . . . What did you just call me?'

'I didn't call you *anything*,' I said. 'I didn't even mention you at all.'

He inclined his head, incredulous. Scarcely able to believe what he had just heard, and anxious to give me every chance to clear up any possible misunderstanding, he said, 'Are you calling me a liar?'

I have no idea why they do this. Whose benefit is it for? Mine? His? Onlookers? Not a single person believes there's been a genuine slight, so why don't they just say, 'I've decided to pick a fight with you. I understand you don't want to fight me, but that's of no consequence: I am resolute in my desire.' No, they always have to go through this moronic ritual. There's never even any attempt to try something new – 'Are you calling into question my ability to process vocal sounds?' or something – always it comes down to 'Are you calling me a liar?' My weary critique of the banality of his performance caused me, instinctively, to roll my eyes, smile and let out a little sigh.

This response broke the tension of the moment – his muscles relaxed and he let out a self-deprecatory chuckle before sitting down with us to share a drink and become, as the years passed, one of my truest and most valued friends.

Wouldn't it be great if you could just stop things at pivotal moments, go home and write what happened next? Actually, of course, he punched me in the throat.

Fortunately, he was a bit obstructed by people around him, and he was crouching, and the angle was awkward, so the blow had very much less power than he could justifiably have hoped for. Despite this, I made a retching sound, grabbed at my neck and spectacularly failed to think, 'Well – that could have been a lot worse.'

'Hey!' George shouted across at Conk. 'Leave him alone!' She started to get up.

'Stay out of this, hen – this is between me and your boyfriend here.' The rest of the people in the pub had gone quiet, watching, and their odd silence made it sound even louder when another voice called out.

'Oi! Stop that right now!' yelled the barman. Phew: the cavalry. 'The pair of you – take it outside.' So, not the cavalry, then: just someone who wanted me to get killed a little farther to the left.

'Come on,' Conk snarled at me. 'You and me. Let's settle this out the front . . . or are you too much of a fucking queer?'

I ought to have said, 'I'm staying right where I am, and phoning the police. Because you're a fuck-witted, juvenile loser with grave self-esteem problems and I couldn't give a shit what you or anyone else in this pub thinks. Moreover, I ridicule the implication that gay men are cowardly and the fact that you reach for such stereotypes shows you are ignorant and prejudiced – possibly it's even a smokescreen produced by the misplaced self-loathing you feel at your own, secret homosexuality.' However, George was there, so I replied, 'Lead the fucking way, mate.'

My reasoning appeared to be, 'I can't let George see I'm afraid. No, it's far better for me and our relationship if instead I let her watch me have the shit kicked out of me.'

George even called, 'Tom – don't . . .' to me, but I waved her protestations aside with a hand. This was a matter of honour: a timeless, male thing. The simple fact was that this tosser had started this – and now he was going to have to damn well learn that I was not the kind of man who was unable to curl up into a ball and whimper while he systematically broke all of my bones and ruptured a few internal organs. I stood up without any signs of hesitation – doing this revealed that he was a good five inches shorter than me. I resist saying that this was 'probably his real problem', lest I too fall into silly stereotyping. But it probably was, right? I felt a small smirk of satisfaction at realising how obvious the causes of his character flaws were, but, well . . . it's odd how quickly you move past every single bit of revelatory gratification that can be squeezed out of the knowledge that you're about to be beaten up by a tiny homosexual.

Conk strode towards the door with his mates and I followed. The other people in the pub parted for us. I moved resolutely: a narrow-eyed, tight-lipped look of determination on my face. Courageously, I hoped I wouldn't start to cry before I got outside – if I could just make it to the fight and get slaughtered, then I'd be in too much of a mess for anyone to notice and it'd be OK.

You'll have picked up, of course, that the idea that I might win here never entered my mind. Conk was shorter than me and also no heavyweight. The trouble was, I'm useless. When I make a fist, I keep having to remind myself to put my thumbs on the outside: *that*'s how useless I am. If I try to kick someone, it's an absolute certainty that I'll miss, and that my shoe will come off. It's impossible for a person to move a hand or an elbow or a head or a knee vaguely towards me in anger without it hitting me on the nose.

But all this, the granite inevitability of my defeat, meant very little: because I couldn't let George see I was afraid of having a fight. That's the reason I was standing outside a pub in Bathgate facing off with a man who'd celebrated every single thought he'd ever had by having it tattooed on to his forearm.

There was about six feet between us. A crowd of people looked on and Conk's two mates growled, 'Gwerrrn – have him,' from behind. We stared at each other menacingly. He moved to the side slightly, as though he might try to outflank me, but I mirrored his movement. That was pretty good, I'd done well there: I must try to recall that move later, after I came to at the hospital. He shuffled a bit more and then started to make a lunge at me. He didn't *actually* lunge at me: he just made the first bit of the movement – feinted an attack, to test me. My reaction was to jump back evasively, bringing up my arms to counter any blows and at the same time bringing every muscle in my body into a state of flexed readiness. Put like that, it sounds OK. In fact, to visualise the effect, try to imagine a set of movements on my part that appeared to be missing only my letting out a high-pitched cry of 'Eek!' A small snigger made its way around the onlookers and Conk's mouth pulled itself into a mocking little smile. I needed to regain the psychological advantage if I were to hold off my inevitable thrashing a little longer.

I decided to spit on the ground.

That's pretty hard, isn't it? Spitting signals you're tough, physical and indefatigable. Athletes spit as they're preparing to throw something. Footballers spit after they've narrowly missed the goal. Seeing that his opponent is the kind of person who enjoys a good spit would surely sow alarm and uncertainty in Conk's mind. So, keeping my eyes fixed on him, I spat off to my side in a sharp, explosive manner. Except that fear had made my lips all rubbery and my spit all viscous. Instead of tearing away to ground like a manly bullet – possibly shattering a section of the pavement on impact – a gooey glob stumbled from my mouth with a 'frrrp' noise, made a clumsy, stringy attempt to break free, and then – defeated by both gravity and its own innate elasticity – fell back on to my shirt. In company with every other person there, I looked down at it. There was only one thing I could do. I reached across with my hand and, very deliberately, wiped it with the heel of my palm – not so much removing it, more smearing it right across my top.

'Yeah,' this silently announced, 'that's right – I spat on *myself*. I *am* Keyser Soze.'

Conk didn't look as if my display had made him newly anxious; it did, however, look as if it had made him utterly bemused. At least it made him pause, though, so that confirmed it as a success as far as I was concerned. Maybe I could buy a little more time by ostentatiously pissing myself – it was certainly an idea to cling on to, given the fact that I might well piss myself anyway.

Just then – as they say in children's books – *just then*, there was a wonderful sound. Cutting through the night came the, blissfully not-too-distant, *'rrRRRrrrrrr'* of a police car flicking its siren on for just a moment as an announcement that it was on its way. I couldn't see it, but the direction the noise was coming from meant it must have been approaching from behind Conk – this was soon confirmed by the people around us peering over there and muttering. The crowd began to break up, Conk blew air through his teeth, and I hissed, 'Fuck,' under my breath (under my breath, very loudly) to convey my disappointment and annoyance. Quickly, Conk changed his whole body language: he went from the tense posture of someone preparing for a fight to the loose, casual manner of 'just a bystander' and he began to saunter towards me – that's to say, away from the approaching police. I remained where I was, putting my hands in my pockets and pretending not to notice him the way spies do when they meet in a park in movies. He strolled past me without saying a word. Though, as he moved by, he did take the opportunity to hit me very hard in the face.

You know how, sometimes, you receive an injury, but it's so abrupt and unexpected that you don't feel anything? Well, this wasn't like that at all. This really, *really* fucking hurt. 'Ergh!' I said, sinking to my knees (and hurting my knees). I pressed my hands to the side of my face, positive that my entire head was broken. After a moment, the initial pain of the impact began to subside and, under it, there was a different, and worse, pain. This one throbbed and squirmed and ran around under my face stinging hot then icy cold then stinging hot again. I clutched harder, trying to somehow press it away. 'Fuck. Fuck. Fuck . . . *Jesus*. Fuck. Fucking *Jesus*. Fuck. Bastard. *Fuck*. Bastard. Bastard . . . Bastard. *Bastard*. Fuck. Fucking . . . *fuck*. Jesus. Fuck-fuck-fuck-fuck-fuck-fuck . . .' I felt a hand on my shoulder.

'Are you all right, sir?' Opening one eye, I looked up at the policeman bending over me.

'Yes, I'm fine, thanks,' I replied.

I should have said, 'No – *he* hit me. Really hard. For no reason,' and pointed at Conk (who hadn't paused and was now nonchalantly strolling off down the street with his mates) but, well, you just don't, do you?

'I see . . . someone called reporting a disturbance here.'

'Really?'

'Aye. Really.'

'Right. Well, I haven't seen anything.'

'Would that be because you were kneeling down on the pavement with your hands over your face, sir?'

There are few things that can quash your swagger more conclusively than a wry Scottish policeman.

'Come on, Jim,' he called wearily to his colleague. 'Let's go inside the pub and check it out.'

At first I thought I was completely alone now, but then I spotted George. She was standing down the road a little; just far enough away so that it looked like she didn't have anything to do with the incident. She hurried over to me.

'God, are you OK?'

'Yeah,' I said, 'it's nothing.'

'I've called a taxi. We could take you to the hospital.'

'No, really, it's fine. I've had much worse than this.'

'Have you?'

'Sure . . . I came off a slide once when I was seven.'

'Right.'

'Needed stitches.'

'I see . . . Has that idiot gone?'

I looked over my shoulder: I couldn't see Conk or his friends anywhere. 'I think so . . . it was lucky the police turned up. I mean, lucky for him.'

'*I* called the police – I was on my mobile before you'd even got out of the door.'

'Oh, right. Well, you saved that twat from the thrashing of his life, then.'

'Getting it or giving it?' She smiled and put her hand on the limited section of my face that I wasn't already holding myself.

223

'I could have taken him.'

'It doesn't matter. He could beat you up a thousand times and you'd still be twice the man he could even *dream* of being . . . He fights because that's *all* he can do.'

'I love you.'

I couldn't have *not* said that at this moment if the fate of the whole human race had depended on my silence. It surged up inside me: even if its irresistible velocity hadn't allowed it to break free, it would have blocked my throat, choking me, until I let it out.

George leaned forward and kissed my sole available eyebrow. 'Saying *that*,' she whispered, 'is always going to attract a girl more than brawling in the street ever will.'

'Good . . .' I smiled and partially released myself for a moment to trace down along the side of her face with my hand. '. . . but, even so, I could have taken him – you do know that, right?'

'Hey – I think this is our taxi.'

She walked over to it as it pulled up, spoke briefly to the driver, then nodded to me and started to get in. I followed. Inside, she laid her head against my shoulder, and the taxi began to take us back to the hotel.

'I could have.'

'I know.'

'No, really – I could have.'

There's something very special about sleeping with a woman. On one level, this is so obvious that it's redundant even to mention it. I mean, if a man's life is dominated by the quest for sex, then waking up to find a bottom pressed to your groin and a pair of tits already in your hands has to be the beau idéal, right? It's like nought to sixty in zero seconds. But that's not what I'm talking about – for a start, my life is far from dominated by hunting for sex: I am, thank you very much, rather more sophisticated and multi-layered than that. I'm referring to how it touches you emotionally. Maybe it's because you're vulnerable when you're asleep. So, by sleeping with you, the woman is showing how completely she trusts you and you, likewise, are showing her the same thing. Maybe that's it. Whatever the reason, it's certainly a surprising truth that sleeping with a woman – without even having sex – somehow feels far more romantic and intimate than hastily fucking her in the alley behind a pub car park. You can get a closeness, in bed together, that's exhilarating without the sexual component being present at all. Which is not to say that George and I didn't have sex when we got back to the hotel – *Christ* no: we went at it like we were both just out of prison – if her tongue had been any more lively I'd have probably suffered friction burns. I'm just pointing out how great it was: we had this whole non-sexual thing there, while at the same time having some really excellent sex. It was perfect. I couldn't have been happier when I woke up next morning lying next to George. I felt like a million dollars. A feeling rather disrupted when I glanced in the bathroom mirror and saw that I looked like £1.75.

My right eye was bloodshot and surrounded by a bruised, many-coloured swelling so fascinatingly alarming that even I, knowing it would hurt me, couldn't help prodding it with an investigative finger. Not attractive. Not attractive at all. I pulled on yesterday's underpants, lit a cigarette that I'd found in the ashtray only two-thirds smoked, and peered in the mirror to give some thought to how I could improve my appearance. George entered, yawning, wrapped in a duvet. Her hair, wild under any circumstances, was here the coiffure equivalent of a terrifying storm sweeping in from the east. It had erratic, swirling currents in its midst, brawling tangles and violent projections like clouds of burning, boiling gas arcing out from a black sun. It was the kind of hair that comes into the bathroom of a morning and *immediately* makes you want to frantically shag its owner while she bends over, supporting herself with arms outstretched against the sink, her groans affected by breathy bursts due to each urgent thrust. I was thinking about the best way to phrase this idea as something we might consider doing, but George spoke first and the word she used was 'Ewww . . .' She was looking at my eye and flinching with sympathetic pain. She moved closer and prodded it with her finger. 'Does it hurt?'

I sucked in air between my teeth as her poke hit and backed away across the bathroom. 'No. It's fine. It looks worse than it is.' She tried to have another prod. I backed away farther.

'I could probably cover the bruise up a little – I've got some foundation in my handbag,' she offered.

'It doesn't matter. It's not like I have a photo-shoot to go to or anything.'

'What will you tell people?'

By people, we both knew she meant Sara. 'Oh, I don't know . . . I'll probably just say someone hit me. There's no point lying about stuff you don't have to, is there? It's perfectly possible for me to get punched in the face without *you* having to be there – ask anyone.'

'Right,' she nodded. 'Well, I'm going to have a shower . . .' She pulled off the duvet and hurled it out of the bathroom. Christ, she was gorgeous. And not just gorgeous, either, but also naked. As she leaned over to turn on the shower I moved behind her and started to kiss her neck.

'Oh, Tom . . . *don't*,' she said, giggling. 'I've just crawled out of bed – I stink.'

'I don't care *how* much you stink,' I whispered, and began running my tongue slowly down her spine. I stopped halfway and straightened up again. 'What I *meant* to say there was "No – you don't stink at all", OK?'

'Yeah, that's what I thought. Still – thanks for saying it eventually.'

I moved my lips over her shoulders. 'You don't . . . stink . . . at all.'

'Mmmm . . . a girl just likes to be told that sometimes, you know?'

She reached her hands behind her back to touch me.

VI

You know what I was thinking about back there? Back when Tom was having that problem with the punk outside the bar? Well, I've got to come clean again here, and tell you that back then I remembered that I cut a few corners, you know, 'physiology-wise'. You see, I didn't really think to put enough space between the cues for 'love' and the cues for 'fear'. I just kind of figured it'd be clear from the context – I mean, why wouldn't I, right? Then I hear that some of your scientists have done this experiment and discovered that, because of the chemicals released, people who experience fear on a first date often 'misinterpret' it as love. Was my face red when I heard that, eh? I simply can't tell you.

Yeah, well – it was just a thought I was having. Never mind.

There is another thing, though. I suppose I should have mentioned this earlier, when I was dropping all the science on you and telling you the names of stuff. But, well, I lost my nerve, you know? One reason I lost it is that this word's no sweetheart to say, I can tell you. Here goes . . . 'phenylethylamine'. What did I tell you, eh? Even your own scientists shorten it to 'PEA' – so as they don't keep screwing up when they try to say it and making an ass of themselves during, I don't know, seminars or whatever. But, I got to admit, the length of it wasn't the only thing that stopped me. Fact is, I'm a bit guilty about it. PEA, you see, is a dirty trick. Sure – like I've told you – I was worried you wouldn't get yourselves together, and that things would fizzle out 'cause of it, but PEA . . . well. OK, I'm just going to say it straight out: PEA kicks in when you're attracted to someone, and here's what it does – it stops you seeing their faults. PEA is, like, your actual rose-tinted glasses. That's bad enough, right? But then . . . Sorry. OK. The length of time varies – it can be years – but after a while . . . it stops working.

Yeah, I know.

I'm not sure I'd have had the guts to tell you this if your scientists hadn't uncovered that bit of evidence already. A dirty trick, like I say. Worse still – a dirty trick, badly done.

Let's just say, I owe you one.

TEN

I paid for a second night, just so we didn't have to check out at eleven and could stay in the hotel room together all day. Later, I popped out briefly and returned with some clean underwear, a couple of toothbrushes, a big bag of scampi and chips and some more cigarettes. Fried food, cigarettes and George: if I wanted for anything at all, it was only a few more hands and an additional mouth. In the afternoon, when we eventually began getting ready to leave, there was that sadness you feel when packing up on the last day of a wonderful holiday. I found myself looking around at things – the view from the window; the shower curtain; the hotel kettle – just to try and seal them under glass for ever in my memory. George and I talked less, and missed no opportunity to share a sorrowful smile. When we got on the train back to Edinburgh, we held hands under the seat. It was as though our souls were intertwined and yet ached that they couldn't melt together entirely.

I sighed with a kind of melancholy joy and slid the catch closed. 'So, have you ever shagged in a train lavatory before?' I asked.

George had suggested it, hissed the idea coquettishly into my ear, and it'd seemed ungentlemanly to appear less than wholeheartedly in favour of giving it a go. But I was concerned that it might lack magic – you generally stay in a train toilet only for as long as you can hold your breath, don't you? All the art and music and literature that humanity has produced through the ages has a devil of a job trying to hold its side of the scales against one glance into a train toilet: if you ever find someone waiting outside as you exit, you're always distraught and have to fight determinedly against the powerful urge to grip them by the shoulders and cry, 'You see all that? That *wasn't me*, OK?' In fact, when we sneaked in together and it turned out that *this* train toilet – alone in the United Kingdom – neither smelled like an open sewer in high summer nor had horrific vileness smeared across every surface, I took it as another sure sign that George and I were being carried along by the miraculous, cradling arms of Destiny.

'No, I haven't,' replied George. 'Have you?'

'Never.'

'Ohhh,' she cooed. 'A first for both of us.'

I did have another concern beyond simply the setting, though. The thing was, I'd had sex quite a few times in the past twenty-four hours. There was some soreness, quite honestly, but even more important than that was . . . Look, let's be honest: it's not a bottomless well, is it? I mean, things get topped up, but it takes time. I wasn't entirely sure I had anything left. What happens if you don't have anything left? I had no idea. Is it like when you have a dry cough? Do you come but, I don't know, it's just air? 'Ffff.' Would George notice? I could fake an orgasm, of course (despite women thinking that this is exclusively *their* party piece, most men have done it at one time or another), but I didn't think I'd be very convincing. I'd be too self-conscious with George. It'd sound like I was reading an orgasm off an autocue. On the other hand, if I *was* up to delivering the goods – production rising to meet demand – would that alter my physiological set-up generally? The way that washing your hair more frequently increases the amount of grease your scalp puts out, say. Would my body expect every day to be like this one now? I imagined the vast overproduction mounting up . . . I pictured a television screen showing a news flash warning that, while out shopping, my testicles had exploded and destroyed two city blocks.

OK. So I was possibly being a little pessimistic – or optimistic – but, still, it was a bit of a worry.

George pulled down her knickers and hitched her skirt up over her hips. I made a snap decision to have sex with her and just hope for the best. You have to follow your instincts sometimes, don't you?

We banged into *everything*. Whoever it was who designed train toilets, they clearly didn't put much thought into the amount of shagging that'd take place in them. With every movement a part of my body knocked into some fixture – directly behind me, pretty much at arse level, was the long, thin, projecting metal tube of the hot-water dispenser: I feared it more than death itself.

'So – you've never – done – this – with – Sara?' George asked, pausing briefly between words as the back of her head banged against the wall. I lost my footing for a second and fell sideways against the button that flushes the toilet – it opened a path directly down to the tracks whipping past only inches below us and the room was filled with a rushing 'Whshhhhhhhhh!' until I lifted my weight off it again.

'Sara!' I half laughed, half shouted, on my first returning thrust. 'No! But forget Sara. When I'm with you, George, you're all I can think about. I'm not thinking about *not* fucking Sara now, I'm thinking about fucking *you*.'

'Then fuck me harder.'

'Fuck you?' I grinned.

'Yes, *fuck me*.'

Have you ever noticed that women most often say the words 'fuck me' when you're already fucking them? They don't ask you to fuck them when – at a party, say, apropos of nothing – you *dearly* wish they would: but then when you *are* fucking them for all you're worth they imply that they can't really tell you've started. It's one vast landscape of pain being a man, it really is.

We stuck to our task tenaciously and, after a little while – with a simply delightful groan – George came. More impressively, so did I: I, quite literally, didn't think I had it in me.

Breathless, we began to slowly pull up and button things: happy, satisfied and, quite honestly, not a little damn proud of ourselves.

'That was good,' beamed George.

'Yeah . . . It needed to be, though – it has to last for . . . for how long? When will I be able to see you again?'

'Hmm . . . I'm not sure. When's good for you? When can you get away from Sara again?'

'Oh, Christ, I can get away from Sara *any time*. You just say when you're free next – as soon as possible, of course – and I'll be there.'

'Well, I've got to go down to . . . What was that?'

'What was what?'

'Shhh . . .' She listened. 'A beep. You beeped.'

'*I* beeped. What do you mean?' I laughed. '*I* don't . . .' I stopped laughing. I scrambled wildly at the holder on the side of my trousers and tore out my mobile phone. It was in the middle of making a call. (I'd set it to beep periodically when in use – to indicate the amount of time I'd been talking.) It was connected, it had beeped, and the display said, 'Sara.' I tentatively raised it to my ear as one might lean to listen to the ticking of a bomb. There was no sound from the other end, but it was definitely making a call.

I stabbed at the button to hang up and looked at my watch.

'What is it?' asked George, anxiously.

'Sara.'

'Sara was on the phone?' she gasped. 'What? Did she ring or . . .'

'No, no, *I* called *her*.'

'How? Speed-dial or something?'

'Maybe. That or voice: I've programmed it to dial certain people if you say their name – you only have to press a single button. If it got banged while we were . . . you know, and then one of us said her name loud enough for it to be picked up, it'd just dial automatically.'

'Jesus.'

'Fucking phones,' I spat. 'Fucking *stupid* fucking mobile fucking phones.'

'So Sara will have heard . . .'

'No, it rang her mobile. She always has it switched off when she's at work.'

'Phew.' She flopped back against the wall, relieved.

'Not bastard "phew", I'm afraid. The call would just go straight to her voicemail. As soon as she finishes work she'll turn on her phone. It'll say, "New Message," and then she'll be treated to a recording of us fucking.'

'Will she know it's us? Did we say anything?'

'I can't remember. She'll know it's from my phone, though, and I bet she'll know it's fucking. Fucking is kind of distinctive, isn't it?'

'Yes . . . and I think we *did* say some things anyway.'

'Yes . . . I think we did . . .' I went cold. My limbs were numb and thousands of thoughts swirled in my head. I couldn't hold on to any of them, though, because, before I could examine one fully, another, even more terrible one would knock it from my hand and take its place.

George chewed her lip. 'When does she finish work?' she asked.

'Five-thirty. We have . . .' I looked at my watch again. '. . . forty-nine minutes until she switches on her phone.'

VII

So, what I want to talk about here is . . . What? No, look, it doesn't really matter about the specifics of Tom and George and Sara – how many times do I have to tell you that? They're only, you know, an illustration of the general principle, right? Sara's just one woman, in Scotland, at one moment in time: her hearing that recording on her cell phone isn't an issue we're concerned with. No, I'm here to tell you . . . What? Hey – don't look at me like that . . . What? Oh, for . . . OK, OK, I'll come back later, then. Really – the phrase 'the bigger picture' just means *nothing* to you people, does it?

ELEVEN

'When do we get into Edinburgh?' asked George.

'The train's supposed to arrive there at four fifty-two, but it'll be late.'

'How do you know?'

'Because it's a fucking *train*,' I replied. George's expression told me I could have said this less ill-temperedly. 'Sorry . . . I'm sorry. I'm just . . .' I kissed her cheek and hugged her. I hugged her incredibly tightly. As though, if I could just hold her hard enough, just keep us close enough together, then somehow I'd be safe. We'd be fused together: an entity of Us that was irreducible and also somehow apart from the rest of the world. Isolated. Protected.

'I can't breathe,' she said.

'I know,' I admitted, 'me neither. It's like a clenched fist in my . . .'

'No – I can't breathe: you're crushing me.'

'Oh, right . . .' I let go and stood back half a pace. 'Sorry.'

'So, what if the train *does* get in on time? Could you get to her shop before she finishes work?'

'Um . . . I don't know. Yes. From the station, in thirty-eight minutes, I might just about be able to get there on foot. If I got a taxi, I'd arrive with quite a bit of time to spare . . . But the problem is *all* that depends on the train getting in on time and my being able to get a taxi, at that time of day, during the Festival.'

'Then we'll be OK.'

'How do you know that?'

'Because it's best to think that way. "Positive Visualisation", my therapist calls it. OK – it's supposed to be more to do with personal interactions . . .'

'Maybe you should call your therapist and ask what visualisation works for trains.'

'*This* will work. It's, um, holistic or something. Our personal energy affects the physical world. If you believe things will be OK, then they will be.'

'They probably won't.'

'They *will* . . . and, even if they aren't, at least you're in better shape, mentally.'

'I believe you should always assume the worst will happen. Because the worst certainly will happen, and then you'll be prepared for it.'

'That's very negative, Tom.'

'Just realistic.'

'Hmm . . . shall we get out of this lavatory?'

'Hold on.'

'What?'

'Just give me a second. It's a big step.'

'What is?'

'Leaving this lavatory. The real world's out there, waiting. Leaving this lavatory is a big step, psychologically.'

'OK.'

I took a deep breath and slowly exhaled.

'Ready?' asked George.

'I . . . No, just give me another second.' I breathed in and out slowly again. 'Right – let's go for it.'

We returned to our seats and hell really set in. I looked at my watch – 4.43. I now had forty-six minutes to get to Sara. Every twenty seconds or so I looked at my watch again, and cursed. The feeling of utter powerlessness, of being trapped in a moving prison, was overwhelming. I knocked my knuckles rapidly on the table top just to have something physical to do, some outlet. Forty-two minutes. Jesus – the time was streaming away like blood from a cut artery. I flattened my face against the window, trying to peer forward to see whether the station was just up ahead, moments away. It wasn't, of course. I tried to pick out some landmark that would tell me, at least, that we were close to it being close. What I was looking for was hope. What I saw was railway embankments. Then the misery moved up another gear entirely – thirty-eight minutes left: we should have been at the station now. Whereas before the desperation had to some extent been for us to hurry up – to give me as much time as possible – now I was watching as any chance of succeeding died before my eyes, second by second. Each tick was a knife in my stomach. Thirty-seven minutes. *Jesus.*

Then, a sliver of light: the PA tone sounded, followed by the driver announcing that we'd be arriving in Edinburgh at any moment. I jumped to my feet and shouted at the nearest loudspeaker.

'About time, you cunt!'

Fortunately – it being both in Britain and on a train – all the other passengers pretended to have completely not noticed my doing this.

I ran to the door. George, looking anxious, followed discreetly behind me. Well, to be honest, she could have been squealing like a pig and she'd still have looked discreet compared to the state I was in. I waited, *furious* with impatience, but it was still well over another minute until we pulled into Edinburgh. And the '. . . doors will remain locked until the train has come completely to a standstill', apparently – if I ever find out which prissy twat on some safety committee came up with *that* one, I'll punch the bastard.

Finally, the train stopped and I was out through the door on to the platform. I raced towards the taxi rank, looking at my watch as I ran: thirty-four minutes. People. In my way. Fuck *off*.

No taxis. Can you *believe* it? Edinburgh, capital of fucking

Scotland, and there're no fucking taxis. What's the point of giving a parliament to a place that can't even sort out *having enough fucking taxis? EH?*

I turned to George. I indicated the area – its taxi-free quality. I made claws of my hands and shook them. 'Fuuuuuuuck!' I said. Everything in the world was against me. Everything. That Doritos bag skidding along the pavement in the breeze, this road, this railway station, Edinburgh, Britain, the Earth, the whole bleeding universe – all of it arranged entirely and solely to fuck me.

'There could be one along at any second,' said George.

'Yes. Or not for another ten minutes – and look . . .' I pointed up at the road. 'The traffic's nose to tail up there. It's not even *moving*. Even if a taxi got here *right now*, I'd never make it across town in time.'

George stuck her thumbnail in between her teeth and gnawed at it anxiously. She glanced up at the road, then back down towards the platforms . . . and then she ran away.

I didn't feel any bitterness as she flew past me – I mean, I couldn't help but see her point. She sped by my ear, and my only thought was, 'Yeah – fair enough.'

I looked over my shoulder at her racing away – God, she was fast. I thought of the first time I'd met her: that very first day when her fitness-programmed legs had been chased by my sometimes-take-the-stairs-just-to-look-virile ones; holding off collapse by nothing but sheer determination to get the book commission. I had no will to follow her now, though – no will to do anything, in fact. I watched her sprint off in the same way as you hear people who claim to have had out-of-body experiences say that they disinterestedly watched the doctors trying to resuscitate their lifeless bodies.

But then she came to a halt in front of someone. She hadn't been running randomly, but had been running over to a particular person. He'd obviously also recently got off a train and – as is not uncommon (Edinburgh seems to attract this type) – he was pushing a bicycle. George was talking to him with great speed and many arm movements. He was looking . . . well, he was looking for the closest exit, quite frankly. I jogged over to them.

'*Please*. Honestly,' George was saying, the words scrambling from her mouth in a jostling stampede. '*Twice* whatever you paid for it. There's bound to be a bike shop in the town. You can get yourself another bike in no time, and still have money left over.'

'Erm . . . Well . . .' replied the man, his eyes searching the station for help.

I pulled at my watch. Thirty-one minutes.

'Look . . .' I began.

'You two are working together?' the man cut in, nervously. The phrase 'working together' beautifully indicating his assessment of the situation.

'We're not work . . . Never mind. *I'll* pay you twice what you paid for it *as well*, OK? That means you'll get four times what it's worth. You give me the bike, I'll leave my cashpoint card – there's a bank just up there – and the two of you can . . .'

'So . . .' The man nodded. 'You don't have the cash? You want me to give you my bike, and *then*, after you've gone . . .'

'Well, *of course* I don't have the cash. I don't carry that much cash around with me – who the hell does? Do *you*?'

'I . . . No: I have no cash on me *whatsoever*. None,' he replied, his voice trembling slightly.

'This is an emergency,' George pleaded. 'Just trust us and . . .'

'Sorry . . .' He began to move away. 'I . . .'

George ran into his path. She pulled off her hat and sunglasses and (subtly, so it wasn't a jarring transformation but just the kind of thing that'd make you think, '. . . and, when I *listened* . . .') turned up the Scottishness of her voice so it was closer to her accent in *The Firth*.

The man stopped dead, just as though he'd hit an invisible barrier. At the same time he changed – *physically changed*: his body posture softened – the stiffness evaporated and his shoulders loosened – while amazed eyes and a broad smile washed the fear and tension from his face.

'Hey!' he said, pointing. 'You're her off the telly, aren't you?'

George lowered her eyes and shyly shrugged an acknowledgement – tricky one to pull off, this, when you've hurled yourself directly in front of someone and practically gone, 'Ta-ra!' but somehow she managed to do it.

'Yes,' I said. I took a step closer and put my arm around the man's shoulders. I glanced around with quite operatically exaggerated stealth and spoke in a conspiratorial whisper. 'Georgina Nye is staying here in Edinburgh – I'm her personal assistant – and it is *vitally* important that I meet someone about business in . . . *Jesus!* . . . sorry. In twenty-nine minutes.'

'What kind of business?' asked the man. Also in a whisper. Also looking around anxiously for eavesdroppers.

I stared right into his eyes and paused for a beat, before replying, 'Television business.'

He looked back at me and – wordlessly – nodded that he understood.

'OK,' I said, 'if I can have your bike, George will go with you to the cashpoint right now and give you the money.'

He waved his hands and looked almost affronted by the suggestion. 'Oh, there's no hurry – you don't have to give me the money right *now*. I mean, if you have other things you need to do first, then . . .'

George had crammed her hair back into her hat and replaced her glasses. She moved me out of the way so that she could stand next to the man and thread her arm through his. 'No, no, I *insist* we go to the cashpoint together right away,' she said, smiling.

'OK,' the man replied, grinning so much it forced his eyes into nothing but tiny dashes. He began to remove the bags from the back of his bicycle, making it more difficult for himself because rather than looking at the fastenings he preferred to keep his eyes fixed on George. 'My sister *loves* you,' he said. 'She's never going to believe that you've bought my bike.'

I pulled my cash card out of my wallet and started to offer it to George, but she waved it away. 'I'll pay the whole lot – Gavin,' she said to me, loudly. Then, with a giggle, added to the man, 'I'll take it all out of his salary.' The man *bellowed* with laughter, this being the funniest thing *he had ever heard*.

I moved in and began helping him to get his bags off the bike. Fortunately for him, I didn't have a knife on me or they'd have been off in three seconds. After a two-figure number of eternities, everything was finally free and I threw myself on to the bicycle. A solemn look at my wristwatch smashed 'twenty-seven minutes' into my face. I glanced over at George. She was looking at me, tense beneath the apparently affable surface. I opened my mouth to say something memorably intrepid – it was clearly a Bruce Willis moment – but I couldn't think of anything so I just sat there for a couple of seconds with my jaw hanging down, and then started cycling as fast as I could.

I had three enemies. One, obviously, was time. The second, related, was distance: while it was, I had no doubt, possible to cycle flat out to Sara's work, whether it was possible for *me* to cycle flat out to Sara's work was another matter. My legs were already beginning to feel the strain, and I hadn't even got out of the service road down to the railway station yet. The final enemy was despair, and this one was the most subtle and the most dangerous of them all. Part of my brain was telling me that I couldn't possibly make it, so why additionally torture myself physically? This part of my brain was concerned for my heart, sympathetic to the increasing pain in my legs and, basically, just wanted what was best for me. I liked this part of my brain. Not only were its arguments compelling, but I also felt real affection there. Against it was a screeching, pitiless bastard of an inner voice that was telling me that I *could* get there in time if I just *pedalled harder*. I despised this voice utterly. It was haranguing and sadistic and also, I felt, anti-intellectual. Fascistic, practically: I really ought to ignore it simply on principle. Yet I had to put these personal feelings aside and somehow keep going. It's amazing how alluring despair is sometimes: how it almost brings tears to your eyes to resist surrendering yourself to the relaxing ecstasy of it.

This bicycle was *so* not the fucking 'Positive Visualisation Express'.

After cycling at top speed for something over an hour and a half, I snatched a look at my watch and was simultaneously encouraged and devastated to see I'd been cycling for eight minutes.

There's a muscle that runs down the top of your leg – the quadriceps femoris – and this muscle has a very special characteristic. If you cycle for, say, something over eight minutes then this muscle will absorb into itself all the distilled human misery of the world. That's 'the distilled human misery of the world,' then, 'in the top section of your leg.' It appears that, where any other muscle would simply cease to function, the quadriceps femoris can keep on going, hurting more and more and more. Yes, it becomes weak and rubbery, but it never *quite* gives up entirely: if you apply enough will, it seems it can always be made to push down one more, agonising, time. Interestingly, the quadriceps femoris is the same muscle that will lose *just* enough strength to ensure that, on the third day of a skiing holiday, the hospital has a nice selection of horrific injuries caused by people not quite making that turn. The quadriceps femoris is the Judas in your leg.

I wasn't going to make it. I had twelve minutes until Sara finished work, switched on her phone and heard me fucking George in the lavatory of the 16.23 from Bathgate to Edinburgh, and I *wasn't going to make it*.

I redoubled my efforts. I can declare with absolute confidence that no one whatsoever who happened to be watching me at this moment said, 'Ah, *there*'s a man who's redoubled his efforts.' It would have been quicker if I'd simply got off the bike, lain down, and allowed a group of small boys to kick my body along the pavement. Quicker, and less painful too. I could taste my ragged lungs in my mouth. My legs were simply sacks filled with some kind of dense, liquid metal. I was clinging, sopping, sagging wet with sweat. It was as though someone had filled a bath with sweat, and I'd fallen into it fully clothed. Where the wind hit my exposed wet skin there was a sensation of fierce chilling, but it was superficial: an icy sheen that stung the surface but didn't reduce my core temperature in any way at all.

I had four minutes left and was no longer checking time remaining against distance remaining and calculating a hope score. It now seemed so impossible I'd get there in time that to analyse it mentally just battered my will to keep going.

At the bottom of a steep hill was the road that eventually led to Sara's work. I turned into it: which would have been lovely, had the bike turned into it too. Instead, its front tyre lost its grip on the tarmac and fled into the air, rearing up like a bucking horse. The bike and I parted ways and it gambolled untidily into a lamp-post while I skidded across the surface of the road on a knee and an elbow. When I scraped finally to a halt, on all fours, I looked up into the face of a dog. Higher up, its owner – an old man with thin white hair – peered down at me with concern and asked, 'Are you all right?' I cupped my hands towards him, pleading.

'Why can't I just *die?*' I asked.

He shrugged.

I grunted to my feet and limped over to where the bicycle had landed. The front mudguard was twisted into the wheel, but I twisted it out again and it seemed that otherwise it was fine. So, I got back on and started to pedal off once more. I had two minutes. It simply wasn't possible to get there in two minutes.

Yet it's funny how the body reacts in times of extreme crisis. You know – like those stories you hear about women lifting a car off their children? There seems to be an override switch on what's physically possible: enough stress and it gets flipped, and you become superhuman. Something like this happened to me, and I pedalled like you simply would not believe. My legs spun, whipping the chain around at hissing speed and sending the bike rocketing along the road. It seemed I had more power than ever before and an infinite supply of energy. Miraculously – with just *three seconds* to go before my time was up – I glanced up and realised that I was nowhere near Sara's work. Absolutely *nowhere* bleeding near it. I was, though, a lot closer than one would have guessed I'd be. I continued to pedal – knowing that I was, at least, within two minutes of getting there. Two minutes later, I revised this assessment. But, three minutes after that, I rounded a corner and could actually see her shop. I gritted my teeth and pumped my legs with every last iota of determination left in my body. Five yards from pulling up alongside the double doors at the front I jerked on the brakes and, the instant I was travelling slowly enough, jumped off the bike and ran – allowing the riderless bicycle to skid off into the wall in front of a newsagent's with a fatal-sounding, clattering crash. It had served its purpose now: bravely given its all to get me there. I hoped I never saw the hateful pile of crap ever again.

I ran the final couple of yards to PolarCity and was, *at last*, standing in front of its glass doors. The sign on it read 'Closed', but Susan – Sara's colleague, whose children I'd come close to traumatising with nudity a few months previously – was just the other side, looking down at a set of keys. I banged frantically on the glass with the flat of my hands and shouted, 'Susan!' She looked up, caught sight of me and all the blood in her face instantly fled the country. To steady her nerves, I bellowed, 'LET ME IN!' and banged on the glass again. She took a step backwards into a promotional display of Cinnamon fucking Grahams, but then she seemed to become aware that, under the injuries, sweat and filth, it was me. This realisation, I have to say, failed to tempt the blood back into her face. She did, however, come over to the door and, after a bit of scrambling with the keys, let me in.

'Tom!' she said. 'Fuck!'

'Where's Sara?' I asked, but I'd spotted her before she answered.

'She's checking a till – we had a . . .'

'Thanks,' I said, heading over to where Sara was standing with a couple of other members of staff and a plump, middle-aged man who was obviously a customer.

'What's happened?' Susan called from behind me, but I didn't bother to answer. I carried on towards Sara. She and the others had heard the commotion of my entry and were now standing motionless, watching my approach. It only took a moment for me to reach them. Sara looked bewildered, her colleagues stunned and the shopper terrified out of his wits (I think he suspected I was the deformed, maniac member of staff they kept in the attic to unleash after-hours on customers who disputed their change). I came to an unsteady halt.

'Can I use your toilet?' I asked.

Sara took a step closer, her eyes racing all over me in alarm. 'Tom – what's happened?'

'Oh, nothing, I'm fine. I've just got back.'

'From London?'

'From London? I mean, yeah – from London, and . . .'

'Jesus – did you *run* all the way?'

'No, I . . .

'God, look at your eye . . .' She reached forward and poked the bruise with her finger. (Why does everyone feel they have to do that?)

'Ow!'

'Sorry,' she said, but looked like she might try for another poke. I backed away a little. 'Sorry,' she said again. 'How did you get that?'

Knowing she was going to ask this question, I'd given it a little thought, as it happens. 'I fell' was uncomplicated enough, but it's what people always say when they're lying about an injury, isn't it? I had no reason to believe that Sara would be suspicious, but this explanation's 'the dog ate my homework' quality seemed to me to invite mistrust. As I'd said to George, it was best to stick to the facts as far as possible and say that someone had hit me – I'd merely change the location. Thinking about it some more, though, I realised I'd forgotten to factor Sara's response into the equation. For example, I'd toyed with 'I was hit by a tramp'. London, as everyone knows, is full of tramps, and telling a Scot that you'd gone to London for the day and been punched in the face, spontaneously, for no reason, by a tramp would be easy to sell. The trouble with this idea, however, was that Sara was unlikely to let it lie. Falling over is simple idiocy; being punched by a tramp is an anecdote. She'd want to know where it happened, what I'd been doing there, if anyone else was around, and, if so, did they help? What did he look like? Did he try to steal anything? Was he on his own? Had I reported it to the police? I'd have to invent a whole narrative – possibly some supporting characters too – and I'd then have to remember it all correctly every time Sara asked me to repeat it to people. (Which she would do – I had no trouble whatsoever hearing Sara saying the words 'Tom – tell Carole about how that tramp beat you up in London'.) These two options – fall or tramp – were still competing for supremacy right up to the time Sara asked, 'How did you get that?' But now she *had* asked it and was standing in front of me waiting for an answer I couldn't dither any longer. She was staring at me. Come on, Tom – you have to reply now.

'I fell over a tramp.'

Bollocks.

'*What?*'

'I fell . . . Look, I'll explain later – can I just use your toilets first?'

She wanted to continue with me, but glanced awkwardly back at the group waiting and watching by the till. 'Aye,' she exhaled. 'Of course . . . you know where they are.'

I scurried off. I did indeed know where they were. They were in the staff area: which was beyond the office and just off the cloakroom, *where everyone left their coats and bags.*

It took me only seconds to get to the cloakroom and locate Sara's coat. About a dozen staff worked at the store and they were a pretty close-knit lot: no one had any misgivings about leaving their things unattended in the staff area. In Sara's pockets, freely accessible to me, were her car keys, her purse and her mobile phone.

Her mobile phone was in my hand!

I'd done it!

Now what?!

Briefly, I thought about smashing it on the floor. Hurling it down with all my strength so it shattered into a thousand pieces. I'd then search through them until I found the SIM card, which I'd eat. I didn't rule this option out, but I did decide that it wouldn't be easy to explain. Easier to explain than a voicemail recording in which George and I spoke in candid fashion to the accompaniment of gasps, grunts and slapping flesh – yes – so, as I say, I didn't rule it out, but I owed it to myself to try simply deleting the message first.

I switched the mobile on. It awoke with a soft glow and,

it seemed to me, the most piercing, deafening electronic trill ever emitted by anything – it was like a two-second rave. 'Shut *uuuup!*' I hissed at it – shaking it in my hand and pointing threateningly at the hard, hard floor, just so it knew I meant business. Sara's mobile – like every mobile in the world except mine – was difficult and confusing to operate. It had some kind of impenetrable menu system that was full of illogically ordered, pointless things I didn't want and moved the wrong way when I tried to scroll through it. I was in far too much of a hurry to give it more than a few seconds of my time. Instead, I decided to try the button marked with those three arcs of increasing size that are the international symbol for 'noise'. I guessed this was probably a quick-access key for her voicemail. Though, with this bleeding phone, I didn't entirely dismiss the possibility that it would instead activate a shrieking, teeth-shatteringly loud, personal attack alarm. I took a breath and pressed it. The phone dialled and after a single ring the call was answered by a slightly posh, vaguely erotic, electronic voice. This high-class robot call-girl welcomed me to my voicemail and said I had one new message which, unprompted, the phone then began to play. Jesus. *Jeeee*sus. If Sara had heard this . . . *Jeee*sus. I stabbed at the '2' key to delete it. This had no effect. Can you believe that? After scientists have worked for *years* to establish that the '2' key is the delete key, after everyone in the world has accepted that this is the most efficient, elegant and instinctive key and have adopted it as a standard as universally accepted as mayday or Greenwich Mean Time, after all this the spiteful, surreal, anarchist network Sara was on had decided it should be something else. Unbelievable.

I heard Sara's voice. She'd come into the staffroom one had to pass through to get to where I was. Quickly, I darted off into the toilet – just a tiny room with a single lavatory and a sink – sat down and locked the door. My fingers hadn't yet let go of the bolt when I head Sara calling me from out in the cloakroom. 'Tom . . . ?' Then, again, 'Tom, are you OK?' Her voice now so close that I could tell she was *right* outside my door – probably almost pressing her ear to it to listen. Even though the locked door was there, she was only inches away from me. It was awfully uncomfortable for me to feel her there when the phone pressed to my head was replaying George and me having sex. I had to tell myself over and over that it was impossible for Sara to hear it.

'Yeah, I'm fine – I'll be out in second,' I called back. Meaning I'd be out when this damn recording ended and the electric bint told me what the bloody delete key was. I thought about pressing all the keys in turn, but it was too risky. What if I pressed one and it said, 'Message saved. Goodbye'? I'd have to start all over again. And anyway, knowing this insistently grisly network, it'd probably say, 'Message saved, and additionally sent to local radio station. Goodbye.' I'd just have to stick with it.

'Are you sure?' Sara asked, unconvinced.

'Yes. I was just really desperate for the toilet.'

'Right . . . So when did you . . .' There were footsteps and I could tell by her voice – the way its tone changed and the way she spoke louder, calling back across to me – that she was moving away from the door. She'd be going to put on her coat. She'd put on her coat and right away reach into the pocket to turn her phone on – she'd do it instinctively, I knew she would.

'Sara,' I called, 'stay here.'

I heard her footsteps return. 'What? What is it? Are you sure you're OK?'

'Yes, I just . . . missed you,' I said, while I continued to fuck George in my ear. Christ – why didn't I hurry up and come? What was I trying to prove?

'What?'

'I missed you. It's nice to be back and have you here with me.'

'While you're on the lavatory?'

'. . . Yes.' Idiot. Quick – say something to distract her, something she won't be able to resist. 'So – how was your day?'

'Oh, you know . . . a wee problem with a customer *right* at the end – it's always *right* at the end. I had to check the till . . .' Footsteps, change of tone – she was heading for her coat again. '. . . but it was . . .'

'Sara – stay there! I'll be finished in a second.'

'And I need to be right outside the door for that, do I? Is there going to be a big finale?'

'No . . . I just . . .' Sweet dancing Jesus – *at last*: the message finished. Robo-Hooker informed me that to erase the message I needed to press '7'. ('7'. '7'! Can you *believe* that? Who the hell uses '7' as the delete key? This network was clearly controlled by some kind of demonic cult.) I did this and was rewarded with the wonderful, wonderful confirmation, 'Message deleted'. What a truly beautiful pair of words. I flushed the toilet, for credibility. 'I'm coming out now . . .' I shouted to Sara: I was completely unable to keep a joyous, euphoric colour out of my voice.

'No, wait a second,' she shouted back, 'the press aren't quite ready . . .'

Keeping the phone behind my back, I opened the door, leapt out and kissed Sara full on the mouth before she could say anything. I used this manoeuvre to circle around, while keeping my back to her, and move on over to her coat. In an easy movement, I took it down from the peg, slipped her mobile back into the pocket and held it out for her to put on. Smooth, flawless and innocuous. Well, apart from the fact that I'd never held out Sara's coat for her to put on before in all the time we'd been together – so she just stared at it, assuming I was holding it up to show her something.

'What?' she asked, peering harder.

'Nothing. I'm just holding your coat out for you.'

'Why?'

'. . . Because I missed you.'

She stared at me in silence for a second or two.

'Riiiight . . .' she said eventually. She worked herself into her coat and looked at me again. 'So, what happened in London, then?'

'I signed the contracts – it was no big deal. Though it did need to be done urgently. But it was no big deal besides that.'

'And then what happened?'

'Nothing happened. I watched a bit of TV at the hotel. Had a drink in the bar. All very dull.'

'Obviously. But the bit of story I'm kind of fishing for here is how you came to turn up at the door to the shop looking like you'd just done a triathlon while being gang-raped.'

I laughed far too much at this, far, far too much. I wouldn't have blamed Sara if she'd assumed I'd become hysterical and slapped me but, as it happens, she was distracted. As I predicted, habit had ensured that one of the first things she did was put her hand into her pocket and pull out her mobile phone to switch it on. However, when she got it out she discovered that it was already on.

'My phone's on,' she said.

'Yes, it is,' I nodded.

I hoped this would put an end to the matter.

'But I turned it off this morning. I always turn it off when I get to work – it's part of my little ritual of getting ready.'

'Maybe you forgot today. What do you fancy eating this evening – perhaps we could go out somewhere?'

'No, I definitely turned it off. I remember because as I was doing it I said to Susan that the battery was very low.'

'Right . . . Well, someone might have knocked into your coat and it switched the phone on accidentally.'

'Can that happen?'

'Oh yes,' I said, with some considerable feeling, 'the buttons on mobiles are *way* too bloody sensitive.'

'Hmm . . .'

She looked at the phone and wrinkled up her nose in thought.

What she was thinking I didn't really know. But I knew precisely what I *didn't* want her to be thinking. I didn't want her to be thinking, 'Hmm . . . I'll just have a quick look at what (and when) the last outgoing call was . . .' That was what I'd do. This thought existed in the world, but had not yet made it into Sara's head. It was my mission now to block its path using all my skill and knowledge of psychology.

'Boo!' I shouted – jumping in front of her, grinning and shaking her by the shoulders.

'Jesus!'

'What?'

'Jesus . . . You scared the shit out of me.'

'Sorry. I was just being playful . . . I've missed you.'

'Tom – what the *fuck* have you been up to? Look at the state of you. You're soaked in sweat, filthy, your clothes are ripped, you've got a black eye and now – Christ help us – you're being *playful*. What the fuck has happened?'

'Right. Yes. Come on, I'll tell you on the way to the car . . .' I said, guiding her towards the door. '. . . it's simply unbelievable.'

That, at least, was perfectly true. I wouldn't say another true thing for the next fifteen minutes.

It was great to soak in the bath. Good for both my muscles and my soul. I even experienced a small, secret moment of satisfaction as I undressed to get in. As everyone knows, the accepted practice is that the wife discovers her husband's infidelity when he takes off his shirt to get changed and she sees scratches on his back. It's an old standard that's still used because it's so flexible. You can have a nice switch – the wife, domestic angel, is perhaps fussing maternally over his clothes when the discovery is made. Or maybe they're about to get into bed when, iconically, the mistress is shown to be with them. You can even work up a nice little metaphor about 'scars' if you fancy. And it would, of course, have been especially gratifying (dramatically) to have the writer caught out by such an old writer's cliché. But it wasn't going to happen here. I allowed myself a smile at the knowledge that I was in such a *fucking awful state* that – even if there'd been any there – a few scratches on my back weren't going to be enough to shop me. I had the black eye, great, raw abrasions on my elbow and my knee and a lucky dip of various other scrapes and bruises all over the place – mostly from the bike crash, but also, I suspected, quite a few from the toilet fucking. Christ, George – in a moment of passion – could have bitten my whole bleeding ear off and I'd have gotten away with it the way I looked now.

I stayed in the bath until my hands became like W.H. Auden's proverbial bollocks. It was sheer joy to lie there, but I was also reluctant to go back down and face Sara again: I'd had more than enough of being cross-examined for one day. She wasn't nasty about it or anything: she simply wanted to clarify bits that she felt she'd misunderstood because they appeared to sound utterly insane. Obviously, you can imagine the position that put me in. It was like doing improv under gunfire.

But, oddly, when I eventually did lace up my courage and go back downstairs, Sara didn't pursue the matter. We had something to eat, watched a little TV, she asked how the book was doing and we chatted about this and that. It was all very pleasant. Comfortable. Being with George was fantastic, but it was lovely to be with Sara and feel comfortable. To sit on the sofa and eat a bag of crisps while she looked through the Argos catalogue for a new hairdryer. When we lay in bed – her head on my chest as I finished reading a magazine article – I felt truly content.

'Why didn't you tell me about the party?' she said.

'Hmm . . . ?' I replied, vaguely. In what I judged to be the manner of a man who, deep in his magazine, hadn't quite heard what she'd said, rather than one who absolutely had heard what she'd said and was wincingly thinking, 'Fuck it.'

'I said, why didn't you tell me about the party?'

'Hmm . . . ?' I tried again, just to reiterate how casual I was. '. . . What party?'

'The party they're having to celebrate the book launch having gone so well.'

Somehow, I stopped myself replying, 'Oh, *that* party.' Instead I turned the page of my magazine (for effect; I wasn't reading – I didn't even know what words were in front of me), and then said, off-handedly, 'Why should I have mentioned it? It's just a dull publicity thing.'

'Because you *know* I've been wanting to meet Georgina Nye, and I could at the party.'

'Not sure they'd let you in. It's for the media, really, and you know what . . .'

'No, I *can* go.' There was a depressing certainty to the way Sara said this.

'Really?' I said, affecting to squint with increased interest at the magazine. (A piece of acting strenuous enough that it did make me actually absorb a little of what was on the page. I turned to another one, briskly – on the hunch that I'd now spent quite long enough appearing to be engrossed in what turned out to be an advert for an anti-thrush cream.)

'Aye. I popped round to Hugh and Mary's while you were away – to collect a video they'd done for me of the Havant International Grand Prix . . .'

'Ah . . . I'm away for an evening, so you settle down with a cycling video . . .'

'No – it wasn't – it was just . . .' She wasn't going to be diverted. 'Look, never mind that. The point is, while I was there they mentioned the party. I can certainly go to it if I want to. They assumed I would be going, in fact.'

'Oh, right.' Oh, bugger. 'Good.' Shit. 'I didn't really think about it. Like I say, it's just a boring media event, really. I wasn't going to go myself.'

'I'll go, even if you don't.'

Nice one – that worked well.

'I *wasn't* going to go myself . . . but then I thought I'd *have* to, or I'd look snotty. Maybe I can network a bit too.'

'Won't Amy be there to do that for you?'

'I suppose so, but . . .'

'Aye – Amy *will* be there. I rang her last night to ask if she was going.'

My stomach was clenched up to the size of a walnut by now. I wasn't at all comfortable with the idea of Sara, George and me being together in the same room. I was hugely *less* uncomfortable about it, however, than about Sara being there alone with her, while I sat at home biting my fingernails. If Sara was going to meet George, I wanted to be there to keep an eye on things. Suppose George let something slip accidentally? It was far better for me to be on hand to fire-fight. Yet the terror of possibilities I'd imagined for the party became positively adorable by comparison now it turned out that Sara had called Amy last night. The only conceivable way I could hear that conversation opening was with Sara saying, 'Amy, as Tom's in London signing that contract thing at the moment . . .' and Amy replying, 'What the fuck are you talking about?'

'You could have called me,' I said. I thought about going on to say, 'Because Amy's been having some mental problems recently – hallucinations, memory loss, pathological lying, that kind of thing.' But I was caught in the indecision of whether it was better to get this in early, or to appear to announce it reluctantly, sadly, in answer to Sara's request to know why Amy had said she didn't know anything about any contract amendments or my being in London. Sara continued before I'd reached a conclusion.

'Oh, I didn't want to bother you, and it just seemed natural to ask Amy herself what she was doing, rather than ask you. It's not like you'd know everything about her, is it? She's just your agent.'

'Right.'

'And it's a wonder you know anything at all, if you ask me – she's very vague . . . or perhaps she's more vague with me than with you . . .'

'Vague?'

'I was on the phone with her for about ten minutes and I don't think she gave me a clear answer to anything apart from that she was going to the party . . . Actually, I'm not sure whether I'd call it "vague" or "evasive", now I come to think about it. She struck me as a bit devious.'

'She's an agent.'

'I know I don't talk to her a great deal – well, she always stays away from me, doesn't she? – but I've never noticed it so much before.'

I shrugged. Because I couldn't think of anything even more non-committal to do.

'Anyway,' Sara continued, 'at least she told me she was going to the party. *You* didn't even mention the party. All this evening I kept bringing up the book and asking how things were going and what was happening, and you never thought to mention it to me. It was like you were hiding it.'

'Hiding it? *Hiding* it? I didn't realise I was being inter-rogated. I simply thought we were chatting and some silly publicity party didn't seem worth mentioning. If you'd simply *asked* me, I'd have told you.'

'Why would I ask you when I didn't know about it?'

'But you did.'

'You didn't know that.'

I was getting whipped here. I evacuated my troops under cover of a huge, theatrical, exasperated sigh. We regrouped and counter-attacked somewhere else in the hope that it'd be less well defended.

'Christ, Sara, I've had a shitty time – rushing about, falling over that tramp, and everything – and now I come back and you start laying into me too. About *nothing*. About not bothering to tell you something that's not very important and that you knew about anyway.' I *was* genuinely indignant here, by the way, not solely faking it for effect. I *did* feel put upon and harassed. I mean – Jesus – as if I weren't under enough stress trying to juggle the lies involved with having an affair, without my girlfriend making it harder for me. I was clearly getting the shitty end of the stick.

Sara looked up into my eyes for an uncomfortable amount of time. Long enough, in fact, for holding my wounded expression to start hurting my eyebrow muscles. Eventually, she sighed, and laid her head back down on my chest.

'I'm sorry, Tom. I just . . .'

She left the 'I just . . .' door open there, inviting me to go through it holding a 'Just what?', I think. I wasn't about to, though. Lord no. I would have liked to have nailed the bugger shut but, as there was no reply that would do that, I simply let the thing flap open in the wind instead. It was the best result available.

After a few moments, I started stroking Sara's hair, appeasingly. I did this for a while, pretending to have gone back to reading the magazine. Because of the position of her head, I couldn't see her eyes, but I sensed that they were open: Sara's eyes were penetrating enough for me to be able to feel them staring even when they were out of view. I didn't let on that I felt her eyes were still peering into the pensive space of the bedroom, though, because then I'd have been caught in the trap of either having to ask, 'What are you thinking?' – which was clearly a frightful direction in which to begin travelling – or be seen to blatantly *not* ask, 'What are you thinking?' – which was tantamount to a comprehensive confession of guilt. Instead I tried to stroke her hair in the way that you'd stroke the hair of someone whose eyes you believed to be closed. Things, as you can see, had now descended to a quite terrifying level of subtlety. I wanted to change my position in the bed, because it was aggravating one of my bruises, but I didn't dare. The situation was *that* brittle. Any sudden movement or noise or even the repositioning of a single buttock could be a catalyst for a discussion flaring up. I continued to stroke her head until I judged I could risk a tiny, tiny signalling yawn and then slowly switched off the light and settled down in bed.

The darkness was silent for a little while, and then Sara, without moving, whispered,

'Do you love me?'

'Like what? Like a bogey loves the underside of a table? More than there are pictures of people's cats on the Internet? Like what?'

'Not like anything. Just . . . do you love me?'

I pulled her tightly to me, almost crushingly tightly.

'Christ, *yes*. Of course, I love you.'

'Anything you'd like to tell me?' asked Amy, a tiny instant before detonating a horizontal explosion of cigarette smoke from between her lips.

'No . . .' I said, rather awkwardly. 'No, not really.'

'Fair enough.'

I hadn't seen or spoken to Amy for over a week. I know some people don't speak to their agent for months on end, but Amy and I hardly ever went more than a few days without meeting up or at least talking on the phone. This was partly Amy's carefully emphasised 'I'm your agent: we are a single spirit' technique. I don't know how many other clients Amy had – it was certainly dozens – but she always made you feel you were not merely her favourite but (a few piffling contractual technicalities aside) actually her only one. I think (and I certainly *like* to think) it wasn't purely artifice, though. I'm sure she sometimes met me for lunch simply because she wanted to have lunch with me. So we could chat and she could order several bottles of wine, without having to worry that I'd drink any of them. It was she who'd suggested we meet today for a general discussion of how *Growing* was doing, and she who'd picked the bar.

'Fair enough,' she repeated, archly. 'But it makes it tricky to know what to say to your girlfriend when I don't know what *not* to say, you get what I mean?'

'Yeah . . . thanks for covering for me the other day. I appreciate it.'

'Uh-huh.'

'It was just a misunderstanding, though.'

'Uhhhh . . . huh.'

'It *was*. Crossed lines.'

'Abso*lutely*.'

I responded by sighing with a huge, extended fizz.

'OK, Tom,' she shrugged, 'don't go into a huffy. I'm not your Jiminy fucking Cricket – don't think I'm going all prying and extra-curricular on you here. OK, yes, I admit, I did sort of hope you'd moved beyond your odd fetish for women who have the special charm of an industrial estate . . .'

'I wasn't seeing Fiona.'

'Did I *say* Fiona?'

'It was just crossed lines.'

'Whatever. I'm simply advising you to think things through . . . People should always think things through.'

She emptied her glass of wine and drew on her cigarette for the time it took her to fill it up again. I'd spent the past week – since George and I had last met – engaged in various sneaks, but the sneaking of cigarettes was perhaps the trickiest. Sara's nose was terrifying. She could easily have made a living sniffing out cigarette smugglers at Dover customs. I was seriously considering renting a flat somewhere, under an assumed name, just so I could have a fag.

'Could I bum a cigarette?' I flicked my chin at Amy's packet on the table.

'When did you start smoking?' she asked. In precisely the annoying kind of way you'd imagine she would.

'I didn't say I'd started smoking, I just asked if I could have a cigarette.'

'Are you going to use it as part of a magic act you're developing?'

'It *is* possible to smoke a cigarette without having "started smoking", you know.'

'Too subtle for me, Tom – I'm just an agent, not a writer, remember?'

'Look, if you don't want to give me one, just say so.'

'No, no, take – please do.'

'*Thank* you. Let it never be said that there's such a thing as a Scot who's tight with their fags.'

I lit the cigarette. It was fantastic.

Amy looked at me quietly for a while. I thought for a moment that she was going to say something I'd rather not hear but fortunately, while any potential statements were still brewing, her peculiar mental thermostat flicked off and she glazed over. I enjoyed a couple of tranquil drags on my cigarette while I waited for her to return. After a few seconds, power was restored to her body, the focus poured back into her eyes and, with a start, she said, 'So ... anyway ... *Growing*, then.'

'I understand it's selling really well. Haven't they done two reprints already?'

'They're doing a *third* now. Paul is gutted.'

'Why?'

'Because he can see that it's going to go through the two

hundred k barrier and he'll have to give us the extra money we agreed on. He'd rather hand over one of his own bollocks than another two per cent. In fact, he's as good as doing that anyway, because he knows I out-manoeuvred him and got the best deal. His bollocks are already mine.'

'Good for you.'

'And *you*. When we cross that two hundred k mark it'll put another thirty thousand pounds in your pocket.'

'I'll begin clearing out a pocket.'

'A little dance would be appropriate around now, Tom. Christ almighty – this deal has earned us twenty times more than we've ever got paid before.'

'No, no, I'm very pleased . . . there *is* more to life than money, though.'

'Well, now you've just started rambling.'

'Amy . . .'

'What?'

'. . . nothing.'

She nodded slowly. 'Yeah, there's a lot of that going round.' She almost seemed to say this to herself as much as to me.

We tapped the ash off our cigarettes together in silence for a few seconds.

'Right!' said Amy, abruptly brightening through an effort of will. 'You sit there, Tom, and smoke cigarettes like a true non-smoker while I get myself *very* drunk indeed.'

'OK.'

'Keep an eye on me. After the third bottle I might try to start a fight with someone but, if I don't, I'll need you to remind me.'

'Righto.'

I was keeping in touch with George mostly through text messages between our mobile phones. This, I have to say, was unbelievably hot. I'd set my 'incoming text alert' to 'vibrate' – each new message from George was signalled by a secret tingling in the area of my waist. If there's anyone who needs me to point out the two different levels at work there, I suggest you forget about everything and just go outside and watch the clouds instead. The texting had been born of necessity (George was massively busy with publicity and didn't have a moment to herself for most of the day) but it actually turned out to be very, *very* erotic. I'd never have thought that exchanging a few blocky words while miles and miles apart could affect my breathing and send tingles racing all over my body (generally racing in the direction of my groin). That's what happened, though. In fact, the few times we managed to speak on the phone were almost an anti-climax compared to the texting. I hoped that, when we got a chance to meet again, we wouldn't be left cold by being physically together and naked – and have to sit on opposite sides of the room texting each other, 'Harder!' and, 'Oh, YES!'

The downside of all this textual intercourse was that I had to conceal it from Sara. This was awful. I'd feel a message arrive and have to sneak off to read it. It was skin-pricklingly exciting to do this – but, as I say, awful. It felt terrible to be deceiving Sara about this thrillingly clandestine communication. Not only that, but I kept popping off to the toilet so often to read and reply to the messages that Sara thought I was developing prostate trouble.

It was especially tricky to hide everything because Sara was watching me. At first I told myself it was nothing but the paranoia that travels with treachery: that she wasn't *really* behaving any differently, it was simply that my overwrought eyes were seeing reflections of their own guilt. I had, after all, imagined in the past that she was scrutinising me – ages before I'd started seeing George, back when I was utterly blameless. It wasn't just imagination this time, though. Sara was definitely behaving differently. She was quieter, for one thing, and she always seemed to look at me intently when I spoke, like she was running a visual polygraph. Any tiny foothold for the hope that I was merely delusional was removed when one day I asked her, 'What's wrong?' Obviously, I wasn't in the habit of asking Sara things like this. I had, however, done it a few times during the years we'd been together when – usually surfing on a wave of lager – I'd snuggle up to her and whisper, 'What's wrong?' on the hunch that she would probably reply, 'Well . . . . I've been wanting you to do something astonishingly dirty to me, but it's *so* filthy that I'm embarrassed to admit that I crave it.' So far, my hunches there had turned out to be wrong. Instead, she had somehow always managed to find other, non-sexual, things that were troubling her to fill up the three or four hours after I'd asked the question. So now, when (hoping I could reset things to normal by an exchange along the lines of 'What's wrong?', 'I think you're sleeping with Georgina Nye', 'I'm not', 'Oh, right – phew') I nestled close to her on the sofa and asked, 'What's wrong?' and got the reply, 'Nothing,' well, I *knew* things weren't right.

I tried not to resent her. I tried to remain unaffected by the fact that everything to do with George was fun and exhilarating and sexy while, over the past week or so, being with Sara increasingly seemed to be a wearing, stressful time spent having to be constantly on my guard. I mean, I loved both George and Sara, and I didn't want to play favourites: Sara made it quite difficult for me on occasion, though, and I was rather proud of my impartial benevolence in not judging her.

I think it's accurate to say that the tension in the house tightened as we approached the party. Nothing actually *happened*, nothing was actually *said*, but there was a definite increase in the air's ambient voltage.

We scarcely said a word as we prepared when the night finally arrived. Sara, who normally took about a minute and a half to get ready to go out anywhere, spent nearly two hours changing in and out of clothes and fiddling with her hair. I told myself that this evening would be the end of it all: Sara would meet George, the suspicions would boil away under the heat of George's charm and our obviously platonic, purely professional relationship and everything would be fine again. (And then, hopefully, George and I could slip away for a rapid, frantic shag somewhere.) Despite trying to convince myself that the party was really a good thing, however, I still wanted it to be over with as soon as possible.

It was being held at a function room in one of the hotels in the city and it didn't start until pretty late (if you're after attracting the media then holding a party after most places have stopped serving drinks is always a good strategy). Sara was adamant that we take a taxi there, rather than go in her car. This meant she intended to get pissed. (I could have driven the car, of course, but if Sara was going to get pissed then my getting pissed too was an option I wanted to keep open.) When the taxi arrived things picked up a little. I called up to Sara, 'The cab's here,' and she called back down, 'OK.' Sadly, however, we failed to build on this conversation. We climbed into the back of the cab and the switch that turns on the little 'doors now locked' red light also seemed to operate as a mute button because Sara and I fell into the type of concentration-demanding silence that one normally only experiences when in a lift with a stranger.

Central Edinburgh fragments at night. It fractures visually as the eclectic whole of the city in daylight – its bony soup – becomes a deep, inky sea erratically strewn with distinct structures. The major landmarks (the National Gallery, say, or the Bank of Scotland – above all, the Castle) shine under powerful floodlights so that they push themselves forward, tearing holes in the night. Sara and I sat in the taxi together, silently looking out at the shattered city through opposite windows.

'Hi, Tom,' sighed Hugh. 'Hello, Sara, you look nice.'

'Thanks.'

'Mary's here somewhere . . .' He looked briefly around the room, but couldn't find her. 'Well, I'm sure you'll run into her at some point. She's off having a good time, I don't doubt . . . It's very entertaining for her, of course, but I swear that the more of these things I come to the more I hate them. There's no art, no creativity, that's all over with by the time we get to these parties. All they are, basically, is the media crawling over the dead flesh seeing what it can devour – like twisting worms eating our corpse . . . There's a table of finger food over there, by the way, if you fancy anything.'

'Maybe later,' I said. 'Is Amy here yet?' I asked, keen to get close to an ally and also knowing that asking for Amy was a less desperate-sounding, but equally effective, way of saying, 'Where's the booze?'

'Yes,' Sara added (pointlessly, I couldn't help thinking), 'is she?'

Hugh peered around the room again. 'I *have* seen her . . . Not sure where she is now, though . . . The wine's over in the far corner, there.'

'Right, I'll head in that direction, then.'

Sara and I moved off, leaving Hugh staring down into his glass: where he appeared to be able to see the entire cold hopelessness of existence laid out before him.

The room was elegant: dignified, Edwardian and illuminated by a soft, warm light that was just dim enough to evoke a feeling of intimacy. The columns that fell from the arches in the ceiling broke up the space and added to this impression, so that it seemed to be a cosy affair, despite the room actually being large enough for perhaps two hundred people to be present without it being remotely overcrowded. Guests were milling around or chatting in huddles of twos, threes and fours, and I threaded through them with Sara at my shoulder, a pace behind.

'Look,' she said suddenly, though not very enthusiastically.

I turned around to her and then away again in the direction she'd indicated with a quick nod. I couldn't see Amy or George.

'What?' I asked.

'It's Paddy Adams.'

I turned back and, now I knew who I was looking for, saw him. He was chatting to (actually 'up', I guessed) a woman of an age, attractiveness and casual dress combination that strongly suggested she was a TV researcher. I could see that he was trying very hard. The fool. The woman was doing things to the stem of her wineglass. She kept pushing stray strands of hair back behind her ears with slow, vastly exaggerated finesse and leaning in closer to him so, fascinated, she could try to hear again a sentence she hadn't quite caught the first time. When she said something to him, her words were spoken in tandem with her fingers reaching out to emphasise her point by touching the back of his hand. The poor woman must have been in absolute despair about whether she'd actually need to get down on all fours and expose her bottom to him before he got the message. 'You've done enough – for Christ's sake call a cab,' her eyes shouted at him, but he kept on determinedly chatting her up when she was already as far up as she could possibly get.

I turned back to Sara. 'Yes,' I said, 'it is.'

'Aren't you going to say hello?'

'Say hello? I don't know him.'

Sara looked at me without replying. I knew pretty quickly that she was saying something by not saying anything, but I wasn't quite sure what that thing might be. I had a little think.

Ah, yes, there it was. Fuck.

'I mean, I don't *know* him. We exchanged a few words at the party after the Benny Barker show . . .' (which, of course, had happened and I'd attended and had stayed at all night and which had occurred precisely as I've told you, Sara, and had not remotely been simply a cover for the time I'd spent in George's hotel room being pornographically and repeatedly unfaithful to you) '. . . but I wouldn't say I *know* him.'

'Right,' said Sara, nodding: nodding slowly, and keeping my eyes fixed directly in the centre of her gaze as she did so.

Oh, crap. Had I remembered right away that I'd said I'd met Paddy Adams I could have brushed this aside. Casually muttered that we'd best not interrupt him while he was so clearly on the pull or something. Now it looked like I was trying to keep Sara away from him. The mood she was in at the moment, she was probably thinking that I was sleeping with him too.

'OK, OK,' I blustered. 'Let's go and say hello, then.'

I strode heavily over to where Paddy Adams was standing. Sara followed behind – far too close for her not to pick it up were I to, say, stab Paddy Adams in the neck with a pencil before he had a chance to utter a word. That meant I had to fall back on Plan B. Adams must meet hundreds, perhaps thousands, of people in his line of work. The barrage of faces was probably especially acute at the moment, what with his successful show at the Festival. Even though he was Irish, I'd have to take the chance that he'd be too English to go anywhere near the awkwardness of revealing that he didn't have a clue who I was, particularly if I raised the embarrassment stakes by implying that we were great, *great* mates.

'Paddy!' My hand was on his shoulder, a knowing grin on my face. 'You old tosser – how are you?'

'Fine,' he replied, while his expression wobbled on a rickety bridge between 'Good to see you' and 'Christ!'

'You *look* fine, you really do,' I said.

'I am,' he confirmed.

The young woman with him seemed unaccountably irritated by my oafish interruption. 'Who . . . ?' she began, looking at Adams. I leapt in before she could get any farther.

'Hi!' I shook her hand. (We didn't 'shake hands': I merely took her hand in mine, and shook it.) 'I'm Tom.' She inclined her head and her lips parted to let out what I suspected might be a 'Tom who? How do you know Paddy?' or 'Paddy, who is this?' or 'Let go of my hand, you fuckwit.' She was still drawing in a preparatory breath, so I cut her off. 'Oh, Paddy – this is my girlfriend, Sara.'

Sara nodded.

Adams nodded back.

'I think you're very funny,' Sara said, with a smile.

Adams's face softened into a boyish grin. Clearly he didn't care who the hell you were so long as you were an attractive young woman and you were saying you thought he was funny. 'Thanks,' he said. Sara smiled even more. *That* was quite enough of that, thank you very much – Sara, *my girlfriend*, I said, Adams. You wanker.

He and Sara stood washing each other with smiles. The Probably A TV Researcher woman glared at Sara in a way that suggested that inside her head she was focusing on her and chanting the word 'cystitis' over and over again.

'Right!' I roared. 'Must be off – maybe we'll catch you again later, Paddy.'

'Yeah,' he replied, noticeably more to Sara than to me. Sara . . . smiled. Christ, why didn't the pair of them just go at it here and now? Maybe ask whether I'd be a sport and bring a table for him to bend her over? He'd better hope I *didn't* catch up with him again during the evening, because if I did it was a good bet that it'd be to push him off a balcony. But then, as it happened, I guessed he'd probably not be around much longer. As we parted, Probably A TV Researcher woman and I shared a glance and I was pretty sure she'd be redoubling her efforts to get him out of here, with her, as soon as possible.

Sara and I moved off together. I gave her a look.

'What?' she asked.

I wanted to say, 'You *know* what. Giving the come-on to Paddy "Listen to my musical Irish brogue" Adams and his twinkling Irish eyes.' I mean, Jesus, here I was half killing myself to keep her from finding out about George – and suffering terrible, *terrible* guilt about the whole thing – and she virtually flings herself at Paddy Adams. Joyfully. *Right in front of my face.* Talk about 'moral high ground': I'd have been well within my rights to have stormed out, there and then. Somehow, though, I managed to stamp down my feelings. 'Nothing,' I replied.

I stared directly ahead (though out of the corner of my eye I could see Sara continuing to look at me) and marched on through the party guests. Eventually, we came to a table laid out with glasses of wine. Two waiters stood behind it, filling new glasses as the ones already there were taken. Close by, possibly trying to out-pace them, was Amy. She was swaying gently to the tune of alcohol.

'Hiya, Tom,' she said. She kissed me on both cheeks, raised her glass, as if to toast my appearance, and then drained it. 'Sara,' she continued, slightly more formally, 'you look well.'

'Thank you. You do too.'

'Well, things are going to plan, so I'm happy.' Amy smiled knowingly at me as she said this to indicate she was thinking of the simply massive pile of extra money we were going to get because *Growing* had sold so well.

'Indeed.' I smiled back, picked up a glass of wine and took a sip. It was vile. (I really do not like wine – I don't know why I keep drinking it.)

Amy took a long draw on her cigarette and reached across the table to a boxy 'No Smoking' sign that she'd overturned and was using as an ashtray. 'I've been running about all over the place, but it's been worth it, I reckon.'

'Running about?' asked Sara.

'Hm? Oh – down to London and back quite a bit . . . sorting stuff out for Tom.' She clinked her glass against mine.

'Och, aye – you were down there when I called you the other week, weren't you?'

'Um . . . no,' replied Amy, using bits of her eyebrows to indicate that she thought this an odd question. 'No, I was in Edinburgh then.'

'Ahh . . .' Sara looked over the glasses of wine on the table, taking quite a time to select a particular one considering they were all identical. '. . . I just thought you might have been there. You never know where people are when you call them on their mobile, do you?'

'I was in Edinburgh,' Amy shrugged.

Sara nodded, 'Right,' and took a drink from her glass.

'Has the woman herself turned up yet?' said Amy.

'You mean George?' I asked, adding a distancing '—ina Nye?' a quarter-second later. 'I don't know.'

'Paul said he'd be driving her over right after they'd finished, erm . . . something or other.'

'A Scottish TV thing in Glasgow,' I said.

'Is that what it is?'

'Um, yes, well, I think so. I read in the paper that she was on some Scottish TV show tonight. I assumed in Glasgow. It was implied in the text. Perhaps I'm wrong, though – I'm only guessing. It's just a guess. What the hell do I know, eh? God, isn't this wine *awful*?'

'Is it?' Amy asked, surprised, and picked up a fresh glass from the table. She drank half of it down. Sara and I looked at her, waiting for a judgement, but she gazed back blankly, appearing never to have considered the possibility of pronouncing upon it.

'So,' asked Sara eventually, 'what do you think you and Tom will be doing next?'

'A holiday might be a good idea, eh, Tom?'

'Off to the South Seas together, maybe?' Sara said, oddly, and smiled, oddly.

'Ha! No, you can have him for the holiday, Sara.'

'Thank you.'

'I get enough of him while we're working.'

'I bet.'

Amy's attention suddenly shifted. There was a small commotion away across the room that almost certainly meant George had arrived. Amy stood on tiptoes, trying to see above the heads of the other guests. I don't think she had much success; affecting complete nonchalance, I didn't look in that direction at all. When it became apparent that I was the only person in the entire room not looking that way – and that standing there at 180 degrees to the direction everyone else was facing appeared not even remotely casual and inconspicuous – I turned around. Through the shifting people, I caught a brief flash of George. She was smiling and looked confident, relaxed and quite unimaginably shaggable.

'Is it Paul and Georgina Nye?' Amy asked.

'Yeah . . .' I said. 'I'm just going to the toilet.'

I'm not going to be melodramatic here and say that I had a panic attack, but there was an element of panic, and it did sort of attack me. George and Sara, for the first time, were in the same place. More than this, I could *see* them both being in the same place. George, real-life George, was visible, just across the room – I turned my head slightly, and there too was Sara, in the flesh. Experiencing them together, visually, tore at the compartmentalising walls: and I liked those walls, I liked those walls a lot. I needed a few moments in the toilet to take a few steady breaths and have a stiff word with myself in the mirror.

When, after some extensive therapeutic hand-washing, I came back out into the main room, George and her agent were standing with Hugh by the drinks table, not that far from Amy and Sara. George and Sara were still very much separate, however. In fact, it was Amy who was obviously peering across, while Sara faced the other way, not even looking in that direction. I wondered whether this was Sara deliberately 'turning her back on George', but it didn't seem like it. She appeared to be genuinely and wholly engaged by whatever she and Amy were talking about. Maybe they'd fallen into a nice 'the amusing effeteness of Englishmen' groove. I strolled over to George's group.

'Good evening,' I . . . well, 'chirped', really. Overdid the untroubled brightness a bit there, Tom.

'Hello, Tom,' replied Hugh.

'Wotchaaaaah,' said Paul.

George just smiled politely.

We chatted for a while about how well the book was doing. Paul swung between remarking what a massive, staggering success it had been (playing to Hugh) and (playing to me) worrying aloud how big the market was and whether they'd manage to sell another copy, ever, and whether this might mean George didn't get the money she'd hoped for. He didn't seem to be troubled by alternately running in two completely opposite directions, though. Whichever line he was taking at the time he threw himself into fully, without any hint of discomfort or self-consciousness. Meanwhile, George and I did a tremendous job of not looking at each other. In fact, I was so determinedly looking at Paul, so as not to be thought to be looking at George, that I didn't notice Sara come over to us. Seemingly instantly, she 'appeared' beside me – as if by teleportation – saying, 'Hi,' and I very nearly jumped back with a comedy 'Agh!' Fortunately, however, I managed to disguise my tense, unnaturally large surprise as a perfectly natural, big, spontaneous nervous twitch.

I leaned across and kissed Sara on the cheek. She looked at me like this was a strange thing for me to do (which it was). 'Paul, George-*ina*: this is Sara, my girlfriend.'

George smiled and nodded.

'She's a cracker, Tom,' said Paul, and winked at Sara. Twat.

'Ahh . . .' Hugh scanned the room. '. . . that reminds me, I still haven't located Mary. Would you all excuse me? I think I'd better engage in a search for my wife.'

'That's what I say to myself every time I go to a party,' cawed Paul. 'Still haven't found a candidate yet. Mind you – I've seen a good few "honourable mentions", if you know what I mean.'

'Yes,' replied Hugh, looking like he didn't. 'Well, see you all later.'

Paul coughed. A purely social cough – just one, carefully placed, 'Hch-arrr' – and took a gulp from his wine. I was surprised that he felt awkward about his joke not being precisely on Hugh's wavelength: I was surprised, in fact, that he was even aware there *were* wavelengths other than his own. 'Well . . .' he continued. '. . . I'll piss off too, if that's OK with you lot. I see your agent's on her own over there, Tom. I'll have a quick chat. See if I can find any pity in the woman, maybe.' He finished his wine, slammed the empty glass down needlessly heavily on a table and strode over to Amy.

This left Sara, George and me together, alone.

'So . . .' I said. I then clicked my teeth, let out some little puffs of air, hummed five or six notes of a non-existent tune and pulled various faces. 'So, then . . .' Sara was looking at me in the strangest way. It wasn't the intense, probing look she'd been carrying around earlier. It was a mixture of bafflement and fascinated inspection. I couldn't even read whether it was affectionate or antagonistic: I'd almost say that she didn't appear to be sure of this herself either. '. . . Sara's a big fan of *The Firth*!' I said, suddenly, pleased to have had a thought.

Sara smiled at George, slightly embarrassed. 'I am, aye,' she said. 'I think you're extremely good in it.'

'Oh, I just say the lines that are written for me,' replied George, switching to a stock modesty that I'd seen her use a couple of times before. 'The crew and the writers do all the work – I simply have to turn up on time and try not to fall over the scenery.'

'Oh, *no* – I think you're a very good actress.'

'I don't know about that . . . but thank you for saying so.'

Well, that seemed to have gone splendidly.

'So – should we think about making a move to leave?' I said to Sara, taking an illustrative half-step in the direction of the exit.

'Leave? We've only just got here.'

'Oh, I wouldn't say "just" . . . or "only" . . . and it's going to be *hell* to get a taxi if we wait until everyone else is leaving.'

Sara turned to George. 'This is Tom for you,' she said with mock despair. 'Hardly ever takes me out, then when he does he wants to get it over with as soon as possible . . . I wouldn't be surprised if he isn't thinking about making it home in time for the late-night film on the telly.'

'No, I . . .'

'Are you sure? When we get back I'll be checking to see if it's circled in the TV guide.'

I looked at George. 'I *do* take her out. I take her out all the time.' I was filled with a strange desire to assure George that I was a good partner. 'Strange' in the sense that I felt I needed to convince George how well I treated my girlfriend: the girlfriend to whom I was being unfaithful, with her.

'All the time?' scoffed Sara.

'We went to B&Q just last Sunday.'

'That's not taking me out.'

'It is – *you* were the one who wanted to go, I didn't want to go. But I went with you.'

'Nice one, Heathcliff,' Sara said. 'I hope *you* managed to have a good time with Tom, Georgina.'

Bwoof. The temperature of my body plummeted by eighty degrees in a single instant.

George didn't display the tiniest flicker, however. She just smiled gently and said, 'He's very professional. I've enjoyed working with him . . . And I'm very pleased with the book, of course. Tom is wonderfully expressive.'

'Oh – *on the page* he's expressive. *On the sofa* I can barely get a word out of him . . . Or maybe he's many-sided: everyone gets a different Tom.'

This was really more information than was needed. I couldn't tell whether Sara was trying to make a point to George (perhaps 'Tom's rubbish – don't bother') or whether it was simply that she'd become excitedly talkative in the presence of a celeb – I'd seen this happen to some of the people at George's book signing.

'Well . . .' George shrugged amiably. 'I don't know about that. I'm just happy we got the chance to work together . . . and relieved that he survived the experience – psychologically *and* physically, eh?' She smiled. 'Though, I must say, your eye looks much better now. No one would ever know.'

Sara smiled too. Then wrinkled her nose up, a little confused. 'You saw Tom's black eye? I didn't know you two had seen each other since the Benny Barker show.'

'Hahaha,' I laughed. I have entirely no idea what I was hoping to achieve by doing this. 'Hahahah . . . yes,' I continued, looking down into my wineglass and shaking my head, as though at some amusing memory. 'Yeeeesss . . .' I glanced up. Sara was looking at me. Like someone who expected they were going to hear an answer within the next day or so. 'Yes, I saw Georgina, briefly, just after I fell over that tramp.'

'Ahhh, right,' Sara nodded. 'You didn't mention Georgina was in London too.'

'Didn't I? Well, I only saw her briefly. She was with her agent when I went in to sign the amended contract.'

'I thought you said you'd fallen over the tramp after that.'

'I went back again after I'd fallen over him.'

'Why?'

'I was shaken up by the fall – I wasn't completely sure I *had* signed.'

'You lost your memory?'

'Just briefly. It didn't seem worth mentioning.'

'I see.'

'Yeah . . . God, this wine is *awful*, isn't it . . . ? Hugh!'

Hugh had returned, and I'd shouted at him and pointed. It's called 'misdirection'.

'What?' asked Hugh, slightly anxiously.

'It's you,' I said.

'Why shouldn't it be?'

'No reason at all. At least none *I* can think of.'

Hugh thought for a moment, and then seemed to accept that this was the case. 'Georgina – I've finally unearthed my wife. She's chatting to someone who buys books for one of the big chain stores. I wonder if you'd come over and charm him a wee bit? It never hurts to plant the idea of an even more prominent display in these people's heads.'

'Of course.' George glanced briefly at Sara and me before following Hugh away. 'Nice to see you again, Tom,' she said, touching my shoulder, 'and it was lovely to meet you, Sara.' Then she was gone.

I stood by Sara and kicked the crap out of my brain – as though it were a captured enemy agent and I was trying to get it to talk. The last thing I wanted was for there to be an awkward silence, because I didn't want it to seem like there was anything to be awkward about, but I simply couldn't think of a single thing to say. Perhaps it was just a few seconds, though it seemed much longer to

279

me, but the uncomfortable lack of speech didn't end until Sara spoke.

'She wasn't what I expected.'

'They never are, are they? Bit of a let-down?'

'No. No, not a let-down, exactly. Just . . .'

'What?'

'Human. I suppose I was surprised to find her so . . . made of flesh.'

'Mmm . . .' I tried to shoo all sorts of images from my mind.

'What do you think of her?'

'I don't know. I don't really think of her at all.'

'You were staring at her.'

'No I wasn't,' I said, rather indignantly – wanting to continue, 'I so bloody *wasn't*. I was half killing myself with nervous exhaustion from the intensity with which I was forcing myself *not* to stare at her so it didn't appear suspicious, in fact – so that shows what *you* know: you and your utterly groundless accusations.' Instead I repeated, 'No I wasn't,' with, for convincingness, a slight pout.

'Oh, you *were*. Furtive staring.'

'*Furtive* now? You're imagining things.'

'Why would I imagine it?'

'I don't know.'

'Why didn't you tell me you'd seen her in London?'

'You didn't ask.'

'I did. I remember doing it specifically: I asked, "Who did you see in London?" and you said, "No one." I tried again – quite a few times – and you finally gave up the precious information that you'd seen Georgina's agent. But you definitely gave the impression that you'd done nothing else at all but sit in your hotel room. Or fall over tramps.'

'Oh, *God*. I didn't "see" Georgina, not really. She was in the office and we exchanged a few words. That doesn't amount to "seeing" someone. Why the interrogation?'

'OK – don't get defensive.'

'I'm not getting bloody defensive.'

'Have you got a crush on Georgina Nye?'

'Jesus! Where did *that* come from?'

'I'm just asking. I mean, she's very attractive, and you've been immersed in thinking about her for the book . . . and you've definitely had something on your mind. In fact, I thought . . .'

'What?'

'Oh, nothing . . .' she replied, shaking her head. 'But is that what the problem has been lately? Have you come down with a case of the Nyes?'

'No, of course not. She's too . . .' What was she 'too'? The woman was perfect. '. . . rich for me.'

'You fancy Madonna – she's absolutely loaded.'

'That's different: she was poor when I started to fancy her. Back when she released "Holiday" she hadn't got two coins to rub together.'

'Well, well . . . I didn't realise you were such a sexual Marxist.'

'Well, *I* didn't realise we'd "had a problem lately".' This was a lie, of course, but a white one. It implied that *I* was perfectly happy and that any 'problem' she'd sensed was non-existent and probably just due to her being premenstrual or wildly oversensitive or stupid or something like that. So, it was basically a white lie I was prepared to take on as it would comfort and reassure her.

'Apparently not,' Sara replied, in a tone unusual for someone who was comforted and reassured.

'What's *that* supposed to mean?'

'Whatever you want it to mean.'

'And what's *that* supposed to mean?'

She shrugged and looked the other way.

I huffed. 'Look, I don't know what you think the problem is, but there *isn't* one as far as I'm concerned. I'm very happy, there's nothing but work between George and me, and I'm going to get something from the buffet now – do you want anything to eat?'

In an evening of curious looks, Sara gave me the most curious look yet. 'No,' she said, finally.

'Fine,' I replied, and strode off to head for the food. Wondering if, when I found it, I'd be able to hold any of it down.

En route, however, I decided to ignore the food entirely and slip outside for a steadying cigarette instead. On the street, around the doorway, there were only slightly fewer people who'd popped out for a quick smoke than there were guests inside. I managed to scrounge a couple of cigarettes without particular shame and smoked them thoughtfully. I told myself to calm down. Myself replied that I'd try.

I finished my final cigarette and flicked the end off into the night: it hit the road with a spray of orange sparks, like the brief, blinking bloom of a fiery flower (is there *anything* about smoking that *isn't* satisfying?). Then I quickly sneaked back into the party and began to look for Sara. I was saved the trouble of searching, however, because when I stopped for a moment to get another drink, she found me.

'Where have you been?' she asked.

'Looking for you.'

'You've been gone ages.'

'I couldn't find you. Where were you?'

'Looking for you.'

'Ah,' I nodded. 'Well, now we've found each other.'

'Yes . . . While I was wandering around, I bumped into Georgina Nye's agent again. I was asking him about the amended contract you'd been down to sign.'

Yaaaaaaaaaaaaaaaaaaaaaaaaaaaaaaaaaaaaaaaaaaaaaaaaaaaaaah hhhhhhhhhhhhhhhhhhhhhhhhhhhhhhhhhhhhhhhhhhhhh!

'Really?' I took a sip of my wine and glanced off around

the room, clearly unconcerned with this fact and only half listening.

Yaaaaaaaaaaaaaaaaaaaaaaaaaaaaaaaaaaaaaaaaaaaaaaaaaaaaaaaaaa ahhhhhhhhhhhhhhhhhhhhhhhhhhhhhhhhhhhhhhhh!

'He said he didn't know what on earth I was talking about.'

'Well, *obviously*,' I said with a roll of my eyes and a sigh. 'That's *obviously* what he's going to say, isn't it? It's obvious.'

'Not to me.'

'Tch – he's an agent. He's not going to discuss contractual details with people, is he? He wants to keep everything private. And, anyway,' I said, visibly hurt, 'why were you checking up on me in the first place?'

'I wasn't "checking up on you". It was simply the first thing I thought of to say: it's the only thing we had in common. I wasn't asking him about contractual details either, I just said something like, "So you and Tom met up to amend the contract the other week, then?", that's all.'

'But that's asking him to give away that the contract's been amended.'

'Well, he could have said, "We did meet for business, yes," or something like that. Rather than, for example, saying, "No, I've never seen Tom in London," and then peering at me like I was a nutter.'

'Pff – he doesn't want to give *anything* away if he can help it.'

'Not even admit he met you?'

'No.'

'Not even to me, your partner?'

'The man's obsessive, clearly.'

'Let's go back and ask him now, then. You come with me.'

'Jesus – we can't do that!'

'Why not?'

Good question, Sara. I'll just take a drink of wine while I think about that one.

'It'll *embarrass* him,' I said finally, in a conspiratorial hiss. 'It's bad manners.'

'How?'

'Look, he particularly didn't want to tell you anything because you're "the girlfriend". He didn't want to say it because it'd seem insulting, but he doesn't know you and he *does* know that it's nearly always the girlfriend who leaks information. Kiss and tell. Revenge. Deliberately broadcasting things after a relationship ends.'

'I didn't know our relationship *was* ending. Who else knows it is, then – besides you and Georgina Nye's agent?'

'Oh, don't be wilfully obtuse. You know what I mean. As far as *he* knows we could be splitting up tonight: he's got to assume the worst.'

Sara didn't look entirely convinced. But neither did she look like this was very close to the biggest load of bollocks she'd ever heard and she was going to hit me in the face with her shoe for even attempting to get her to accept it. So, pretty much a staggeringly fabulous triumph on my part, I reckoned.

She didn't reply. That was good. We needed to stick with that. I grabbed a glass of wine from the table and thrust it into her hands. Drink. Relax. Alcohol and silence was the way we should go here. She took a sip, while continuing to stare at me, but still didn't say anything. Things improved even more when Hugh and Mary wandered over. While Sara was distracted and definitely not hurling herself completely into the conversation, the amiable chatter engaged her enough so that she didn't simply stand there and brood. As the night went on, in fact, she drank several more glasses of wine and the four of us had what it wouldn't be entirely unreasonable to call an acceptably good time.

We talked for calm ages about wonderfully unimportant

things until Hugh glanced at his watch and said, 'I'd better make one last tour of the room.' It was late and many of the guests had already gone (the place was sparsely populated enough now for it to be possible to look around and see everyone who was there: I noted that George had obviously left – though Paul was still here, talking to Amy).

'Yeah, we ought to get back home,' I said.

'We'll take you,' Mary offered. 'We've got a taxi ordered – we can drop you off.'

'It's a bit out of your way,' said Sara.

Hugh waved the objection away with great nobility. 'Tch – McAllister and Campbell are paying for the cab . . . we can go via Inverness if you want.'

Hugh went to say a final, warm and genuine goodbye to anyone who might help book sales and Mary went to keep a lookout for the taxi, which was due to arrive in about ten minutes. Sara and I slowly ambled over to the coat-check counter. I put my arm around her as we moved across the room. She looked up at me and seemed on the verge of saying something, but then bit her lip, stayed silent and put her arm round me too. We recovered our coats and I was pleased that, after we put them on, we returned easily to each other's arms. Sara even laid her head sleepily on my shoulder as we walked away towards the exit. I was looking down at her, so a falsely friendly, over-loud 'Tom!' was the first I knew that by not watching where I was going I'd trodden in something unfortunate.

'Hello, Fiona.'

'Super evening, wasn't it? I thought it went off awfully well.' She was her usual chill self, but seemed to be a bit tipsy underneath the ice.

'Yes.'

'And this must be the girlfriend?' To build on the casually insulting 'the', she pronounced 'girlfriend' as though it were the most tentative of suggestions: a risky idea she was proposing almost from desperation at the lack of alternatives.

'This is Sara, yes. Sara, this is Fiona. Fiona is in McAllister and Campbell's publicity department.'

Sara lifted her head from me and smiled. 'Hi there. I'm very pleased to meet you.'

'Ahh – a Scotswoman, I hear!' exclaimed Fiona. 'Tom clearly has a special fondness for the Scots.' She smiled like a snake: the kind you'd want to pick up by the tail, swing its head repeatedly against a tree, and then throw into a fire.

'I'm sorry?' squinted Sara.

'Oh, I just meant that he clearly likes you, and you're a Scot.'

'Well,' I said, 'we've got to be off, Fiona . . .'

'Shagged out, are you? Talking of which, did you see Georgina tonight?'

She was toying with me, like a cat: the kind you'd want to pick up by the tail, swing its head repeatedly against a tree, and then throw into a fire.

'Yes, Sara and I did speak to her, briefly.'

'Sara too?' she replied with great surprise. 'How lovely. Are you a fan, Sara?'

'I think she's a good actress, aye.'

I thought I could feel Sara's body tightening. Perhaps it was simply that my arm was subconsciously tightening *around her* and giving the impression that she was tensing up.

'Yes, wonderful, isn't she? Tom's a big fan too, aren't you, Tom?'

'Not especially.'

I tried to begin moving off, without it looking like I was trying to get away, but Fiona out-manoeuvred me. She moved to block my path, while giving the impression that she wasn't doing anything but randomly changing where she was standing.

'Oh, Tom, don't pretend you're not star struck. I know

you've loved every minute of it – and you've certainly put an awful lot of yourself into her . . .' She took a sip from her wine. '. . . book.'

'I work hard on all the books I do.' I was edging sideways, crab-like, pulling Sara along with me. A column blocked Fiona's way as – trying to maintain her position in front of us – she moved sideways too. As her shoulder pressed against the column, I made to begin a quick spurt of speed towards the exit. But Fiona was quicker off the mark: she nipped around the column and popped out on the other side, right in front of us again.

'Well, your effort certainly wasn't wasted on Georgina, was it? From what I've picked up, you've made her utterly delighted that she got her hands on you.'

'Fiona?' said Sara.

'Yes, darling? Sorry to be such a bore with the shop talk, you must be fed up with it – I bet that Tom just *loves* to keep both you and Georgina filled in.'

'Fiona,' she repeated, 'you appear to be hinting – clumsily, I have to say – that Tom is fucking Georgina Nye.'

Fiona's face lurched from smug into alarmed with an ugly crashing of gears. (My face, as far as I could tell, fell off entirely.) 'No, I . . .' she began, but Sara wasn't finished.

'But, you see, we've got a taxi waiting, so can we please forget the childish innuendo now? I'm sorry if it spoils your surprise, but I'm already perfectly well aware that Tom is fucking Georgina Nye – that's very old news. So, if there's nothing else . . . ?'

'I . . .'

'Good. We'll be off, then.' Sara guided us both away towards the exit (I was too stupefied to do anything but dumbly follow her lead), while Fiona remained immobilised by flat-footed confusion.

'Sara?' Fiona called, suddenly regaining her ability to function and starting after us. 'I'm . . . You must have entirely misunderstood me . . . There's . . .' She caught up and put her hand on Sara's shoulder, bringing us to a halt and pulling Sara around. 'I . . .' she began, and then stopped as Sara glared directly into her face. Sara's eyes then looked across coldly at Fiona's hand on her shoulder. Fiona's eyes followed them. I saw Fiona's hand grip tighter, making it clear she wasn't going to let go until she'd been allowed to say her piece. Sara's eyes moved back to stare right at Fiona again; Fiona's eyes swung to meet them. They looked at each other in silence for a second. Then Sara head-butted Fiona right on the nose.

Right on it. Nnch! Like that – Nnch! It was a terrible sound: the kind of noise you'd imagine a boundary-making hit would produce if you were playing cricket with a hamster.

Fiona went rigid and glassy eyed. Too stunned – psychologically, or physically, or both – to do anything. I rather hoped she might topple over satisfyingly, like a tree falling. (It was probably too much to hope for in a hotel function room, but I further cherished the image that – as she lay there insensible – she'd then be trampled by horses.) I never got to see what happened, though, because Sara pulled me away while Fiona was still dancing the Lot's Wife.

We hurried along, Sara dictating the pace, and were very quickly outside.

'Hey!' Mary looked out of the window of a taxi right in front of the hotel. 'Get in. Hugh should be here soon.'

'Thanks,' said Sara, brightly, and we clambered inside. She sat on the pull-down seat, opposite Mary. I flopped on to the long rear one next to the window and looked at her, but she didn't look back. Instead she chatted cheerfully to Mary about how they'd be glad to get out of their shoes and so on. Hugh arrived and we drove home. Sara and Mary continued to chat, and Hugh talked to me about something or other, but it didn't make it into my brain.

Eventually, we reached our house and got out. We waved

goodbye to Hugh and Mary as they pulled away in the taxi, Sara fiddling with her key in the lock at the same time. The door opened after some coaxing – Sara half falling into the hall when it finally gave in. I followed her inside and she flicked on the light, kicked off her shoes, began to remove her coat and, most noticeably, turned to me and said, 'You fucking cunt.'

My first instinct was to say, 'What?' in an innocently bemused fashion. I mean, literally, it was my 'instinct'. I didn't for a moment consider it to be an option worth trying (I'd been searching for 'options worth trying' for the whole taxi journey and hadn't come up with a single one), but it very nearly popped out, instinctively. I managed to capture it in time, though, and instead said nothing at all.

'Well?' said Sara. She looked very angry. I'd hardly ever seen her angry: not *really* angry. It was scary. All I could think was, 'Christ – she's going to head-butt me.' She let me dither for a moment before repeating, even more insistently, '*Well?*'

I sighed, wearily. 'Fiona's a bitch,' I said. 'She's always hated me.'

'You're saying it's not true, then? Is that what you're saying?'

'Good God, *of course* it's not true. I don't know why you told her you knew about it.'

'I told her because I didn't want that snotty English tart thinking she was better than me. That she could play with this juicy secret right there – while the poor, poor wee girlfriend didn't really understand what was going on right in front of her face.'

'But it's not true.'

'Of course it's fucking true. You think I haven't seen that something was going on? All the secretiveness and the weirdness and the ridiculous stories and the secrecy . . .'

'You already said secre—'

289

'I know what I've fucking said! With everything that's been happening, I knew that something was up. Until I got her alone at the party and realised her eyes were on someone else, I'd thought you were sleeping with Amy . . .'

'Amy!' I laughed out loud at this.

If I'm ever in this situation again, I will never, ever, *ever* laugh out loud at any point. It really is one of those lessons you only need to learn once.

'You *cunt*!' Sara came at me in a flurry of blows. She was completely overwhelming: none of the impacts was very heavy, but she seemed suddenly to be attacking me with five times the number of arms I had available to defend myself. 'You complete fucking *bastard*!'

'Jesus!' I said, covering my head. 'Calm down!'

She did stop hitting me and back off a little, but I didn't delude myself that it had anything to do with my negotiating skills.

I held my hands out in front of me – imploringly (and, if we're being strictly accurate, also half in readiness in case she went for me again). 'I'm sorry. It's just so unbelievable that you could think I was seeing Amy.'

Sara laughed now, but it was dry and humourless. 'More bloody believable than the thought of you and Georgina Nye!'

That stung a little. Fair enough, Georgina Nye – famous, beautiful actress adored by half of Great Britain – was a hell of a catch, but to suggest that it was *unbelievable* that she'd sleep with me? That she was completely out of my league? I mean, come on – you expect a little more backing than that *from your girlfriend*, for God's sake. That was hardly a confidence booster, was it? Your own girlfriend finding it incredible that you could pull Georgina Nye? I could have said, stroppily, that her astonishment just reflected badly on herself at the end of the day. If I was such a no-hoper at the top level, then what did that say about her? Eh?

I judged that this probably wasn't the time to mention this, however.

'But I'm not sleeping with Georgina Nye,' I insisted, 'so that's irrelevant.'

'Don't, Tom.' There were tears in her eyes now, but I think they were still as much from anger as anything. Or, rather, her shifting expressions seemed to suggest that they were produced by a massive blend of emotions, none of which she could hold in. She was leaking sadness and fury and incomprehension and hurt and a thousand other things all at the same time. There wasn't a single name for what was in her eyes . . . but it was exactly the kind of psychological state you could imagine being used later, as a defence at a murder trial. 'Don't you *dare* do that to me. That would be truly sickening. After all that's happened . . . your moods, your stupid cover stories . . . all those little slips you've made – like when I simply said *you* had a crush on that fucking woman, and you replied that there was "nothing *between* you" . . .'

'I just . . .'

'The way you were looking at her tonight. Her agent not knowing about the contract meeting, *your* agent being so vague that I knew she was covering up *something*, that Fiona tart . . . and, above all, the look on your face *right now*. Don't you *dare* show so little respect for me as to think I'm gullible enough to believe you're not sleeping with her. Is that how much respect you have for me? *Is it?*'

'I . . .' My throat was swollen; I could barely speak.

'I'll say it again: you're sleeping with Georgina Nye, aren't you?'

My head dropped. 'Yes,' I said. Hardly louder than a whisper, and choking on the word.

'You . . . fucking . . . *cunt*.'

I somehow managed to raise my eyes to look at her.

'You . . . *fucking* . . . *cunt*!' she repeated. 'So – that's how much respect you have for me, is it? I'm not even worth

fucking *lying* for? No, no: just come straight out with it –
spit it right into my face.'

'You said . . .'

'You disgusting, arrogant bastard. Being dragged around by
your dick I can understand, but I never knew you thought so
little of me as to be prepared to calmly kick me in the teeth
like *that.*'

'But you . . . I'm sorry, but . . .'

'*Jesus.* Well, I hope you'll treat Georgina fucking Nye better
than this now you're with her.'

'*With her?* I'm not "with her". I mean, I *am*, but I'm not,
and I'm with *you* at least as much, if not more. It's . . . oh,
I don't know what it is. I'm confused.'

'If you think you're going to be "with me" *and* "with
Georgina Nye", then "confused" is not *nearly* the fucking
word for what you are.'

'I didn't mean . . . I just don't know what to think or
what to do.'

'Really? Poor you and your inner turmoil. I'm not nearly
so deep, apparently, because *I* know what to think: I think
you're a cunt. *And* I know what to do too.' She moved
over, opened the front door and held it wide. 'Fuck off,'
she said.

'Come on, Sara . . . can't we talk about this?'

'Ha! Mr Talk About Our Feelings all of a sudden? Goodbye,
Mr Sit On The Fucking Sofa, Not Say A Word And Sigh
Wearily If I Try To Get A Conversation Going – Can't It
Wait Until After *Newsnight*: I'm Listening to This Report?,
and hello, Mr Talk About Our Feelings. What a sudden
and remarkable change – what *can* have brought it on!
You *cunt*!'

'Sara . . .'

'If you want to talk, go and talk to your slag of an
actress.'

'She's not a slag.' I felt I couldn't let George continually be called that. I wanted to be fair and it was, well, dishonourable not to defend her against such things. 'I thought you liked her.'

'*What?* You ... oh, I *see* ... You mean, "like her as an actress"? Rather than "like her as some rich slut who's been fucking my boyfriend behind my back"?'

'Come on, Sara, be reasonable. I understand you're upset, but let's try to behave like adults. This doesn't change who she is, and you liked her. She *is* a lovely person.'

'Doesn't change who she is? Of course it changes it. She's now the kind of person who can have it all – all the money and the fame and the success – but not be able to resist taking what *I* have, when I've got so little.'

'It's not like that. In fact, you're quite similar people.'

'We are not – in *any* fucking way – similar.'

'That's not true. Look, for a start, you're a supervisor at your work, and she's one in that factory in *The Firth*.'

'She *plays* a supervisor, you shithead!'

'But she knows how it feels – she spent two weeks in a real factory shadowing a supervisor to prepare for that part.'

'Give me one good reason why I shouldn't knife you *right* fucking now.'

'I didn't say it was *identical* . . .'

'Good for you, Tom. Because she's a wee, spoilt, rich tart who just takes whatever she fancies on a whim, and I'm a nobody. A nobody with three pairs of shoes to my name, in a dead-end job, in a dead-end life, and she can just drop by and take my boyfriend because . . . because *she can*. Because she's the big star who's in the newspapers and on TV, and I'm nothing but the boring girlfriend who sells bleeding Wall's Viennettas and fucking microwave fucking Calorie Counter fucking *cannelloni alla Besciamella*, and I'll be doing exactly the same thing until the day I fucking die. Jesus – she must be laughing at the very thought that I could possibly compete with her.'

'It's not a competition, for Christ's sake – and I don't care that she's a famous actress, that's just stupid.'

'Right. Of course. It had no effect on you at all.'

'It *didn't*.'

'Sure. You never once thought, "Wa-hey! I'm fucking *Georgina Nye* here!" Never even crossed your mind.'

'No. Never. If that'd been the case, I'd have been attracted to her even before we met – but I wasn't. The whole thing just happened gradually, without my even being aware of it.'

'I can imagine. It must have been a terrible bleeding shock to look down one day and notice you're shagging her brains out – "Christ! I'm fucking an actress!"'

'It . . . Look, it simply wasn't like that. It was just . . .' I wanted to say 'destiny', but that seemed ludicrous at this point, for some reason. 'I can't explain it, but I love you both and . . .'

'Och, you *love* her, do you?'

'I love you *both*.'

Sara grabbed me and physically hurled me out of the door.

'I'm charmed by your huge capacity for love, Tom. Well fucking done . . . Now fuck off.'

'Where to?'

'I don't care. Just leave. You can come back during the day, while I'm out, and collect your stuff. You can do that all next week. After that I'm changing the locks and anything of yours that's still here I'll burn.'

I leaned towards her. 'I love you, Sara. I know you're hurt, but I do still love you . . . more than I can say.'

'I'm closing this door now. I'll be back in two minutes to see if you're still here, and when I come back to check on that I'll be carrying a hammer.'

She slammed the door in my face.

I decided she needed some time to cool down.

*   *   *

'Sorry,' I said, for about the twentieth time. 'I didn't know where else to go . . . well, to tell the truth, there was nowhere else I *wanted* to go.'

'It's OK,' said George, 'I was still awake anyway.' She lit a cigarette and tossed the packet over to me. I took one greedily. There ought to be special cigarettes for times like this: rapid, super-strength ones, in the same way as you can get those isotonic, glucose-rich sports drinks. They ought to make crisis cigarettes that you simply have to tap on a table to ignite and that race down from tip to filter in a single drag.

After the unfortunate scene with Sara, I'd phoned George's mobile and then taken a taxi to her hotel. The night staff there obviously assumed I was one of the other guests and had let me walk right up to her room without anything beyond a 'Good evening, sir' from the reception desk.

'Anyway,' I said, 'I thought you'd want to know.'

'Yes,' replied George, and served up just the most basic components of a smile.

'I'm sorry.'

'It's not your fault, Tom. If it's anyone's fault then, well . . .' She took a long draw on her cigarette. '. . . it's Fiona's.'

'Bitch. I'm sure she only meant to torment me . . . but she'd had a bit of wine and she misjudged the level – and misjudged Sara too, for that matter. Still . . . bitch.'

'I'll call Paul first thing in the morning – he'll take care of her.'

In my head, I heard Paul hissing the words, 'I'll take care of her.' And then, perhaps, tapping the side of his nose.

'He's not going to kill her, is he?' I asked, a little anxiously.

'Kill her?'

'Well – get someone from the London gangland to do it.'

'Er, no, I don't expect so. I was thinking more that he'd phone and tell her that if she said another word then she'd be flushing her publicity career away – that he'd put the word out that anyone who employed her certainly wouldn't be working with me or anyone else Paul has any influence with. Why on earth did you think he'd *kill* her?'

'Well ... you know ... his accent.' Put like that it sounded stupid.

'Ah.'

'Don't tell him I said that.'

'Of course not ... You'd be a dead man.'

We treated ourselves to a couple of proper, if puny, smiles.

'So,' I said, 'what are we going to do?'

'What's Sara going to do?'

'I don't know. She's taken this much worse than I imagined.'

'You imagined her finding out?'

I had, in fact. Often. She'd discover some telltale clue and it'd all come out. She'd be in floods of tears. Upset almost to the point of collapse: distressed by the discovery and also terrified that she'd lost me. It'd be awful and very, very emotional. I'd hold her as she sobbed; hold her tightly and tell her how it was a dreadful, cruel thing that Fate had visited upon all of us. How most people are lucky enough never to face a situation where they meet the two people they were meant for, and meet them at the same time. I'd cry a little too, and say how I loved her just as much as I'd always done. That I couldn't bear the thought that finding love with George would mean I'd lose my love with her. We'd cling to each other, desperately, into the night. Then, the next morning – Sara a little red eyed from the tears but confident now of my continued love for her – we'd try to find some way for the three of us to move forward: a way of making this three-cornered relationship work.

I didn't imagine her just getting very, very angry indeed and throwing me out of the house. I seemed to remember she implied she might attack me with a hammer too, at one point – I'd definitely never imagined that bit at all.

'No,' I said, shaking my head animatedly, 'I don't mean I imagined her finding out. I meant she reacted much worse than I would have imagined, she would react, to it, if she had, done. Which she did.'

'I see.'

'Well, whatever . . . I don't know what she's going to do. I'll give her the night to calm down and call her tomorrow. She did have quite a few glasses of wine at the party, so maybe it was just the alcohol talking.' (Yes – that was probably it, actually.)

'Hmm . . .' George bit her lip. 'Do you think she'll keep talking when the alcohol wears off?'

'I'm sure she'll talk more reasonably.'

'No – I meant, do you think she'll *talk*?' she asked.

I looked at her, squinting that I didn't quite know what she meant.

'To the press,' she said. 'Do you think she'll talk to the press?'

'God – *no* – of course not.' No, she wouldn't. Would she? No, it was unthinkable. For one thing, Sara had more class than that. And, for another, she'd surely realise how damaging such a thing would be. Giving her story to the press – doing something so spiteful and ill considered – would be dreadful: it'd create a wound in our relationship that it'd be terribly difficult to heal. I couldn't believe she'd do something like that. 'No, Sara would never do that.'

'How many books have you ghost-written for women whose husbands have thought they'd never do such a thing?' Jesus.

'Sara's different.'

George's face humoured me with an 'OK – if you say so' expression. 'Practical things, then – where are you planning to stay?'

'Well, I thought I could stay here tonight.'

'Yes.' George squeezed my hand, briefly. '*Of course* you can. But what about after that?'

'Well ... hopefully Sara will get a little less volcanic and let me back into the house ... the spare bedroom, or something. But I suppose, just in case, I'll get a hotel room in the meantime.'

'Not in this hotel, though.'

'Christ no – I could never afford to stay in ... Oh, right. I see what you mean. No, I'll get a room in a different hotel. A long way from here.'

'You're very sweet, Tom.' She touched my face, briefly. 'Especially with all you're going through.'

We talked for another half an hour or so, chain-smoking and running over hundreds of 'what about's and 'what if's. Then, quietly, we went to bed. We just slept together, we didn't have sex. Which was absolutely fine with me, obviously. We were both exhausted – emotionally as much as physically – and, in any case, having sex in these circumstances, with what had happened still very much raw in our minds, well, that would have been completely inappropriate. *Coarse*, even. Actually, I was glad it never seemed to be an option. Phew.

The following morning, I went to book a room in a hotel – a reasonably nice one, in fact. Well, I wasn't remotely poverty stricken, not with the money I was going to get from *Growing*, so I was sure I could easily afford a night or two in a fairly decent place. After that, I went and had a quite astonishingly ugly ten minutes with Sara.

I'd never have thought she could be so nasty, quite frankly. I called round the house with the perfectly acceptable excuse that I needed to pick up just a few things that couldn't wait until next week when she was out – my shaver, some clothes, the charger for my mobile and so on. I even rang the doorbell, rather than using my key to let myself in. She did allow me into the house to collect the stuff, but she was rigid faced, cold and monosyllabic: it was like trying to talk to the Terminator. However, it wasn't until I suggested that this was a silly situation – shouldn't I stay so we could try to work things through? – that she really turned savage. She said that if I ever turned up again while she was there she'd destroy everything of mine without even giving me the week's grace and, what was more, if I didn't leave in the next fifteen seconds she'd call the police. (I may have lived there for several years – and, if I'd been looking at it from the position of preparing for a vile and gruelling legal battle, also partly paid the upkeep – but it was solely her house on paper.)

I left carrying a suitcase of my things and a completely new, sober perspective on the situation. Clearly, it could be several days – perhaps even a whole week – before Sara calmed down again.

Once I'd set myself up with a room, I gave George a call. We talked for a few minutes but she was just about to set off to meet Paul (she had to tour around the country doing more publicity work for the next few days). So, I stayed in my hotel for the rest of the day, and all the next day too. Even more so than usual, I kept my mobile to hand – to the extent of leaving it switched on all night while I charged it. I didn't want to miss it if Sara rang to begin patching things up. I could understand it'd be quite a struggle, internally, for her to make that first call and I wanted to make sure I was there for her when she did.

I didn't feel like going out, but there wasn't much to do where I was. I spent some time in the hotel bar, smoking and drinking whisky (whisky is the drink in these situations – aesthetically: you can't picture Marlowe or Spade having dame trouble and sitting at the bar with a glass of Belgian lager or a dry sherry, can you?). There's only so long you can hang around in a hotel bar drinking on your own, though, without straying into lonely saddo territory. So, I got out before that set in, and went up to my room, where I drank from the mini-bar and sat on the edge of my bed watching the telly instead.

Hugh stared at me like an unflattering photograph of himself: a still image caught for ever in the instant between complete disbelief and utter horror.

I hadn't been looking forward to telling him, but I'd judged it'd be best to get it over with. For one thing, it was possibly appropriate that he know about the situation quickly for professional reasons – what with M&C handling George's book. For another, Sara might very well talk to Mary about it soon, so he could easily hear of it that way: I preferred to tell him myself before this happened. It seemed the decent thing to do, but I was also keen that the first he heard of it wasn't some distorted version of events – passed on from Sara, through his wife – that would reflect poorly on me. I was worried, in fact, that he might have heard already, before I'd come to his office this morning. His current facial expression very much indicated that this was not the case.

However, someone who *had* been on the receiving end of some information, in my estimation, was Fiona. When I'd walked into the office, Fiona had been going somewhere carrying a bundle of manuscripts. She'd glanced up, seen me, gone bloodless, then dropped her head and scurried – yes, *scurried* – away. It was attractive to imagine that her own awareness of her mistake coupled with nothing more than my stern gaze had been sufficient to provoke this reaction, but I doubted it. I guessed that she'd had a call from Paul on Saturday morning, pointing out how it would look if news of George's other-woman status were to get out when her book was singing a sisterhood hymn: and how poorly it would serve Fiona's reputation when it got around that *she* was the one who'd revealed the secret, while *she was actually in charge of the publicity for the book*. I'm sure Paul would have made it very clear that, in those circumstances, her publishing career was likely to shift gear pretty quickly from head of publicity at McAllister & Campbell's Scottish offices to unpacking the boxes at a discount bookstore in Rhyl. (Despite George's assurances, I couldn't get the idea that he'd additionally threatened to have her thrown into a car compactor in Deptford out of my mind, either.)

Hugh was still frozen with that expression on his face.

'Oh,' he said, finally.

'Yes. It's a bit of a mess, I'm afraid.'

'So . . . Have . . . How long have you and Georgina Nye been . . . ?'

'Just two or three weeks, really. Though . . .' I shrugged, '. . . you know.'

'No, not really,' said Hugh, 'I haven't got a clue . . . Dear me – poor Sara.'

'Yes . . . yes . . . but "poor me" too, obviously.'

'You?'

I was a bit hurt by this. 'Yes – me,' I said. 'I'm the one who's sitting on his own in a hotel room, drinking tiny – *obscenely* expensive – bottles of Drambuie and watching reruns of *Mister* bloody *Ed*. Sara's kicked *me* out, not the other way round.'

'But, well, Tom . . . it is, you know, your fault.'

'Oh, *right*. It's always the man's fault, isn't it? Have you ever noticed that? Whenever someone's unfaithful, it's *always* the man's fault. If he strays, then he's some thoughtless, selfish bastard who's so shallow that he'll risk everything because he can't resist the chance of a quick shag. But if the *woman* is unfaithful, then that'll be because she felt "unloved" or "ignored" or "undervalued", and it's the man's fault again. A man has an affair and it's a drooling, dumb, dick-over-brains thing or a pathetic mid-life crisis, but a woman has one and it just shows how bloody complex she is – how she knew "the relationship wasn't working", even though it seemed to be working perfectly to her poor, bovine other half. But that's not her being selfish, never satisfied and twisting the truth of the situation, oh no – *she* can decide that about the relationship as a whole completely unilaterally and that just means she's *sensitive*: if he doesn't see it that way, well, that's actual proof he's brutish and self-obsessed. Amazing, isn't it, how – whoever does what – it's *always* the man's fault?'

'Tom? *You've been sleeping with Georgina Nye.*'

'Oh, for Christ's . . . I'm talking culturally, Hugh – *culturally*. Do you have to be so bloody literal about things?'

'Well . . .'

'And, anyway, suppose we say for a second that this *is* about me . . .'

'Um . . .'

'You love Mary, don't you?'

'Of course.'

'And your sex life is still good?'

'Mary's very interested in gardening nowadays.'

'Eh . . . ? What's that supposed to mean? Is gardening the antidote to sex or something?'

'Personally or culturally? Because . . .'

'Whatever, whatever, it doesn't matter. You're not sexually unsatisfied with Mary, though, are you?'

'Tom . . .' Hugh wriggled, as though he were embarrassed.

'*Are* you?'

'No, Tom – I'm not.'

'Good. So, you love her and your sex life is fine . . . but that doesn't mean you're not a human being any more: that you don't have exactly the same emotions as any other human being. You still fancy other women.'

'No I don't.'

'Of course you do.'

'I don't.'

'You *do* . . . what about Cameron Diaz?'

'That's hardly the same thing, Tom.'

'Why not?' I sat back in my chair, challenging him to give a convincing explanation.

'Because I might look at Cameron Diaz and think she's attractive, but that's a very different thing to *sleeping with* Cameron Diaz. I think Nicole Kidman is attractive too . . . And Tori Amos. Courteney Cox, Angelina Jolie, Catherine Zeta-Jones, Liz Hurley, Gwyneth Paltrow, Sheryl Crow, Katie Jameson . . .'

'Katie Jameson?'

Hugh leaned over and pointed out of his window, across the McAllister & Campbell office. 'Katie Jameson . . .' he said. '. . . in Legal and Copyright . . . Sandra Bullock, Nigella Lawson, Natalie Imbruglia, Jenny Agutter, Kirsty Wark, my daughter's geography teacher, the woman who's on the cheese and cooked meats counter at the supermarket, Mary's sister-in-law in Kinlochewe . . .'

'OK, OK.'

'. . . but the point is I've never done anything about it. I've never actually slept with *a single one of them*.'

'But you would if you had the chance.'

'No. I wouldn't.'

'You bloody *would*.'

'No, I *wouldn't*. Because Mary would find out and leave me.'

'Ahhh – but suppose you knew Mary would never find out.'

'It's impossible to know that.'

'Hypothetically.'

'Well if, in a hypothetical context, I knew she'd never find out then maybe, in a hypothetical context, I'd sleep with one of them. But then, in a hypothetical context, I'm sleeping with one of them hypothetically now, just so I can consider your question.'

'There you go, then – you're sleeping with Cameron Diaz.'

'No, because – non-hypothetically – I'd never, ever do it. Mary would find out and leave me.'

'But that doesn't alter the fact that you *want* to, right? Whether you do it – whether the action or the intent is the crucial thing – is Sartre versus Kant, isn't it? *At the very least*, you have to admit it's a central dilemma of moral philosophy that it'd be awfully glib of you to say you've categorically solved this morning, Hugh.'

'Mmm . . .'

'*Wouldn't* it?'

'Well, I suppose . . .'

'So . . .' I leaned forward and began jabbing my finger down on Hugh's desk for emphasis. '. . . here I am, genuinely emotionally engaged with two women – through a random act of chance that meant I met both of them. In moral terms it's perfectly arguable that I'm no more culpable than any other sexually mature human being on the planet, and yet I'm stranded in a society where infidelity is – axiomatically – *always* judged to be the man's fault on some level or other. Christ! Talk about loaded dice. Even *you* aren't on my side! What have I done that's so wrong?'

'Um . . .'

'Tell me – what have I done?!'

'Erm . . .'

'I'm a fucking idiot, aren't I?'

'Would you like a cup of tea?'

I slumped back in my chair, suddenly very tired, and said, hardly louder than a whisper, 'Yes . . . yes, please.'

I called George a few times during the day but her mobile was switched off. I left messages asking her to phone me back. I was upset and . . . I was upset, and frightened, and I wanted to talk to her: she would listen and be able to sympathise. She, more than anyone, knew how much I loved Sara and so she would be able to understand how hard this whole thing had hit me. Then something interesting happened: at about nine o'clock in the evening George sent me a text message that said, 'i need some time to think about things.'

The interesting aspect of this was that I knew she had lots of free text messages included in her mobile contract. Dumping me via text wasn't even costing her the 8 1/2p it would have cost me to dump her that way. This seemed brutally unfair. Nauseous and shaking, I did – somehow – manage to convince myself I'd misinterpreted her words. Doing this in the face of such evidence took an impressive effort of will, as you can imagine: I don't like to brag, but suffice it to say that I've *certainly* been dumped by enough women to recognise a dumping as roaringly explicit as 'I need some time to think about things'. I texted her back, 'are you saying its over?'

A little later, she replied, 'i didn't say that. i just need some time to think about things.'

So, that was it, then: she'd definitely dumped me.

I sent her multiple further messages, but got no reply. I tried to ring, but got diverted to her voicemail. This was an astonishingly cruel thing to happen to me. On the very day I'd come to realise that my relationship with Sara might be in serious jeopardy (obviously, I'd known before this morning that the situation was serious, but I hadn't quite understood how it was so, erm . . . *serious*. You know, 'really serious'), on this very day George had also deserted me. I couldn't understand it.

Yes – self-evidently – George was ambitious and would be terrified of anything that might damage her image, but I simply couldn't accept she'd drop me so quickly and so coldly when things got rough. She wasn't that mercenary and unfeeling. I'd had sex with her – so I knew what she was really like. Pretty quickly I realised that it must be her agent who was making her do it. I couldn't delude myself: I had to face the facts now. George was probably sitting in some hotel – her eyes raw from crying, her voice hoarse from sobbing, nervous shivers running through her hunched, emotionally drained frame – clutching her mobile phone and staring inconsolably at the message Paul had insisted she send to me. And there was no hope of my competing, of course: George was completely under his control. He'd guided her for so long that he'd now become a father figure she couldn't defy, and there was no doubt that his calculating outlook would mean he'd want to protect his investment in her. What could I do about it? Nothing. For all I knew, Paul had even confiscated her mobile phone by now and any messages I sent would go to him instead. Moreover, George was George, so I couldn't simply contact her the way one would a normal person. In fact, if I tried to get in touch with any real determination then Paul would probably report me to the police as a stalker. Most of all, if he'd broken George psychologically – made her give in, deny our love and do his bidding – then she was already lost to me.

There was only one thing for me to do now. I needed to get very, very drunk and then phone Sara.

First of all, I got very, very drunk. The initial phase of this took about an hour. To avoid the sadistically inflated prices charged for drinks from the mini-bar, I went downstairs and put in the groundwork there. I hurled an eclectic selection of spirits and beers into myself, which was all the more effective as they landed on a virtually empty stomach (not completely empty as, forty-five minutes and a significant number of drinks into the exercise, I was absolutely overcome with hunger for three bags of dry-roasted peanuts – something which, by amazing good fortune, they sold at the bar). I then took a little stroll around the inside of my brain to inspect my condition and reported back to myself that I wasn't 'drunk', as such, but 'relaxed and perhaps a little light headed'. Still, I felt, I'd done enough to move back upstairs now. Some other guests were in the lift, but I was so cleverly slow, measured and precise both in my demeanour and in the way I took my time pressing the correct button for my floor that I doubt they suspected for one moment that I'd been drinking. A deception I successfully maintained, as the lift doors shut (removing me from their view) after I got out and it thus didn't matter that I walked along to my room by bouncing from one side of the corridor to the other.

I opened my door and made straight for the mini-bar. I knew I'd made more alcoholic headway than I'd first imagined when my progress across the room was staged so it began with my drifting off to the left through a conveniently open doorway and falling magnificently into the bath. I lay in it for a few minutes, and giggled uncontrollably at something I forget now, before pulling myself out again (knocking a spare toilet roll into the lavatory in the process – ahhh . . . I'll get that out in the morning: I don't think I'll need to use the lavatory at all tonight) and heading back to the bedroom. I opened the mini-bar and was surprised and delighted to find that, now I looked again, the drinks didn't seem all that expensive at all.

I sat on the edge of the bed and opened the first bottle – it made a satisfying cr-r-r-ick as all the tiny metal connectors on the lid snapped under my expert and dashing twist. The spirit was pleasingly sharp. It stung my tongue and lips and felt like a penance, like an alcoholic Hail Mary. My determination for absolution spurred me to drink another almost right away. I sat still for a moment . . . Christ – I felt really, really sick. I was going to puke in a second . . . No, hold on . . . it was OK: it had passed. I reached forward and opened a Pernod.

Just the *tiniest* little bit after midnight I telephoned Sara.

'Hello?' she said. She sounded sleepy.

'It's me . . . I love you.'

'Tom . . .'

'I really, really, really, really, really, *really* love you, Sara.'

'Tom?'

'What?'

'I want you to piss off now, and never call me again – OK?'

'But I *love* you. Don't you care that I *love you*? You *bitch*! You – no! I didn't mean that!'

'Tom . . .'

'Don't hang up! *Please* . . . It's . . . I love you.'

'Yeah – me, Georgina Nye . . .'

'It's over between George and me. Finished.'

'Ahhh . . .'

'You're the only one I want.'

'So, she dumped you.'

'She *didn't* dump me . . . the *bitch* . . . it's that agent of hers – I'm going to smash his fucking face in . . . She didn't . . . I mean, this is about me and you – it's got nothing to do with her.'

'Goodbye, Tom.'

'No! No – I need to tell you something . . .'

''Bye.'

'No – *please*. Listen. I've got to tell you this, OK . . . ? Just let me say this *one thing*.'

'What? What is it?'

'It's . . . right. Sara?'

'What?'

'*I love you*.'

'I'm disconnecting the phone from the wall.'

The line went dead.

I looked my mobile right in the face. '*Bitch!*' I shouted at it. 'Well, fuck you, then! Right, if that's the way you want it . . . Fuck . . . You.'

I rang the land line again, but it was disconnected. I rang Sara's mobile. It was switched off, so I left a message explaining that I loved her. There was nothing else I could do now but return to the mini-bar.

I don't know when I finally drifted off to sleep, but I didn't wake up until about 11.30 the next morning. All I could recover about the previous night's events, using the physical evidence available rather than my memory, was: (a) I'd continued to drink – the mini-bar was ravaged; (b) at some point I'd smashed a vase, and then tried to hide the bits from the hotel staff by pushing them inside the air-conditioning grille; (c) I couldn't say how many text messages I'd sent, but the last five were retained by my phone and were 'i love you', 'I LOVE YOU', 'you fucking BITCH', 'im missing you' (that one was sent to George) and (back to Sara again) 'I Loooooooooove you'; (d) I was deeply, *deeply* wrong about not needing to use the toilet again.

I tried to ring Sara's mobile to apologise for my behaviour the previous night. Possibly with a view to then moving on to apologise about various other things too. I got a 'number unavailable' message, though. I couldn't think of any reason for this except that Sara had either changed her number or had had me barred from calling it. I was drenched by misery. Not that grandiose, Gothic misery either: just an ugly, wretched bleakness. It was the emotional equivalent of sitting there in wet clothes – like I'd been caught in some kind of grim downpour and left damp with pathetic sadness.

I was miserable, I was a twat, and the cause of my misery was that I was a twat. Rearrange those pieces any way you fancy and you're not going to be able to avoid the conclusion that you are, definitively, a 'miserable twat'.

I called Amy and arranged to meet her that evening. I'd prepared a little speech, 'Never mind *why* . . . it's just important that I see you. There's something I need to say,' but she never gave me the chance.

'Amy? Are you free this evening?'

'Um, yeah. Eight-thirty, at Galluzzi's, OK?'

'Yeah . . . I . . .'

'Right, see you then. 'Bye.'

I bet she was about to see another client. Everybody was trying to emphasise how unspecial I was, it seemed.

I took a shower and changed into the only alternative set of clothes I had with me. After that I did nothing. Nothing at all. I lay half sitting up on the bed, without even turning the TV on (any noise seemed harsh and painful: not because I had a hangover – I didn't, in fact – but simply because it was a vulgar intrusion into my sorrow: inappropriate and grating) and smoked and smoked until, by the time I had to leave to meet Amy, my breathing sounded like a bicycle pump.

'Christ, Tom – *well done!*'

Amy had paused for only a couple of seconds after my, apropos of nothing, announcement that I'd been sleeping with George and now, as she replied, her eyes were sparkling. She reached across, grabbed my shoulder and gave it a tiny, congratulatory shake. '*Well done*,' she repeated.

'You said she was a Fuck Monster.'

'That's what I've heard, aye – but a completely A-list Fuck Monster. If you divide the number of people who've poked her by the number of people who'd've *liked to have* poked her you probably get a figure that's actually smaller than for the world's top nun.'

'So you think having sex with Georgina Nye is . . . what? An achievement to be proud of?'

'Abso*lutely*. It's Georgina Nye. I mean . . . Christ, Tom – *well done*.'

'Sara doesn't see it quite like that.'

'Ah, right . . . So Sara knows, then?'

I lit a cigarette. 'Yeah . . . she's thrown me out.'

'How did she find out about it?'

'Fiona. Well, really, it was lots of things: a steady drip of things. But, for brevity, let's just say it was that fucking bitch Fiona.'

'That makes sense.'

'What do you mean by that?'

'Well, you'd gone off her, hadn't you?'

'I was never "on" her . . .' I said, tapping my cigarette repeatedly against the rim of the ashtray. '. . . and even if – for argument's sake – we say I was, then she never fancied me back.'

Amy tutted. 'Tch – what's that got to do with it?'

'So why should she care? And I'm sure she didn't mean to give me away, in any case – she'd just had a bit too much to drink and . . .'

'Her subconscious desire slipped out.'

'But she *didn't fancy* . . .'

'Not *that* desire, you bampot: her desire for revenge. With Fiona, everything's about Fiona. She might not have fancied you, but she wanted *you* to fancy *her*. And she certainly didn't want you to stop fancying her because you'd moved on to someone else. And certainly not someone with a far better arse than she has.'

'I . . .'

'Ha!' Amy clapped her hands together in delight. 'Georgina Nye's arse – officially the UK's best arse according to the readers of at least two national magazines! Fucking *brilliant*! Fiona must have been near-suicidal – I can't wait to see her.'

'I think George's agent has already given her a hard time.'

'Not as hard as . . . Hold on, you mean Paul knows about this already?'

'I think so . . . I think he's made sure George won't be seeing me any more too.'

'How long has Paul known?'

'Um, I can't say. Since Saturday morning, maybe.'

'Right . . .'

Amy topped up her Chianti. The wine sloshed in flamboyantly and a bit spilt over the edge of the glass. I watched it snake down the side, like a tear of blood.

Jesus – 'like a tear of blood'. I'd actually thought that. When you find yourself thinking in the kind of similes that normally remain safely in the diaries of fourteen-year-old girls, then you *know* you're in a bad way. 'Like a tear of blood.' *Jesus.*

'Amy . . . I'm a bit fucked up,' I said.

'Aye. That's understandable, Tom. I can imagine what you're going through. Still, there *are* positives – I mean, you're going to make fucking *thousands* from the book.'

'The book?'

'The book. *I Poked Georgina Nye* . . . The *book.*'

'I'm not going to do a book.'

'Oh, I wasn't serious about the title . . . Though, come to think of it, if we used asterisks, that'd be great: *I asterisk, asterisk, asterisk-ed Georgina Nye.* If pushed, we'd just say it was "loved". But that we blanked it because "love" is a dirty word for her. Christ – this thing writes itself!'

'It'll have to, because *I'm* not writing it.'

'Tom, Tom – you've *got* to write it. You can't possibly pass up an opportunity like this. You'll be financially secure for life.'

'I'm not writing a book.'

'Tom . . .' She lowered her voice and took on a sorrowful look. 'This is your chance to give a true account: to tell *your* side of the story.'

'Jesus, Amy! You can't use that line on me. That's *our line* – how can you sit there and use our line on me?'

'Because it always works.'

'Well, it's not going to this time. I'm not writing a book.'

'And Sara? You think Sara isn't going to sell the story?'

'She won't.'

'You're sure about that?'

'Yes.'

'Because you know her.'

'Yes.'

'Tell me . . . since she found out about you and George,

has she been just like the woman you've known for the past however many years it is?'

God, she was good. I was *so* lucky to have Amy as my agent.

'That's not the point.'

'In what way isn't it exactly, irrefutably, overwhelmingly the point?'

'Sara has no story to sell. She's an unknown supermarket supervisor whose nobody boyfriend slept with Georgina Nye, and she didn't know anything about it. There's a magazine feature in it . . .'

'Two-page, non-exclusive: I'm thinking one of the more upmarket women's mags – say, *marie claire*?'

'Yeah, they pay quite – No! Shut up. She *could* make a few pounds, but she has no details . . . or anything, really. Sara wouldn't do it, but she *definitely* wouldn't do it for what would be on offer.'

'Tch – and *that*'s your point?'

'No. My point is that – even if she did do it – *I* won't. We both know that we always try to make it about somebody else – reactive: "setting the record straight", or "not allowing him to get away with it", or "letting the world know what you're *really* like". But, really, it's about me. And I don't think it's right. If I did it I'd be demeaning myself, it's about my own sense of what's honourable.'

'Holy fucking shite! Drink up, Tom – you're wanted back in *The Iliad*. Listen to yourself. You don't hold the morality of Great Britain in the balance here. It's a simple business deal. If you pass this up all that happens is that you miss out on *hundreds of thousands of pounds*. That's all. *You* miss out. Georgina Nye – Georgina Nye and fucking Paul Dugan – walk away smiling. *You* miss out and life goes on – they don't start erecting statues of you or anything.'

'I don't care. Like I said, it's about me, and *I* don't want to do it.'

'Then you're nuts.'

'Quite probably. But I'm afraid this is a time when you're getting ten per cent of bugger all.'

'I wasn't thinking about my ten per cent.'

I did a thing with my eyes.

'OK,' she said, 'I mean I wasn't *only* thinking about my ten per cent. I was thinking about what was best for you too. I know how people can have these conflicts between their emotions and good financial sense – *believe* me, I do – and I just wanted you to think this through. If you're determined to piss away a fortune because of the samurai fucking code or whatever, then fine. I think you're wrong, but I'll go along with it because it's what you want.' Amy scrunched her cigarette out in the ashtray. 'I'm your agent – but I'm your friend too.'

'Which are you most?'

'Hey – don't push it, OK? I've reached out now, so just don't fucking push it.'

There was a short silence. I turned the cigarette packet over and over on top of the table.

'Well,' I said, 'I suppose I'd better tell you why I wanted to see you.'

'What? You mean it wasn't to tell me about poking Nye? Christ – what now? Are you going to peel your face back and confess you're from the planet Zerg?'

'I want you to arrange for me to see George. Call her agent and set it up.'

'Not very likely, Tom. Celebrity? Spurned lover? Paul isn't going to allow that. He'll assume you're going to attack her.'

'I'm not going to attack her . . .'

'Right – that'll be my negotiating position, then.'

'Listen – you and Paul can be there too. Set it up somewhere public – though, obviously, not *too* public – and all four of us can meet. I need to see her face to face one more time, that's all . . .'

Amy stared at me and nodded slowly.

'. . . Oh, for Christ's sake,' I said, 'I *am not* going to attack her.'

'I didn't say . . .'

'Quite apart from anything else,' I added, sadly, 'she'd easily be able to kick the shit out of me.'

'I still can't see Paul allowing it. You and me are the last people he wants to have sitting across the table.'

'He will. Public place, all of us present – that'll help. But what's more, he'll be terrified I'm going to write the story. If he thinks there's *any* chance he can prevent it with his cockney banter – backed up by George being there to play on my affection – then he won't be able to resist.'

'Mmmm . . .' Amy admitted. 'You've got something there.'

'I'll be fine. Really. I just need to see her. I can't make it end for me without seeing her.'

'You poor bastard.'

'I know. Pathetic.'

Amy shook her head. 'No. It's . . . What about you and Sara? Think you can fix it?'

'I thought so at first, but now . . . No, I can't see her taking me back. Why should she?'

'I'm sorry.'

'Whatever.'

'It's a bit shitty for you all round, then, really?' She reached across and put her hand over mine, giving it a tiny squeeze. Funny: we'd been kissing each other's cheeks for years, but I think this was the first time our hands had ever touched. I was ludicrously grateful for the contact. I turned my hand over and squeezed hers back: too hard, I think – a little desperately. I just wanted someone to hang on to. Amy smiled. 'Oh well . . .' she said, with a sigh. 'It'll pass, eventually. You'll get over it and, at the end of the day, you still got to poke Georgina Nye – no one can ever take that away from you.'

*   *   *

Everything in the house heckled me. The sofa called, 'This is where you and Sara used to sit together'; the wardrobe nagged, 'Get your clothes out of me – I'm for Sara alone now'; the grill cackled, 'Won't be making any cheese on toast under me again. Twat.'

I'd come to collect some more of my stuff and it was awful. On a specific level, it put a hollow ache in my stomach to walk around in a place so familiar, so ours, that now seemed resolute in excluding me. Every thing was a thing lost. More generally, it made me confront the fact that I would have to make a declaration of defeat soon. OK, I'd got an attractive sum heading my way for *Growing*, but I couldn't afford to live in a hotel – even a not very nice hotel – for ever. And, even if I could have, there wasn't room for all my things. I'd have to find a bedsit or a flat or something. Doing that would be a practical admission, to myself, that Sara and I weren't going to be getting back together. The tricky thing was that I wanted to give it time: it'd been less than a week, *maybe* Sara would soften. But she'd told me that anything I hadn't removed by Friday night she'd destroy or throw away. And I believed her. I believed her because of everything she'd said to me, and the absolutely unwavering way she'd said it. I believed her because she now wasn't saying anything to me at all. And I believed her because of the answerphone.

Sara had dug the old answerphone out of the attic. With our both having mobiles, we didn't really need it any more, so we'd thrown it up there along with every other electrical appliance we owned that had outlived its era. We kept the land line, though, for my Internet access and so that people could call us without having to pay mobile rates all the time. I went over to the answerphone and pressed the 'announce' button . . . just to hear Sara's voice. After a whirr and a click its tinny loudspeaker crackled, 'Hi, this is Sara. I can't get to the phone at the moment but, if you'd like to leave a message, then speak after the tone. Unless you're Tom, in which case, please just fuck off.' The announcement – though somewhat indicative of her feelings – wasn't the crucial thing. Nor was the fact that the only credible reason for her to have reattached the answerphone was so that she could hear who was calling before picking up the phone and, if it was me, *not* pick up the phone. No, neither of those things was the real kick in the stomach. What hit home was purely that she'd brought it down and set it up. Sara had never been able to set it up – nor programme the timer on the VCR, nor use any of the zillion different food type/defrost settings on the microwave. Just being in the *same room* as our digital camcorder used to make her angry. Had I been there, I know she'd have insisted that I 'set this bloody stupid thing up'. There used to be no middle ground between it being set up by me, or Sara outside on the lawn, hitting it with a shovel. But now, here it was. Sought out, attached, and set up perfectly. The answerphone was Sara psychologically accepting that I wasn't there, and then tacitly announcing that it wasn't a problem. You know how some men are threatened by their wife having a vibrator? Well, that's nothing to how comprehensively redundant this answerphone made me feel. Jesus: rate *that* for depressing – in the movies, electronics don't show you how expendable you are until they achieve sentience with the awesome artificial intelligence of HAL or that military computer in *War Games* or something ... I was being put in my place by a bloody answerphone.

I gathered two suitcases full of belongings and called a taxi to take me back to the hotel. While I waited for it to arrive I wrote a note to Sara (telling her how I loved her and how I hoped we could work things out) and left it on the table in the dining room. When I closed my eyes, I could imagine her – so strongly I could hear the fabric of her coat and smell the scent of her skin – coming home from work, seeing my note lying there, and throwing it unread into the bin.

*   *   *

Paul reached across the table and shook my hand with great enthusiasm. Tosser. Anyone would have thought that *he'd* called the meeting and was buzzing with delight to see me. Amy had said that he hadn't wanted the meeting until she'd hinted at my writing about what had happened. 'Wouldn't have met me if his bollocks had been in a vice,' she'd said with an acrid laugh. 'But, as soon as I made the tiniest wee threat of you leaking things about Nye ... well, he simply couldn't *wait* to meet.' So, here we all were, just a few days later. Paul's aim was clearly to control those events he couldn't avoid. His smiles and expansively open body language were ribbons and bows on a dog turd. George, on the other hand, didn't rise from her seat when Amy and I came in and didn't look at me as I sat down. She just gazed off to the side at nothing fascinating and absently twiddled with a strand of hair that was dangling from under her hat.

We'd deliberately come to an out-of-the-way restaurant very early in the day. I suppose the owners hoped a few people might arrive later for lunch, but for now we were the only ones there.

'Good to see you again, mate,' said Paul. 'Amy?' He raised a wine bottle questioningly. Amy nodded and he filled a glass for her. 'Tom?'

'No thanks,' I replied.

He sat back in his chair and clapped his hands together. 'Okey-dokey. So . . .'

Amy lit a cigarette. 'Paul,' she said, 'we wanted this meeting so we could get a few things straight.' There was, obviously, no reason at all for this meeting. Amy had the task, therefore, of rambling on pointlessly for a while, just for the look of the thing. 'I'm sure you know what I mean,' she added, meaningfully.

'I'm not sure I do, darling. We've got everything signed and sorted, haven't we?'

'Absolutely – abso*lute*ly . . . but there are other issues. Personal issues.'

I fixed my eyes on George, hoping she'd look towards me on hearing this – out of reflex if nothing else. But she continued to stare away from the table.

'Oh, I reckon it's always best to keep that stuff private – you know what I mean?' replied Paul. 'Personal stuff's personal, isn't it? It's *well* poor if you start chucking all your personal affairs about . . . makes for an ugly situation all round.'

'That's all very well, Paul. But I think some acknowledgement, just between the parties involved, would be, um . . . decent. Let's say, a way to put things on good terms, for the future?'

Paul kept his gaze locked on Amy for a few seconds of serious thought and scratching himself under the armpit. Amy stared back equally unblinking.

'I'm sure my client never intended to cause any distress,' said Paul at last.

'You tell us that, but my client is naturally going to *be* distressed when he finds himself in such a situation and yet receives no explanation of how it came about,' Amy replied.

'Perhaps my client has been a *bit*, erm . . .'

'Upsettingly cold?'

'I was going to say "unforthcoming". But, given my client's position, it's, you know, an instinctive response.'

'But how do you think that makes my client feel? My client is in exactly the same position and has precisely the same fears, yet suddenly has no idea where he stands.'

I thought this was pushing our case a tad hard: I could hardly argue that I was in 'exactly the same position' as George and, because that wasn't true, I couldn't really claim to have 'precisely the same fears' either. But Amy was certainly making the argument with impressive passion, so I didn't really care. Her delivery alone would surely keep the meeting going a little longer. Hopefully long enough so I could get

George to look me in the eyes. That was all I wanted: one genuine moment of contact.

Paul dropped his gaze to the table. 'My client is sorry if your client took it the wrong way.'

'How the fuck was my client *supposed* to take it?' Amy refilled her wineglass. 'Eh? This wasn't something my client was used to doing, or did casually – you know that. But he took the chance, exposed himself because he thought it was worth it and might really be going somewhere . . . and then the next thing he knows it all ices over and he's left standing there like a fucking idiot.'

Had I been talking to Paul, I wouldn't have been quite *that* unflinching in the characterisation of how I was left, I must admit.

'Your client never looked like an idiot,' Paul replied quietly.

'Well . . . he certainly *felt* like one!'

'Amy . . . ?' I began, but she hadn't finished.

'The biggest fucking idiot in Edinburgh.'

'I wouldn't exactly . . .' I said, but she didn't appear to be listening.

'Everyone laughing at how silly and naive he'd been. "Ha ha – what a sucker."'

'No one was laughing – no one even knew,' said Paul. 'And did your client think for a second that my client might have clammed up because *she* was scared she'd been naive and left herself open?'

George had stopped peering determinedly away now. Instead she was staring at Paul. She put her hand on his shoulder, but he took no notice at all and continued talking to Amy.

'My client has to be careful – my client has her client to think of,' he said.

Now that didn't even make sense.

'And my client doesn't?' replied Amy, with bitter, mock surprise.

'Oh, come on, love – it's hardly the same level, is it?'

'Right, so my client's shite? Is that what you're saying? I have a worthless, unimportant client? I'm small-time?'

'Don't get hysterical: I didn't say that at all. Be realistic, though. If you stay calm and look at it . . .'

'I'm *sick* of staying fucking calm! Calm, businesslike Amy. *She* won't cause any bother – she's so *realistic* and bloody bollocking *calm!*' Amy chewed at her lip and began, clumsily, trying to scramble another cigarette out of her packet.

'Amy, I never . . .'

'You never *anything*. That's the problem.'

'Woah, woah, woah!' I said, slapping my hand down on the table repeatedly. 'Hold on a bleeding minute . . .' Without looking at him, because I was focusing on Amy, I pointed a finger at Paul. 'Have you and him been at it?'

Amy didn't reply but merely thumbed her lighter furiously (and fruitlessly – it rasped and shot sparks but no flame came).

'I don't *believe* it!' I said. 'You and him have been at it! Jesus. You've been at it, and you didn't tell me.'

'So?' said Amy, rather annoyed. 'You didn't tell me you were poking her.' She jabbed a finger towards George.

'That's completely different.'

'How is it?'

'Because you're my bloody *agent* – you *have* to tell me who you're sleeping with.'

'Bollocks do I.'

'You do if you're sleeping with the enemy.'

'Paul?' asked George, clearly as an abbreviation of all sorts of questions.

'Yes . . .' Paul said to her, awkwardly. '. . . we had a thing.'

'Why didn't you tell me?' she asked, amazed.

'Christ!' He nodded sharply at me. 'You didn't tell me that *he* was poking you!'

'Can everyone,' insisted George, 'stop saying I've been "poked", please?'

'How *could* you?' I said to Amy. 'He's a wanker.' Out of the corner of my eye, I saw Paul stiffen a little as this escaped from my mouth. I turned to placate him. 'That's what *she* said, I mean – *she* said you were a wanker: she was always saying it.'

'I didn't say he was a *wanker* . . .' mumbled Amy.

'You bloody did.'

'Well, even if I did . . . you know . . . what you say to people – and to yourself – and what you feel don't always end up matching, do they?'

George tugged at Paul's sleeve. 'When did this all happen, Paul? Paul? *Paul?* Answer me. How long . . . I mean, when did it end?'

'End?' said Paul, with a snort. 'Ask her.'

'Amy?' said George.

Amy looked off to the side and shrugged with massively theatrical carelessness. 'Ask *him.*'

I wearily blew air out between my lips and then glanced back and forth between Amy and Paul. 'Look . . . you pair – sort this out, OK?' I looked at George, caught her eye and jerked my head in the direction of the door. 'We'll give you a couple of minutes alone. Get your problems . . .'

'*I* don't have a problem,' Amy cut in, smiling humourlessly.

'Well . . .' began Paul.

'*Both of you* . . .' I said, sternly. '. . . Get your problems under control. You're supposed to be *agents*, for God's sake – behave like them.' I stood up, and looked at George again. She was hesitant, but she eventually stood up too and followed me out of the restaurant.

I paced about outside, glancing back through the large glass front window at Amy and Paul. Paul was saying something and touching Amy's hand. She wasn't responding, but she wasn't withdrawing either.

George was standing indicatively away from me, looking off into the distance with her arms folded across her chest. She was rocking slightly from side to side, transferring her weight alternately from one foot to the other like someone might do if they were trying to keep warm. I knew I'd been wrong in my assumption (well, let's be honest, 'my dreamy hope') that Paul had made her stop seeing me. Her body language here was all her own, and it clearly said she wanted to be somewhere I wasn't.

I lit a cigarette. 'Want one?' I called, offering the packet. She shook her head.

I poked at a pebble with my toe, moving it around for a while and then making a shot for the drain at the edge of the road. It was deflected by an uneven kerbstone and missed, shooting off to the left.

'*Fuck*,' I hissed quietly to myself with great irritation.

The council really ought to do something about the kerb-stones in this city.

I took another drag on my cigarette and looked over at George. 'I wouldn't sell the story, you know,' I said.

She looked back at me, briefly. 'I know,' she said, then looked away again. 'Paul is scared to death . . . but I never thought you would. It just wouldn't be you.'

'Do you love me?'

'No.'

She could have hesitated. Couldn't she? You know, just for a second – what would it have hurt?

'Did you love me at all?' Well, you have to ask, don't you? You're going to get second prize with a 'Yes . . . once': that or a 'No – not really' that provides you with a full-blown feeling of victimhood, misery, martyrdom and self-pity. Either way you'll have *something* to take home.

George took a heavy breath. Pulling lots of air in, holding it for a time, and then releasing it abruptly. She briefly glanced over at me. 'I think I loved the idea of you.'

'Right . . . right . . .' I nodded. 'So . . . what the fuck does *that* mean, then?'

'I loved what you had – what you were. Settled, secure, comfortable, not controlled by ambition . . . Sara, the semi and the steady, quiet jobs. How your girlfriend never needed to worry about what you saw in her – whether it was false: whether you didn't love her but really just . . .'

'The *idea* of her?'

'Touché.'

I tossed my cigarette on to the ground and stubbed it out viciously with my foot – tearing it to pieces, smearing its innards across the pavement. It seemed the perfect thing to do at that moment – required, really. Trouble was, I hadn't finished it. In fact, I'd only had a few drags: Christ – it was only half smoked. What a waste. And I still wanted to smoke, too. I lit another one. Bugger.

'It wasn't conscious, you know?' George went on. 'I didn't realise what was really attracting me to you until later.'

'When it wasn't there.'

'I suppose.'

'Well . . . I see . . . Attracted to me because of the life I had, rather than who I was . . .' I nodded that I understood. 'Bit of a fucking psycho, aren't you, really?'

'My therapist says I have problems with security and self-esteem.'

'Ah – that's different, then.'

George became a little angry and looked at me properly for the first time. 'Can you honestly say that you weren't attracted to me partly because I'm "Georgina Nye"? Under all that loud dismissal of celebrity, weren't you *remotely* excited at the thought of having sex with someone who was on the telly?'

I wanted to say, 'No. That *never* mattered at all,' as I had to Sara. But I didn't. The dreadful thing was, I wasn't sure now. Could I say that it never mattered *at all*? That it didn't for one moment pass through my mind and give me a tiny thrill? And, if it did, if I was – even partly – attracted to her not because of anything she was but because of the life she had, then was I just as much of a fucking psycho as she was? This was pretty fundamental stuff about my personality.

Best not to think about it.

I shrugged.

'Well,' said George, rather triumphantly, 'there you go.'

Ha. Got her – because actually, of course, I'd admitted *nothing*.

George peered through the window at Amy and Paul. They were hunched close, still talking. 'I think they need more than a few minutes,' she said. 'I'm going to find a cab – tell Paul I'm making my own way back, would you?'

'Sure.'

'You know,' she said, turning across to look at me apologetically, 'I never meant to . . .'

'Oh – *don't*,' I smiled. 'Let's keep at least one cliché in the box.'

George smiled back. 'Well . . . look after yourself, Tom. I hope things turn out right for you.'

'Yeah. And I hope you . . . well, that you stay hugely famous and unbelievably rich. If nothing else, I think this whole mess has taught you what's *really* important to you, and you'll never again be tempted by the chimera of relentless anonymity and far, far less money.'

She laughed and punched me playfully in the chest. I smiled back (even though she'd actually hit a pen that was in my pocket and knocked it *right* into my nipple and it really hurt). Then she leaned forward and kissed me on the cheek, before turning around and walking away down the street. I watched her go, wondering whether she would turn around. Indulge in a brief glance, maybe – for 'one last look'. She didn't, though. She simply kept on walking until she rounded the bend and there was nothing left but an empty road.

'First time she mentioned her therapist,' I said to myself. 'I should have known right then.'

That would have made quite a good bit in a script, I reckoned. I could see it now: bitter-sweet, certainly, but ultimately the amiable closing of a chapter. Tom – a little sad, but a little wiser too – was ready to make a fresh start.

In fact, I just felt like shit.

Or so I thought. When people say, 'I couldn't be happier!' they may well be right. When they say, 'I couldn't be any more miserable,' they are almost certainly grossly underestimating. I'd *thought* I'd felt like shit that day, but really I'd barely even entered the intestine.

The days and weeks that followed were filled – stuffed to bursting point – with the absence of Sara. I sat in my hotel room and wanted to cry. I did cry too, obviously, but even worse was the wanting to cry: the feeling of being filled with agonising despair that needed to be released somehow – crying, shouting, punching the wall, *anything* that might vent the awful pressure of it inside me. Sitting there with clenched fists and clenched teeth. Pleading with the air in the hope that there might be a deity passing who'd be prepared to strike a deal; begging that the physical horror of this choking, viscous misery be cut out of me at any price.

Simply being awake hurt. Consciousness was something that had to be borne like an open wound until sleep gave me a little respite. And sleep was pretty half hearted about doing that, too. I'd lie in bed all day, and sleep fitfully through the night. Combined with this, I drank as much as I could and thus spent great sheets of time bobbing about on the surreal ocean between sleep and wakefulness – sometimes just below the surface, sometimes just above it, but at all times never quite sure which was which.

I think I went mad, to be honest. I certainly did things that only a mad person would do. I didn't wash, shave, change my clothes, sleep properly or get sober for three days, and I then went to stand outside Sara's store as she left work . . . in the belief that seeing me like this might prompt her to take me back. Seriously – that's where my mind was: 'Tom! You stink! Oh – how I've missed you!' I telephoned – over and over again – just to hear Sara's voice on the answerphone. Then, when the time came to leave a message, I'd stay on the line, silently. There was this lunatic notion in my mind that maybe – just . . . maybe – one time she'd be sitting there, listening to the silence, knowing it was me and, sensing my pain, she'd pick up and suggest we gave it another try. That was where my mind was. I wasn't some mute, disturbing phone stalker: I was a desperate man, reaching out – reassuring her that I still loved her and was waiting. I'd go to places where I thought I might see her. I don't mean to our . . . to her house or anything as literal as that. I mean that I'd think and think about where she might be at any given time – a pub she liked, or a shop, or anywhere at all – and get myself over to that place. The idiot idea here was that we'd 'accidentally' meet – I'd be as surprised as she was, 'Well, *fancy* bumping into you' – and then . . . well, I don't know: but it'd end up with her inviting me back and everything returning to how it had been before. *That*'s where my mind was – in the entirely insane belief that it might *somehow* lead to a reconciliation, I'd spend six hours on a Sunday wandering endlessly around the B&Q on Ingles Green Road. And after the first four hours, unsurprisingly, at least one security guard tends to start wandering around a few paces behind you. Worst of all, I began to hate couples. I'd see a couple on the street and hate that they were together and happy and blithely – carelessly – unmindful of the dizzying good fortune of their situation.

I was useless. Completely surplus to the Earth's require-ments in every sense. It might be a standard image – the writer, haemorrhaging despair, a bottle of bourbon by his side, racing against the keyboard to keep up with the outpouring of words

– but depression isn't really a creative fire at all, it's actually a smothering blanket. I couldn't even raise the will to switch on my laptop, let alone drag out a few leaden sentences. All I had the energy or desire to do was sit around feeling weak and ghastly and sick. And if I was no good to myself, then I was a positive impediment to the lives of those around me. I'd turn up at Hugh's office and talk. Rambling, repetitive, self-pitying near-monologues half full of needy, awkward silences. Hugh tried to help. He attempted to get me to move on, or consider other things, or just get some kind of grip at all. That in itself was a crushing situation to be in: *Hugh* trying to cheer me up. What kind of miserable fucker must you be if *Hugh* is telling you to count your blessings? It was like being talked down from a ledge by Sylvia Plath.

And, in an irony whose sweetness I can only compare to being hit in the mouth with a spanner, there was also the splendid and timely fact that Amy and Paul had become an open, official pairing. Amy tried to keep it from my view as much as possible, but I knew it was there. For a start, she was unpleasantly happy. How *anyone*, anyone *in the entire world*, could have the sheer, thoughtless vulgarity to be happy when *this was happening to me* made me bitter and angry at humanity's selfishness, but for *Amy* to be happy – with George's agent moreover – was almost disloyal. I was saved from hating her only by the knowledge that it wasn't her fault. It wasn't really Amy who was against me – it was the universe. Fate was a sadistic bully and I was its target: I was a victim of malicious providential harassment.

Naturally, I realised that Sara was the only woman in the world for me – would always be the only woman for me – in an agonising epiphany fairly early on in this period. Armed with this new and world-altering knowledge, I wrote long letters to her explaining my discovery. The first one I ended with the words, '. . . it's unbearable that I've come to see this only now. I know it's too late and you won't take me back, but I needed to tell you how I felt anyway. Don't worry – I don't expect a reply.'

When, after about five days, I hadn't received a reply (a reply hinting that, on the basis of this new evidence, she'd take me back), I wrote another letter. This one began by asking I be excused for the second intrusion, but there were a few technical points I'd forgotten to include in the previous letter and I thought they ought to be mentioned for the sake of completeness. I also cleverly tried to win her over by, very subtly, implying that she was cold and pitiless and indifferent to the pain I was feeling. I got no reply to this letter either. Naturally, therefore, I wrote more letters. However, the letters I wrote after the two openers had a steadier rhythm and a more reliable format and could pretty much be relied upon to begin by apologising self-loathingly for what I'd said in the previous letter, and to end by saying it again.

I can't quite remember the moment when I realised what I needed to do if I ever wanted to have Sara forgive me. I'd known for a long time that she'd need to believe that I was different now, but I can't say when the specific sign that would convince her of this became obvious to me. I think the understanding grew, piece by piece, over a period of many days and nights. Tellingly, as it did, I began to see also that it wasn't something I needed to do just for Sara. I saw that it was important for me as well. I'd been a shit. A thoughtless, pompous shit, and I needed to change. Not just because that way I stood a chance of being with Sara again, but also because I *simply needed to change*. Old Tom had to be cast aside for ever and New Tom had to step up and take over. After accepting this, everything else was just details. I had a purpose now, and hope: I felt better than I had in weeks.

(Though, to be honest, I still felt like shit. But, you know, *better* shit.)

*   *   *

I'd picked the day based on nothing. It was simply 'two Saturdays away' from when I judged that I'd got all the arrangements in place, or at least knew what they all were. Given that it was that day by chance – but couldn't be changed on the spur of the moment: moved on a couple of days because it was raining, say – I was lucky beyond anything I deserved that it was glorious. A dry, clear, sunny autumn day. The kind of day that seems, above all else, *clean*. The kind of day when even the far distance is as sharp as glass. The kind of day that, stepping out into it, somehow provokes you, completely against your character, to take a big, purifying breath of air and then stand there smiling, arms akimbo.

Learning from experience, I'd had a haircut earlier in the week rather than taking the risk of waiting until the day itself. I'd prepared almost everything else earlier too. The chauffeur-driven limo was one thing that could, conceivably, go wrong – because that wasn't arriving until later in the day – but I simply had to rely on it being there: the chauffeur not being sick and so on. There was no way around that, though. I wasn't about to *buy* a limo and *employ* a chauffeur just so I could use them for this one day – hiring them for a few hours was wincingly expensive enough. And, anyway, at least a stretch limo, even if it broke down, was better than a coach and horses. The coach and horses was what I'd thought of first, of course, but I rapidly realised that a coach and horses was just stupid. The limo had a DVD player in it, for a start.

There was one other major thing that was unarranged, but this one was also out of my hands, really. I'd booked the holiday (Venice – where else? I mean, I have heard that it stinks, but still, well, it *has* to be Venice, right?) and bought the plane tickets. I couldn't call Sara's work to make sure they'd secretly sort out her having the time off, however. That's to say, I *could* have done that, but I didn't think they'd be able to keep it a secret. Most of the specialness of all this came from it being a complete surprise. It had cost a fortune, yes (though I didn't mind about that in the least: even though – I have to make clear – it had cost an absolute *fortune*), and there was pampering and luxury and fun, but the real heart of the thing was the surprise. There was no way I was prepared to risk losing that because someone, for whatever reason, had decided they ought to tell Sara about it or give it away through jokey, giggling idiocy – mention that she ought to bring in a nose clip the next day, in case she went anywhere smelly, or something like that. We'd wing the getting leave bit: Sara would be away for a couple of weeks, and they'd simply have to adapt to it. They'd have to if she came down with amoebic dysentery or something, wouldn't they? This was no different, really.

I'd bought a morning suit. Don't even *begin* to guess how much this had cost: just know that the truth is more frightening than you could ever imagine. I didn't really have any choice, though, as I wouldn't have had time to return it had I hired one. I just hoped that I'd be best man several dozen times over the years ahead – in fact, given the price of the suit, I was prepared to determinedly make many, many new friends for no other reason than to encourage this, if need be. Initially, I'd thought a bunch of flowers would also be required. However, when I thought about it more deeply, I realised that Sara wasn't really that interested in flowers. I'd certainly never known her bring any home for herself and the one, tiny vase that was in the house had always been used to store Biros. Bringing her flowers, then, seemed pretty pointless. A gift of flowers was for people who liked flowers: I should bring her something *she* liked. I had a careful think and eventually remembered her saying once that she liked fudge, so I'd bought a bag of that instead.

I can't tell you how nervous I was getting ready. Even caked in anti-perspirant, my armpits were like tiny tropical swamps. I left my shirt off for as long as possible, and when I did finally put it on in the last ten minutes before leaving my hotel room I paced around with my arms stuck out to the side: dangling down at the elbows, in the pose dancers always strike when they're supposed to be imitating a puppet. I opened my collar and blew air down at my armpits too. I was determined to pull out all the stops to get things right.

Just ahead of time I went to the hotel lobby and waited. I'd decided I wouldn't have a cigarette – just so I didn't smell of smoke, and I'd therefore be utterly perfect for Sara – but I was simply too nervous not to have one. Anyway, I told myself, in a short while I'd be giving up smoking as part of my new, Sara-containing life, so I might as well have a final cigarette or few now. And, I discovered, I'd absently put a two-thirds-full packet and a lighter in my jacket pocket too: which was a lucky coincidence that, to be honest, made the final decision for me.

Slightly late – a good forty seconds by my watch – the limo arrived to pick me up. The driver knew where he was supposed to go, but double-checked with me just in case wires had got crossed and misunderstandings had occurred. 'Best I make sure . . .' he said. '. . . only if there's a load of people waiting at a church somewhere, while I'm parked outside a supermarket specialising in frozen food, then there's bound to be unfortunate repercussions. You can see my position.' I assured him he'd been told the right location and explained what I wanted him to do as we drove along.

We took a route that passed through the town centre and I was worried we'd get caught in traffic. There was no precise time when I needed to be at Sara's work, half an hour later wouldn't make any difference, but I was psychologically committed to everything happening exactly as I'd planned it so the possibility of a delay sent another four or five pints of sweat dashing to my armpits. However, I switched from anxiety to joy and relief as we were going down Princes Street.

'Stop!' I called to the driver.

'I can't stop here, sir,' he replied.

'Just for a moment – *please*.'

'You can't just pull up in Princes Street, especially in a car this size. We'll block traffic and I'll get done for it in thirty seconds flat.'

'I need to jump out here. I'll be back in less than thirty seconds.'

He sighed heavily, replied, 'You'd better be, sir,' and pulled over.

A storm of car horns began almost immediately.

I didn't care, though, because I'd just realised the one thing that I'd forgotten. The element I'd overlooked, the missing letter needed to spell out 'perfection', was music. This leapt into my brain as we passed the Waverley Shopping Centre and, out of the window of the limo, I saw four Ecuadorian musicians: pan pipes, ponchos, hats – the lot. I saw them there busking and immediately I *knew* I must have them.

Persuading them to pack up – *right now* – and pile into a limo with me took some skilfully frantic negotiating and the promise of a stinging amount of money. (Ecuadorian pan-pipe music – to go – while your car is snarling up Princes Street on a Saturday afternoon is, I'll warn you now, very much a seller's market.) Still, it would haunt me for ever if I didn't get the final thing I needed to make the event I was staging complete. The deal struck, I hurried the four of them into the car and we pulled away again. They sat opposite me as we drove along and I explained what I was doing and how they could stand just a little behind me, providing the scene with a romantic and magical soundtrack. They listened carefully as I spoke and then hunched together for a small burst of Spanish muttering.

The one I took to be the leader (he had the biggest hat) asked, 'What music would you like us to play?'

'Oh, you know . . .' I shrugged, and pointed to the instruments they were holding.

'We can do "Just The Way You Are",' the leader replied. He looked around at his companions for confirmation. They nodded without hesitation.

'Billy Joel,' said one.

'Very romantic,' the leader added.

I grimaced my uncertainty about this. 'I . . . erm . . . I don't think so. That might be just the tiniest bit . . . tacky.'

'It's a wonderful piece of music. Very romantic,' the leader said, a little defensively.

'Billy Joel is hugely underrated,' chipped in the Ecuadorian holding the guitar.

'Yes,' I replied, 'obviously . . . um . . .'

'*52nd Street* is one of my all-time top-ten albums.'

'Yes, yes, but I think something more *Ecuadorian* would be better here.'

The leader shrugged. 'Whatever you say . . . you're paying.' He sat back in the seat and looked deliberately out of the window, away from me, for the rest of the journey.

I guided the driver so he pulled up some distance from Sara's store. I didn't want her to see the car until the end. I'd carry her out . . . no, hold on – that was being silly . . . we'd walk out together and I'd wave my hand and the limo would appear to take us to the airport. I instructed the driver to wait for my wave before coming. He asked if it would be a special wave. I said no, just a normal wave.

'Ugh,' said the Ecuadorian holding the guitar as he stood up to get out of the car. 'I *thought* this seat was uncomfortable . . .' He handed me a very flat bag of fudge. I peered inside. It was squashed, but seemed OK otherwise. At least, it did if you had no idea why it felt so warm.

All that was left now was to go into that low-cost freezer store and find the woman I loved. The Ecuadorians and I strode down the road to the entrance. Outside the glass

doors I paused for a second and took a deep breath ...
The Ecuadorians waited for their cue. I nodded to them,
they began to play, and we swept in.

I moved along the end of the checkouts and peered down
the aisles but I couldn't see Sara. For a second – obviously
prone to paranoia – I thought I might have screwed up and
that she wasn't working this Saturday. I'd worked it out,
though – repeatedly checked the dates – and I was sure she
should be. Everyone in the shop, staff and customers, had
come to a halt and was watching me – carrier bags were
dangling in frozen hands, shopping was pouring unnoticed
along checkout conveyor belts and gathering into little piles
at the end. I jogged over to Susan, who was sitting at the end
till staring at me with a look that might almost have been
mistaken for sheer terror.

'Hi, Susan ... is Sara in the office?'

'I don't ...' she began, but the store manager, Terry,
appeared at her shoulder.

'No,' he cut in, 'I've just come out of there. What's all this,
then, Tom?'

'I'm looking for Sara.'

He turned his head slightly, in the vague direction of the
other checkouts, but kept his eyes locked on me. 'Anyone
know where Sara is?' he called.

'I think she's in the lavatory,' shouted back the woman on
the next checkout down, whose name I couldn't remember.

'Would you go and get her for me, please, Pam?'

Ah, yes, 'Pam'. She'd had a hysterectomy, I recalled being
repeatedly told against my will.

'So ...' said Terry. He smiled. He clicked his teeth. He
sucked in some air, and then let it out again. He patted
the top of the till slowly, in time with the Ecuadorian
mood music.

'Business seems good,' I said, nodding around at the
motionless shoppers.

'Oh, you know, can't complain . . . Head office is always – ah, Sara! There you are.'

She appeared around the side of him, Pam hurrying a few steps behind her.

'Well . . .' Terry said, and he retreated: walking backwards, slightly bowed – like a butler leaving a room.

Sara looked stunning. Her hair was tied back and she was wearing her pink, nylon, corporate overall – both of her hands pushed deep into the side pockets. I went weak at the sheer beauty of her. Her mouth alone was so lovely you could spend your whole life just staring at it in awe. Her nose was heartbreakingly wonderful – each nostril more emotionally affecting than an entire symphony. Her eyes . . . Oh, *Jesus* – her *eyes* . . . the things that had first attracted me to her all those years ago. They were beyond anything in the world. So glorious that the sheer, perfect fabulousness of them tore at me: they were lovely to the extent that it hurt me to look at them. But to stand there and have *them* look at *me*? Well, that was akin to being blessed – her gaze had weight and substance; it washed over me like cleansing water.

I took a step towards her. She didn't say anything, or move, but simply continued to look at me with an expression of what seemed to be disengaged curiosity.

'Sara,' I said. 'I know that I did a terrible thing. I know that I hurt you. But, believe me, I've suffered for it too – suffered more than you could ever imagine. I see now that I was awful not just because of what I did, but also because of what I didn't do. I always took the easy way, did what required the least effort and caused me the smallest amount of trouble. I thought of myself when I should have been thinking of you: because without you – I realise now – I'm nothing. All that's happened has brought home to me how – for years – I haven't deserved you. Well, I've changed, Sara. I've changed and what I want, all I want, is a chance.' I reached into my pocket. 'I've booked a holiday for us – the plane is leaving in a couple of hours – and . . .' I opened the box containing the ring and offered it to her. '. . . I want to ask you to marry me . . . Sara – give me the chance to deserve you.'

I paused for a moment, and then raised my other hand. 'Oh – and I've bought you some fudge too.'

Sara peered down at the ring: slowly, emotion began to fill her, until now, impassive face.

'I don't know,' she began, 'what the *fuck* you think you're doing.'

'I'm asking you to marry me,' I replied, a little confused. (Well, it was obvious, wasn't it?)

'And what the hell makes you think I want to marry you? What's that, then? The magic bait women can't resist? The "real thing"? I can't believe you'd be so conde-fucking-scending as to think that the offer of a ring and a register office would blow my little girlish mind. Have I *ever* been interested in marriage, as far as you can remember?'

'Well . . . no – but it's the gesture, isn't it? The declaration that . . .'

'You're prepared to "make the ultimate sacrifice"? Is that it? "Christ – he's prepared to *get married*: that's like taking a bullet for me, that is." You insulting, arrogant twat.'

'It's about commitment . . .'

'I was committed to you anyway . . . and I *thought* you were committed to me too.'

'I'm sorry. I just . . .'

'Never mind. It's all irrelevant. The important issue here is that – surprisingly – I do not want to marry you. I'll go farther. I don't want to go out for a few drinks with you either. I don't want to talk to you, see you or even have a vague awareness that you're alive somewhere. I do *not* want to marry you: what I *want* is for you to fall down a fissure in the Earth's crust . . . Tom?'

'Yes?'

'Fuck off.'

She started to turn around, but I quickly moved so as to remain facing her.

'But Sara, *please* . . . I'm in agony without you. I'm an absolute fucking mess. You wouldn't believe it. There's nothing in me – *nothing* – but a terrible, terrible aching for you. I can't sleep, I can't concentrate, I can't think of anything else but you. The food I try to eat sticks in my throat, Sara. My mouth is dry, and the food sticks in my throat. It goes dry when I think about you and I think about you all the time. I can barely speak properly now – my stupid dry tongue is huge and clumsy in my mouth. *Sara* . . .' I reached out and touched her arm. '. . . without you I have no spit.'

She looked down coolly at my hand on her. I let it fall away.

'Aye – it's all about *you* and how *you* feel, so it is. OK, as you're clearly the *real* issue here, let's say a few words about *you*, then, shall we? You're self-obsessed. Your feet stink. And you're shite in bed. Worst of all, though, you're a coward. I've listened to *years* of you ranting on pompously about fame, and how it's empty and stupid and you're so clever and well adjusted to be above all that nonsense, and poor, poor old misguided Hugh and "Who in the world *cares* about a photo of Russell Crowe buying lip balm?" *Years* of you saying how you want to keep in the background. Well . . . it's bollocks. Because I've seen you reading the Review section of the *Guardian* every bloody week with your jaw muscles twitching, and then going off into your room and being in a foul mood for the rest of the day. Hmm . . . and why *is* it that every time an author is interviewed on the telly you *have* to watch, and yet every time you sit there snorting "wanker" all the way through it? Why *is* that, Tom? It's because you want the fame and recognition so badly it knots up your insides . . . but you're too fucking *scared* to even try for it. You're frightened to death of the bad reviews and the failures and people not liking you. So what do you do? You

338

write things you can claim or disown as it suits you. Hedge your bets. Never get the credit you want, but never risk the humiliation either. You're always outside the medals, but at least you're not last, eh? "Respected within the industry." *Second fucking rate by your own design.*'

I thought I was going to throw up. I was definitely going to cry – I could feel my lips trembling and I opened my eyes wider in an attempt to give the tears more room so they'd stay inside my lids rather than spill down my cheeks. I tried to hold my voice steady, but it wobbled in all directions.

'So, what you're saying is it's all part of the same thing? That I won't take the chance – the all-or-nothing, big risk – with relationships either?'

'Jesus! No. There you go again. *That*, Tom, would be how you'd write yourself. That'd be your character motivation in the TV miniseries. You, in reality, aren't that fucking deep. You just want to have your cake and eat it: that's it. But *please* try to fucking grasp that· I'm not attempting to explain your psychology here. I'm simply rubbishing you. Because you betrayed me by going off with some tart, and so *I get to do that*. Do you understand? You look like a fool when you run. You're nowhere *near* as clever as you think you are. Every time I watched the cycling I wished that you had an arse even *half* as good as any one of the riders up there. You're completely fucking useless, Tom.'

'Sara . . . I just wanted . . .'

'You wanted to get away with it. And I bet you thought you could – because that's how you'd already written it for yourself in your head. And now you think that an idiot proposal, some piss-weak "big scene" idea out of some piss-weak romantic movie and a bag of fudge will make everything all right. On the basis of that self-serving delusion, you come here and embarrass me in front of the people I work with. For the final time, Tom: I don't want you any more. Go . . . *away* . . . *from me*.'

I searched her face, and came back empty handed. She looked at me and there wasn't even hatred there. What was there was even more painful: I was simply no one special. I nearly stumbled as I turned round – my legs suddenly seemed to have been fitted with all the wrong joints – but I somehow managed to stay on my feet and walk unsteadily out into the street.

I was still sick to my stomach, but now I was also dizzy. Disorientated and confused. I must have appeared like a drunk. I had no idea whatsoever where I was going and my steps were awkward and arrhythmic – I didn't appear to know exactly where the ground was: my feet banging into it unexpectedly soon or judging it to be two inches higher than was actually the case. There was no time: it didn't exist where I was. There was just a nauseous, roaring instant extended for ever. To tell the truth, I felt like I was dying.

Then, from behind me, a hand touched my shoulder.

The relief that Sara had relented at least enough to come after me exploded inside my body. It was a leap from the cripplingly unbearable to the ringingly wondrous in the space of a single heartbeat. A wave of euphoria rushed through every part of me: instantaneously snatching my face into a grin, unbinding my lungs and giving me new skin. I spun round to look at her.

The biggest-hatted Ecuadorian looked back at me a little uncomfortably. Behind him trailed the others: they'd obviously been following me down the street, like we were a train.

'I'm sorry,' he said. 'We played, though. We played as we agreed.'

'Yes,' I replied quietly.

'So . . .' He raised his eyebrows.

'So, what? Oh . . . right. Your money.'

We took the llam back into town. The driver dropped us near the centre and, wearing a morning suit and with four

Ecuadorian musicians shuffling in a solemn line behind me, I went off to find a cashpoint.

'Thanks,' said the leader as I handed him the wad of notes that meant I probably wouldn't be able to withdraw any more money for the rest of the week. 'If you ever need us again . . .'

I gave him a look and he hurried away with his companions.

Nothing in Edinburgh seemed right. I swung my head to look all about me and things appeared misshapen, or dirty, or not quite the colour they should have been. Most of all, though, I didn't seem a part of any of it any longer. The city was going on everywhere, but it flowed around me like a foreign body in its bloodstream. I headed off downhill, purely because it *was* downhill. There was no energy left in me; I was empty – wrung out. A few shops ahead I spotted a café and, when I reached it, I fell in through the door and flopped down at the nearest table. There was absolutely no part of me that had the will to move another step.

I pulled out a cigarette and lit it. I took a long drag and then stared, fascinated, at the glowing end creeping along the paper. A waitress's stomach appeared in my field of view and, after a moment considering it without point, meaning or conclusion, I looked up at her face.

'What can I get you?' Her pen was waiting on her pad.

I knocked my cigarette on the ashtray. 'Don't serve mashed bananas and tuna in gravy, do you?'

She looked down at me with an 'Ugh' expression on her face.

'No,' I said, turning my attention back to the ashtray. 'No – I didn't think so.'

VIII

Hey, I'm no great thinker, but even *I* could see that was going to end badly. But, like I said, that was why I showed you the thing in the first place. You get me? I picked Tom and Sara and Georgina for a couple a reasons. One reason I picked them was that there was no particular reason to pick them, yeah? The names, the time, the jobs, the superficial details of stuff that happened – the paint job – all that might belong to them, but, really, they could have been anyone, anywhere. The story, if you know what I mean, the *story* is pretty much fixed: all they can do is use their own handwriting to put it down. Tom might feel like he's hurting 'cause he's lost Sara, but he's just hurting 'cause that's what happens to anyone at this point. The chemicals he's been getting are close to cocaine or nicotine not just 'cause they induce the same kind of pleasure, but 'cause they're addictive like them too. Really, I'm not kidding you here; these things aren't all that different at all. It's no wonder that now he's feeling just like someone who's going cold turkey. And, yeah – it's my doing, again. I wanted you people to keep things going . . . and that not only meant making it good to get together, but bad to be apart. Carrot and stick, you see what I'm saying?

But he's not missing *Sara;* he's just missing his partner. All that stuff about people being meant for each other or . . . what is it some of you say? 'Somewhere, there's one person for everyone – it's just down to the two of them finding each other.' *What?* I ask you, is that any way to run a species? Your 'special person' is simply a person who's available. 'Just one person for each other person'? You'd die out. The fact is, the reason your partner is beside you right now hasn't got anything to do with destiny and paired souls – it's just 'cause they were around. They were around – a few smells and features were close enough to fit you – and the way your head works meant that you came to believe that they were 'special'. You see that, right? I mean, if you think about it for just a moment, even, you're bound to realise I'm being straight with you here.

George is famous. Dick Cheney is famous too – you think Tom would have been attracted to Dick Cheney, if they'd met? I know it's against your nature, OK, but don't complicate things. Things are simple. Mostly, you just pair off by attractiveness – I figured this was as a good a way to do it as any. All the things that strongly influence a friendship – similar interests, personal beliefs, intelligence, yadda, yadda, yadda – are *completely* outweighed when men and women pair up in relationships by how similar they are in the good-looks stakes. I can't count the number of your scientists who've done experiments that have shown this. One guy at UCLA even did this study and found that the *closer* matched pairs were in physical attractiveness, the *more likely* they were to have 'fallen more deeply in love'. Ha! – am I *good*, or what? Another one of these study things found there was a *really* high hit rate when people tried to match husbands and wives together from their wedding pictures based on *nothing* but how close they were when ranked by looks. I mean – come *on* – I don't even need to tell you all about this, do I? It can't be like you haven't noticed it, right?

I'm not saying you don't feel anything, but you feel it 'cause of oxytocin and vasopressin and endorphins and 'cause that's the game plan, not 'cause of anything mystic. There *isn't* anything mystic. When a junkie wants his fix, he *really* wants his fix – it's *real*. But – whatever he tells himself – you can see it's just the drug pulling the strings, yeah? I know it's tough to step outside on this one, but it's the same thing here – it's just different drugs.

Which kind of brings me to the second reason I picked Tom: it's because we got to see a little of the aftermath. I'm kind of hoping that by understanding Tom's misery – how it came about and what it is – you'll understand your own when it happens. And that understanding it will make it be not so bad. I know I screwed up – I've told you that, and I'm not trying to avoid anything here – but maybe it'll be a bit better if you realise that this is all nothing but, you know, molecules and opportunity.

344

OK, OK, sure: I've simplified stuff. Who wouldn't? Makes my head ache just thinking about all the biochemistry and the whatever – the neurology – and the variations and all that. But, overall, it's always pretty much the same. And, all the time, however complex the mixture might be, *there's no pixie dust in it*, you know what I'm saying? Like that guy said . . . what was he called? Whatever – it doesn't matter – he said – Ryle! That was his name. Cheesh – I'm losing it, I really am. Anyways, like I was saying, however much you're going to say it's complicated and you can't get some big computer to work out all the interactions and all that, however complex it is . . . there's no 'ghost in the machine', OK?

I'm hoping that'll give you some comfort. I really should have guessed that, the way you are, you'd see meaning and magic in love: because you like to see meaning and magic in yourselves and you believe love is the most human thing there is – the thing that makes you what you are. I never intended that, but I should have guessed it. So, I came here to tell you straight how things really work. To make amends for my oversight. So that the next time you feel like crap 'cause of all this stuff, you can say, 'Sure, I feel like crap. But it's just molecules – I'm not being crushed by, you know, *destiny* or anything.' It'll still hurt, but you'll have perspective, yeah? Stick your hand in a flame, and it hurts like crazy – but you don't take it *personal*, right? You don't let it break your spirit.

So, Tom and Sara didn't work out. That's a shame – I like things to work out: I was really cut up about the Neanderthals, for example. But they'll get over it. They weren't meant to be together – or *not* meant to be together – they just met and *were* together for a while. Molecules and opportunity. That's the way you've got to look at these things. I hope you understand now, and it'll help you all and, you know, that my explaining everything here makes up for the way I took my eye off the ball a little with this one.

You all take good care of yourselves, OK?

345

IX

Look, I don't think you're being very fair with me here. I'm getting all these, you know, bad vibes, and that's not right. Not when I've levelled with you like I have. And, what's more important, by thinking I should intervene in some way, you're not taking on board all the stuff I've been telling you. I picked Tom and Sara 'cause they fell apart, and I wanted some guys who fell apart. So you could see how they fell apart and how in – oh, I don't know . . . in a *cosmic* sense, or whatever – it didn't really matter. And now you're giving me this attitude like *I* caused it. Well, OK, yeah, I did cause it – but only 'cause of a few flaws in my design. It wasn't deliberate. And I wasn't going after Tom and Sara *specifically*, was I? What do you think? I'm General Motors or something? You want me to recall the whole human race, after all this time, 'cause of this?

Get out of here.

You're never grateful, are you, you people? And even if I was to do something about Tom and Sara – which I'm not saying I'm going to, right – even 'if I was, what good does that do? They're just two people, it won't change anything overall. You know what I think? I think this is just a way of you avoiding things. You're focussing on them, so you can ignore the real issue here.

And, anyways, I don't do that kind of thing. I set things up, is what I do. Start things running and let them go. I'm a hands-off kind of God. I don't mess around with the day-to-day business. It's kind of a rule, in fact.

So.

I . . .

Awww . . . right. OK, then. If it makes you happy – and *just this once* – I'll give things a nudge or two. But I'm not going to force everything just to suit you, OK? I'll arrange some stuff . . . see what happens. That's all. The rest goes off as it goes off, OK? And you better not tell anyone I got involved on a personal level, yeah? What do you think all those people killed by mudslides and falling masonry would say if they found out I'd intervened on a personal level like this? Those people whine like you wouldn't believe as it is.

So. OK. Wait there. I'll see what I can do. And you know that PEA thing I screwed you with? Well, I'm doing this as payback for it – *capite?* After this, we're even.

TWO YEARS LATER

X

Yeah, that's right, 'two years later'. You got a problem with that? You thought I was going to appear to Sara the very next day as a golden elephant or something? Get over yourselves.

TWELVE

Hugh tapped his pen on the notepad in front of him: holding it vertically, so that he was making lots of dots – randomly, but rhythmically – on the paper.

'You don't like it?' I'd just pitched him my idea for the second novel, and he was noticeably not scrambling for his phone and panting that he wanted the lawyers in there with a contract for me to sign *right now*. 'It doesn't *have* to be robots,' I added. 'It could be aliens, say. Or the Dutch.'

'No, no, robots are fine,' he replied, and made a great many tiny, rapid nods. 'I see what you're trying to do – thematically – and robots are fine.'

'So what is it? What is it, then? It's the vagina thing, isn't it? It is, isn't it? Christ, Hugh – this is the twenty-first century: people can . . .'

'No, Tom it's not the v— it's not that thing. The idea sounds very . . . intriguing. I'm sure we can go somewhere with it. It's just that, well, I'm turning forty next week . . .'

'Really? But, Hugh, you never mentioned it! Why didn't you flag it up to me by, oh, I don't know – going on about it in this very office during endless, miserable reflections on your own mortality for months and months and months? Say?'

'It's not that . . .'

'Isn't it?'

'No . . . Well, I *am* going to be forty. I hoped I'd have my book finished by the time I was . . . I rewrote a bit last night, you know? It's crap, Tom – *utter crap*.'

'Still sounds like it's about you turning forty to me. Despite all those protestations there.'

Hugh dropped his eyes.

'No,' he said. 'Really, it's that I've been meaning to tell you I'm having a party.'

'*You're* having a party?' I laughed out loud. 'And to celebrate turning forty, too? I thought you'd set your heart on spending the whole day locked in the toilet, sobbing.'

'I had. I don't know what it is, but now I sort of feel obliged to have one. It's a feeling that won't leave me alone: like it's impolite of me not to have a party. Very odd. Mary has been going on at me too. Insisting I do it.'

'Right . . . will it be fancy dress?'

'Very funny. But anyway . . . the thing is . . . Mary and I would like to invite you.'

'Thanks. Sure – I'd love to come. Don't know why you've made such a big deal about it. Surely you can't have been worried I wouldn't, and that the festivities would simply wither without me?'

'No, that's not it . . . It's just we want to invite Sara too.'

I hadn't seen Sara for two years.

'Oh, right.'

'Both Sara and you are our friends, Tom. We'd like you both to be there, but we don't want it to . . .' He let the sentence fade before saying . . . well, I don't know what. Perhaps, '. . . we don't want it to end up with you two throwing trifle at each other in our living room.'

'Come on, Hugh . . . Sara and I split up *two years ago* – it's ancient history. I've got no problem with her being there at all.' I gave a little laugh. 'Maybe you'd be better off asking *her* if she's OK with *my* being there, eh?'

'Good Lord, Tom – don't you think we asked Sara if it was OK *first*?'

'Oh. Right. Of course.' I nodded, and then – very off-handedly indeed – added, 'And she was fine with it?'

He stared at me evenly. 'She said you two were "ancient history".'

'Tch – don't go looking for subtexts, Hugh. It's a common phrase. I've moved on, and I'm sure Sara's moved on too. Hasn't she?'

'Yes.'

'Has she? Completely? Well . . . that's good. I wouldn't like to think that she still had some kind of residual thing there, when I've moved on so utterly. That wouldn't be fair.'

'Maybe you could try to stay in different rooms?'

'Oh, Hugh, get a grip. It's fine – really . . . Will she be bringing her boyfriend?'

'Tom . . .'

'I'm kidding, I'm kidding . . . It'll be fine.'

I was sure it would be. Fun, even. I think the rule of thumb is that, kept away from absolutely any further provocation whatsoever, Scottish women come down from being murderously angry after about eighteen months. So, hopefully, Sara and I could talk to each other like adults now. We'd got the history, but without the emotion to stir things up. It'd just be like meeting someone you used to fight with at primary school. I was quite looking forward to it, out of curiosity. I was disinterestedly keen to see her. No more than that, though. I had, after all, moved on.

'Glad you could make it, Tom,' said Mary.

I handed her a bottle of wine. 'Wouldn't miss Hugh becoming officially "past it" for the world.'

'Ha – well, you're about fifteen years too late for that party. We were worried you couldn't come for some reason, though.'

I had arrived pretty late. I'd deliberately hung back, you see. Waited before turning up – pacing away a couple of hours in my flat. I didn't want to look, oh, I don't know, 'desperate' or like I hadn't got a life. Not that anyone would be looking at me to think this, of course. But . . . well, I just felt better not arriving until everyone else was there, that was all.

354

'Sorry,' I said, 'I got bogged down with some work.'

'No problem – just as long as you've managed to get here, that's the important thing.'

'Is Sara here?'

You fucking *idiot*, Tom.

'No, not yet.'

Fuck. Fuck. Fuck. Maybe I could say I'd forgotten something and needed to go back home to look for it, until after she'd arrived. Or perhaps I could just hang a placard around my neck reading, 'Tom. Desperate. No life. Pity me'. At least it was nice to have options.

Mary looked at me and I felt my face start to heat up and redden: which is bad enough when you're six, but quite the worst thing imaginable when you're thirty and a professional writer with your own flat. Quickly, I became intensely wrapped up in the task of undoing the zip on my jacket. Mary continued, 'She's coming later . . . Tom . . .' She hesitated for an uneasy inhalation before continuing, which gave me the chance to head her off.

'Only I know Hugh was *really* . . .' I laughed and shook my head incredulously. '. . . uptight about our both being here. I thought he might have her under armed guard in the kitchen or something.'

Mary paused for a moment and her eyes frisked my face for concealed thoughts before she nodded, 'Right,' and took my jacket. Then she threw on some cheeriness. 'You go in and get yourself a drink, OK? Circulate. Mingle. From what I've picked up, the living room's "Amis" and the dining room's "Movie Adaptations" and the conservatory is "The Tyranny of the Genre" – or, if you search around, you might even be able to find some of *my* friends and have a normal conversation.'

'Thanks – but, if experience has taught me anything, I know I'll probably get a few drinks inside me then start on Amis.'

I walked, eyes favouring the carpet, into the dining room

and over to the food and drink table. There was a selection of things. I drank a glass of red wine and stared pensively at the crostini.

The irksome thing – I told myself, slightly annoyed – was that it really wasn't a big deal, my seeing Sara again. It was just that Hugh and Mary seemed to *think* it was and I was slipping into confirming their suspicions simply because I was trying so hard to show that they weren't true. Like that game where you lie in bed at night and try *not* to think about breasts. Erm . . . possibly that's a game only I play – but you get the idea. I wasn't remotely hung up on Sara any more. Sure, I *had* been, immediately after we'd split up. For a time there I was insane, no doubt about it. Unbalanced, irrational, fixated, self-destructive, drainingly depressed – a complete basket case. But that had only lasted, say, two or three weeks or a year. I hadn't laid eyes on her since that slight unfortunateness at her work – nor had I even heard all that much about her, in fact. Our few mutual friends clearly worked hard never to mention her in my presence and I'd only come by the odd bit of information after overhearing others talking, or on rare occasions when someone slipped up and forgot I was there. One reason I'd been looking forward to this evening was it was an opportunity to show everyone, including Sara, that all that nonsense was in the past now.

I was on my second glass of wine, and chatting to a couple who were nervous because they suspected that they weren't quite sure they knew what 'the new pornography' was this year, when Sara walked into the room with Mary.

The instant I saw her, my throat seemed to swell, my stomach shivered and my . . . well, let's just say that it was not a good moment anywhere along the entire length of my digestive tract. *Immediately*, I pulled my eyes away from her, back to the people I was talking to – I did it the picosecond I saw her. This instantaneous reaction was aeons too slow to avoid her randomly glancing in my direction and seeing that I was looking at her. I recovered by nodding with vigour and intense concentration in response to what the man I was talking to was saying: I also laughed very loudly at his amusing remark. He flinched slightly.

'I don't think child slavery is terribly funny, actually,' he said.

'What? Oh, no, I wasn't laughing at that – it just reminded me of . . . a joke.'

'A joke about child slavery?'

'No.' I took a sip of my wine, then shook my head, gravely. 'But, that child slavery, eh? Terrible thing. Terrible.'

This was ridiculous. It must have been a good two months since even the concept of Sara's existence had, for any reason at all, passed through my brain. Yet a fraction of a glimpse of her, and now my palms were sweating. It was surely just a purely reflexive response – something triggered by a former habit. Like an old soldier one day jumping at a car backfiring: it doesn't mean he's still shell-shocked, it's simply an instinctive twitch – an echo of past conditioning, maybe, or the itching of a phantom limb. I was fine. It wasn't *me*: it was just my dumb-ass autonomic nervous system.

I forced myself into an hour of the smallest talk there has ever been at any party, anywhere in the world, ever. It was *tiny*. Punishingly unengaging . . . nanotalk. Oddly, though, all the time I was doing this I could sense where Sara was: directly behind me, off to the left, away in the next room, etc. My skin seemed to prickle to indicate her position, as though my body were a compass. This sensation and the conversations I was forcing myself to have became too much eventually. An hour was enough for the look of the thing, surely? So, precisely one hour after I'd first seen that Sara was in the house, I apologised to the person I was with for suddenly realising that another matter meant I was unable to listen to the rest of the sentence he was speaking, and went to lay things to rest. Say hello to Sara, earth the current, get rid of all this silliness and allow myself to exhale.

I found her (I made sure it didn't seem like I was *looking for* her, obviously) in the kitchen, talking to a man who I assumed made, sold or fitted wall tiles – he was talking about the wall tiles in the room, and I can't think of a single reason anyone would do that were they not in the business of making, selling or fitting them.

'*Hi, Sara!*' I said, flashing my eyes wide and taking a half-step back from the surprise of stumbling across her. Of all people. There.

'Hello, Tom,' she replied.

I wasn't sure how I should read that.

'This is Iain,' she continued.

We shook hands and then Iain talked about tiles until no one at all would have blamed me had I opened the kitchen drawer, taken out a knife and viciously slain him.

Neither Sara nor I spoke more than an 'I see' or a 'Really?' but that didn't make Iain protest that he was having to do all the talking and the one-sidedness was draining him. He went on and on. And on. I could feel my fingernails growing. Couldn't he see that I wanted him to go away? I think Sara wanted him to go away too. Iain's place in society was 'away': that was where he could do the most good. Christ – now he'd moved on to grouting. No one could be this dull. I'd rather have spent the time listening to that woman who tells you you haven't hung up your telephone properly. Forty-five minutes waiting in a bus shelter on a freezing, wet Tuesday evening would be *less* interesting if Iain were there. Jesus. *Please – let him stop.*

Finally – decades after he'd started – Iain waggled his glass in the air and said, 'Well . . . I need a refill.'

'You need a fucking good kicking is what you need,' I said. (I was addled by Iain-fatigue, OK? Anyone would have said the same thing – honestly.)

Iain balanced a squint between surprise and distress.

'Ahhh!' I added, pointing my finger at him and grinning.

'Oh – ha ha! Nice one,' he replied, grinning back happily, and went off to get another drink. (And then, I hoped, to emigrate and die.)

Sara and I stood together in silence for a moment. I sipped at my glass of wine and looked with interest at those things in the kitchen that most unmistakably weren't her.

'You look well,' Sara said (very, very suddenly, it seemed to me).

'Thanks – so do you . . . I see you've cut your hair short.'

She reached up and ruffled it, as though checking it was still there, and still short. 'Och – aye. I did that *years* ago . . . As a statement, to be honest.' She laughed. 'I went out and did it just because I knew you'd hate it short.'

'Right.'

'. . . And I hated it.'

I nodded.

'But,' she said, running her fingers through it again, 'it's kind of grown on me now.'

'Hair does that.'

'Funny.'

I sipped at my wine some more.

'Amy couldn't come, I understand?' Sara said.

'That's right. She thought it was too long a trip up from London – until the baby's older.'

'Aye. Of course. She's still your agent, though, right? Even now she lives down there, and everything?'

'Oh, yeah. Marriage and motherhood haven't slowed her down – quite the opposite, in fact. She's *forever* telling me that London is simply the only place to be if you're a literary agent.'

Sara smiled. 'How things change.'

'How they do . . . indeed.'

Another wine-sipping pause.

'So,' I asked, much as I'd ask any acquaintance about their partner, just to show interest, 'you're going out with a professional cyclist, I hear?'

About ten months ago, this piece of information had slipped out of Hugh's mouth, and all over me, while he was taking a phone call from Mary as we were having lunch together. He'd immediately become flusteringly apologetic. I'd ribbed him mercilessly, of course. That he could tumble into hysteria simply because he'd let it out that Sara was seeing someone? Good Lord – as though after all this time the idea of her being with someone else had the slightest impact on me! Bless. What an old mother hen you are, Hugh! Then, still chuckling visibly all the way, I popped off briefly to the restaurant's toilet and threw up.

For a while afterwards, whenever I thought about her having sex with this other man (which I tended to do rather a lot), I'd gag with nausea. Then, perhaps, get spinning, stumbling drunk and spend an evening scrawling 'BITCH' and 'SLAG' on bits of paper until I felt I was ready to move on to punching the wardrobe and crying.

But that's all a normal part of the healing process, right? And, anyway, it was *months* ago: obviously I was over all that now.

Sara huffed out a little laugh. 'I *was*.'

'Broke up?' I asked: enduring actual physical pain from forcing my expression into one of concern and sympathy.

'Aye . . . aye.'

'I'm sorry.'

'Aww – no big deal. It wasn't meant to be.'

'Right.'

'And seeing him shave his legs creeped me out.'

'Fair enough.'

We did a bit of throat clearing. It seemed like the time for it.

'And you?' Sara asked. 'Are you seeing anyone?'

'Nah – I haven't seen anyone since we split up.' I immediately realised that this sounded astonishingly unimpressive or, even worse, as though I were clumsily trying to imply that she'd always be the only one for me: that my sexual side had disappeared the day she left. 'I've done an *awful* lot of wanking, though,' I hastily added.

'Naturally – you're a writer.' She flicked the rim of her wineglass with her fingernail. It rang out with a pure but deeply, deeply irritating note. 'I read your book, by the way.'

'You didn't have to.'

'Oh – I think I *did*, actually. Anyway, I enjoyed it.'

'*Enjoyed* it?'

'Well, not "enjoyed" . . .'

'The *Observer* called it "unremittingly grisly and harrowing – a suppurating wound of a novel".'

'Aye, well – what do they know?'

'Oh – they were praising it. It's serious literary fiction. I didn't write it to be *enjoyed*: I hope I'm a good enough writer to be beyond that.'

'OK, then. I found it "raw". Is that all right?'

'What about "uncomfortable"?'

'Oh, *aye* – definitely.'

'Excellent.'

'I've heard it sold quite well.'

'Hmm . . .'

'Didn't it?'

'It was a "cult hit".'

'What's that?'

'You know what a "hit" is?'

She shrugged. 'I suppose so.'

'This was a "cult hit".'

'Ah.'

I made a dismissive wave. 'It doesn't matter. The important thing is that I stay true to myself . . . and I think the next one will do better: it's got robots.'

'Killer robots?'

'Too soon to say. I've missed you, you know?'

It wouldn't stay in any longer. I was amazed I'd managed to keep it in this long, quite frankly.

'Aye, well . . .' She looked down and flicked her glass again. The shrill chime it made annoyed my teeth.

'I . . .' Oh, Jesus. 'Do you want another drink? Only I'm keen to try some of the stuff Mary and Hugh smuggled back from the Gambia – they say it's used over there to celebrate special occasions, flavour stews and as a traditional way of executing goat thieves. You want to try some? It'll be fun. The label has a picture of a defibrillator on it. What do you say? Eh?'

She showed me the outer layer of a smile. 'No – you go ahead. I'm just going to have a wee chat with some folk . . . catch up on the gossip . . . you know.'

'OK, sure. Well – I'll be off to tackle that drink then . . . It was good to see you, Sara.'

'Aye. You too, Tom.'

With a show of buoyant energy, I left the kitchen and headed off through the house.

So – that was that. What was there left to do? Or say? I'd wanted – no, I'd *needed* – to tell her I'd missed her, and I'd done it. Before I'd seen her again tonight I hadn't realised how much I'd needed to tell her that. To tell her it while I was sober and rational. So that, hopefully, it didn't sound like nothing but a jilted boyfriend whining about his own feelings but instead assured *her* that she was a person who was special enough always to be missed. Well, it was out of my system now. That was everything, surely? There wasn't any air left to clear. Anything from now on could only count as wilful digging up, not finally laying to rest. Hmm . . . if this was closure, then it was vastly overrated.

Awww – crap.

Crap, crap, crap. You're going to regret this, Tom . . . The trouble is, you'll regret it even more if you don't try.

I spent the remainder of the evening talking to people I didn't know very well about things I didn't care about at all. Mary proposed a toast that luridly drove embarrassment into Hugh's shattering chest, we sang what a jolly good fellow he was and he made a short speech, which somehow brought together his appreciation that everyone had come with how bacteria had now developed immunity to all the antibiotics available and a new plague era must surely be upon us – it was classic Hugh, and provoked an enthusiastic round of applause and some cheering. All the time, however, I had Sara in the corner of my eye and the front of my mind.

At last, I spotted her telling Hugh and Mary that she was leaving. (I couldn't hear what she was saying – I was across the room – but the 'Weeeeell, I'd better be making a move now . . .' speech is unmistakable even with no sound.) I nipped over to them all with my most rapid casualness.

'Weeeeell,' I said, glancing at my watch, 'I'd better be making a move. It's been great fun, Hugh . . . Mary.' I looked across and smiled. 'I leave the rest of the wine to you, Sara.'

'Oh, I'm leaving now too.'

'*Are* you?'

'Aye – my cab's outside.'

'Really? Um, look, I couldn't use it as well, could I? You can get out at your place and I'll carry on with it. It'll save me having to call a cab for myself and wait around for it to arrive – I'll pick up the whole tab, obviously . . .' I raised my eyebrows questioningly, and left them there, for ages. I noticed Hugh and Mary tighten: as though someone had increased the tension of their spines by a half-turn or so.

'I'm sure it won't take long for another cab to arrive, Tom,' said Mary. 'And Sara's house and your flat aren't really in the same direction – you'll be paying a lot for the detour.'

'Tch – it's only money,' I tutted. 'Sara?'

'Aye, fine – whatever,' she replied with a shrug.

'Sara, you . . .' began Mary, but Sara showed that she had

a general idea of what Mary was about to say – and that it was all right and Mary shouldn't worry about it – by riding right over the top of her before she could say it.

'OK – let's go – don't want to keep the driver waiting. Hugh – happy birthday. Mary – I'll phone you in the week, OK? Come on, Tom.'

We hurried out to the cab.

The whole journey was occupied with my thinking of things to say that couldn't possibly be taken as hinting at anything else. It was the conversational equivalent of playing Taboo. Sara seemed genuinely OK with me being there, though, if a little quiet. The real moment, the one that started the buzzing in my ears, came when we finally pulled up outside her house.

'Well . . .' said Sara.

'Well . . .' I nodded in agreement.

'My house,' she said, with a wave in its direction.

I peered out at it standing cold in the eerie semi-darkness of the sodium street lights. 'Still looks the same.'

'It is. You ought to see inside – I haven't even vacuumed since you were last there.' She laughed. 'I'm Miss fucking Havisham.'

'*Could* I see inside?'

Sara let her laugh die gently and stared at me with those eyes of hers. (Not that she could have stared at me with anything else, obviously: I simply mean that her look was all the more piercing because of the eyes she had available.) She didn't say anything, and neither did I. There was just the hum of the taxi's engine, the small creaks of the seats and our breathing, yet the intensity of it was both exhilarating and utterly unbearable. The air was completely still, but I felt as though a wind were blowing into my face.

'If I were to say you could come in for a coffee . . .' Sara said evenly – and about half a second before the impossibly taut atmosphere in the back of that cab would have been broken anyway by my pissing myself, because of the impossibly taut atmosphere in the back of that cab – '. . . would you have the good sense to realise that there wasn't, and I don't want there to be, any more to it than that?'

'Jesus – *of course.*'

'OK . . . would you like to come in for a coffee?'

'Yeah – why not.'

Sara went to the house while I paid for the cab. She left the door open: I pushed it back and stepped inside.

The hallway ambushed me. I wasn't expecting it to be armed with such an unsettling mixture of familiarity and otherness. And it smelled. Not badly: it didn't stink. But it smelled of 'our house'. That says it all, really. Because you can't smell your own house – everyone else's house smells to some extent, but you can't smell your own house at all: your nose is dead to it. So, for me to be able to smell it and for it to smell like our house, which is something you can't smell . . . that's also my emotional response for you, right there.

Sara made some coffee and we sat down in the living room. I sat on the sofa; she sat separately, in a chair.

I looked around the room, which was exactly as it had always been. (I couldn't help especially noticing that it still had the same carpet.) 'I like what you've done with it,' I said.

'Aye – I was going for a kind of retro feel.'

I blew on my coffee.

'Was I really shite in bed?' I asked.

'Ha! That's the one thing that's stuck in your mind, isn't it?'

'No, no . . . I just . . .'

'You were OK.'

'OK?'

Sara sat and smiled at me.

I nodded. 'I see,' I said. 'You're going to leave me here, holding "OK", aren't you?'

She sat and smiled.

I looked down into my mug. 'Do you ever have any regrets?' I asked.

'Regrets? That I went off and fucked someone else, you mean? Yes, I – no, hold on, wait a minute . . .'

'Right, I deserve that, obviously. I just meant . . . do you ever wonder if it might have worked out differently?'

'Had there not been that whole "massive betrayal" thing?'

'Do you ever wonder?'

'If you hadn't decided to throw away everything for a quick shag with an actress?'

'Do you ever wonder?'

'. . . Sometimes. Of course I think about it, sometimes.'

I put my coffee down on the table and leaned towards her. She started with alarm. 'On the coaster!' she said.

'Oh . . . sorry.' I moved the mug and leaned closer to her again. 'Sara – we were really great together, once. And I think about you all the time . . .'

'When you're doing all that wanking?'

'No.'

She blew on her coffee and stared at me.

'Seriously,' I said. 'I think about you every time I walk past the freezer section in Safeway, for example. And I hardly ever wank in there.'

'Oh, aye – you say that *now* . . .'

'I'd like to try again.'

'Don't you remember what I said when we were in the cab? Coffee is as far as I want to go, Tom.'

'I've changed, Sara. I *really* have.'

'Tom . . . *so have I*. A lot.'

'I can see that . . . But I still love you. It's as simple as that. Filter out the noise, look past the scenery, and it *is* as simple as that: when I look at you, I know I still love you.'

'It is *not* as simple as that . . . OK, I'll admit that I've missed you sometimes, and even that I still have feelings for you, but

I could never trust you again. And, without trust, it's never going to work.'

'But you *can* trust me. I'm perhaps the only man in the world you *can* trust.'

She took a mouthful of coffee and nodded slowly. 'Canny . . . very canny. You have me now, don't you? Because you know there's no way on earth I'll ask you to leave before I've heard how you're going to try to justify a statement as utterly fucking arse-headed as that . . . Canny.'

I moved so I was facing her as directly as possible. 'Here's the thing about being unfaithful, Sara . . . it's absolutely *fantastic*.'

'I think you're losing the audience already, Tom.'

'No, listen to me. The proportion of people who are unfaithful is huge – maybe even sixty per cent, I read somewhere. It's not some kind of aberration: it's the norm. And that should be no surprise because, as I say, it's *fantastic*. You have all the excitement and freshness and novelty you have when you're first getting together with someone *plus* this whole extra layer of thrilling secrecy and intrigue. And lots of sex. Who could resist that? Hardly anyone. Most of those people who *aren't* unfaithful have simply not had the chance to be. I'm not justifying it . . .'

'*Lord* no.'

'I'm *not*. I'm just presenting the facts. So, how do you stay faithful when being unfaithful is something so attractive and thrilling and sexy? Something that makes you feel both desired – valued – and also like you're seventeen again?'

'You need to not be an arsehole.'

'Good. Point one: you need to not be an arsehole. If you're an arsehole, all else will fail – I should know, I was an arsehole. But even if you aren't an arsehole there are other points. Point two is that you've got to want to keep what you have. *Really* want to keep it – even when tempted with something as flattering, as exhilarating, and as quite simply *fantastic* as an affair. Point three flows from this, and it's the most important one of all. You have to be completely – com*pletely* – sure that you won't be able to get away with it. That your partner will *not* – however much you lie and plead and cajole – will *not* let you get away with it. You'll be out. It'll be over. *Definitely.*'

Sara took another mouthful of coffee and continued to stare at me, but she didn't say anything.

'Don't you see?' I said. 'I *know* you'd never let me get away with it. I'm the only man in the world who absolutely *knows* that if I were ever unfaithful to you I'd be fucked.'

She drained her mug and put it down.

'OK,' she said. 'Logical flaws . . . First, if I was prepared to have another try with us, then it'd show you *could* get away with it.' She got up and began to move out into the hallway. I scampered after her. 'Your case only holds up if I never take you back. The second I take you back, the case for having you back collapses.'

'That, I admit, is a dilemma. But, against it, I'll point out that, all the time you *refuse* to give me another chance, I'm the perfect person to be given one. The two things cancel each other out . . . I reckon.'

She reached the front door and paused.

'The second problem,' she said, 'is me. If infidelity is *so* amazing – and you've talked it up that much that I'm simply gagging to try it myself now – then you're heading for heart-break, aren't you? *I'm* bound to be unfaithful to *you*.'

'I'm perfectly willing to take that chance.'

'Why?'

'Because I'm a fucking idiot.'

'Clearly.'

'And I still love you.'

She dropped her eyes and took a long, slow breath.

I reached out and put my hand on her arm. Touching her skin again made the hairs on my neck prickle. 'I can't know how you feel, Sara,' I said, 'but if I don't do everything I can, this one last time, to persuade you to give me a chance, then I'll never forgive myself. I'll be a bigger coward than I ever was before, and I'll suffer for it for the rest of my life. Let's try again? . . . What do you say?'

She raised her eyes and I saw them run over my face, examining all my features before returning to look straight into me. Then she took a step forward and kissed me. Her lips were warm and soft and brought with them an embrace of ecstasy and relief. We wrapped our arms around each other and kissed harder, more deeply. I was like a man coming up after being under water until his lungs had almost burst. Joy, release, elation – she opened up and I fell into her. Sara slid her mouth away from mine, returned it once more, then took it away again and stepped back from me.

'No,' she said.

'What?'

'No. I can't try again – I don't *want* to try again.'

'But . . .'

She opened the door and moved round so that it was clear my role here was to step out. 'It's tempting in some ways,' she said, 'and you've made a reasonable theoretical case for it – don't think I didn't appreciate that . . . but, at the end of the day, it's a bad idea.'

'Why? Fucking *why*?'

'Because it's over. It's the past. It's easy to get all dreamy about the past, but the fact is, if it was that fucking great, it wouldn't *be* the past, would it? You'll always be special to me, Tom . . . but let's not kid ourselves, eh? Life moves on. You can never go back – and you shouldn't try.'

'I was looking to go forward.'

'Well put.'

'But you're still holding the door open.'

'Aye . . . You can call a cab from your mobile.'

I swallowed a couple of times – which was no easy matter, I can tell you – then stepped outside.

I turned back and stood there for a moment, trying to think of something apposite, moving and yet awfully clever to say as a final goodbye.

'Goodbye, Sara,' I said.

'Goodbye, Tom,' she replied, and closed the door.

XI

Well . . . I tried. OK? Just for you, I gave them one more shot at it. And it wasn't easy, I can tell you. Just getting Hugh to have that party was a job I wouldn't wish on anyone – cheesh: the man's like some kind of misery anchor, you know what I mean? He holds on to the bottom and dragging him towards a little joy nearly pulls his arms out of their sockets.

Maybe Sara's going to look back and kick herself one day: could be she's become a bit too cool and logical – and way too stubborn – for her own good. It's definitely tough for Tom. Men are hit harder by this: harder and longer. But then, they get to avoid the slight discomfort that comes from my not quite remembering what I'd done with the anatomy layout when I hit upon the idea of childbirth. So – it's swings and roundabouts, really. The bottom line is what I've been saying all along: It Doesn't Matter. Molecules, not magic. That's the truth. It's painful – but nothing mystic: think of it like food poisoning. You know the set-up now, and that should make it easier. I made it involve all your senses: now I'm giving you that extra sense, the one that can hopefully take the edge off it all . . . a sense of perspective.

OK? Give it a try, yeah? Anyways, I'm going now – stuff to do.

See you soon.

The distorted shape behind the semi-transparent glass paused for a second, then pulled the door open.

'Och – Tom! How *are* you? Lord – what's it been? Four minutes?'

'They always come back, don't they? In the movies you like? The men always try *one more time* after it seems it's too late.'

'Aye . . . and can I point out that your success rate from copying what works in the movies has been – historically – fucking *tragic*?'

'Abysmal.'

'And that "winningly persistent suitor" or "creepy bleeding stalker" is not a call that you get to make?'

'No – you get to make that call.'

'Aye, that's right . . . That's right: I get to make that call.'

'So?'